PORT MORTUARY

PATRICIA CORNWELL

LARGE PRINT PRESS
A part of Gale, Cengage Learning

GALE
CENGAGE Learning

Detroit • New York • San Francisco • New Haven, Conn • Waterville, Maine • London

GALE
CENGAGE Learning

Copyright © 2010 by CEI Enterprises, Inc.
A Kay Scarpetta Novel.
Large Print Press, a part of Gale, Cengage Learning.

LIBRARY OF CONGRESS CATALOGING-IN-PUBLICATION DATA

Cornwell, Patricia Daniels.
   Port mortuary / by Patricia Cornwell.
     p. cm. — (Thorndike Press large print basic)
   "A Kay Scarpetta novel."
   ISBN-13: 978-1-4104-3158-5
   ISBN-10: 1-4104-3158-4
     1. Scarpetta, Kay (Fictitious character)—Fiction. 2. Medical examiners (Law)—Fiction. 3. Forensic pathologists—Fiction. 4. Women physicians—Fiction. 5. Terrorism—Prevention—Fiction. 6. United States. Dept. of Defense—Fiction. 7. Cambridge (Mass.)—Fiction. 8. Large type books.
   I. Title.
   PS3553.O692P575 2010
   813'.54—dc22   2010042422

ISBN 13: 978-1-59413-479-1 (pbk. : alk. paper)
ISBN 10: 1-59413-479-0 (pbk. : alk. paper)

Published in 2011 by arrangement with G. P. Putnam's Sons, a member of Penguin Group (USA) Inc.

Printed in the United States of America
   2 3 4 5 6   15 14 13 12 11

ED258

A NOTE TO MY READERS

While this is a work of fiction, it is not science fiction. The medical and forensic procedures, and technologies and weapons, you are about to see exist now, even as you read this work. Some of what you are about to encounter is extremely disturbing. All of it is possible.

Also real and fully operational at this writing are various entities, including the following:

Port Mortuary at Dover Air Force Base
Armed Forces Medical Examiner (AFME)
Armed Forces DNA Identification Laboratory (AFDIL)
Armed Forces Institute of Pathology (AFIP)
Department of Defense (DoD)
Defense Advanced Research Projects Agency (DARPA)
Royal United Services Institute (RUSI)

5

Special Weapons Observation Remote Direct-Action System (SWORDS)

Although completely within the realm of possibility, the Cambridge Forensic Center (CFC), the Georgia Prison for Women, Otwahl Technologies, and the Mortuary Operational Removal Transport (MORT) are creations of the author's imagination, as are all of the characters in this story and the plot itself.

My thanks —
To all the fine men and women of the Armed Forces Medical Examiner System and the Armed Forces Institute of Pathology, who have been kind enough during my career to share their insights and highly advanced knowledge, and to impress me with their discipline, their integrity, and their friendship.

As always, I'm deeply indebted to Dr. Staci Gruber, director of the Cognitive and Clinical Neuroimaging Core, McLean Hospital, and assistant professor, Harvard Medical School, Department of Psychiatry.

And, of course, my gratitude to Dr. Marcella Fierro, former chief medical examiner of Virginia, and Dr. Jamie Downs, medical examiner, Savannah, Georgia, for their expertise in all things pathological.

To Staci
You have to live with me
while I live it —

1

Inside the changing room for female staff, I toss soiled scrubs into a biohazard hamper and strip off the rest of my clothes and medical clogs. I wonder if *Col. Scarpetta* stenciled in black on my locker will be removed the minute I return to New England in the morning. The thought hadn't entered my mind before now, and it bothers me. A part of me doesn't want to leave this place.

Life at Dover Air Force Base has its comforts, despite six months of hard training and the bleakness of handling death daily on behalf of the U.S. government. My stay here has been surprisingly uncomplicated. I can even say it's been pleasant. I'm going to miss getting up before dawn in my modest room, dressing in cargo pants, a polo shirt, and boots, and walking in the cold dark across the parking lot to the golf course clubhouse for coffee and something to eat before driving to Port Mortuary, where I'm not in charge. When I'm on duty for the Armed Forces Medical Examiner, the AFME, I'm no longer a chief. In fact, I'm outranked by quite a number of people, and critical decisions aren't mine to make, assuming I'm even asked. Not so when I return to Massachusetts, where I'm depended on by everyone.

It's Monday, February 8. The wall clock above the shiny white sinks reads 16:33 hours, lit up red like a warning. In less than ninety minutes I'm supposed to appear on CNN and explain what a forensic radiologic pathologist, or RadPath, is and why I've become one, and what Dover and the Department of Defense and the White House have to do with it. In other words, I'm not just a medical examiner anymore, I suppose I'll say, and not just a habeas reservist with the AFME, either. Since 9/11, since the United States invaded Iraq, and now the surge of troops in Afghanistan — I rehearse points I should make — the line between the military and civilian worlds has forever faded. An example I might give: This past November during a forty-eight-hour period, thirteen fallen warriors were flown here from the Middle East, and just as many casualties arrived from Fort Hood, Texas.

12

Mass casualty isn't restricted to the battle-field, although I'm no longer sure what constitutes a battlefield. Maybe every place is one, I will say on TV. Our homes, our schools, our churches, commercial aircraft, and where we work, shop, and go on vacation.

I sort through toiletries as I sort through comments I need to make about 3-D imaging radiology, the use of computerized tomography, or CT, scans in the morgue, and I remind myself to emphasize that although my new headquarters in Cambridge, Massachusetts, is the first civilian facility in the United States to do virtual autopsies, Baltimore will be next, and eventually the trend will spread. The traditional postmortem examination of dissect as you go and take photographs after the fact and hope you don't miss something or introduce an artifact can be dramatically improved by technology and made more precise, and it should be.

I'm sorry I'm not doing *World News* tonight, because now that I think of it, I'd rather have this dialogue with Diane Sawyer. The problem with my being a regular on CNN is that familiarity often breeds contempt, and I should have thought about this before now. The interview could get personal, it occurs to me, and I should have mentioned the possibility to General Briggs. I should have told him what happened this morning when the irate mother of a dead soldier ripped into me over the phone, accusing me of hate crimes and threatening to take her complaints to the media.

Metal bangs like a gunshot as I shut my locker door. I pad over tan tile that always feels cool and smooth beneath my bare feet, carrying my plastic basket of olive oil shampoo and conditioner, an exfoliant scrub made of fossilized marine algae, a safety razor, a can of shaving gel for sensitive skin, liquid detergent, a washcloth, mouthwash, a toothbrush, a nail brush, and fragrant Neutrogena oil I'll use when I'm done. Inside an open stall, I neatly arrange my personal effects on the tile ledge and turn on the water as hot as I can stand it, hard spray blasting as I move around to get all of me, then lifting my face up, then looking down at the floor, at my own pale feet. I let water pound the back of my neck and head in hopes that stiff muscles will relax a little as I mentally enter the closet inside my base lodging and explore what to wear.

General Briggs — John, as I refer to him when we're alone — wants me in an airman battle uniform, or better yet, air force blues, and I disagree. I should wear civilian clothes, what people see me in most of the time when I do television interviews, probably a simple dark suit and ivory blouse with a collar, and the understated Breguet watch on a leather strap that my niece, Lucy, gave me. Not the Blancpain with its oversized black face and ceramic bezel, which also is from her, because she's obsessed with timepieces, with anything technically complicated and expensive. Not pants but a skirt and heels, so I come across as nonthreatening and accessible, a trick I learned long ago in court. For some reason, jurors like to see my legs while I describe in graphic anatomical detail fatal wounds and the agonal last moments of a victim's life. Briggs will be displeased with my choice in attire, but I reminded him during the Super Bowl last night when we were having drinks that a man shouldn't tell a woman what to wear unless he's Ralph Lauren.

The steam in my shower stall shifts, disturbed by a draft, and I think I hear someone. Instantly, I'm annoyed. It could be anyone, any military personnel, doctor or otherwise, whoever is authorized to be inside this highly classified facility and in need of a toilet or a disinfecting or a change of clothes. I think about colleagues I was

15

just with in the main autopsy room and have a feeling it's Captain Avallone again. She was an unavoidable presence much of the morning during the CT scan, as if I don't know how to do one after all this, and she drifted like ground fog around my work station the rest of the day. It's probably she who's just come in. Then I'm sure, because it's always her, and I feel a clenching of resentment. *Go away.*

"Dr. Scarpetta?" her familiar voice calls out, a voice that is bland and lacking in passion and seems to follow me everywhere. "You have a phone call."

"I just got in," I shout over the loud spatter of water.

It's my way of telling her to leave me be. *A little privacy, please.* I don't want to see Captain Avallone or anyone right now, and it has nothing to do with being naked.

"Sorry, ma'am. But Pete Marino needs to talk to you." Her unemphatic voice moves closer.

"He'll have to wait," I yell.

"He says it's important."

"Can you ask him what he wants?"

"He just says it's important, ma'am."

I promise to get back to him shortly, and I probably sound rude, but despite my best intentions I can't always be charming. Pete

Marino is an investigator I've worked with half my life. I hope nothing terrible has happened back home. No, he would make sure I knew if there was a real emergency, if something was wrong with my husband, Benton; with Lucy; or if there was a major problem at the Cambridge Forensic Center, which I've been appointed to head. Marino would do more than simply ask someone to let me know he's on the phone and it's important. This is nothing more than his usual poor impulse control, I decide. When he thinks a thought, he feels he must share it with me instantly.

I open my mouth wide, rinsing out the taste of decomposing charred human flesh that is trapped in the back of my throat. The stench of what I worked on today rises on swells of steam deep into my sinuses, the molecules of putrid biology in the shower with me. I scrub under my nails with anti-bacterial soap I squirt from a bottle, the same stuff I use on dishes or to decon my boots at a scene, and brush my teeth, gums, and tongue with Listerine. I wash inside my nostrils as far up as I can reach, scouring every inch of my flesh, then I wash my hair, not once but twice, and the stench is still there. I can't seem to get clean.

The name of the dead soldier I just took

care of is Peter Gabriel, like the legendary rock star, only this Peter Gabriel was a private first class in the army and had been in the Badghis Province of Afghanistan not even a month when a roadside bomb improvised from plastic sewer pipe packed with PE-4 and capped with a copper plate punched through the armor of his Humvee, creating a molten firestorm inside it. PFC Gabriel took up most of my last day here at this huge high-tech place where the armed forces pathologists and scientists routinely get involved in cases most members of the public don't associate with us: the assassination of JFK; the recent DNA identifications of the Romanov family and the crew members of the *H.L. Hunley* submarine that sank during the Civil War. We're a noble but little-known organization with roots reaching back to 1862, to the Army Medical Museum, whose surgeons attended to the mortally wounded Abraham Lincoln and performed his autopsy, and I should say all this on CNN. Focus on the positive. Forget what Mrs. Gabriel said. I'm not a monster or a bigot. *You can't blame the poor woman for being upset,* I tell myself. She just lost her only child. The Gabriels are black. *How would you feel, for God's sake? Of course you're not a racist.*

I sense a presence again. Someone has entered the changing room, which I've managed to fog up like a steam shower. My heart is beating hard because of the heat.

"Dr. Scarpetta?" Captain Avallone sounds less tentative, as if she has news.

I turn off the water and step out of my stall, grabbing a towel to wrap up in. Captain Avallone is an indistinct presence hovering in haze near the sinks and motion-sensitive hand dryers. All I can make out is her dark hair and her khaki cargo pants and black polo shirt with its embroidered AFME gold-and-blue shield.

"Pete Marino . . ." she starts to say.

"I'll call him in a minute." I snatch another towel off a shelf.

"He's here, ma'am."

"What do you mean *'here'*?" I almost expect him to materialize in the changing room like some prehistoric creature emerging from the mist.

"He's waiting for you out back by the bays, ma'am," she informs me. "He'll take you to the Eagle's Rest so you can get your things." She says it as if I'm being picked up by the FBI, as if I've been arrested or fired. "My instructions are to take you to him and assist in any way needed."

Captain Avallone's first name is Sophia.

She's army, just out of her radiology residency, and is always so damn military-correct and obsequiously polite as she lingers and loiters. Right now is not the time. I carry my toiletry basket, padding over tile, and she's right behind me.

"I'm not supposed to leave until tomorrow, and going anywhere with Marino wasn't part of my travel plans," I tell her.

"I can take care of your vehicle, ma'am. I understand you're not driving. . . ."

"Did you ask him what the hell this is about?" I grab my hairbrush and my deodorant out of my locker.

"I tried, ma'am," she says. "But he wasn't helpful."

A C-5 Galaxy roars overhead, on final for 19. The wind as usual is out of the south.

One of many aeronautical principles I've learned from Lucy, who is a helicopter pilot among other things, is that runway numbers correspond to directions on a compass. Nineteen, for example, is 190 degrees, meaning the opposite end will be 01, oriented that way because of the Bernoulli effect and Newton's laws of motion. It's all about the speed air needs to flow over a wing, about taking off and landing into the wind, which in this part of Delaware blows in from the sea, from high pressure to low, from south to north. Day in and day out, transport planes bring the dead and take them away along a blacktop strip that runs like the River Styx behind Port Mortuary.

The shark-gray Galaxy is the length of a football field, so huge and heavy it seems scarcely to move in a pale sky of feathery clouds that pilots call mare's tails. I would know what type of airlifter it is without looking, can recognize the high pitch of its scream and whistle. By now I know the sound of turbine engines producing a hundred and sixty thousand pounds of thrust, can identify a C-5 or a C-17 when it's miles out, and I know helicopters and tilt rotors, too, can tell a Chinook from a Black Hawk or an Osprey. During nice weather when I have a few moments to spare, I sit on a bench outside my lodgings and watch the flying machines of Dover as if they're exotic creatures, such as manatees or elephants or prehistoric birds. I never tire of their lumbering drama and thundering noise, and the shadows they cast as they pass over.

Wheels touch down in puffs of smoke so close by I feel the rumble in my hollow organs as I walk across the receiving area with its four enormous bays, high privacy wall, and backup generators. I approach a blue van I've never seen before, and Pete Marino makes no move to greet me or open my door, and this bodes nothing one way or another. He doesn't waste his energy on manners, not that being gracious or particularly nice has ever been a priority of his for as long as I can remember. It's been more than twenty years since the time when we first met in Richmond, Virginia, at the morgue. Or maybe it was a homicide scene where I first was confronted with him. I really can't recall.

I climb in and shut the door, stuffing a duffel bag between my boots, my hair still damp from the shower. He thinks I look like hell and is silently judging. I can always tell by his sidelong glances that survey me from head to toe, lingering in certain places that are none of his business. He doesn't like it when I wear my AFME investigative garb, my khaki cargo pants, black polo shirt, and tactical jacket, and the few times he's seen me in uniform I think I scared him.

"Where'd you steal the van?" I ask as he backs up.

"A loaner from Civil Air." His answer at least tells me nothing has happened to Lucy.

The private terminal on the north end of the runway is used by nonmilitary personnel who are authorized to land on the air

22

force base. My niece has flown Marino here, and it crosses my mind they've come as a surprise. They showed up unannounced to spare me from flying commercial in the morning, to escort me home at last. Wishful thinking. That can't be it, and I look for answers in Marino's rough-featured face, taking in his overall appearance rather much the way I do a patient at first glance. Running shoes, jeans, a fleece-lined Harley-Davidson leather coat he's had forever, a Yankees baseball cap he wears at his own peril, considering he now lives in the Republic of the Red Sox, and his unfashionable wire-rim glasses.

I can't tell if his head is shaved smooth of what little gray hair he has left, but he is clean and relatively neat, and he doesn't have a whisky flush or a bloated beer gut. His eyes aren't bloodshot. His hands are steady. I don't smell cigarettes. He's still on the wagon, more than one. Marino has many wagons he is wise to stay on, a train of them working their way through the unsettled territories of his aboriginal inclinations. Sex, booze, drugs, tobacco, food, profanity, bigotry, slothfulness. I probably should add mendacity. When it suits him, he's evasive or outright lies.

"I assume Lucy's with the helicopter . . . ?"

23

I start to say.

"You know how it is around this joint when you're doing a case, worse than the damn CIA," he talks over me as we turn onto Purple Heart Drive. "Your house could be on fire and nobody says shit, and I must have called five times. So I made an executive decision, and Lucy and me headed out."

"It would be helpful if you'd tell me why you're here."

"Nobody would interrupt you while you were doing the soldier from Worcester," he says to my amazement.

PFC Gabriel was from Worcester, Massachusetts, and I can't fathom why Marino would know what case I had here at Dover. No one should have told him. Everything we do at Port Mortuary is extremely discreet, if not strictly classified. I wonder if the slain soldier's mother did what she threatened and called the media. I wonder if she told the press that her son's white female military medical examiner is a racist.

Before I can ask, Marino adds, "Apparently, he's the first war casualty from Worcester, and the local media's all over it. We've gotten some calls, I guess people getting confused and thinking any dead body with a Massachusetts connection ends up with us."

24

"Reporters assumed we'd done the autopsy in Cambridge?"

"Well, the CFC's a port mortuary, too. Maybe that's why."

"One would think the media certainly knows by now that all casualties in theater come straight here to Dover," I reply. "You're certain about the reason for the media's interest?"

"Why?" He looks at me. "You know some other reason I don't?"

"I'm just asking."

"All I know is there were a few calls and we referred them to Dover. So you were in the middle of taking care of the kid from Worcester and nobody would get you on the phone, and finally I called General Briggs when we were about twenty minutes out, refueling in Wilmington. He made Captain Do-Bee go find you in the shower. She single, or does she sing in Lucy's choir? Because she's not bad-looking."

"How would you know what she looks like?" I reply, baffled.

"You weren't around when she stopped by the CFC on her way to visit her mother in Maine."

I try to remember if I was ever told this, and at the same time I'm reminded I have no idea what has gone on in the office I'm supposed to run.

"Fielding gave her the royal tour, the host with the most." Marino doesn't like my deputy chief, Jack Fielding. "Point being, I did try to get hold of you. I didn't mean to just show up like this."

Marino is being evasive, and what he's described is a ploy. It's made up. For some reason he felt it necessary to simply appear here without warning. Probably because he wanted to make sure I would go with him without delay. I sense real trouble.

"The Gabriel case can't be why you just showed up, as you put it," I say.

"Afraid not."

"What's happened?"

"We've got a situation." He stares straight ahead. "And I told Fielding and everybody else that no way in hell the body was being examined until you get there."

Jack Fielding is an experienced forensic pathologist who doesn't take orders from Marino. If my deputy chief opted to be hands-off and defer to me, it likely means we've got a case that could have political implications or get us sued. It bothers me considerably that Fielding hasn't tried to call or e-mail me. I check my iPhone again. Nothing from him.

"About three-thirty yesterday afternoon in

Cambridge," Marino is saying, and we're on Atlantic Street now, driving slowly through the middle of the base in the near dark. "Norton's Woods on Irving, not even a block from your house. Too damn bad you weren't home. You could have gone to the scene, could have walked there, and maybe things would have turned out different."

"What things?"

"A light-skinned male, possibly in his twenties. Appears he was out walking his dog and dropped dead from a heart attack, right? Wrong," he continues as we pass rows of concrete and metal maintenance facilities, hangars, and other buildings that have numbers instead of names. "It's broad daylight on a Sunday afternoon, plenty of people around because there was an event at whatever that building is, the one with the big green metal roof."

Norton's Woods is the home of the American Academy of Arts and Sciences, a wooded estate with a stunning building of timber and glass that is rented out for special functions. It is several houses down from the one Benton and I moved into last spring so I could be near the CFC and he could enjoy the close proximity of Harvard, where he is on the faculty of the medical school's Department of Psychiatry.

"In other words, eyes and ears," Marino goes on. "A hell of a time and a place to whack somebody."

"I thought you said he was a heart attack. Except if he's that young, you probably mean a cardiac arrhythmia."

"Yeah, that was the assumption. A couple of witnesses saw him suddenly grab his chest and collapse. He was DOA at the scene — supposedly. Was transported directly to our office and spent the night in the cooler."

"What do you mean *'supposedly'*?"

"Early this morning Fielding went into the fridge and noticed blood drips on the floor and a lot of blood in the tray, so he goes and gets Anne and Ollie. The dead guy's got blood coming out of his nose and mouth that wasn't there the afternoon before, when he was pronounced. No blood at the scene, not one drop, and now he's bleeding, and it's not purge fluid, obviously, because he sure as hell isn't decomposing. The sheet he's covered with is bloody, and there's about a liter of blood in the body pouch, and that's fucked up. I've never seen a dead person start bleeding like that. So I said we got a fucking problem and everybody keep your mouth shut."

"What did Jack say? What did he do?"

"You're kidding, right? Some deputy you got. Don't get me started."

"Do we have an identification, and why Norton's Woods? Does he live nearby? Is he a student at Harvard, maybe at the Divinity School?" It's right around the corner from Norton's Woods. "I doubt he was attending whatever this event was. Not if he had his dog with him." I sound much calmer than I feel as we have this conversation in the parking lot of the Eagle's Rest inn.

"We don't have many details yet, but it appears it was a wedding," Marino says.

"On Super Bowl Sunday? Who plans a wedding on the same day as the Super Bowl?"

"Maybe if you don't want anybody to show up. Maybe if you're not American or are un-American. Hell if I know, but I don't think the dead guy was a wedding guest, and not just because of the dog. He had a Glock nine-mil under his jacket. No ID and was listening to a portable satellite radio, so you probably can guess where I'm going with this."

"I probably can't."

"Lucy will tell you more about the satellite-radio part of it, but it appears he was doing surveillance, spying, and maybe whoever he was fucking with decided to

29

return the favor. Bottom line, I'm thinking somebody did something to him, causing an injury that was somehow missed by the EMTs, and the removal service didn't notice anything, either. So he's zipped up in the pouch and starts bleeding during transport. Well, that wouldn't happen unless he had a blood pressure, meaning he was still alive when he was delivered to the morgue and shut inside our damn cooler. Forty-something degrees in there and he would have died from exposure by this morning. Assuming he didn't bleed to death first."

"If he has an injury that would cause him to bleed externally," I reply, "why didn't he bleed at the scene?"

"You tell me."

"How long did they work on him?"

"Fifteen, twenty minutes."

"Possible during resuscitation efforts a blood vessel was somehow punctured?" I ask. "Antemortem and postmortem injuries, if severe enough, can cause significant bleeding. For example, maybe during CPR a rib was fractured and caused a puncture wound or severed an artery? Any reason a chest tube might have been placed presumptively and that caused an injury and the bleeding you've described?"

But I know the answers even as I ask the

questions. Marino is a veteran homicide detective and death investigator. He wouldn't have commandeered my niece and her helicopter and come to Dover unannounced if there was a logical explanation or even a plausible one, and certainly Jack Fielding would know a legitimate injury from an accidental artifact. *Why haven't I heard from him?*

"The Cambridge Fire Department's HQ is maybe a mile from Norton's Woods, and the squad got to him within minutes," Marino says.

We are sitting in the van with the engine off. It is almost completely dark, the horizon and the sky melting into each other with only the faintest hint of light to the west. *When has Fielding ever handled a disaster without me? Never.* He absents himself. Leaves his messes for others to clean up. That's why he's not tried to get hold of me. Maybe he's walked off the job again. How many times does he need to do that before I stop hiring him back?

"According to them, he died instantly," Marino adds.

"Unless an IED blows someone into hundreds of pieces, there's really no such thing as dying instantly," I reply, and I hate it when Marino makes glib statements. Dy-

31

ing instantly. Dropping dead. Dead before he hit the ground. Twenty years of these generalities, no matter how many times I've told him that cardiac and respiratory arrests aren't causes of death but symptoms of dying, and clinical death takes minutes at least. It isn't instant. It isn't a simple process. I remind him again of this medical fact because I can't think of anything else to say.

"Well, I'm just reporting what I've been told, and according to them, he couldn't be resuscitated," Marino answers, as if the EMTs know more about death than I do. "Was unresponsive. That's what's on their run sheet."

"You interviewed them?"

"One of them. On the phone this morning. No pulse, no nothing. The guy was dead. Or that's what the paramedic said. But what do you think he's going to say — that they weren't sure but sent him to the morgue anyway?"

"Then you told him why you were asking."

"Hell, no, I'm not retarded. You don't need this on the front page of the *Globe*. This hits the news, I may as well go back to NYPD or maybe get a job with Wackenhut, except no one's hiring."

"What procedure did you follow?"

"I didn't follow shit. It was Fielding. Of course, he says he did everything by the book, says Cambridge PD told him there was nothing suspicious about the scene, an apparent natural death that was witnessed. Fielding gave permission for the body to be transferred to the CFC as long as the cops took custody of the gun and got it to the labs right away so we could find out who it's registered to. A routine case, and not our fault if the EMTs fucked up, or so Fielding says, and you know what I say? It won't matter. We'll get blamed. The media will go after us like nothing you've ever seen and will say everything should move back to Boston. Imagine that?"

Before the CFC began doing its first cases this past summer, the state medical examiner's office was located in Boston and was besieged by political and economic problems and scandals that were constantly in the news. Bodies were lost or sent to the wrong funeral homes or cremated without a thorough examination, and in at least one suspected child-abuse death the wrong eyeballs were tested. New chiefs came and went, and district offices had to be shut down due to a lack of funding. But nothing negative ever said about that office could compare to what Marino is suggesting about us.

"I'd rather not imagine anything." I open my door. "I'd rather focus on the facts."

"That's a problem, since we don't seem to have any that make much sense."

"And you told Briggs what you just told me?"

"I told him what he needed to know," Marino says.

"The same thing you just told me?" I repeat my question.

"Pretty much."

"You shouldn't have. It was for me to tell. It was for me to decide what he needs to know." I'm sitting with the passenger's door open wide and the wind blowing in. I'm damp from the shower and chilled. "You don't raise things up the chain just because I'm busy."

"Well, you were busy as hell, and I told him."

I climb out of the van and reassure myself that what Marino has just described can't be accurate. Cambridge EMTs would never make such a disastrous mistake, and I try to conjure up an explanation for why a fatal wound didn't bleed at the scene and then bled profusely, and I contemplate computing time of death or even the cause of it for someone who died inside a morgue refrigerator. I'm confounded. I haven't a clue, and most of all I worry about him, this young man delivered to my door, presumed dead. I envision him wrapped in a sheet and zipped inside a pouch, and it's the stuff of old horrors. Someone coming to inside a casket. Someone buried alive. I've never had such a ghastly thing happen, not even close, not once in my career. I've never known anyone who has.

"At least there's no sign he tried to get out of the body bag." Marino tries to make both of us feel better. "Nothing to indicate he might have been awake at some point and started panicking. You know, like clawing at the zipper or kicking or something. I guess if he struggled he would have been in a weird position on the tray when we found him this morning, or maybe rolled off it. Except I wonder if you would suffocate in one of those bags, now that I think of it. I guess so, since they're supposed to be watertight. Even though they leak. You show me a body bag that doesn't leak. And that's the other thing. Blood drips on the floor leading from the bay to the fridge."

"Why don't we continue this later." It's check-in time. There are plenty of people in the parking lot as we walk toward the inn's modern but plain stucco entrance, and Marino has a big voice that projects as if he's perpetually talking inside an amphitheater.

"I doubt Fielding has bothered to watch the recording," Marino adds anyway. "I doubt he's done a damn thing. I haven't seen or heard from the son of a bitch since first thing this morning. MIA once again, just like he's done before." He opens the glass front door. "I sure as hell hope he doesn't shut us down. Wouldn't that be something? You do him a fucking favor and give him a job after he walked off the last one, and he destroys the CFC before it's even off the ground."

Inside the lobby with its showcases of awards and air force memorabilia, its comfortable chairs and big-screen TV, a sign welcomes guests to the home of the C-5 Galaxy and C-17 Globemaster III. At the front desk I silently wait behind a man in the muted pixilated tiger stripes of the army combat uniform, or ACU, as he buys shaving cream, water, and several mini bottles of Johnnie Walker Scotch. I tell the clerk that I'm checking out earlier than planned, and yes, I'll remember to turn in my keys, and of course I understand I'll be charged the usual government rate of thirty-eight dollars for the day even though I'm not staying the night.

"What is it they say?" Marino goes on. "No good deed goes unpunished."

"Let's try not to be quite so negative."

"You and me both gave up good positions in New York, and we shut down the office in Watertown, and this is what we're left with."

I don't say anything.

"I hope like hell we didn't ruin our careers," he says.

I don't answer him because I've heard enough. Past the business center and vending machines, we take the stairs to the second floor, and it is now that he informs me that Lucy isn't waiting with the helicopter at the Civil Air Terminal. She's in my room. She's packing my belongings, touching them, making decisions about them, emptying my closet, my drawers, disconnecting my laptop, printer, and wireless router. He's waited to tell me because he knows damn well that under ordinary circumstances, this would annoy me beyond measure — doesn't matter if it's my computer-genius, former-federal-law-enforcement niece, whom I've raised like a daughter.

Circumstances are anything but ordinary, and I'm relieved that Marino is here and

Lucy is in my room, that they have come for me. I need to get home and fix everything. We follow the long hallway carpeted in deep red, past the balcony arranged with colonial reproductions and an electronic massage chair thoughtfully placed there for weary pilots. I insert my magnetic key card into the lock of my room, and I wonder who let Lucy in, and then I think of Briggs again and I think of CNN. I can't imagine appearing on TV. What if the media has gotten word of what's happened in Cambridge? I would know that by now. Marino would know it. My administrator, Bryce, would know it, and he would tell me right away. Everything is going to be fine.

Lucy is sitting on my neatly made bed, zipping up my cosmetic case, and I detect the clean citrus scent of her shampoo as I hug her and feel how much I've missed her. A black flight suit accentuates her bold green eyes and short rose-gold hair, her sharp features and leanness, and I'm reminded of how stunning she is in an unusual way, boyish but feminine, athletically chiseled but with breasts, and so intense she looks fierce. Doesn't matter if she's being playful or polite, my niece tends to intimidate and has few friends, maybe none except Marino, and her lovers never last.

Not even Jaime, although I haven't voiced my suspicions. I haven't asked. But I don't buy Lucy's story that she moved from New York to Boston for financial reasons. Even if her forensic computer investigative company was in a decline, and I don't believe that, either, she was making more in Manhattan than she's now paid by the CFC, which is nothing. My niece works for me pro bono. She doesn't need money.

"What's this about the satellite radio?" I watch her carefully, trying to interpret her signals, which are always subtle and perplexing.

Caplets rattle as she checks how many Advil are in a bottle, deciding not enough to bother with, and she clunks it in the trash. "We've got weather, so I'd like to get out of here." She takes the cap off a bottle of Zantac, tossing that next. "We'll talk as we fly, and I'll need your help copiloting, because it's going to be tricky dodging snow showers and freezing rain en route. We're supposed to get up to a foot at home, starting around ten."

My first thought is Norton's Woods. I need to pay a retrospective visit, but by the time I get there, it will be covered in snow. "That's unfortunate," I comment. "We may have a crime scene that was never worked

39

as one."

"I told Cambridge PD to go back over there this morning." Marino's eyes probe and wander as if it is my quarters that need to be searched. "They didn't find anything."

"Did they ask you why you wanted them to look?" That concern again.

"I said we had questions. I blamed it on the Glock. The serial number's been ground off. Guess I didn't tell you that," he adds as he looks around, looking at everything but me.

"Firearms can try acid on it, see if we can restore the serial number that way. If all else fails, we'll try the large-chamber SEM," I decide. "If there's anything left, we'll find it. And I'll ask Jack to go to Norton's Woods and do a retrospective."

"Right. I'm sure he'll get right on it," Marino says sarcastically.

"He can take photographs before the snow starts," I add. "Or someone can. Whoever's on call —"

"Waste of time," Marino says, cutting me off. "None of us was there yesterday. We don't know the exact damn spot — only that it was near a tree and a green bench. Well, that's a lot of help when you're talking about six acres of trees and green benches."

"What about photographs?" I ask as Lucy continues going through my small pharmacy of ointments, analgesics, antacids, vitamins, eyedrops, and hand sanitizers spread over the bed. "The police must have taken pictures of the body in situ."

"I'm still waiting for the detective to get those to me. The guy who responded to the scene, he brought in the pistol this morning. Lester Law, goes by Les Law, but on the street he's known as Lawless, just like his father and grandfather before him. Cambridge cops going back to the fucking *Mayflower*. I've never met him."

"I think that about does it." Lucy gets up from the bed. "You might want to make sure I didn't miss anything," she says to me.

Wastebaskets are overflowing, and my bags are packed and lined up by a wall, the closet door open wide, nothing inside but empty hangers. Computer equipment, printed files, journal articles, and books are gone from my desk, and there is nothing in the dirty-clothes hamper or bathroom or in the dresser drawers I check. I open the small refrigerator, and it is empty and has been wiped clean. While she and Marino begin carrying my belongings out, I enter Briggs's number into my iPhone. I look out at the three-story stucco building on the other side

41

of the parking lot, at the large plate-glass window in the middle of the third floor. Last night I was in that suite with him and other colleagues, watching the game, and life was good. We cheered for the New Orleans Saints and ourselves, and we toasted the Pentagon and its Defense Advanced Research Projects Agency, DARPA, which had made CT-assisted virtual autopsies possible at Dover and now at the CFC. We celebrated mission accomplished, a job well done — and now this, as if last night wasn't real, as if I dreamed it.

I take a deep breath and press send on my iPhone, going hollow inside. Briggs can't be happy with me. Images flash on the wall-mounted flat-screen TV in his living room, and then he walks past the glass, dressed in the combat uniform of the army, green and sandy brown with a mandarin collar, what he typically wears when he's not in the morgue or at a scene. I watch him answer his phone and return to his big window, where he stands, looking directly at me. From a distance we are face-to-face, an expanse of tarmac and parked cars between the armed forces chief medical examiner and me, as if we're about to have a standoff.

"Colonel." His voice greets me somberly.

"I just heard. And I assure you I'm taking

care of this, will be on the helicopter within the hour."

"You know what I always say," his deep, authoritative voice sounds in my earpiece, and I try to detect the degree of his bad mood and what he's going to do. "There's an answer to everything. The problem is finding it and figuring out the best way to do that. The proper and appropriate way to do that." He's cool. He's cautious. He's very serious. "We'll do this another time," he adds.

He means the final briefing we were scheduled to have. I'm sure he also means CNN, and I wonder what Marino told him. What exactly did he say?

"I agree, John. Everything should be canceled."

"It has been."

"Which is smart." I'm matter-of-fact. I won't let him sense my insecurities, and I know he sniffs for them. I know damn well he does. "My first priority is to determine if the information reported to me is correct. Because I don't see how it can be."

"Not a good time for you to go on the air. I don't need Rockman to tell us that."

Rockman is the press secretary. Briggs doesn't need to talk to him because he already has. I'm sure of it.

"I understand," I reply.

"Remarkable timing. If I was paranoid, I might just think someone has orchestrated some sort of bizarre sabotage."

"Based on what I've been told, I don't see how that would be possible."

"I said if I was paranoid," Briggs replies, and from where I stand, I can make out his formidable sturdy shape but can't see the expression on his face. I don't need to see it. He's not smiling. His gray eyes are galvanized steel.

"The timing is either a coincidence or it's not," I say. "The basic tenet in criminal investigations, John. It's always one or the other."

"Let's not trivialize this."

"I'm doing anything but."

"If a living person was put in your damn cooler, I can't think of much worse," he says flatly.

"We don't know —"

"It's just a damn shame after all this." As if everything we've built over the past few years is on the precipice of ruin.

"We don't know that what's been reported is accurate —" I start to say.

"I think it would be best if we bring the body here," he interrupts again. "AFDIL can work on the identification. Rockman

44

will make sure the situation is well contained. We've got everything we need right here."

I'm stunned. Briggs wants to send a plane to Hanscom Field, the air force base affiliated with the CFC. He wants the Armed Forces DNA Identification Lab and probably other military labs and someone other than me to handle whatever has happened, because he doesn't think I'm competent. He doesn't trust me.

"We don't know if we're talking about federal jurisdiction," I remind him. "Unless you know something I don't."

"Look. I'm trying to do what's best for all involved." Briggs has his hands behind his back, his legs slightly spread, staring across the parking lot at me. "I'm suggesting we can dispatch a C-Seventeen to Hanscom. We can have the body here by midnight. The CFC is a port mortuary, too, and that's what port mortuaries do."

"That's not what port mortuaries do. The point isn't for bodies to be received, then transferred elsewhere for autopsies and lab analysis. The CFC was never intended to be a first screening for Dover, a preliminary check before the experts step in. That was never my mandate, and it wasn't the agreement when thirty million dollars was spent

45

on the facility in Cambridge."

"You should just stay at Dover, Kay, and we'll bring the body here."

"I'm requesting you refrain from intervening, John. Right now this case is the jurisdiction of the chief medical examiner of Massachusetts. Please don't challenge me or my authority."

A long pause, then he states rather than asks, "You really want that responsibility."

"It's mine whether I want it or not."

"I'm trying to protect you. I've been trying."

"Don't." That's not what he's trying. He doesn't have confidence in me.

"I can deploy Captain Avallone to help. It's not a bad idea."

I can't believe he would suggest that, either. "That won't be necessary," I reply firmly. "The CFC is perfectly capable of handling this."

"I'm on the record as having offered."

On the record with whom? It occurs to me uncannily that someone else is on the line or within earshot. Briggs is still standing in front of his window. I can't tell if anyone else might be in the suite with him.

"Whatever you decide," he then says. "I'm not going to step on you. Call me as soon as you know something. Wake me up if you

46

have to." He doesn't say good-bye or good luck or it was nice having me here for half a year.

2

Lucy and Marino have left my room. My suitcases, rucksacks, and Bankers Boxes are gone, and there is nothing left. It is as if I was never here, and I feel alone in a way I haven't for years, maybe decades.

I look around one last time, making sure nothing has been forgotten, my attention wandering past the microwave, the small refrigerator-freezer and coffeemaker, the windows with their view of the parking lot and Briggs's lighted suite, and, beyond, the black sky over the void of the empty golf course. Thick clouds pass over the oblong moon, and it glows on and off like a signal lantern, as if telling me what is coming down the tracks and if I should stop or go, and I can't see the stars at all. I worry that the bad weather is moving fast, carried on the same strong south wind that brings in the big planes and their sad cargo. I should hurry, but I'm distracted by the bathroom mirror, by the person in it, and I pause to look at myself in the glare of fluorescent lights. *Who are you now? Who really?*

My blue eyes and short blond hair, the strong shape of my face and figure, aren't so different, I decide, are remarkably the same, considering my age. I have held up well in my windowless places of concrete and stainless steel, and much of it is genetic, an inherited will to thrive in a family as tragic as a Verdi opera. The Scarpettas are from hearty Northern Italian stock, with prominent features, fair skin and hair, and well-defined muscle and bone that stubbornly weather hardship and the abuses of self-indulgence most people wouldn't associate with me. But the inclinations are there, a passion for food, for drink, for all things desired by the flesh, no matter how destructive. I crave beauty and feel deeply, but I'm an aberration, too. I can be unflinching and impervious. I can be immutable and unrelenting, and these behaviors are learned. I believe they are necessary. They aren't natural to me, not to anyone in my volatile, dramatic family, and that much I know is true about what I come from. The rest I'm not so sure about.

My ancestors were farmers and worked for the railroads, but in recent years my

49

mother has added artists, philosophers, martyrs, and God knows what to the mix as she has set about to research our genealogy. According to her, I'm descended from artisans who built the high altar and choir stalls and made the mosaics at Saint Mark's Basilica and created the fresco ceiling of the Chiesa dell'Angelo San Raffaele. Somehow I have a number of friars and monks in my past, and most recently — based on what, I don't know — I share blood with the painter Caravaggio, who was a murderer, and have some tenuous link to the mathematician and astronomer Giordano Bruno, who was burned at the stake for heresy during the Roman Inquisition.

My mother still lives in her small house in Miami and is prepossessed with her efforts to explain me. I'm the only physician in the family tree that she knows of, and she doesn't understand why I've chosen patients who are dead. Neither my mother nor my only sibling, Dorothy, could possibly fathom that I might be partly defined by the terrors of a childhood consumed by tending to my terminally ill father before I became the head of the household at the age of twelve. By intuition and training, I'm an expert in violence and death. I'm at war with suffering and pain. Somehow I always end up in charge or to blame. It never fails.

I shut the door on what has been my home not just for six months but more than that, really. Briggs has managed to remind me where I'm from and headed. It's a course that was set long before this past July, as long ago as 1987, when I knew my destiny was public service and didn't know how I could repay my medical school debt. I allowed something as mundane as money, something as shameful as ambition, to change everything irrevocably and not in a good way — indeed, in the worst way. But I was young and idealistic. I was proud and wanted more, not understanding then that more is always less if you can't be sated.

Having gotten full rides through parochial school and Cornell and Georgetown Law, I could have begun my professional life unburdened by the obligations of debt. But I'd turned down Bowman Gray Medical School because I wanted Johns Hopkins badly. I wanted it as badly as I'd ever wanted anything, and I went there without benefit of financial aid, and what I ended up owing was impossible. My only recourse was to accept a military scholarship as some of my peers had done, including Briggs, whom I was acquainted with in the earliest stage of my profession, when I was assigned to the Armed Forces Institute of Pathology, the AFIP, the parent organization of the AFME. A quiet stint of reviewing military autopsy reports at Walter Reed Army Medical Center in Washington, D.C., Briggs led me to believe, and once my debt was paid, I'd move on to a solid position in civilian legal medicine.

What I didn't plan on was South Africa in December of '87, what was summertime on that distant continent. Noonie Pieste and Joanne Rule were filming a documentary and about my same age when they were tied up in chairs, beaten, and hacked, broken bottle glass shoved up their vaginas, their windpipes torn out. Racially motivated crimes against two young Americans. "You're going to Cape Town," Briggs said to me. "To investigate and bring them home." Apartheid propaganda. Lies and more lies. *Why them and why me?*

As I take the stairs down to the lobby, I tell myself not to think about this right now. *Why am I thinking about it at all?* But I know why. I was yelled at over the phone this morning. I was called names, and what happened more than two decades ago is now before me again. I remember autopsy reports that vanished and my luggage gone through. I remember being certain I would turn up dead, a convenient accident or suicide, or staged murder, like those two women I still see in my head. I see them as clearly as I did then, pale and stiff on steel tables, their blood washing through drains in the floor of a morgue so primitive we used handsaws to open their skulls, and there was no x-ray machine, and I had to bring my own camera.

I drop off my key at the front desk and replay the conversation I just had with Briggs, and I have clarity. I don't know why I didn't see the truth instantly, and I think of his remote tone, his chilly deliberateness, as I watched him through glass. I've heard him talk this way before, but usually it is directed at others when there is a problem of a magnitude that places it out of his hands. This is about more than his personal opinion of me. This is about something beyond his typical calculations and our conflicted past.

Someone has gotten to him, and it wasn't the press secretary, not anyone at Dover but higher up than that. I feel certain Briggs conferred with Washington after Marino divulged information, running his mouth and spinning his wild speculations before I'd had the chance to say a word. Marino shouldn't have discussed the Cambridge case or me. He's set something into motion he doesn't understand, because there's a lot he doesn't understand. He's never been military. He's never worked for the federal government and is clueless about international affairs. His idea of bureaucracy and intrigue is local police department policies, what he rubber-stamps as bullshit. He has no concept of power, the kind of power that can tilt a presidential election or start a war.

Briggs would not have suggested sending a military plane to Massachusetts for the transfer of a body to Dover unless he's gotten clearance from the Department of Defense, the DoD — in other words, the Pentagon. A decision has been made and I'm not part of it. Outside, in the parking lot, I climb into the van and won't look at Marino, I'm so angry.

"Tell me more about the satellite radio," I say to Lucy, because I intend to get to the bottom of this. I intend to find out what Briggs knows or has been led to believe.

"A Sirius Stiletto," Lucy says from the dark backseat as I turn up the heat because Marino is always hot while the rest of us freeze. "It's basically nothing more than storage for files, plus a power source. Of course, it also works as a portable XM radio, just as it's designed to, but it's the headphones that are creative. Not ingenious but technically clever."

"They've got a pinhole camera and a microphone built in," Marino offers as he drives. "Which is why I think the dead guy was the one doing the spying. How could he not know he had an audiovisual recording system built into his headphones?"

"He might not have known. It's possible someone was spying on him and he had no idea," Lucy says to me, and I sense she and Marino have been arguing about it. "The pinhole is on top of the headband but in the edge of it and hard to see. Even if you noticed, it wouldn't necessarily cross your mind that built inside is a wireless camera smaller than a grain of rice, an audio transmitter that's no bigger, and a motion sensor that goes to sleep after ninety seconds if nothing's moving. This guy was walking around with a micro-webcam that was recording onto the radio's hard drive and an additional eight-gig SD card. It's too soon for me to tell you if he knew it — in other words, if he rigged this up himself. I know that's what Marino thinks, but I'm not at all sure."

"Does the SD card come with the radio, or was it added aftermarket?" I inquire.

"Added. A lot of storage space, in other

words. What I'm curious about is if the files were periodically downloaded elsewhere, like onto his home computers. If we can get hold of them, we might know what this is about."

Lucy is saying that the video files she has looked at so far don't tell us much. She has reason to suspect the dead man has a home computer, possibly more than one of them, but she hasn't found anything that might tell us where he lived or who he is.

"What's stored on the hard drive and SD card go back only as far as February fifth, this past Friday," she continues. "I don't know if that means the surveillance just started or, more likely, these video files are large and take up a lot of space on the hard drive. They probably get downloaded some-where, and what's on the hard drive and SD card gets recorded over. So what's here may be just the most recent recordings, but that doesn't mean there aren't others."

"Then these video clips were probably downloaded remotely."

"That's what I would do if it were me do-ing the spying," Lucy says. "I'd log in to the webcam remotely and download what I wanted."

"What about watching in real time?" I then ask.

"Of course. If he was being spied on, whoever's doing it could log on to the webcam and watch him as it's happening."

"To stalk him, to follow him?"

"That would be a logical reason. Or to gather intelligence, to spy. Like some people do when they suspect their person is cheating on them. Whatever you can imagine, it's possible."

"Then it's possible he inadvertently recorded his own death." I feel a glint of hope and at the same time am deeply disturbed by the thought. "I say 'inadvertently' because we don't know what we're dealing with. For example, we don't know if he intentionally recorded his own death, if he's therefore a suicide, and I'm not ready to rule out anything."

"No way he's a suicide," Marino says.

"At this point, we shouldn't rule out anything," I repeat.

"Like a suicide bomber," Lucy says. "Like Columbine and Fort Hood. Maybe he was going to take out as many people as he could in Norton's Woods and then kill himself, but something happened and he never got the chance."

"We don't know what we're dealing with," I say again.

"The Glock had seventeen rounds in the

57

magazine and one in the chamber," Lucy tells me. "A lot of firepower. You could certainly ruin someone's wedding. We need to know who got married and who attended."

"Most of these people have extra magazines," I reply, and I know all about the shootings at Fort Hood, at Virginia Tech, at far too many places, where assailants open fire without necessarily caring who they kill. "Usually these people have an abundance of ammunition and extra guns if they're planning on mass murder. But I agree with you. The American Academy of Arts and Sciences is a high-profile place, and we should find out who got married there yesterday and who the guests were."

"I figure you're a member," Marino says to me. "Maybe you got a contact for getting a list of members and a schedule of events."

"I'm not a member."

"You're kidding."

I don't offer that I haven't won a Nobel Prize or a Pulitzer and don't have a Ph.D., just an M.D. and a J.D., and they don't count. I could remind him that the Academy may not be relevant anyway, because non-members can rent the building. All it takes is connections and money. But I don't feel like giving Marino detailed explanations.

He shouldn't have called Briggs.

"Good news and not so good about the recordings." Lucy reaches over the back of the seat and hands me her iPad. "Good news, as I've pointed out, is it doesn't appear anything's been deleted, at least not recently. Which could be an argument in favor of him being the one doing the spying. You might speculate that if someone had him under surveillance and had something to do with his death, that person likely would have logged on to the Web address and scrubbed the hard drive and SD before people like us could look."

"Or how about remove the damn radio and headphones from the damn scene?" Marino says. "If he was being stalked, hunted down, and whoever's doing it whacked him? Well, if it was me, I'd grab the headset and radio and keep walking. So I'm betting he was the one doing the recording. I don't believe for a minute someone else was. And I'm betting this guy was involved in something, and whatever the reason for the spy equipment, he was the only one who knew about it. What sucks is there's no recording of the perp, of whoever whacked him, which is significant. If he was confronted by someone while he was walking his dog, why didn't the headphones record it?"

"The headphones didn't record it because he didn't see the person," Lucy replies. "He wasn't looking at whoever it was."

"Assuming there was a person who somehow caused his death," I remind both of them.

"Right," she says. "The headphones pretty much pick up whatever the wearer is looking at, the camera on the crown of his head, pointing straight out like a third eye."

"Then whoever whacked him came up from behind," Marino states conclusively. "And it happened so fast the victim never even turned around. Either that or it was some kind of sniper attack. Maybe he was shot with something from a distance. Like a dart with poison. Aren't there some poisons that cause hemorrhaging? May sound far-fetched, but shit like this happens. Remember the KGB spy poked with an umbrella that had ricin in the tip? He was waiting at a bus stop, and no one saw a thing."

"It was a Bulgarian dissident who worked for the BBC, and it's not a certainty it was an umbrella, and you're getting deeper into the woods without a map," I tell him.

"Ricin wouldn't drop you in your tracks, anyway," Lucy says. "Most poisons won't. Not even cyanide gas. I don't think he was poisoned."

"This isn't helpful," I answer.

"My map is my experience as a cop," Marino says to me. "I'm using my deductive skills. They don't call me Sherlock for nothing." He taps his baseball cap with a thick index finger.

"They don't call you Sherlock at all." Lucy's voice from the back.

"It's not helpful," I repeat, looking at his big shape as he drives, at his huge hands on the wheel, which rubs against his gut even when he's in what he considers his fighting shape.

"Aren't you the one always telling me to think outside the box?" Defensiveness hardens his tone.

"Guessing isn't helpful. Connecting dots that might be the wrong dots is reckless, and you know it," I say to him.

Marino has always been inclined to jump to conclusions, but it's gotten worse since he took the job in Cambridge, since he went to work for me again. I blame it on a military presence in our lives that is as constant as the massive airlifters flying low over Dover. More directly, I blame it on Briggs. Marino is ridiculously enamored of this powerful male forensic pathologist who is also a general in the army. My connection to the military has never mattered to him or even been acknowledged, not when it was part of my past, not when I was recalled to a special status after 9/11. Marino has always ignored my government affiliations as if they don't exist.

He stares straight ahead, and headlights of an approaching car illuminate his face, touched by disgruntledness and a certain lack of comprehension that is part of who he is. I might feel sorry for him because of the affection I can't deny, but not now. Not under the circumstances. I won't let on that I'm upset.

"What else did you share with Briggs — in addition to your opinions?" I ask Marino.

When he doesn't answer, Lucy does. "Briggs saw the same thing you're about to see," she says. "It wasn't my idea, and I didn't e-mail them, just so we're clear."

"Didn't e-mail what exactly?" But I know what exactly, and my incredulity grows. Marino sent evidence to Briggs. It's my case, and Briggs has been given information first.

"He wanted to know," Marino says, as if that's a good enough reason. "What was I supposed to tell him?"

"You shouldn't have told him anything. You went over my head. It's not his case," I reply.

"Yeah, well, it is," Marino says. "He was appointed by the surgeon general, meaning he basically was hired by the president, so I'd say that means he outranks everyone in this van."

"General Briggs isn't the chief medical examiner of Massachusetts, and you don't work for him. You work for me." I'm careful how I say it. I try to sound reasonable and calm, the way I do when a hostile attorney is trying to dismantle me on the witness stand, the way I do when Marino is about to erupt into an unseemly display of loud profanities and slammed doors. "The CFC has a mixed jurisdiction and can take federal cases in certain situations, and I realize it's confusing. Ours is a joint initiative between the state and federal governments and MIT, Harvard. And I realize that's an unprecedented concept and tricky, which is why you should have let me handle it instead of bypassing me." I try to sound easygoing and matter-of-fact. "The problem about involving General Briggs prematurely, about involving him precipitously, is things can take on a life of their own. But what's done is done."

"What do you mean? 'What's *done*'?" Marino sounds less sure of himself. I detect an anxious note, and I'm not going to help him out. He needs to think about what has been done, because he's the one who did it.

"What's the not-so-good news?" I turn around and ask Lucy.

"Take a look," she says. "It's the last three recordings made, including a minute here and there when the headset was jostled by the EMTs, the cops, and this morning by me when I started looking at it in my lab."

The iPad's display glows brightly, colorfully, in the dark, and I tap on the icon for the first video file she has selected, and it begins to play. I see what the dead man was seeing yesterday at three-oh-four p.m., a black-and-white greyhound curled up on a blue couch in a living room that has a heart-of-pine floor and a blue-and-red rug.

The camera moves as the man moves because he has the headphones on and they are recording: a coffee table covered with books and papers neatly stacked, and what looks like architectural or engineering drafting vellum with a pencil on top; a window with wooden blinds that are closed; a desk with two large flat-screen monitors and two silver MacBooks, a phone plugged into a charger, possibly an iPhone, and an amber glass smoking pipe in an ashtray; a floor lamp with a green shade; a fleece dog bed and scattered toys. I get a glimpse of a door that has a dead bolt and a sliding lock, and on a wall are framed photographs and posters that go by too abruptly for me to see the details. I will wait to study them later.

So far I observe nothing that tells me who the man is or where he lives, but I get the impression of the small apartment or maybe the house of someone who likes animals, is financially comfortable, and is mindful of security and privacy. The man, assuming this is his place and his dog, is highly evolved intellectually and technically, is creative and organized, possibly smokes marijuana, and has chosen a pet that is a needy companion, not a trophy but a creature that has suffered cruelty in a former life and can't possibly fend for itself. I feel upset for the dog and worry about what has happened to it.

Certainly the EMTs, the police, didn't leave a helpless greyhound in Norton's Woods yesterday, lost and alone in the New England weather. Benton told me it was eleven degrees this morning in Cambridge, and before the night is out, it will snow. Maybe the dog is at the fire department's headquarters, well fed and attended to around the clock. Maybe Investigator Law took it home or some other police person did. It's also possible no one realized the dog belonged to the man who died. Dear God, that would be awful.

"What happened to the greyhound?" I have to ask.

"Got no idea," Marino says, to my dismay. "Nobody knew until this morning when Lucy and me saw what you're looking at. The EMTs don't remember seeing a greyhound running loose, not that they were looking, but the gate leading into Norton's Woods was open when they got there. As you probably know, the gate's never locked and is wide open a lot of the time."

"He can't survive in freezing conditions. How could people not notice the poor thing unleashed and running loose? Because I can't imagine he wasn't running around in the park for at least a few minutes before he ran out of the open gate. Common sense would tell you that when his master collapsed, the dog didn't suddenly flee from the woods and onto the street."

"A lot of people take their dogs off the leashes and let them run loose in the parks like Norton's Woods," Lucy says. "I know I do with Jet Ranger."

Jet Ranger is her ancient bulldog, and he doesn't exactly run.

"So maybe nobody noticed because it

didn't look out of the ordinary," she adds.

"Plus, I think everybody was a little pre-occupied with some guy dropping dead," Marino states the obvious.

I look out at military housing on a poorly lit road, at aircraft that are bright and big like planets in the overcast dark. I can't make sense of what I'm being told. I'm surprised the greyhound didn't stay close to his master. Maybe the dog panicked or there's some other reason no one noticed him.

"The dog's bound to show up," Marino goes on. "No way people in an area like that are going to ignore a greyhound wandering around by itself. My guess is one of the neighbors or a student has it. Unless it's possible the guy was whacked and the killer took the dog."

"Why?" I puzzle.

"Like you've been saying, we need to keep an open mind," he answers. "How do we know that whoever did it wasn't watching nearby? And then at an opportune moment, took off with the dog, acting like it belonged to him?"

"But why?"

"It could be evidence that would lead to the killer for some reason," he suggests. "Maybe lead to an identification. A game. A thrill. A souvenir. Who the hell knows? But you'll notice from the video clips at one point the leash was taken off him, and guess what? It hasn't showed up. It didn't come in with the headphones or the body."

The dog's name is Sock. On the iPad's display, the man is walking and clucking his tongue, telling Sock it's time to go. *"Let's go, Sock,"* he coaxes in a pleasant baritone voice. *"Come on, you lazy doggie, it's time for a walk and a shit."* I detect a slight accent, possibly British or Australian. It could be South African, which would be weird, a weird coincidence, and I need to get South Africa off my mind. *Focus on what's before you,* I tell myself as Sock jumps off the couch, and I notice he has no collar. Sock — a male, I assume, based on the name — is thin, and his ribs show slightly, which is typical for greyhounds, and he is mature, possibly old, and one of his ears is ragged as if once torn. A rescue retired from the racetrack, I feel sure, and I wonder if he has a microchip. If so and if we can find him, we can trace where he's from and possibly who adopted him.

A pair of hands enters the frame as the man bends over to loop a red slip lead around Sock's long, tapered neck, and I notice a silver metal watch with a tachymeter on the bezel and catch the flash of yellow gold, a signet ring, possibly a college ring. If the ring came in with the body, it might be helpful, because it might be engraved. The hands are delicate, with tapered fingers and light-brown skin, and I get a glimpse of a dark-green jacket and baggy black cargo pants and the toe of a scuffed brown hiking boot.

The camera fixes on the wall over the couch, on wormy chestnut paneling and the bottom of a metal picture frame, and then a poster or a print rises into view as the man stands up, and I get a close look at a reproduction of a drawing that is familiar. I recognize da Vinci's sixteenth-century sketch of a winged flapping device, a flying machine, and I think back a number of years — when was it exactly? The summer before 9/11. I took Lucy to an exhibition at London's Courtauld Gallery, "Leonardo the Inventor," and we spent many entranced hours listening to lectures by some of the most eminent scientists in the world while studying da Vinci's conceptual drawings of water, land, and war machines: his aerial screw, scuba gear, and parachute, his giant crossbow, self-propelled cart, and robotic knight.

The great Renaissance genius believed

that art is science and science is art, and the solutions to all problems can be found in nature if one is meticulous and observant, if one faithfully seeks truth. I have tried to teach my niece these lessons most of her life. I have repeatedly told her we are instructed by what is around us if we are humble and quiet and have courage. The man I am watching on the small device I hold in my hands has the answers I need. *Talk to me. Tell me. Who are you, and what happened?*

He is walking toward the door that is dead-bolted with the slide lock pulled across, and the perspective abruptly shifts, the camera angle changes, and I wonder if he has adjusted the position of the head-phones. Maybe he didn't have them completely over his ears and now he's about to turn on music as he heads out. He walks past something mechanical and crude-looking, like a grotesque sculpture made of metal scrap. I pause on the image but can't get a good look at whatever it is, and I decide that when I have the luxury of time I'll replay the clips as often as I want and study every detail carefully, or if need be, get Lucy to forensically enhance the images. But right now I must accompany the man and his dog to the wooded estate not even a block from Benton's and my house. I must witness what happened. In several minutes he will die. *Show me and I'll figure it out. I'll learn the truth. Let me take care of you.*

The man and the dog go down four flights of stairs in a poorly lit stairwell, footsteps sounding light and quick against uncarpeted wood, and the two of them emerge on a loud, busy street. The sun is low, and patches of snow are crusty on top with black dirt, reminding me of crushed Oreo cookies, and whenever the man glances down, I see wet pavers and asphalt, and the sand and salt from snow removal. Cars and people move jerkily and lurch as he turns his head, scanning as he walks, and music plays in the background, Annie Lennox on satellite radio, and I hear only what is audible outside the headphones, what is being picked up by the mike inside the top of the headband. The man must have the volume turned up high, and that's not good, because he might not hear someone come up behind him. If he's worried about his security, so worried that he double-locks his apartment door and carries a gun, why isn't he worried about not hearing what is going on around him?

But people are foolish these days. Even reasonably cautious people multitask ridiculously. They text-message and check e-mail while driving or operating other dangerous machinery or while crossing a busy street. They talk on their cell phones while riding bicycles and while Rollerblading, and even while flying. How often do I tell Lucy not to answer the helicopter phone; doesn't matter that it's Bluetooth-enabled and hands-free. I see what the man sees and recognize where he's walking, on Concord Avenue, moving at a good clip with Sock, past redbrick apartment buildings and the Harvard Police Department and the dark-red awning of the Sheraton Commander Hotel across the street from the Cambridge Common. He lives very near the Common, in an older apartment building that has at least four floors.

I wonder why he doesn't take Sock into the Common. It's a popular park for dogs, but he and his greyhound continue past statues and cannons, lampposts, bare oak trees, benches, and cars parked at meters lining the street. A yellow Lab chases a fat squirrel, and Annie Lennox sings, *"No more 'I love you's' . . . I used to have demons in my room at night . . ."* I am the man's eyes and ears at the time the headphones are recording, and I have no reason to suspect he knows about the hidden camera and mike or that any such thing is on his mind at all.

I don't get the sense he has a dark plan or is spying as he walks his dog. Except that he has a Glock semiautomatic pistol and eighteen rounds of nine-millimeter ammunition under his green jacket. Why? Is he on his way to shoot someone, or is the gun for self-protection, and if so, what did he fear? Maybe it was a habit of his, a normal routine to walk around armed. There are people like that, too. People who don't think twice about it. Why did he grind the serial number off the Glock, or did someone else do it? It enters my mind that the hidden recording devices built into his headphones might be an experiment of his or a research project. Certainly Cambridge and its surrounds are the mecca of technical innovations, which is one of the reasons the DoD, the Commonwealth of Massachusetts, Harvard, and MIT agreed to establish the CFC on the north bank of the Charles River in a biotech building on Memorial Drive. Maybe the man was a graduate student. Maybe he was a computer scientist or an engineer. I watch what is on the iPad's display, abrupt, shaky images of Mather Court apartments, a playground, Garden Street, and the tilted, worn headstones of the Old Burying Ground.

In Harvard Square, his attention fixes on the Crimson Corner newsstand, and he seems to think of walking in that direction, perhaps to buy a paper from the overstocked selection that Benton and I love. This is our neighborhood, where we prowl for coffee and ethnic food, and papers and books, ending up with takeout and armloads of wonderful things to read that we pile on the bed on weekends and holidays when I'm home. The *New York Times* and the *Los Angeles Times*, the *Chicago Tribune*, and the *Wall Street Journal*, and if one doesn't mind news a day or two old, there are fat papers from London, Berlin, and Paris. Sometimes we find *La Nazione* and *L'espresso*, and I read to us about Florence and Rome, and we look at ads for villas to rent and fantasize about living like the locals, about exploring ruins and museums, the Italian countryside and the Amalfi Coast.

The man pauses on the crowded sidewalk and seems to change his mind about something. He and Sock trot across the street, on Massachusetts Avenue now, and I know where they are headed, or I think I do. A left on Quincy Street, and they are walking more briskly, and the man has a plastic bag in his hand, as if Sock isn't going to hold out much longer. Past the modern Lamont

Library and the Georgian Revival brick Harvard Faculty Club and Fogg Museum, and the Gothic stone Church of the New Jerusalem, and they turn right on Kirkland Avenue. It is the three of us. I am with them, cutting over to Irving, turning left on it, minutes from Norton's Woods, minutes from Benton's and my house, listening to Five for Fighting on the satellite radio . . . *"even heroes have the right to bleed . . ."*

I feel a growing sense of urgency with each step as we move closer to the man dying and the dog being lost in the bitter cold, and I desperately don't want it. I'm walking with them as if leading them into it because I know what's ahead and they don't, and I want to stop them and turn them back. Then the house is on our left, three-story, white with black shutters and a slate roof, Federal-style, built in 1824 by a transcendentalist who knew Emerson, Thoreau, and the Norton of *Norton's Anthology* and Norton's Woods. Inside the house, Benton's and my house, are original woodwork and molding, and plaster ceilings with exposed beams, and over the landings of the main staircase are magnificent French stained-glass windows with wildlife scenes that light up like jewels in the sun. A Porsche 911 is in the narrow brick driveway, exhaust fog-

75

ging out of the chrome tailpipes.

Benton is backing up his sports car, the taillights glowing like fiery eyes as he brakes for a man and his dog walking past, and the man has his headphones turned toward Benton, maybe admiring the Porsche, a black all-wheel-drive Turbo Cabriolet that he keeps as shiny as patent leather. I wonder if he will remember the young man in the bulky green coat and his black-and-white greyhound or if they really registered at the time, but I know Benton. He'll become obsessed, maybe as obsessed with the man and his dog as I am, and I search my memory for what Benton did yesterday. Late afternoon he dropped by his office at McLean because he'd forgotten to bring home the case file of the patient he was to evaluate today. A few degrees of separation, a young man and his old dog, who are about to be parted forever, and my husband alone in his car heading to the hospital to pick up something he forgot. I'm watching it all unfold as if I'm God, and if this is what it's like to be God, how awful that must be. I know what's going to happen and can't do a thing to stop it.

3

I realize the van has stopped and Marino and Lucy are getting out. We are parked in front of the John B. Wallace Civil Air Terminal, and I stay put. I continue to watch what is playing on the iPad as Lucy and Marino begin unloading my belongings.

Cold air rushes in through the open tailgate while I puzzle over the man's decision to walk Sock in Norton's Woods, in what's called Mid-Cambridge, almost in Somerville. Why here? Why not closer to where he lived? Was he meeting someone? A black iron gate fills the display, and it is partially opened and his hand opens it wide, and I realize he has put on thick black gloves, what look like motorcycle gloves. Are his hands cold, or is there another reason? Maybe he does have a sinister plan. Maybe he intends to use the gun. I imagine pulling back the slide of a nine-millimeter pistol and pressing the trigger while wearing bulky gloves, and it seems illogical.

I hear him shake open the plastic bag, and then I see it as he looks down and I catch a glimpse of something else, what looks like a tiny wooden box. *A stash box,* I think. Some of them are made of cedar and even have a tiny hygrometer in them like a humidor, and I recall the amber glass smoking pipe on the desk inside the apartment. Maybe he likes to walk his dog in Norton's Woods because it is remote and usually quite private, and of little interest to the police unless there is a VIP or high-level event that requires security. Maybe he enjoys coming here and smoking weed. He whistles at Sock, bends over, and slips the lead off him, and I can hear him say, *"Hey, boy, do you remember our spot? Show me our spot."* Then he says something that's muffled. I can't quite make it out. *"And for you,"* it sounds like he says, followed by, *"Do you want to send one . . . ?"* Or *"Do you send one . . . ?"* After playing it twice I still can't understand what he is saying, and it may be that he is bent over and talking into his coat collar.

Who is he talking to? I don't see anyone nearby, just the dog and the gloved hands, and then the camera angle shifts up as the man straightens up and I see the park again, a vista of trees and benches, and off to one side a stone walkway near the building with the green metal roof. I catch glimpses of people and conclude by the way they are bundled up for the cold that they aren't wedding guests but most likely are walking in the park just like the man is. Sock trots toward shrubs to leave his deposit, and his master moves deeper into the gracious wooded estate of ancient elms and green benches.

He whistles and says, *"Hey, boy, follow me."*

In shaded areas around thick clumps of rhododendrons the snow is deep and churned up with dead leaves and stones and broken sticks that make me think morbidly of clandestine graves, of sloughed-off skin and weathered bones that have been gnawed on and scattered. He is scanning, looking around, and the hidden camera pauses on the three-tier green metal roof of the glass-and-timber building I can see from the sun-porch at Benton's and my house. As the man turns his head, I see a door on the first floor that leads outside, and the camera pauses again on a woman with gray hair standing outside the door. She is dressed in a suit and a long brown leather coat and is talking on her phone.

The man whistles and makes a gritty

sound as he walks on the slate gravel path toward Sock, to pick up what the dog has left . . . *"and this emptiness fills my heart . . ."* Peter Gabriel sings. I think of the young soldier with the same name who burned up in his Humvee, and I smell him as though his foul odors are still trapped deep inside my nose. I think of his mother and her grief and anger on the phone when she called me this morning. Forensic pathologists aren't always thanked, and there are times when those left behind act as if I am the reason their loved one is dead, and I try to remember that. *Don't take it personally.*

The gloved hands shake out the rumpled plastic bag again, the type one gets at the market, and then something happens. The man's gloved hand flies up at his head, and I hear the jostle of his hand hitting the headphones as if he's swatting at something, and he exclaims, *"What the . . . ? Hey . . . !"* in a breathy, startled way. Or maybe it is a cry of pain. But I don't see anything or anyone, just the woods and distant figures in it. I don't see his dog, and I don't see him. I back up the recording and play it again. His black gloved hand suddenly enters the frame, and he blurts out, *"What the . . . ?"* then, *"Hey . . . !"* I decide he sounds stunned and upset, as if something has knocked the wind out of him.

I play it again, listening for anything else, and what I detect in his tone is protest and maybe fear, and, yes, pain, as if someone has elbowed him or bumped him hard on a busy sidewalk. Then the tops of bare trees rush up and around. Chipped bits of slate zoom in and get large as he thuds down on the path, and either he is on his back or the headphones have come off. The screen is fixed on an image of bare branches and gray sky, and then the hem of a long black coat swishes past, flapping as someone walks swiftly, and another loud jostling noise and the picture changes again. Bare branches and a gray sky but different branches showing through the slats of a green bench. It happens so fast, so unbelievably fast, and then the voices and the sounds of people get loud.

"Someone call nine-one-one!"

"I don't think he's breathing."

"I don't have my phone. Call nine-one-one!"

"Hello? There's . . . uh, yeah, in Cambridge. Yes, Massachusetts. *Je-sus!* Hurry, hurry; they fucking have me on hold. Je-sus, hurry! I can't believe this. Yes, yes, a man, he's collapsed and doesn't seem to be breathing . . . Norton's Woods at the corner of Irving and Bryant . . . Yes, someone is trying CPR. I'll stay on . . . I'm staying on. Yes, I mean, I don't . . . She wants to know if he's still not breathing. No, no, he's not breathing! He's not moving. He's not breathing! . . . I didn't really see it, just looked over and noticed he was on the ground, suddenly he was on the ground . . ."

I press pause and get out of the van, and it is cold and very windy as I walk quickly into the terminal. It is small, with restrooms and a sitting area, and an old television is turned on. For a moment I watch Fox News and fast-forward the video on the iPad while Lucy leans against the front desk and pays the landing fee with a credit card. I continue to stare at images of bare branches showing between the slats of green-painted wood, certain now that the headphones ended up under a bench, the camera fixed straight up as the XM radio plays. . . . *"Dark lady laughed and danced . . ."* The music is louder because the headphones aren't pressed against the man's head, and it seems absurdly incongruous to be listening to Cher.

Voices off-camera are urgent and excited, and I hear the sounds of feet and the distant wail of a siren as my niece chats with an older man, a retired fighter pilot now working at Dover part-time as a fixed base operator, he is happy to tell her.

". . . In 'Nam. So that would have been, what, an F-Four?" Lucy chats with him.

"Oh, yeah, and the Tomcat. That was the last one I flew. But Phantoms were still around, you know, as late as the eighties. You build them right and they last like you wouldn't believe. Look how long the C-Five's been around. And still some Phantoms in Israel, I think. Maybe Iran. Nowadays those left in the U.S., we use them for unmanned targets, as drones. One hell of an aircraft. You ever seen one?"

"In Belle Chasse, Louisiana, at the Naval Air Station. Took my helicopter down there to help with Katrina."

"They've been experimenting with hurricane-busting, using Phantoms to fly into the eye." He nods.

The screen on the iPad goes black. The headphones weren't recording anymore, and I'm convinced that when the man fell to the ground they must have ended up some distance away under a bench. The motion sensor wasn't detecting enough activity to prevent it from dozing, and that's curious to me. How exactly did his headphones get knocked off and end up where they did? Maybe someone kicked them out of the way. It could have been accidental if that's

83

what happened, perhaps by a person trying to help him, or it could have been deliberate by a person who was covertly recording him, stalking him. I think of the hem of the black coat flapping by, and I fast-forward intermittently, looking for the next images, listening for sounds, but nothing until four-thirty-seven p.m., when the woods and the darkening sky swing wildly, and bare hands loom large and paper crackles as the headphones are placed inside a brown bag, and I hear a voice say, ". . . Colts all the way." And another voice says, "Saints are gonna take it. They got . . ." Then murky darkness and muffled voices, and nothing.

Finding the TV remote on the arm of a couch inside the terminal, I switch the channel to CNN and listen to the news and watch the crawl, but not a word about the man on the video clips. I need to ask about Sock again. Where is the dog? It's not acceptable that no one seems to know. I fix on Marino as he enters the sitting area, pretending not to see me because he is sulking, or maybe he regrets what he's done and is embarrassed. I refuse to ask him anything, and it feels as if the missing dog is somehow his fault, as if everything is Marino's fault. I don't want to forgive him for e-mailing the video clips to Briggs, for talking to him first.

If I don't forgive Marino for once, maybe he'll learn a lesson for once, but the problem is I'm never quite able to convince myself of any case I make against him, against anyone I care about. Catholic guilt. I don't know what it is, but already I am softening toward him, my resolve getting weaker. I feel it happening as I search channels on the television, looking for news that might damage the CFC, and he walks over to Lucy, keeping his back to me. I don't want to fight with him. I don't want to hurt his feelings.

I walk away from the TV, convinced at least for the moment that the media doesn't know about the body waiting for me in my Cambridge morgue. Something as sensational as that would be a headline, I reason. Messages would be landing nonstop on my iPhone. Briggs would have heard about it and said something. Even Fielding would have alerted me. Except I've heard nothing from Fielding about anything at all, and I try to call him again. He doesn't answer his cell phone, and he's not in his office. Of course not. He never works this late, for God's sake. I try him at his home in Concord and get voicemail again.

"Jack? It's Kay," I leave another message. "We're about to take off from Dover. Maybe you can text or e-mail me an update. Investigator Law hasn't called back, I assume? We're still waiting for photographs, and have you heard anything about a missing dog, a greyhound? The victim's dog, named Sock, last seen in Norton's Woods." My voice has an edge. Fielding is ducking me, and it's not the first time. He's a master at disappearing acts, and he should be. He's staged enough of them. "Well, I'll try you again when we land. I assume you'll meet us at the office, probably sometime between nine-thirty and ten. I've sent messages to Anne and Ollie, and maybe you can make sure they are there. We need to take care of this tonight. Maybe you could check with Cambridge PD about the dog? He might have a microchip. . . ."

It sounds silly to belabor my point about Sock. What the hell would Fielding know about it? He couldn't be bothered to go to the scene, and Marino's right. Someone should have gone.

Lucy's Bell 407 is black with dark tinted glass in back, and she unlocks the doors and baggage compartment as wind buffets the ramp.

A wind sock is stiffly pointed north like a horizontal traffic cone, and that's good and bad. The wind will still be on our tail but so will the storm front, heavy rains mixed with sleet and snow. Marino begins to load my luggage while Lucy walks around the helicopter, checking antennas, static ports, rotor blades, the emergency pop-out floats and the bottles of nitrogen that inflate them, then the aluminum alloy tail boom and its gear box, the hydraulic pump and reservoir.

"If someone was spying on him, covertly recording him, and realized he was dead, then the person had something to do with it," I say to her, apropos of nothing. "So wouldn't you expect that person to have remotely deleted the video files recorded by the headphones, at least gotten rid of them on the hard drive and SD card? Wouldn't such a person want to make sure we didn't find any recordings or have a clue?"

"Depends." She grabs hold of a handle on the fuselage and inserts the toe of her boot into a built-in step, climbing up.

"If it were you doing it," I ask.

"If it were me?" She opens fasteners and props open a panel of the lightweight aluminum skin. "If I didn't think anything significant or incriminating had been recorded, I wouldn't have deleted them." Using a small but powerful SureFire flashlight, she inspects the engine and its mounts.

"Why not?"

Before she can answer, Marino walks over to me and says to no one in particular, "I got to make a visit. Anybody else needs to, now's the time." As if he's the chief steward and reminding us that there is no restroom on the helicopter. He's trying to make up to me.

"Thanks, I'm fine," I tell him, and he walks off across the dark ramp, back to the terminal.

"If it were me, this is what I'd do after he's dead," Lucy continues as the strong light moves over hoses and tubing, as she makes sure nothing is loose or damaged. "I'd download the video files immediately by logging on to the webcam, and if I didn't see anything that worried me, I'd leave them be."

She climbs up higher to check the main rotor, its mast, its swashplate, and I wait until she is back on the tarmac before I ask, "Why would you leave them be?"

"Think about it."

I follow her around the helicopter so she can climb up and check the other side. She almost seems amused by my questions, as if what I'm asking should be obvious.

"If they're deleted after he's dead, then someone else did it, right?" she says, checking under cowling, the light probing carefully.

Then she drops back down to the ramp.

"Of course he couldn't do it after he was dead." I wait to answer her, because she could get hurt climbing all over her helicopter, especially when she's up around the rotor mast. I don't want her distracted. "So that's why you would leave them if you were the one spying on him and knew he was dead or were the one responsible for his death."

"If I were spying on him, if I followed him so I could kill him, hell, yes, I'd leave the last video recordings made, and I wouldn't grab the headphones from the scene, either." She shines the brilliant light along the fuselage again. "Because if people saw him wearing them out there in the park or on his way to the park, why are they now missing? The headphones are rather beefy and noticeable."

We walk around to the nose of the helicopter.

"And if I take the headphones, I'd have to take his satellite radio, too, dig in his coat pocket and get that out, have to take time to go to all this trouble after he's on the ground, and hope nobody saw me. And what about earlier files downloaded somewhere, assuming the spying has gone on for a while? How is that explained if there's no recording device that shows up and we find recordings on a home computer or server somewhere? You know what they say." She opens an access panel above the pitot tube and shines the light in there. "For every crime, there are two — the act itself and then what you do to cover it up. Be smarter to leave the headphones, the video files, alone, to let cops or someone like you or me assume he was recording himself, which is what Marino believes, but I doubt it."

She reconnects the battery. Her rationale for disconnecting it whenever she leaves the helicopter for any period of time is that if someone manages to get inside the cockpit and is lucky while fiddling with the throttle and switches, they could accidentally start the engine. But not if the battery is disconnected. Doesn't matter her hurry, Lucy always does a thorough preflight, especially if she's left her aircraft unattended, even if it's on a military base. But it doesn't escape my attention that she is checking everything more thoroughly than usual, as if she suspects something or is uneasy.

"Everything A-okay?" I ask her. "Everything in good shape?"

"Making sure of it," she says, and I feel

her distance more strongly. I sense her secrets.

She trusts no one. She shouldn't. I never should have trusted some people, either, going back to day one. People who manipulate and lie and claim it is for a cause. The right cause, a godly or just cause. Noonie Pieste and Joanne Rule were smothered to death in bed, probably with a pillow. That's why there was no tissue response to their injuries. The sexual assaults, the hacks with machetes and slashes with broken glass, and even the ligatures binding them when they were tied up in the chairs, all of it postmortem. A godly cause, a just cause, in the minds of those responsible. An unthinkable outrage, and they got away with it. To this day they did. *Don't think about it. Focus on what is before you, not on the past.*

I open the left-front door and climb up on a skid, the wind gusting hard. Maneuvering myself around the collective and cyclic and into the left seat, I fasten my four-point harness as I hear Marino opening the door behind me. He is loud and big, and I feel the helicopter settle from his weight as he climbs into the back, where he always sits. Even when Lucy flies with only him as a passenger, he isn't allowed up front where there are dual controls that he can nudge or bump or use as an armrest because he doesn't think. He just doesn't think.

Lucy gets in and begins another preflight, and I help her by holding the checklist, and together we go through it. I've never had a desire to fly the various aircraft my niece has owned over the years, or to ride her motorcycles or drive her fast Italian cars, but I'm fine to copilot, am handy with maps and avionics. I know how to switch the radios to the necessary frequencies or enter squawks and other information into the transponder or Chelton Flight System. If there was an emergency, I probably could get the helicopter safely to the ground, but it wouldn't be pretty.

". . . Overhead switches in the off position," I continue going down the list.

"Yes."

"Circuit breakers in."

"They are." Lucy's agile fingers touch everything she checks as we go down the plastic-laminated list.

Momentarily, she flips on the boost pumps and rolls the throttle to flight idle.

"Clear to the right." As she looks out her side window.

"Clear to the left." As I look out at the dark ramp, at the small building with its lighted windows and a Piper Cub tied down a safe distance away in the shadows, its tarp shaking in the wind.

Lucy pushes the start switch, and the main rotor blade begins to turn slowly, heavily, thudding faster like a heartbeat, and I think of the man. I think of his fear, of what I detected in those three words he exclaimed.

"What the . . . ? Hey . . . !"

What did he feel? What did he see? The lower part of a black coat, the loose skirt of a black coat swishing past. Whose coat? A wool dress coat or a trench coat? It wasn't fur. Who was wearing the long, black coat? Someone who didn't stop to help him.

"What the . . . ? Hey . . . !" A startled cry of pain.

I replay it in my mind again and again. The camera angle dropping suddenly, then fixing straight up at bare branches and gray sky, then the hem of the long, black coat moving past in the frame for an instant, maybe a second. Who would step around someone in distress as if he was an inanimate object, such as a rock or a log? What kind of human being would ignore someone who grabbed his chest and collapsed? The person who caused it, perhaps. Or someone who didn't want to be involved for some reason. Like witnessing an accident or assault and speeding off so you don't become part of the investigation. A man or a woman? Did I see shoes? No, just the hem or skirt of the coat flapping, and then another jostling sound and the picture was replaced by different bare trees showing through the underside of a green-painted bench. Did the person in the long black coat kick the headphones under the bench there so they didn't record something else that was done?

I need to look at the video clips more closely, but I can't do it now. The iPad is in back, and there isn't time. The blades rapidly beat the air, and the generator is on-line. Lucy and I put our headsets on. She flips more overhead switches, the avionics master, the flight and navigation instruments. I turn the intercom switch to "crew only" so Marino can't hear us and we can't hear him while Lucy talks to the air traffic controller. The strobes, the pulse and night scanner landing lights, blaze on the tarmac, painting it white as we wait for the tower to clear us for takeoff. Entering destinations in the touch-screen GPS and in the moving map display and the Chelton, I correct the altimeters. I make sure the digital fuel indicator matches the fuel gauge, doing most things at least twice, because Lucy believes in redundancy.

The tower releases us, and we hover-taxi to the runway and climb on course to the northeast, crossing the Delaware River at eleven hundred feet. The water is dark and ruffled by the wind, like molten metal flowing thickly. The lights of land flicker through trees like small fires.

4

We change our heading, veering toward Philadelphia, because the visibility deteriorates closer to the coast. I flip the intercom switch so we can check on Marino.

"You all right back there?" I'm calmer now, too preoccupied with the long black coat and the man's startled exclamation to be angry with Marino.

"Be quicker to cut through New Jersey," his voice sounds, and he knows where we are, because there is an in-flight map on a video screen inside the rear passenger compartment.

"Fog and freezing rain, IFR conditions in Atlantic City. And it isn't quicker," Lucy replies. "We'll be on 'crew only' most of the time so I can deal with flight following."

Marino is cut out of our conversation again as we are handed off from one tower to the next. The Washington sectional map is open in my lap, and I enter a new GPS destination of Oxford, Connecticut, for an eventual fuel stop, and we monitor weather on the radar, watching blocks of solid green and yellow encroach upon us from the Atlantic. We can outrun, duck, and dodge the storms, Lucy says, as long as we stay inland and the wind continues to favor us, increasing our ground speed to what at this moment is an impressive one hundred and fifty-two knots.

"How are you doing?" I keep up my scan for cell towers and other aircraft.

"Better when we get where we're going. I'm sure we'll be fine and can outrun this mess." She points at what's on the weather radar display. "But if there's a shadow of a doubt, we'll set down."

She wouldn't have come to pick me up if she thought we might have to spend the night in a field somewhere. I'm not worried. Maybe I don't have enough left in me to worry about yet one more thing.

"How about in general? How are you doing?" I say into the mike, touching my lip. "You've been on my mind a lot these past few weeks." I try to draw her out.

"I know how hard it is to keep up with people under the circumstances," she says. "Every time we think you're coming back,

something changes, so we've all quit thinking it."

Three times now the completion of my
fellowship was delayed by one urgent matter or another. Two helicopters shot down
in one day in Iraq with twenty-three killed.
The mass murder at Fort Hood, and most
recently, the earthquake in Haiti. Armed
forces MEs got deployed or none could be
spared, and Briggs wouldn't release me
from my training program. A few hours ago,
he attempted to delay my departure again,
suggesting I stay in Dover. As if he doesn't
want me to go home.

"I figured we'd get to Dover and find out
you had another week, two weeks, a month,"
Lucy adds. "But you're done."

"Apparently, they're sick of me."

"Let's hope you don't get home only to
turn around and go back."

"I passed my boards. I'm done. I've got
an office to run."

"Someone needs to run it. That's for
sure."

I don't want to hear more damning comments about Jack Fielding.

"And things are fine elsewhere?" I ask.

"They've almost finished the garage, big
enough for three cars even with the washing
bay. Assuming you tandem park." She starts

on a construction update, reminding me how disengaged I've been from what's going on at my own home. "The rubberized flooring is in, but the alarm system isn't ready. They weren't going to bother with glass breakers, and I said they had to. Unfortunately, one of the old wavy-glass windows original to the building didn't survive the upgrade. So you've got a bit of a breeze in the garage at the moment. Did you know all this?"

"Benton's been in charge."

"Well, he's been busy. You got the freq for Millville? I think one-two-three-point-six-five."

I check the sectional and affirm the frequency and enter it into Comm 1. "How are you?" I try again.

I want to know what I'm coming home to in addition to a dead man awaiting me in the morgue cooler. Lucy won't tell me how she is, and now she's accusing Benton of being busy. When she says something like that, she doesn't mean it literally. She's very tense. She's obsessively watching the instruments, the radar screens, and what's outside the cockpit, as if she's expecting to get into a dogfight or to be struck by lightning or to have a mechanical failure. I'm sensing something is off about her, or maybe I'm the one in a mood.

"He has a big case," I add. "An especially bad one."

We both know which one I mean. It's been all over the news about Johnny Donahue, the patient at McLean, a Harvard student who last week confessed to murdering a six-year-old boy with a nail gun. Benton believes the confession is false, and the cops, the DA, are unhappy with him. People want the confession to be genuine, because they don't want to think someone like that might still be loose. I wonder how the evaluation went today, as I envision Benton's black Porsche backing out of our driveway on the video clips I just watched. He was on his way to McLean to pick up Johnny Donahue's case file when a young man and a greyhound walked past our house. Several degrees of separation. The human web connecting all of us, connecting everyone on earth.

"Let's keep one-two-seven-point-three-five on Comm Two so we can monitor Philly," Lucy is saying, "but I'm going to try to stay out of their Class B. I think we can, unless this stuff pushes in any tighter from the coast."

She indicates the green and yellow shapes on the satellite weather radar display that show precipitation moving closer, as if trying to bully us northwest into the bright skyline of downtown Philadelphia, fly us into the high-rises.

"I'm fine," she then says. "Sorry about him, because I can tell you're pissed." She points her thumb toward the back, meaning Marino. "What'd he do besides be his usual self?"

"Were you listening when he talked to Briggs?"

"That was in Wilmington. I was busy paying for fuel."

"He shouldn't have called him."

"Like telling Jet Ranger not to drool when I get out the bag of treats. It's Pavlovian for Marino to shoot off his mouth to Briggs, to show off. Why are you more surprised than usual?" Lucy asks as if she already knows the answer, as if she's probing, looking for something.

"Maybe because it's caused a worse problem than usual." I tell her about Briggs wanting the body transported to Dover.

I tell her that the chief of the Armed Forces Medical Examiners has information he's not sharing, or at least I suspect that he is withholding something important from me. Probably because of Marino, I say. Because of what he's managed to stir up by going over my head.

"I don't think that's all of it by a long shot," Lucy says as her tail number is called out over the air.

She presses the radio switch on her cyclic and answers, and as she talks to flight following, I enter the next frequency. We hopscotch from airspace to airspace, the shapes on the weather radar mostly yellow now and bird-dogging us from the southeast, indicating heavy rains that at this altitude will create hazardous conditions as supercooled water particles hit the leading edges of the rotor blades and freeze. I watch for moisture on the Plexiglas windscreen and don't see anything, not one drop, while I wonder what Lucy is referring to. What's not it by a long shot?

"Did you notice what was in his apartment?" Lucy's voice in my headset, and I assume she means the dead man and what I watched on the video clips recorded by his headphones.

"You said that's not all of it." I go back to that first. "Tell me what you're referring to."

"I'm about to and didn't want to bring it up in front of Marino. He didn't notice, wouldn't know what it was, anyway, and I didn't point it out because I wanted to talk to you and I'm not sure he should know about it, period."

"Didn't point out what?"

"My guess is Briggs didn't need it pointed out," Lucy goes on. "He had a lot more time to look at the video clips than you did, and he or whoever else he's showed them to would have recognized the metal contraption near the door, sort of looks like a six-legged creepy crawler welded together with wires and composite pieces and parts, about the size of a stackable washer and dryer. Picked up by the camera for a second when the man and Sock were on their way out to Norton's Woods. I'm sure it wasn't lost on you, of all people."

"I caught a glimpse of what I thought was a crude metal sculpture." Obviously, I missed a connection she's made. A big one.

"A robot, and not just any robot," Lucy informs me. "A prototype developed for the military, what was supposed to be a tactical packbot for the troops in Iraq, and then another creative purpose was suggested that went over like the proverbial lead balloon."

A glint of recognition, and an ominous feeling begins working its way up from my gut, tightening my chest, creating awareness, then a memory.

"This particular model didn't last long," she continues, and I think I know what she's talking about.

MORT. Mortuary Operational Removal Transport. *Good God.*

"Never made it into service and is obsolete if not silly now, replaced by biologically inspired legged robots that can carry heavy loads over rough or slippery terrain," she says. "Like the quadruped called Big Dog that's all over YouTube. Damn thing can carry hundreds of pounds all day long in the worst conditions imaginable, jumps like a deer and regains its balance if it trips or slips or you kick it."

"MORT," I go ahead and say it. "Why would he have a packbot like MORT in his apartment? I think I'm misunderstanding something."

"You ever see it in person back then, when you got into a debate about it on Capitol Hill? And you're not misunderstanding anything. I'm talking about MORT."

"I never saw MORT in person." I saw it on videotaped demonstrations only, and I got into more than one debate, especially with Briggs. "Why would he have something like that?" I ask again about what Lucy claims is in the dead man's apartment.

"Creepy as hell. Like a giant mechanical ant, gas-powered," she says. "Sounds like a chain saw when it's ambulating slowly on its short, clunky legs with two sets of grippers in front like Edward Scissorhands. If you saw it coming at you, you'd run like hell or maybe lob a grenade at it."

"But in his apartment? Why?" I remember demonstrations that I found horrifying, and heated discussions that became nasty skirmishes with colleagues including Briggs at the AFME, at Walter Reed, and in the Russell Senate Office Building.

MORT. The epitome of wrongheaded automation that became the source of a controversy in military and medical intelligence. It wasn't the technology that was such a terrible idea, it was the suggestion of how it should be used. I remember a hot summer morning in Washington, the heat rising off a sidewalk crowded with Boy Scouts touring the capital as Briggs and I argued. We were hot in our uniforms, frustrated and stressed, and I remember walking past the White House, people everywhere, and wondering what would be next. What other inhumanities would be offered by technology? And that was almost a decade ago, almost the Stone Age compared to now.

"I'm pretty sure — in fact, more than pretty sure — that's what's parked inside the guy's apartment," Lucy is saying. "And you don't buy something like that on eBay."

"Maybe it's a model," I suggest. "A facsimile."

"No way. When I zoomed in on it, I could see the composite parts in detail, some wear and tear on it from usage, probably from R-and-D on hard terrain and it got scraped up a little. I could even see the fiber-optic connectors. MORT wasn't wireless, which was just one of a number of things wrong with it. Not like what they're doing today with autonomous robots that have onboard computers and receive information through sensors controlled by man-wearable units instead of lugging around a cumbersome Pelican case–based one. Like the military guys are doing so their field-embedded operators are hands-free when they're out with their robotic squads. This whole new thing with lightweight ruggedized processors that you can wear in your vest, say you're operating an unmanned ground vehicle or the armed robots, the SWORDS unit, the Special Weapons Observation Remote Direct-Action System. A robotic infantry armed with M-two-forty-nine light machine guns. Not something I'm comfortable with, and I know how you feel about that."

"I'm not sure that there are words for how

I feel about it," I reply.

"Three SWORDS units so far in Iraq, but they haven't fired their weapons yet. Nobody's sure how to get a robot to have that kind of judgment. Artificial EQ. A rather daunting prospect but I'm sure not impossible."

"Robots should be used for peacekeeping, surveillance, as pack mules."

"That's you but not everyone."

"They should not make decisions about life and death," I go on. "It would be like autopilot deciding whether we should fly through these clouds rolling toward us."

"Autopilot could if my helicopter had moisture and temperature sensors. Throw in force transducers and it will land all by itself as light as a feather. Enough sensors and you don't need me anymore. Climb in and push a button like the Jetsons. Sounds crazy, but the crazier, the better. Just ask DARPA. You got any idea how much money DARPA invests in the Cambridge area?"

Lucy lowers the collective, losing altitude and bleeding off speed as another ghostly patch of clouds rolls toward us in the dark.

"Besides what it's invested in the CFC?" she then says.

Her demeanor is different, even her face is different, and she's no longer trying to hide what has come over her. I know this mood. I know it all too well. It is an old mood I haven't seen in a while, but I know it like I know the symptoms of a disease that has been in remission.

"Computers, robotics, synthetic biology, nanotechnology, the more off the wall, the better," she continues. "Because there's no such thing as mad scientists anymore. I'm not sure there's any such thing as science fiction. Come up with the most extreme invention you can imagine, and it's probably being implemented somewhere. It's probably old news."

"You're suggesting this man who died in Norton's Woods is connected to DARPA."

"Somehow he is, in some capacity. Don't know how directly or indirectly," Lucy answers. "MORT isn't being used anymore, not by the military, not for any purpose, but was *Star Wars* stuff about eight or nine years ago when DARPA stepped up funding for military and intelligence-gathering applications of robotics, bio and computer engineering. And forensics and other applications germane to our war dead, to what happens in combat, in theater."

It was DARPA that funded the research and development of the RadPath technology we use in virtual autopsies at Dover and now at the CFC. DARPA funded my four-month fellowship that turned into six.

"A substantial percentage of research grants are going to Cambridge area labs, to Harvard and MIT," Lucy says. "Remember when everything became about the war?"

It's getting harder to remember a time when that wasn't true. War has become our national industry, like automotives and steel and the railroads once were. That's the dangerous world we live in. I don't believe it can change.

"The brilliant idea that robots like MORT could be utilized in theater to recover casualties so troops didn't risk their lives for a fallen comrade?" Lucy reminds me.

Not a brilliant idea but an unfortunate one. A supremely stupid one, I thought at the time and still do. Briggs and I weren't on the same side about it. He'll never give me credit for saving him from a PR misstep that could have injured him badly.

"The idea was aggressively researched for a while and then got tabled," Lucy adds.

It got tabled because using robots for such a purpose supposes they can decide a fallen soldier, a human being, is fatally injured or dead.

"DoD got a lot of shit for it, at least internally, because it seemed cold-blooded and inhumane," she says.

Deservedly. No one should die in the grippers of something mechanical dragging them off the battlefield or out of a crashed vehicle or from the rubble of a building that has collapsed.

"What I'm getting at is the early generations of this technology have been buried by DoD, relegated to a classified scrap yard or salvaged for pieces and parts," Lucy says. "Yet your guy in the cooler has one in his apartment. Where'd he get it? He's got a connection. He has drafting paper on the coffee table. He's an inventor, an engineer, something like that, and somehow involved in classified projects that require a high level of security clearance, but he's a civilian."

"How can you be so sure he's a civilian?"

"Believe me, I'm sure. He's not experienced or trained, and he sure as hell isn't military intel or a government agent or he wouldn't walk around listening to music turned up loud and armed with an expensive pistol that has the serial number ground off — in other words, he probably bought it on the street. He'd have something that would never be traced to him or anyone, something you use once and toss. . . ."

"We don't know who the gun is traced to?" I want to make sure.

"Not that I know of, not yet, which is ridiculous. This guy isn't undercover. Hell, no. I think what he is is scared," Lucy says as if she knows it for a fact. "Was," she adds. "He *was*. And someone had him under surveillance — my belief, anyway — and now he's dead. In my opinion, it's not a coincidence. I suggest you exercise extreme caution when talking to Marino."

"Sometimes he has terrible judgment, but he's not trying to do me in."

"He's also not medical intel like you are, and his understanding only goes so far as not discussing cases with his buddies at the bowling alley and not talking to reporters. He thinks it's perfectly fine to confide in people like Briggs, because he's got no sense when it comes to military brass." Lucy's demeanor is as uneasy and somber as I've seen her since I can't remember when. "In a case like this one, you talk to me, you talk to Benton."

"Have you told Benton what you just told me?"

"I'll let you explain about MORT, because he's not likely to understand what it is. He wasn't around when you went through all that with the Pentagon. You tell him, and then all of us can talk. You, him, me, and that's it, at least for now, because you don't know who is what, and you damn well better have your facts straight and know who's us and who's them."

"If I can't trust Marino with a case like this, or any case, for that matter, why do I have him?" Defensiveness sharpens my tone, because Marino was her idea, too.

She encouraged me to hire him as CFC's chief of operational investigations, and she talked him into it, too, although it wasn't exactly a hard sell. He'd never admit it, but he doesn't want to be anywhere I'm not, and when he realized I was going to be in Cambridge, he suddenly got disenchanted with the NYPD. He lost interest in Assistant DA Jaime Berger, whose office he was assigned to. He got into a feud with his landlord in the Bronx. He started complaining about New York taxes, even though he'd been paying them for several years. He said it was intolerable having no place to ride a motorcycle and no place to park a truck, even though he owned neither at the time. He said he had to move.

"It's not about trust. It's about acknowledging limitations." It's an uncharacteristically charitable thing for Lucy to say. Usually, people are simply bad or useless and deserve whatever punishment she decides.

She eases up on the collective and makes

subtle adjustments with the cyclic, increasing our speed and making sure we don't climb into the clouds. The night around us is impenetrably dark, and there are stretches where I can't see lights on the ground, suggesting we are flying over trees. I enter the frequency for McGuire so we can monitor its airspace while keeping an eye on the Traffic Collision Avoidance System, the TCAS. It is showing no other aircraft anywhere. We might be the only ones flying tonight.

"I don't have the luxury to allow for limitations," I tell my niece. "Meaning I probably made a mistake hiring Marino. I probably made a bigger one hiring Fielding."

"Not probably, and not the first time. Jack walked out on you in Watertown and went to Chicago, and you should have left him there."

"In all fairness, we lost our funding in Watertown. He knew the office was probably going to close, and it did."

"That's not why he left."

I don't respond, because she's right. It isn't why. Fielding wanted to move to Chicago because his wife had been offered a job there. Two years later, he asked if he could come back. He said he missed working for me. He said he missed his family. Lucy, Marino, Benton, and me. One big, happy family.

"It isn't just them. You have a problem with everybody there," Lucy then says.

"So nobody should have been hired. Including you, I suppose."

"Probably not me, either. I'm not exactly a team player." She was fired by the FBI, by ATF. I don't think Lucy can be supervised by anybody, including me.

"Well, this is a nice thing to come home to," I reply.

"That's the danger with a prototype installation that no matter what anyone says is in fact both civilian and military, has both local and federal jurisdiction and also academic ties," Lucy says. "You're neither-nor. Staff members don't exactly know how to act or aren't capable of staying within boundaries, assuming anyone even understands the boundaries. I warned you about that a long time ago."

"I don't remember you warning me. I just remember you pointing it out."

"Let's enter the freq for Lakehurst and squawk VFR, because I'm ditching flight following," she decides. "We get pushed any farther west and we're going to have a crosswind that will slow us down more than twenty knots and we'll be grounded for the night in Harrisburg or Allentown."

5

Snowflakes are crazed like moths in landing lights and the wind of our blades as we set down on the wooden dolly. The skids tentatively touch, then spread heavily as the weight settles, and four sets of headlights begin to move toward us from the security gate near the FBO.

The headlights move slowly across the ramp, illuminating snow that is falling fast, and I recognize the silhouette of Benton's green Porsche SUV. I recognize the Suburban and the Range Rover, both of them black. I don't know the fourth car, a sleek, dark sedan with a chrome mesh grille. Lucy and Marino must have driven here separately today and left their SUVs with the line crew, which makes sense. My niece always arrives at the airport well in advance of everyone else so she can get the helicopter ready, so she can check it from the pitot tube on its nose to the stinger on its tail boom. I haven't seen her like this in a while, and as we wait the two minutes in flight idle before she finishes the shutdown, I try to remember the last time, pinpoint it exactly, in hopes of figuring out what's happening. Because she isn't telling me.

She won't unless it fits into her overall plan, and there is no getting information out of her when she's not ready to offer it, which can be never in extreme situations. Lucy thrives on covert behavior, is far more comfortable being who she's not than who she is, and that's always been the case, going back to her earliest years. She feeds on the power of secrecy and is energized by the drama of risk, of real danger. The more threatening, the better. All she's revealed to me so far is that an obsolete robot in the dead man's apartment is a DARPA-funded packbot called MORT that at one time was intended for mortuary operations in theater, in other words, body removal in war, a mechanical Grim Reaper. MORT was insensitive and inappropriate, and I fought it aggressively years ago, but the peculiarity of the dead man having such a thing in his apartment doesn't explain Lucy's behavior.

When was it that she scared me so badly, not that it's been only once, but the time I thought she might end up in prison? Seven or eight years ago, I decide, when she came back from Poland, where she was involved in a mission that had to do with Interpol, with special ops that to this day I'm unclear about. I'll never know just how much she would tell me if I pushed hard enough, but I won't. I've chosen to remain foggy about what she did over there. What I know is enough. It's more than enough. I would never say that about Lucy's feelings, health, or general well-being, because I care intensely about every molecule of her, but I can say it about some complex and clandestine aspects of the way she has lived. For her own good and mine, there are details I will not ask about. There are stories I don't want to be told.

During the last hour of our flight here to Hanscom Field, she got increasingly preoccupied, impatient, and impossibly vigilant, and it is her vigilance that has a special caliber. That's what I recognize. Vigilance is the weapon she draws when she feels threatened and goes into a certain mode I used to dread. In Oxford, Connecticut, where we stopped for fuel, she wouldn't leave the helicopter unattended, not for a second. She supervised the fuel truck and made me stand guard in the cold while she trotted

118

inside the FBO to pay because she didn't trust Marino with guard duty, as she put it. She told me that when they had refueled in Wilmington, Delaware, earlier today en route to Dover, he was too busy on the phone to care about security or notice what was going on around them.

She said she watched him through the window as he paced on the tarmac, talking and gesturing, no doubt swept up in telling Briggs about the man who allegedly was still alive when he was locked inside my cooler. Not once did Marino look at the helicopter, Lucy reported to me. He was oblivious when another pilot strolled over to check it out, squatting so he could inspect the FLIR, the Nightsun, and peering through Plexiglas into the cabin. It didn't enter Marino's mind that the doors were unlocked, as was the fuel cap, and of course there is no such thing as securing the cowling. One can get to the transmission, the engine, the gear boxes, the vital organs of a helicopter, by the simple release of latches.

All it takes is water in the fuel tank for a flameout in flight, and the engine quits. Or sprinkle a small amount of contaminant into the hydraulic fluid, maybe dirt, oil, or water into the reservoir, and the controls will fail like power steering in a car, but a little more serious when you're two thousand feet in the air. If you really want to create havoc, contaminate both the fuel and the hydraulic fluid so you have a flameout and a hydraulic failure simultaneously, Lucy described in gory detail as we flew with the intercom on "crew only" so Marino couldn't hear. That would be especially unfortunate after dark, she said, when emergency landings, which are difficult enough, are far worse, because you can't see what's under you and had better hope it isn't trees, power lines, or some other obstruction.

Of course, the sabotage she fears most is an explosive device, and she's obsessed in general with explosives and what they're really used for and who is using them against us, including the U.S. government using them against us if it suits certain agendas. So I had to listen to that for a while before she went on to depress me further by explaining how simple it would be to plant such a thing, preferably under luggage or a floor mat in back so that when it detonates it takes out the main fuel tank beneath the rear seats. Then the helicopter turns into a crematorium, she told me, and this made me think of the soldier in the Humvee again and his devastated mother lashing out at me over the phone. I was making unfortunate associations most of the time we were flying, because for better or worse, any disaster described evokes vivid examples from my own cases. I know how people die. I know exactly what will happen to me if I do.

Lucy cuts the throttle and pulls the rotor brake down, and the instant the blades stop turning, the driver's door of Benton's SUV opens. The interior light doesn't go on. It won't in any one of the three SUVs on the ramp, because cops and federal agents, including former ones, have their quirks. They don't sit with their backs to the door. They hate to fasten their seat belts, and they don't like interior lights in their vehicles. They are imprinted to avoid ambushes and restraints that might impede their escape. They resist turning themselves into illuminated targets. They are vigilant but not as vigilant as Lucy has been these past few hours.

Benton walks toward the helicopter and waits near the dolly with his hands in the pockets of an old black shearling coat I gave him many Christmases ago, his silver hair mussed by the wind. He is tall and lean against the snowy night, and his features are keen in the uneven shadow and light. Whenever I see him after a long separation, it is with the eyes of a stranger, and I'm drawn to him all over again, just like the first time long ago in Virginia when I was the new chief, the first woman in America to run such a large medical examiner system, and he was a legend in the FBI, the star profiler and head of what was then the Behavioral Science Unit at Quantico. He walked into my conference room, and I was suddenly unnerved and unsure of myself, and it had nothing to do with the serial murders we were there to discuss.

"You know this guy?" he says into my ear as we hug. He kisses me lightly on the lips, and I smell the woodsy fragrance of his aftershave and feel the soft leather of his coat against my cheek.

I look past him to a man climbing out of the sedan, what I now can see is a dark-blue or black Bentley that has the throaty purr of a V12 engine. He is big and overweight, with a jowly face and a fringe of thinning hair that flails in the wind. Dressed in a long overcoat, the collar up around his ears, and with gloves on, he stands a polite distance away with the detached demeanor of a limo driver. But I sense his awareness of us. He seems most interested in Benton.

"He must be waiting for someone else," I decide as the man looks at the helicopter, then looks at Benton again. "Or he's mixed up."

"Can I help you?" Benton steps closer to him.

"I'm looking for Dr. Scarpetta?"

"And why might you be looking for Dr. Scarpetta?" Benton is friendly but firm, and he gives nothing away.

"I was sent here with a delivery, and the instructions I got is the party would be on Dr. Scarpetta's helicopter or meeting it. What branch of service you with, or maybe you're Homeland Security? I see it's got a FLIR, a searchlight, a lot of special equipment. Pretty high-tech; how fast does it go?"

"What can I do for you?"

"I'm supposed to give something directly to Dr. Scarpetta. Is that you? I was told to ask for identification." The driver watches Lucy and Marino carry my belongings out of the passenger and baggage compartments. The driver isn't interested in me, not so much as a glance. I'm the wife of the tall, handsome man with silver hair. The driver thinks Benton is Dr. Scarpetta and that the helicopter is his.

"Let's get you out of here before this turns into a blizzard," Benton says, walking toward the Bentley in a way that gives the driver no choice but to follow. "I hear we're getting six to eight inches, but I think we're in for more, like we need it, right? What a winter. Where are you from? Not here. The south somewhere. I'm guessing Tennessee."

"You can tell after twenty-seven years? Guess I need to work on talking Yankee. Nashville. Was stationed here with the Sixty-sixth Air Base Wing and never got around to leaving. I'm not a pilot, but I drive pretty good." He opens the passenger door and leans inside. "You fly that thing yourself? I've never been in one. I knew right away your chopper wasn't air force. I guess if you're CIA, you're not going to tell me. . . ."

Their voices drift back to me as I wait on the ramp where Benton left me. I know better than to follow him to the Bentley but am unwilling to sit inside our car when I have no idea who the man is or what delivery he's talking about or how he knew someone named Scarpetta would be at Hanscom, either on a helicopter or meeting it, and what time it would land. The first person who comes to mind is Jack Fielding. It's likely he knows my itinerary, and I check my iPhone. Anne and Ollie have answered my text messages and are already at the CFC, waiting for us. But nothing from Fielding. *What is going on with him?* Something is, something serious. This can't be

124

nothing more than his usual irresponsibility or indifference or erratic behavior. I hope he's all right, that he's not sick or injured or fighting with his wife, and I watch Benton tuck something into a coat pocket. He heads straight to the SUV, and that's his message to me. Get in and don't ask questions on the ramp. Something just transpired that he doesn't like, despite his relaxed, friendly act with the driver.

"What is it?" I ask him as we shut our doors at the same time Marino opens the back and starts shoving in my boxes and bags.

Benton turns up the heat and doesn't answer as more of my belongings are loaded, and then Marino comes around to my door. He raps a knuckle on the glass.

"Who the hell was that?" He stares off in the direction of the Bentley, and snow is falling thick and hard, frosting the bill of his baseball cap and melting on his glasses.

"Did many people know you and Lucy were heading out to Dover today?" Benton leans his shoulder against me as he talks to him.

"The general. And Captain What's-her-name, Avallone, when I called trying to get a message to the Doc. And certain people at our office knew. Why?"

"Nobody else? Maybe a mention in passing to the EMTs, to Cambridge police?"

Marino pauses, thinking, and a look passes over his face. He's not sure whom he told. He's trying to remember, and he's calculating. If he did something foolish, he won't want to admit it, has heard quite enough about how indiscreet he is. He doesn't intend to be chastised yet again, although, to be fair, he wouldn't have had a reason to behave as if it was classified information that he and Lucy were flying to Delaware to pick me up. It's not a state secret where I've been, only why I've been there, and I was supposed to come home tomorrow, anyway.

"No big deal if you did." Benton seems to be thinking the same thing I am. "I'm just trying to figure out how a messenger knew to meet the helicopter here, that's all."

"What kind of messenger drives a Bentley?" Marino says to him.

"Apparently, the kind who's been told your itinerary, including the helicopter's tail number," Benton replies.

"Goddamn Fielding. What the hell's he doing? He's fucking lost it, that's what." Marino takes off his glasses and then has nothing to wipe them with, and his face looks naked and strange without his old

126

wire-rims. "I mentioned to a few people that you were probably coming back today instead of tomorrow. I mean, obviously certain people knew because of the problem we have with the dead guy bleeding and everything else." He directs this at me. "But Fielding's the one who knew exactly what you were doing, and he sure as hell knows Lucy's helicopter, since he's been in it before. Shit, you don't know the half of it," he adds darkly.

"We'll talk at the office." Benton wants him to shut up.

"What the hell do we really know about him? What the fuck's he up to? It's damn time to quit protecting him. He's sure as hell not protecting you," he says to me.

"Let's talk about this later," Benton replies with a warning in his tone.

"Setting you up somehow," Marino says to me.

"Now's not the time to get into it." Benton's voice flattens out.

"He wants your job. Or maybe he just doesn't want you to have it." Marino looks at me as he digs his hands into the pockets of his leather jacket and steps away from my window. "Welcome home, Doc." Flakes of snow blowing into the car are cold and wet on my face and neck. "Good to be

reminded who you can really trust, right?"
He stares at me as I roll up the glass.

Anticollision beacons flash red and white on the wingtips of parked jets as we drive slowly across the ramp toward the security gate, which has just swung open.

The Bentley drives through, and we are right behind it, and I notice its Massachusetts plate doesn't have *livery* stamped on it, suggesting the car isn't owned by a limousine company. I'm not surprised. Bentleys are unusual, especially around here, where people are understated and conservation-minded, even those who fly private. I seldom see Bentleys or Rolls-Royces, mostly Toyotas or Saabs. We pass the FBO for Signature, one of several flight services on the civilian side of the airfield, and I place my hand on the soft suede of Benton's coat pocket without touching the creamy white envelope barely protruding from it.

"Would you like to tell me what just happened?" It appears he was given a letter.

"Nobody should know you just flew here or that you might be here, shouldn't know anything about you personally or your whereabouts, period," Benton says, and his face and voice are hard. "Obviously, she called the CFC and Jack told her. She's certainly called there before, and who else but Jack?"

He says it as if it's really not a question, and I have no idea what he is referring to.

"I can't understand why he or anyone would talk to her, for Christ's sake," Benton goes on, but I don't believe he doesn't understand whatever it is he's talking about. His tone says something else entirely. I don't sense that he's even surprised.

"Who?" Because I have no idea. "Who's called the CFC?"

"Johnny Donahue's mother. Apparently, that's her driver." Indicating the car up ahead.

The windshield wipers make a loud rubbery sound as they drag across the glass, pushing away snow that is turning to slush as it hits. I look at the taillights of the Bentley in front of us and try to make sense of what Benton is telling me.

"We should look at whatever it is." I mean the envelope in his pocket.

"It's evidence. It should be looked at in the labs," he says.

"I should know what it is."

"I finished evaluating Johnny this morning," Benton then reminds me. "I know his mother has called the CFC several times."

"How do you know?"

"Johnny told me."

"A psychiatric patient told you. And that's reliable information."

"I've spent a total of almost seven hours with him since he was admitted. I don't believe he killed anyone. There are a lot of things I don't believe. But I do believe his mother would call the CFC, based on what I know," Benton says.

"She can't really think we would discuss the Mark Bishop case with her."

"These days people think everything is public information, that they're entitled," he says, and it's not like him to make assumptions and to indulge in generalities. His statement strikes me as glib and evasive. "And Mrs. Donahue has a problem with Jack," Benton adds, and that comment strikes me as genuine.

"Johnny's told you his mother has a problem with Jack. And why would she have an opinion about him?"

"Some of this I can't get into." He stares straight ahead as he drives on the snowy road, and the snow is falling faster and slashes through the headlights and clicks against glass.

I know when Benton is keeping things from me. Usually, I'm fine with it. Right now I'm not. I'm tempted to slide the

130

envelope out of his pocket and look at what someone, presumably Mrs. Donahue, wants me to see.

"Have you met her, talked to her?" I ask him.

"I've managed to avoid that so far, although she's called the hospital, trying to track me down, called several times since he was admitted. But it's not appropriate for me to talk to her. It's not appropriate for me to talk about a lot of things, and I know you understand."

"If Jack or anyone has divulged details about Mark Bishop to her, that's about as serious as it gets," I reply. "And I do understand your reticence, or I think I do, but I have a right to know if he's done that."

"I don't know what you know. If Jack's said anything to you," he says.

"About what specifically?"

I don't want to admit to Benton and most of all to myself that I can't remember precisely when I talked to Fielding last. Our conversations, when we've had them, have been perfunctory and brief, and I didn't see him at all when I was home for several days over the holidays. He had gone somewhere, presumably taken his family somewhere, but I'm not sure. Long months ago, Fielding quit sharing the details of his personal life with me.

"Specifically, this case, the Mark Bishop case," Benton says. "When it happened, for example, did Jack discuss it with you?"

Saturday, January 30, six-year-old Mark Bishop was playing in his backyard, about an hour from here in Salem, when someone hammered nails into his head.

"No," I answer. "Jack hasn't talked about it with me."

I was in Dover when the boy was murdered, and Fielding took the case, which was extraordinarily out of character, and I thought so then. He's never been able to deal with children but for some reason decided to deal with this one, and it shocked me. In the past, if the body of a child was en route to the morgue, Fielding absented himself. It made no sense at all that Fielding would take the Mark Bishop case, and I'm sorry I didn't return home, because that was my first impulse. I should have acted on it, but I didn't want to do to my second in command what Briggs just did to me. I didn't want to show a lack of faith.

"I've reviewed it thoroughly, but Jack and I haven't discussed it, although I certainly indicated I would make myself available if there was a need." I feel myself getting defensive and hate it when I get that way.

"Technically, it's his case. Technically, I wasn't here." I can't stop myself, and I know it sounds weak, like I'm making excuses, and I feel annoyed with myself.

"In other words, Jack hasn't tried to share the details. I should say he's not shared his details," Benton says.

"Consider where I've been and what I've been doing," I remind him.

"I'm not saying it's your fault, Kay."

"What's my fault? And what do you mean, 'his' details?"

"I'm asking if you've asked Jack about it. If maybe he's avoided discussing it with you."

"You know how he is when it's kids. At the time, I left him a message that one of the other medical examiners could handle it, but Jack took care of it. I was surprised he did, but that's how it went. As I've said, I've reviewed all of the records. His, the police, the lab reports, et cetera."

"So you really don't know what's going on with it."

"It seems you're saying I don't."

Benton is silent.

"Know what's going on in addition to the latest? The confession made by the Donahue boy?" I try again. "Certainly I know what's been in the news, and a Harvard student confessing to such a thing has been all over it. Obviously, what you're getting at is there are details I've not been told."

Again Benton doesn't answer. I imagine Fielding talking to Johnny Donahue's mother. It's possible Fielding gave her details about where I would be tonight, and she sent her driver to deliver an envelope to me, although the driver didn't seem to know Dr. Scarpetta was a woman. I look at Benton's black shearling coat. In the dark, I can make out the vague white edge of the envelope in his pocket.

"Why would anyone from your office talk to the mother of the person who's confessed to the crime?" Benton's question sounds more like a statement. It sounds rhetorical. "We absolutely sure nothing was leaked to the media about your leaving Dover today, maybe because of this case?" He means the man who collapsed in Norton's Woods. "Maybe there's a logical explanation for how she knew. A logical explanation other than Jack. I'm trying to be open-minded."

It doesn't sound like he's trying to be open-minded at all. It sounds like he believes Fielding told Mrs. Donahue for a reason, one I can't begin to fathom. Unless it's what Marino said minutes ago, that Fielding wants me to lose my job.

134

"You and I both know the answer." I hear the conviction in my tone and realize how certain I am of what Jack Fielding could be capable of. "Nothing's been in the news that I'm aware of. And even if Mrs. Donahue found out that way, it doesn't explain her knowing the tail number of Lucy's helicopter. It doesn't explain how she knew I was arriving by helicopter or would land at Hanscom or at what time."

Benton drives toward Cambridge, and the snow is a blizzard of flakes that are getting smaller. The wind is beating the SUV, gusting and shoving, the night volatile and treacherous.

"Except the driver thought you were me," I add. "I could tell by the way he was dealing with you. He thinks you're Dr. Scarpetta, and Johnny Donahue's mother certainly must know I'm not a man."

"Hard to say what she knows," Benton answers. "Fielding's the medical examiner in this case, not you. As you said, technically you have nothing to do with it. Technically, you're not responsible."

"I'm the chief and ultimately responsible. At the end of the day, all ME cases in Massachusetts are mine. I do have something to do with it."

"It's not what I meant, but I'm glad to

hear you say it."

Of course it's not what he meant. I don't want to think about what he meant. I've been gone. Somehow I was supposed to be at Dover and at the same time get the CFC up and running without me. Maybe it was too much to ask. Maybe I've been deliberately set up for failure.

"I'm saying that since the CFC opened, you've been invisible," Benton says. "Lost in a news blackout."

"By design," I reply. "The AFME doesn't court publicity."

"Of course it's by design. I'm not blaming you."

"Briggs's design." I give voice to what I suspect Benton is getting at.

He doesn't trust Briggs. He never has. I've always chalked it up to jealousy. Briggs is a very powerful and threatening man, and Benton hasn't felt powerful or threatening since he left the FBI, and then there is a past Briggs and I share. He is one of very few people still in my life who predates Benton. It feels as if I was barely grown up when I first met John Briggs.

"The AFME didn't want you giving interviews about the CFC or publicly talking about anything relating to Dover until the CFC was set up and you were finished with your training," Benton goes on. "That's kept you out of the limelight for quite a while. I'm trying to remember the last time you were on CNN. At least a year ago."

"And coincidentally, I was supposed to step back into the limelight tonight. And coincidentally, CNN was canceled. The third time it's been canceled, as my return here was delayed and delayed."

"Yes. Coincidentally. A lot of co-incidences," Benton says.

Maybe Briggs has compromised me and done so intentionally. How brilliant it would be to groom me for a bigger job, the biggest job so far, while systematically making me less visible. To silence me. Ultimately, to get rid of me. The idea of it is shocking. I don't believe it.

"Whose coincidences, that's what you would need to know," Benton then says. "And I'm not stating as fact that Briggs did anything Machiavellian. He's not the entire Pentagon. He's just one gear in a very big machine."

"I know how much you dislike him."

"It's the machine I don't like. It's always going to be there. Just make sure you understand it so you don't get chewed up by it."

Snow clicks and bounces against glass as

we pass stretches of open fields and dense woods, and a creek runs hard against the guardrail to our right as we pass over a bridge. The air must be colder here, the snow small and icy as we drive in and out of pockets of changing weather that I find unsettling.

"Mrs. Donahue knows that the chief medical examiner and director of the CFC, someone named Dr. Scarpetta, is Jack's boss," Benton then says. "She had to know that if she went to the trouble to have something delivered to you. But maybe that's all she knows," he summarizes, offering an explanation for what just happened at the airport.

"Let's look at whatever it is." I want the envelope.

"It should go to the labs."

"She knows I'm Jack's boss but doesn't know I'm a woman." It seems preposterous, but it's possible. "Even though all she had to do was Google me."

"Not everybody Googles."

I'm reminded of how easy it is for me to forget that there are still technically unsophisticated people in the world, including someone who might have a chauffeur and a Bentley. Its taillights are far ahead of us now on the narrow two-lane road, getting smaller and more distant as the car drives too fast for the conditions.

"Did you show the driver your identification?" I ask.

"What do you think?"

Of course Benton wouldn't. "So he didn't realize you're not me."

"Not from anything I did or said."

"I guess Mrs. Donahue will continue to think Jack works for a man. Strange that Jack would tell her how to find me and not indicate how her driver might recognize me, at least indicate I'm not a man. Not even use pronouns that might indicate it. Strange. I don't know." I'm not convinced of what we're conjecturing. It doesn't feel right.

"I wasn't aware you were having so many doubts about Jack. Not that they aren't warranted." Benton is trying to draw me out. The FBI agent in him. I've not seen it in a while.

"Just don't say I'm twice bitten or thrice bitten or whatever. Please," I say with feeling. "I've heard it enough today."

"I'm saying I wasn't aware."

"And all I've been aware of is my usual misgivings and denials about him," I reply. "I've not had sufficient information to be more concerned than usual." My way of asking Benton to give me sufficient information if he has it, to not act like a cop or a mental-health practitioner. *Don't hold back,* I'm telling him.

But he does hold back. He doesn't say a word. His attention is fixed straight ahead, his profile sharp in the low illumination of the dashboard lights. This is the way it's always been with us. We step around confidential and privileged information. We dance around secrets. At times we lie. In the beginning, we cheated, because Benton was married to someone else. Both of us know how to deceive. It isn't something I'm proud of, and I wish it didn't continue to be necessary professionally. Especially right this minute. Benton is dancing around secrets, and I want the truth. I need it.

"Look, we both know what he's like, and yes, I've been invisible since the CFC opened," I continue. "I've been in a vacuum, doing the best I can to handle things long distance while working eighteen-hour days, not even time to talk to my staff by phone. Everything's been electronic, mostly e-mails and PDFs. I've hardly seen anyone. I should never have placed Jack in charge under the circumstances. When I hired him yet again and rode out of town, I set everyone up for exactly what's happened. And you did tell me so, and you aren't the only one."

"You've never wanted to believe you've got a serious problem with him," Benton says in a way that unsteadies me further. "Even if you've had plenty of them. Sometimes there's simply no sufficient evidence that will make us accept a truth we can't bear to believe. You can't be objective when it comes to him, Kay. I'm not sure I've ever understood the reason."

"You're right, and I hate it." I clear my throat and calm my voice. "And I'm sorry."

"I just don't know if I'll ever figure it out." He glances over at me, both hands on the wheel, and we're alone on a snow-blown road that is poorly lit, driving through a snowy darkness. The Bentley is no longer visible up ahead. "I'm not judging you."

"He wrecks his life and needs me again."

"It's not your fault he wrecks his life unless you haven't told me something. Actually, no matter what, it wouldn't be your fault. People wreck their own lives. They don't need others to do it."

"That's not entirely true. He didn't choose what happened to him as a child."

"And that's not your fault, either," Benton says, as if he knows more about Fielding's past than I've ever told him, what few details I have. I've always been careful not to probe my staff, especially not to probe

Fielding. I know enough about his early tragedies to be mindful of what he might not want to talk about.

"Of course it sounds stupid," I add.

"Not stupid. Just a drama that will always end the same way. I've never completely understood why you feel the need to act it out with him. I feel like something happened. Something you've not told me."

"I tell you everything."

"We both know that's not true about either of us."

"Maybe I should just stick with dead people." I hear the bitterness in my tone, the resentment seeping through barriers I've carefully constructed most of my life. Maybe I don't know how to live without them anymore. "I know how to handle dead people just fine."

"Don't talk like that," Benton says quietly.

It's because I'm tired, I tell myself. It's because of what happened this morning when the black mother of a dead black soldier disparaged me over the phone and called me names, referred to my following not the Golden Rule but the *White Rule.* Then Briggs tried to override my authority. It's possible I've been set up by him. It's possible he wants me to fail.

"It's such a goddamn stereotype," Benton

then says.

"Funny thing about stereotypes. They're usually based on something."

"Don't say things like that."

"There won't be any more problems with Jack. The drama will end, I promise. Assuming he hasn't already ended it, hasn't walked off the job. He's certainly done that before. He has to be fired."

"He's not you, never was or could be, and he's not your damn child." Benton thinks it is as simple as that, but it isn't.

"He has to be let go," I answer.

"He's a forty-six-year-old forensic pathologist who's never earned the trust you show him or anything the hell you do for him."

"I'm done with him."

"You are done with him. I'm afraid that's true and you're going to have to let him go," Benton says, as if a decision was made already, as if it isn't up to me. "What is it you feel so guilty about?" There's something in his tone, something about his demeanor. I can't put my finger on what it is. "Way back in your Richmond days when you were just getting started with him. Why the guilt?"

"I'm sorry I've caused so many problems." I evade his question. "I feel I'm the one who's let everybody down. I'm sorry I've not been here. I can't begin to express how sorry I am. I take responsibility for Jack, but I won't allow it anymore."

"Some things you can't take responsibility for. Some things aren't your fault, and I'm going to keep reminding you of that, and you'll probably keep believing it's your fault, anyway," my husband the psychologist says.

I'm not going to discuss what is my fault and what isn't, because I can't talk about why I've always been irrationally loyal to Jack Fielding. I came back from South Africa, and my penance was Fielding. He was my public service, what I sentenced myself to as punishment. I was desperate to do right by him because I was convinced I'd wronged everyone else.

"I'm taking a look." I mean at what is in Benton's coat pocket. "I know how to look at a letter without compromising it, and I need to see what Mrs. Donahue wrote to me."

I slide the envelope out, holding it lightly by its edges, and discover the flap is sealed with gray duct tape that partially covers an address engraved in an old-style serif typeface. I recognize the street as one in Boston's Beacon Hill, near the Public Garden, very close to where Benton used to own a brownstone that was in his family for generations. On the front of the envelope is *Dr. Kay Scarpetta: Confidential* written elaborately with a fountain pen, and I'm careful about touching anything else with bare hands, especially the tape. It is a good source for fingerprints, for DNA and microscopic materials. Latent prints can be developed on porous surfaces such as paper by using a reagent such as ninhydrin, I calculate.

"Maybe you've got a knife handy." I place the envelope in my lap. "And I need to borrow your gloves."

Benton reaches across me and opens the glove box, and inside is a Leatherman multitool knife, a flashlight, a stack of napkins. He pulls a pair of deerskin gloves out of his coat pockets, and my hands are lost in them, but I don't want to leave my fingerprints or eradicate those of someone else. I don't turn on the map-reading light, because the visibility is bad and getting worse. Illuminating what I'm doing with the flashlight, I slip a small blade into a corner of the envelope.

I slit it along the top and slide out two folded sheets of creamy stationery that are of heavy stock with a watermark I can't make out clearly, what looks like some type of emblazonment or family crest. The letterhead is the same Beacon Hill address,

and the two pages are typed with a typewriter that has a cursive typeface, which is
something I haven't seen in many years,
maybe a decade at least. I read out loud:

Dear Dr. Scarpetta,
I hope you will excuse what I'm sure
must seem an inappropriate and pre-
sumptuous gesture on my part. But I am
a mother as desperate as a mother could
possibly be.
My son Johnny has confessed to a
crime I know he did not commit and
could not have committed. Certainly
he's had difficulties of late that resulted
in our seeking treatment for him, but
even so, he's never demonstrated any
serious behavior problems, not even
when he began Harvard as a withdrawn
and bullied fifteen-year-old. If he was
going to have a breakdown, I should
think it would have been then, having
left home for the first time and not pos-
sessing the normal skills for interacting
with others and making friends. He did
remarkably well until this past fall semes-
ter of his senior year, when his personality became alarmingly altered. But he
did not kill anyone!
Dr. Benton Wesley, a consultant for the

146

FBI and a member of the McLean Hospital staff, knows quite a lot about my son's background and developmental obstacles, and perhaps he is at liberty to discuss these details with you, since he hasn't seemed inclined to discuss them with your assistant, Dr. Fielding. Johnny's is a long, complex story, and I need you to hear it. Suffice it to say that when he was admitted at McLean last Monday, it was because he was deemed to be a danger to himself. He had not harmed anybody else or so much as intimated that he might. Then suddenly out of the blue he confessed to such a vicious and horrible crime, and in short order was transferred to a locked ward for the criminally insane. I ask you, how is it possible the authorities have been so quick to believe his ludicrous and deluded tales?

I must talk to you, Dr. Scarpetta. I know your office performed the autopsy on the little boy who died in Salem, and I believe it is reasonable to request a second opinion. Of course you know Dr. Fielding's conclusion — that the murder was premeditated, carefully planned, a cold-blooded execution that was an initiation for a satanic cult. Something as monstrous as that is absolutely inconsistent with anything my son could do to anyone, and he has never had anything to do with cults of any description. It is outrageous to assume that his fondness for books and films with a horror or supernatural or violent theme might have influenced him to "act out."

Johnny suffers from Asperger's syndrome. He is spectacularly gifted in some areas and completely incompetent in others. He has very rigid habits and routines that he is obsessive about, and on January 30, he was eating brunch at The Biscuit with the person he is closest to, a supremely gifted graduate student named Dawn Kincaid, just as they do every Saturday morning from ten a.m. until one p.m. He could not, therefore, have been in Salem when the little boy was killed mid-afternoon.

Johnny has the remarkable ability to remember and parrot the most obscure details, and it is clear to me that what he has said to the authorities has come straight from what he's been told about the case and what's been in the news. He truly does seem to believe he is guilty (for reasons I can't begin to comprehend), and even claims that a

148

"puncture wound" to his left hand was from the nail gun misfiring when he used it on the boy, which is fabricated. The wound is self-inflicted, a stab wound from a steak knife, and one of the many reasons we took him to McLean to begin with. My son seems determined to be severely punished for a crime he didn't commit, and the way things are going, he will get his wish.

Below are numbers to contact me. I hope you will have compassion and that I hear from you soon.

Sincerely,
Erica
Erica Donahue

6

I return the sheets of heavy, stiff stationery to their envelope, then wrap the letter in napkins from the glove box to protect it as much as possible inside the zip-up compartment of my shoulder bag. If I have learned nothing else, it is that you can't go back. Once potential evidence has been cut through, contaminated, or lost, it's like an archaeologist's trowel shattering an ancient treasure.

"She doesn't seem to know you and I are married," I comment as trees thrash in the wind along the roadside, snow swirling whitely.

"She might not," Benton replies.

"Does her son know?"

"I don't discuss you or my personal life with patients."

"Then she may not know much about me."

I try to work out how it might be possible

that Erica Donahue wouldn't tell her driver that the person he was to deliver the letter to is a small blonde woman, not a tall man with silver hair.

"She uses a typewriter, assuming she typed this herself," I continue to deduce. "And anyone who would go to so much trouble taping up the envelope to ensure confidentiality probably isn't going to let someone else type the letter. If she still uses a typewriter, it's unlikely she goes on the Internet and Googles. The watermarked engraved stationery, the fountain pen, the cursive typeface, possibly a purist, someone very precise, who has a very certain and set way of doing things."

"She's an artist," Benton says. "A classical pianist who doesn't share the same high-tech interests as the rest of her family. Husband's a nuclear physicist. Older son's an engineer at Langley. And Johnny, as she pointed out, is incredibly gifted. In math, science. Writing that letter won't help him. I wish she hadn't."

"You seem very invested in him."

"I hate it when people who are vulnerable are an easy out. Because someone is different and doesn't act like the rest of us, he must be guilty of something."

"I'm sure the Essex County prosecutor

wouldn't be happy to hear you say that."
I've assumed that's who hired Benton to
evaluate Johnny Donahue, but Benton isn't
acting like a consultant, certainly not like
one for the DA's office. He's acting like
something else.

"Misleading statements, lack of eye contact, false confessions. A kid with Asperger's
and his never-ending isolation and search
for friends," Benton says. "It's not uncommon for such a person to be overly influenced."

"Why would someone want to influence
Johnny to take the blame for a violent
crime?"

"All it takes is the suggestion of something
suspicious, such as what a weird coincidence
that you were talking crazy about going to
Salem, and then that little boy was murdered there. Are you sure you hurt your
hand when you stuck it in a drawer and got
stabbed by a steak knife, or did it happen
some other way and you don't remember?
People see guilt, and then Johnny sees it.
He's led to say what he thinks people want
to hear and to believe what he thinks people
want to believe. He has no understanding
of the consequences of his behavior. People
with Asperger's syndrome, especially teen-
agers, are statistically overrepresented

among innocent people who are arrested and convicted of crimes."

Snowflakes are suddenly large and blowing wildly like white dogwood petals in a violent wind. Benton downshifts the Tiptronic transmission and lightly touches the brakes.

"Maybe we should pull over." I can't see the road as the headlights bounce off whiteness swarming all around us.

"Some freakish storm cell, like a microburst." He leans close to the steering wheel, peering straight ahead, as angry gusts of wind buffet us. "I think the best thing is to drive out of it."

"Maybe we should stop."

"We're on pavement. I can see which lane we're in. Nothing's coming." He looks in the mirrors. "Nothing's behind us."

"I hope you're right." I'm not just talking about the snow. Everything seems ominous, as if sinister forces surround us, as if we're being warned.

"It wasn't a smart thing for her to do. An emotional thing, maybe even a well-intended thing, but not smart." Benton drives very slowly through chaotic whiteness. "It's hearsay, but it won't be helpful. It's best you don't call her."

"I'll need to show the letter to the police,"

I reply. "Or at least tell them about it, so they can decide what they want to do."

"She's just made things worse." He says it as if he's the one deciding things. "Don't get mixed up in this by calling her."

"Other than her trying to influence the medical examiner's office, how has she made things worse?" I ask.

"Several key points she incorrectly makes. Johnny doesn't read horror or supernatural or violent fiction or go to movies like that, at least not that I'm aware of, and that detail won't help him. Also, Mark Bishop wasn't murdered mid-afternoon. It was closer to four. Mrs. Donahue may not realize what she just implied about her son," Benton says as the white squall ends as suddenly as it began.

Flakes are small and icy again, swirling like sand over pavement and accumulating in shallow drifts on the roadsides.

"Johnny was at The Biscuit with his friend, that's true," Benton continues, "but according to him, he was there until two, not one. Apparently, he and his friend had been there numerous times, but I'm not aware of him having some rigid regimen of being there every Saturday with her from ten to one."

The Biscuit is on Washington Street,

barely a fifteen-minute walk from our house in Cambridge, and I think of Saturdays when I've been home, when Benton and I have wandered into the small café with its chalkboard menu and wooden benches. I wonder if Johnny and his friend were ever in there when we were.

"What does his friend say about what time they left the café?" I ask.

"She claims she got up from the table around one p.m. and left him sitting there because he was acting strange and refused to leave with her. According to her statement to the police, Johnny was talking about going to Salem to get his fortune read, was talking wildly about that, and was still at the table when she walked out the door."

I find it interesting that Benton would have looked at a police statement or know the details of what a witness said. His role isn't to determine guilt or innocence or even to care but to evaluate if the patient is telling the truth or malingering and is competent to stand trial.

"Someone with Asperger's would have a hard time with the concept of a fortune being read or cards being read or anything of that nature," Benton is saying, and the more he tells me, the more perplexed I am.

He's talking to me as if he's a detective

and we're working the case together, yet he's cryptic when it comes to Jack Fielding. There's nothing accidental about it. My husband rarely lets information slip, even if he gives the appearance otherwise. When he thinks I should know information he can't tell me, he finds a way for me to figure it out. If he decides it's best I don't know, he won't help me. It's the frustrating way we live, and at least I can say I'm never bored with him.

"Johnny can't think abstractly, can't comprehend metaphors. He's very concrete," Benton is saying.

"What about other people inside the café?" I ask. "Could anybody in the café verify what the friend said or what Johnny claims?"

"Nothing more definitive than he and Dawn Kincaid were in there that Saturday morning," Benton says, and I don't remember when I've seen him so disturbed by someone he has evaluated. "Don't know about it being a weekly routine, and by the time Johnny confessed, several days had passed. Amazing what shitty memories people have, and then they start guessing."

"Then all you have is what Johnny says and now what his mother says in this letter," I reiterate what I'm hearing. "He says he left The Biscuit at two, which might not have given him enough time to get to Salem and commit the murder at around four. And his mother is saying he left at one, which could have given him enough time to do it."

"As I said, it's not helpful. What's in his mother's letter is quite bad for him. So far the only real alibi anyone can offer that might show his confession is bullshit is a problematic timeline. But an hour makes all the difference, or it could."

I imagine Johnny getting up from his table at The Biscuit at around one p.m. and heading to Salem. Depending on traffic and when he was actually out of Cambridge or Somerville and heading north on I-95, he could have been at the Bishops' house in the historic district by two or two-thirty.

"Does he have a car?" I ask.

"He doesn't drive."

"A taxi, the train? Not a ferry this time of year. They don't start running again until spring, and he would have had to board it in Boston. But you're right. Without a car, it would have taken him longer to get there. An hour would make a difference for someone who had to find transportation."

"I just don't understand where she got that detail," Benton says. "Well, maybe from him. Maybe he's changed his story yet again. Johnny said he left The Biscuit at two, not one, but maybe he's changed that rather critical detail because he thinks it's what someone wants to hear. However, it would be unusual, very unusual."

"You were just with him this morning."

"I'm not the one who would influence him to change a detail."

Benton is saying that the detail is new and he doesn't believe that Johnny has changed his story about what time he left the café. It would seem Mrs. Donahue simply made a mistake, but when I try to imagine that, something feels wrong.

"How would he have gotten to Salem at all?" I ask.

"He could have taken a taxi or a train, but there's no evidence he did either. No sightings of him, no receipts found, nothing to prove he was ever in Salem or had any connection with the Bishop family. Nothing except his confession," Benton says as his eyes cut to the rearview mirror. "And what's important about that is his story is exactly what's been in the news, and he changes the details as news accounts and theories change. That part of his mother's letter is accurate. He parrots details word for word. Including if somebody suggests a scenario or information — leads him, in other words.

Suggestibility, vulnerable to manipulation, acting in a way that generates suspicion, hallmark signs in Asperger's." He glances in the mirror again. "And attention to detail, to minutiae that can seem bizarre to others. Like what time it is. He's always maintained he left The Biscuit at two p.m. Three minutes past two, to be exact. You ask Johnny what time it is or what time he did something, and he'll tell you practically to the second."

"So why would he change that detail?"

"In my opinion, he wouldn't."

"Seems like he'd be better off saying he left earlier if he really wants people to believe he murdered Mark Bishop."

"It's not that he wants people to believe it. It's that he believes it. Not because of what he remembers but because of what he doesn't remember and because of what's been suggested to him."

"By whom? Sounds like he confessed before he was ever a suspect and interrogated. So he wasn't enticed into a false confession by the police, for example."

"He doesn't remember. He's convinced he suffered a dissociative episode after he left The Biscuit at two p.m., somehow got to Salem and killed a boy with a nail gun —"

"He didn't," I interrupt. "That much I can tell you with certainty. He didn't kill Mark Bishop with a nail gun. Nobody did."

Benton doesn't say anything as he speeds up, the snowflakes small again and sounding like grit hitting the car.

"Mrs. Donahue's also clearly misunderstood Jack's medical opinion." I talk with conviction as another part of me won't stop worrying about how I should handle her. I consider doing what Benton said and not calling her. I'll have my administrative assistant, Bryce, contact her instead, first thing in the morning, and say I'm sorry but I'm not able to discuss the Mark Bishop case or any case. It's important Bryce not give the impression that I'm too busy, that I'm unmoved by Mrs. Donahue's distress, and that makes me think of PFC Gabriel's mother again, of the painful things she said to me this morning at Dover. "I assume you've reviewed the autopsy report," I say to Benton.

"Yes."

"Then you know there is nothing in Jack's report that mentions a nail gun, only that injuries caused by nails penetrating the brain were the cause of death." I decide I can't possibly let Bryce make such a call on my behalf. I'll do it myself and ask Mrs.

Donahue not to contact me again. I'll emphasize it's for her own protection. Then I'm filled with doubt, going back and forth on what to do with her, no longer so sure of myself. I've always had confidence in my ability to handle devastated people, bereft and enraged people, but I don't understand what happened this morning. Mrs. Gabriel called me a bigot. No one has ever called me a bigot before.

"A nail gun hasn't been ruled out by the people who count," Benton informs me. "Including Jack."

"I find that almost impossible to believe."

"He's been saying it."

"First I've heard of it."

"He's been saying it to whoever will listen. I don't care what's in his written report, the paperwork you've seen," Benton repeats as he looks in the rearview mirror.

"Why would he say something contrary to lab reports?"

"I'm simply relaying to you what I know for a fact that he's been saying about a nail gun being the weapon."

"Saying a nail gun was used is absolutely contrary to scientific and medical fact." In my sideview mirror I see headlights far behind us. "A nail gun leaves tool marks consistent with a single mechanized blow,

161

similar to a firing-pin impression on a cartridge case. Instead, what we have in this instance are tool marks on nails that are consistent with a handheld hammer, and there were hammer marks on the boy's scalp and skull and underlying pattern contusions. Nail guns often leave a primer residue similar to gunshot residue, but Mark Bishop's wounds were negative for lead, for barium. A nail gun wasn't used, and I'm frankly amazed if what you're implying is that the police, the prosecutor, believe otherwise."

"Not hard to understand a number of things people choose to believe in this case," Benton says, and he's sped up, driving the speed limit.

I look in my sideview mirror again, and the headlights are much closer. Bright bluish-white lights blaze in the mirror. A large SUV with xenon headlights and fog lamps. *Marino,* I think. And behind him, I hope, is Lucy.

"Wanting to believe that Johnny's confession is true, as I've said," Benton continues. "Wanting to think that it had to be a blitz attack, that Mark Bishop couldn't have seen it coming or he would have struggled like hell. No one wants to think a child was held down and knew what was about to happen to him as someone drove nails into his skull with a hammer, for Christ's sake."

"He had no defense injuries, no evidence of a struggle, no evidence of being held down. It's in Jack's report. I'm sure you've seen it, and I'm sure he explained all this to the prosecutor, to the police."

"I wish you'd done the damn autopsy." Benton cuts his eyes to his mirrors.

"What exactly has Jack been saying beyond what I've read in his paperwork? Besides the possibility of a nail gun."

Benton doesn't answer me.

"Maybe you don't know," I then say, but I believe he does.

"He said he couldn't rule out a nail gun," Benton replies. "He said it isn't possible to tell definitively. He said this after he was asked because of what Johnny claimed in his confession. Jack was specifically and directly asked if a nail gun could have been used."

"The answer's definitively no."

"He would debate that with you. He said it isn't possible to tell definitively in this case. He said it's possible it was a nail gun."

"I'm telling you it's not possible, and it is possible to tell definitively," I reply. "And this is the first I've heard about a nail gun except for what's been on the Internet, which I have dismissed, since I dismiss most things in the news unless I am certain of the sources."

"He suggested if you pressed a nail gun against someone's head, you'd get what's similar to the muzzle mark made by a contact gunshot wound. And it's possible that's what we're seeing on the scalp and underlying tissue. And that's why there's no evidence of a struggle or that the boy knew what was happening."

"You wouldn't get a muzzle mark similar to a contact gunshot wound, and it's not possible," I reply. "The injuries I saw in photographs are hammer marks, and just because there was no evidence of a struggle doesn't mean the boy wasn't somehow coerced or coaxed or manipulated into cooperating. It sounds to me as if certain parties are choosing to ignore the facts of the case because of what they want to believe. That's extremely dangerous."

"I think Fielding is the one who might be ignoring the facts of the case. Maybe intentionally."

"Good God, Benton. He might be a lot of things . . ."

"Or it's negligence. It's one or the other," Benton says, and he has something in mind, I believe he does. "Listen. You did the best you could these past six months."

"What's that supposed to mean?" I know what it means. It means exactly what I've feared every single day that I've been gone.

"Remember when he was your fellow in the dark ages, in Richmond?" Benton is getting close to an area that is off-limits, even though he couldn't possibly know it. "From day one, he couldn't stand doing kids, that's absolutely true, as you've pointed out. If a kid was coming in, he'd run like hell, sometimes disappearing days at a time. And you'd drive around, trying to find him, going to his house, his favorite bar, the damn gym or tae kwon do, drinking himself into a stupor or kicking the shit out of someone. Not that any of us like dealing with dead children, for Christ's sake, but he's got a real problem."

I should have encouraged Fielding to go into surgical pathology, to work in a hospital lab, looking at biopsies. Instead, I mentored and encouraged him.

"But he took the Mark Bishop case," Benton says. "He could have passed him off to one of your other docs. I just hope he didn't lie; I sure as hell hope he didn't do that on top of everything else." But Benton thinks Fielding is lying. I can tell.

"On top of what else?" I ask as I look into

my sideview mirror, wondering why Marino is on our bumper.

"I hope someone didn't encourage him to suggest the possibility of a nail gun even if he knows better." Benton has a way of looking in his mirrors without moving his head. All his years of undercover work, of watching his back because he really had to. Some habits never die.

"Who?" I ask.

"I don't know."

"You sound like you do know. You're not going to tell me." It is useless to push him. If he's not telling me, it's because he can't. Twenty years of the dance and it never gets easier.

"The cops want this case solved, that's for damn sure," Benton says. "They want a nail gun to be the weapon, because it's what Johnny has confessed to and because the thought is easier to deal with than a hammer. It concerns me that someone has influenced Jack."

"Someone has? Or you're just guessing that someone has."

"It concerns me that it might be Jack who is influencing people," Benton says next, and that's what he really thinks.

"I wish Marino would get off our bumper. He's blinding me with his damn lights.

166

What's he doing?"

"It's not Marino," Benton says. "His Suburban doesn't have lights like that, and he has a front plate. This one doesn't. It's from out of state, a state that doesn't require a front plate, or it's been removed or is covered with something."

I turn around to look and the lights hurt my eyes. The SUV is only a few car lengths behind us.

"Maybe someone trying to pass us," I wonder aloud.

"Well, let's see, but I don't think so." Benton slows down, and so does the SUV. "I'll make you pass us, how about that," and he's talking to the driver behind us. "Grab the number from the rear plate as he goes by," Benton says to me.

We are almost stopped in the road, and the SUV stops, too. It backs up quickly and makes a U-turn, going the other way, fishtailing as it speeds off in the snowy night on the snowy road. I can't make out the plate on its rear bumper or any detail about the SUV except that it is dark and large.

"Why would someone be following us?" I say to Benton as if he might know.

"I have no idea what that was," Benton says.

"Someone was following us. That's what

that was. Staying too close because of the weather, because visibility is so bad you would have to stay close or you could easily lose the person if they turned off."

"Some jerk," Benton says. "Nobody sophisticated. Unless he deliberately wanted us to know he was back there or thought we wouldn't notice."

"How's it even possible? We just drove through a blizzard. Where the hell did it come from? Out of nowhere?"

Benton picks up his phone and enters a number.

"Where are you?" he says to whoever answers, and after a pause he adds, "A large SUV with fog lights, xenons, no front plate, on our ass. That's right. Made a U-turn and sped off the other way. Yes, on Route Two. Anything like that just pass you? Well, that's weird. Must have turned off. Well, if . . . Yes. Thanks."

Benton places his phone back on the console and explains, "Marino's a few minutes behind us, and Lucy's right behind him. The SUV's vanished. If someone's stupid enough to follow us, he'll try again and we'll figure it out. If the point was to intimidate, then whoever it is doesn't know his target."

"Now we're a target."

"Anyone who knows wouldn't try it."

"Because of you."

Benton doesn't answer. But what I said is true. Anyone who knows anything about Benton would be aware of how foolhardy it is to think he can be intimidated. I feel his hard edge, his steely aura. I know what he can do if threatened. He and Lucy are similar if confronted. They welcome it. Benton's simply cooler, more calculating and restrained than my niece will ever be.

"Erica Donahue." That's the first thought to come to mind. "She's already sent one person to intercept us, and I doubt she realizes how dangerous her son's charming, handsome Harvard psychologist is."

Benton doesn't smile. "Wouldn't make sense."

"How many people know our whereabouts?" There is no point in trying to lighten the mood, which is unrelentingly intense. Benton has his own caliber of vigilance. It is different from Lucy's, and he is far better at concealing it. "Or my whereabouts. How many people know?" I go on. "Not just the mother or the driver. What did Jack do?"

Benton speeds up again and doesn't answer me.

"You're not thinking Jack has some reason

to intimidate us. Or try," I then say.

Benton doesn't reply, and we drive in silence and there is no sign of the SUV with the fog lamps and xenon headlights.

"Lucy suspects he's drinking a lot." Benton finally starts talking again. "But you should get that from her. And from Marino." His tone is flat, and I hear the unforgiveness in it. He has nothing but disdain for Fielding, even if he is silent about it most of the time.

"Why would Jack lie? Why would he try to influence anyone?" I'm back to that.

"Apparently, he's been coming in late and disappearing, and he's having his skin problems again." Benton doesn't answer my question. "I hope to hell he's not doing steroids on top of everything else, especially at his age."

I resist the usual defense that when Fielding is acutely stressed, he has problems with eczema, with alopecia, and that he can't help it. He's always been obsessed with his body, is a classic case of megarexia or muscle dysmorphia, and most likely this can be attributed to the sexual abuse he suffered as a young boy. It would sound absurd to go down the list, and I'm not going to do it this time. For once, I won't. I continue checking my sideview mirror. But the xenon headlights and fog lamps are gone.

"Why would he lie about this case?" I ask again. "Why would he want to influence anybody about it?"

"I can't imagine how you could make a kid stay still for that," Benton says, and he's thinking about Mark Bishop's death. "The family was inside the house and claim they didn't hear screams, didn't hear anything. They claim that Mark was playing one minute and the next he was facedown in the yard. I'm trying to envision what happened and can't."

"All right. We'll talk about that, since you're not going to answer my question."

"I've tried to picture it, to reconstruct it, and draw a blank. The family was home. It's not a big yard. How is it possible no one saw someone or heard anything?"

His face is somber as we drive past Lanes & Games, where Marino bowls in a league. What is the name of his team? *Spare None.* His new buddies, law enforcement and military people.

"I thought I'd seen it all, but I just can't picture how it happened," Benton again says, because he can't or won't tell me what is really on his mind about Fielding.

"A person who knew exactly what he was doing." I can envision it. I can imagine in painful detail what the killer did. "Someone who was able to put the boy at ease, perhaps lure him into doing what he was told. Maybe Mark thought it was part of a game, a fantasy."

"A stranger showed up in his yard and got him to play a game that involved having nails hammered into his head — or pretending to, which is more likely," Benton considers. "Maybe. But a stranger? I don't know about that. I've missed talking to you."

"It wasn't a stranger, or at least didn't seem like one to Mark. I suspect it was someone he had no reason to distrust — no matter what he was asked to do." I base this on what I know about his injuries or lack of them. "The body showed no signs that he was terrified and panicky, someone trying to fight or escape. I think it's likely he was familiar with the killer or felt inclined to co-operate for some reason. I've missed talking to you, but I'm here now and you're not talking to me."

"I am talking to you."

"One of these days I'm going to slip Sodium Pentothal into your drink. And find out everything you've never told me."

"If only it worked, I would reciprocate. But then we'd both be in serious trouble. You don't want to know everything. Or you shouldn't. And I probably shouldn't, either."

"Four p.m. on January thirtieth." I'm thinking about how dark it would have been when Mark was murdered. "What time did the sun set that day? What was the weather?"

"Completely dark at four-thirty, cold, overcast," says Benton, who would have found out those details first thing if he was the one investigating the case.

"I'm trying to remember if there was snow on the ground."

"Not in Salem. A lot of rain because of the harbor. The water warms up the air."

"So no footprints were recovered in the Bishops' yard."

"No. And at four it was getting dark and the backyard was in shadows because of shrubbery and trees," Benton says, as if he's the detective on the case. "According to the family, Mrs. Bishop, the mother, went out at four-twenty to make Mark come into the house, and she found him facedown in the leaves."

"Why are we assuming he had just been killed when she found him? Certainly his physical findings would never allow us to pinpoint his time of death to exactly four p.m."

"The fact that the parents recall looking out the window at approximately a quarter of four and seeing Mark playing," Benton says.

" 'Playing'? What does that mean exactly? What kind of playing?"

"Don't know exactly." Benton and his evasiveness again. "I'd like to talk to the family." I suspect he's already talked to them. "There are a lot of missing details. But he was playing by himself in the yard, and when his mother looked out the window at around four-fifteen, she didn't see him. So she went out to make him come into the house and found him, tried to rouse him, and picked him up and rushed him inside. She called nine-one-one at exactly four-twenty-three p.m., was hysterical, said that her son wasn't moving or breathing, that she was worried he had choked on something."

"Why would she think he might have choked?"

"Apparently, before he went out to play, he'd put some leftover Christmas candy into his pocket. Hard candies, and the last thing she said to him as he was going out the door was not to suck on candy while he was running or jumping."

I can't help but think that this is the sort of detail Benton would have gotten from the Bishops in person. I feel he has talked to them.

"And we don't know what kind of playing he was doing? He's by himself, running and jumping?" I ask.

"I just got involved in this case after Johnny confessed to it." Benton is evasive again. For some reason, he doesn't want to talk about what Mark was doing in his backyard. "Mrs. Bishop later told police she didn't see anybody in the area, that there was no sign of anybody having been on their property, and she didn't know until Mark got to the emergency room that he'd been murdered. The nails had been hammered in all the way, and his hair hid them, and there was no blood. And his shoes were missing. He was wearing a pair of Adidas while playing in the yard, and they were gone and haven't shown up."

"A boy playing in his yard in the near dark. Again, hard to imagine he would cooperate with a stranger. Unless it was someone who represented something he instinctively trusted." I continue making that point.

"A fireman. A cop. The guy who drives the ice-cream truck. That sort of thing," Benton considers easily, as if this is safe to talk about. "Or worse. A member of his own family."

"A member of his family would kill him in such a sadistic, hideous fashion and then take his shoes? Taking the shoes sounds like a souvenir."

"Or supposed to look like one," Benton says.

"I'm no forensic psychologist," I then say. "I'm playing your role, and I shouldn't. I'd like to see where it happened. Jack never went to the scene, and he should have made a retrospective visit." My mood settles lower as I say that. He didn't go to Mark Bishop's scene, and he didn't go to Norton's Woods.

"Or another kid. Kids playing a game that turned deadly," Benton says.

"If it was another kid," I reply, "he was remarkably well informed anatomically."

I envision the autopsy photographs, the boy's head with his scalp reflected back. I envision the CT scans, three-dimensional images of four two-inch iron nails penetrating the brain.

"Whoever did it couldn't have picked more lethal locations to drive the nails," I explain. "Three went through the temporal bone above the left ear and penetrated the pons. One was nailed into the back of the skull, directed upward, so it damaged the cervicomedullary junction, or upper cervical spinal cord."

"How fast would that have killed him?"

"Almost instantaneously. The nail to the back of the head alone could have killed him in minutes, as little time as it takes to die after you can no longer breathe. Injury at the C-one and C-two levels of the spinal cord interferes with breathing. The police, the prosecutor, a jury, for that matter, would have a hard time believing another child could have done that. It seems that causing death, almost immediate death, was the intention, and it was premeditated, unless the hammer and nails were at the scene, in the yard or house, and by all accounts they weren't. Correct?"

"A hammer, yes. But what house doesn't have a hammer? And the tool marks don't match. But you know that from lab reports. No nails like the ones that killed him. Those weren't found at the family's home, and no nail gun," Benton says.

"These were L-head nails, typically used in flooring."

"According to the police, no nails like that were found at the residence," he repeats.

"Iron, not stainless steel." I continue with details from photographs, from lab reports, and all the while I hear myself, I'm aware that I'm going over the case with Benton as if it's mine. As if it's his. As if we are work-

177

ing it the way we used to work cases in our early days together. "With traces of rust despite their protective zinc coating, which suggests they weren't just purchased," I go on. "That maybe they'd been lying around somewhere and exposed to moisture, possibly saltwater."

"Nothing like that at the scene. No L-head flooring nails, no iron nails at all," Benton says. "The father's been spreading the rumor about a nail gun, at least publicly."

"Publicly. Meaning he told the media," I assume.

"Yes."

"But when? He told the media when? That's the important question. Where did the rumor come from and when? Do we know for a fact it started with the father, because if it did, that's significant. It could mean he's offering an alibi, suggesting a weapon he doesn't have, that's he trying to lead the police in the wrong direction."

"We're thinking the same thing," Benton says. "Mr. Bishop might have suggested it to the media, but the question is, did someone suggest it to him first?"

I detect more subtleties. It occurs to me that Benton knows how the rumor about a nail gun started. He knows who started it, and it's not difficult to guess what he's implying. Jack Fielding is trying to influence what people think about this case. Maybe Fielding is the one behind the rumor that is now all over the news.

"We should do a retrospective. I'm trying to remember the name of the Salem detective." There's so much to do, so much I've missed. I hardly know where to start.

"Saint Hilaire. First name James."

"Don't know him." I'm a stranger to my own life.

"He's convinced of Johnny Donahue's guilt, and I'm really concerned it's just a matter of time before he's charged with first-degree murder. We have to move fast. When Saint Hilaire reads what Mrs. Donahue just wrote to you, it will be worse. He'll be more convinced. We have to do something quickly," Benton says. "I'm not supposed to give a damn, but I do because Johnny didn't do it and no jury is going to like him. He's inappropriate. He misreads people, and they misread him. They think he's callous and arrogant. He laughs and giggles when something isn't funny. He's rude and blunt and has no idea. The whole thing is absurd. A travesty. Probably one of the most classic examples of false confessions I've ever seen."

"Then why is he still on a locked unit at

McLean?"

"He needs psychiatric treatment, but no, he shouldn't be locked up on a unit with psychotic patients. That's my opinion, but no one's listening. Maybe you can talk to Renaud and Saint Hilaire and they'll listen to you. We'll go to Salem and review the case with them. While we're there, we'll look around."

"And Johnny's breakdown?" I ask. "If his mother is to be believed, he was fine his first three years at Harvard and suddenly has to be hospitalized? He's how old?"

"Eighteen. He returned to Harvard last fall to begin his senior year and was noticeably altered," Benton said. "Aggressive verbally and sexually, and increasingly agitated and paranoid. Disordered thinking and distorted perceptions. Symptoms similar to schizophrenia."

"Drugs?"

"No evidence whatsoever. Submitted to testing when he confessed to the murder and was negative; even his hair was negative for drugs, for alcohol. His grad-school friend Dawn Kincaid is at MIT, and she and Johnny were working together on a project. She became so concerned about him she finally called his family. This was in December. Then a week ago, Johnny was admitted to McLean with a stab wound to his hand and told his psychiatrist that he'd murdered Mark Bishop, claiming he took the train to Salem and had a nail gun in a backpack, said he needed a human sacrifice to rid him of an evil entity that had taken over his life."

"Why nails? Why not some other weapon?"

"Something to do with the magical powers of iron. And most of this has been in the news."

I recall seeing something on the Internet about devil's bone, and I mention that.

"Exactly. What iron was called in ancient Egypt," Benton replies. "They sell devil's bone in some of the shops in Salem."

"Lashed together in an X that you carry in a red satin pouch. I've seen them in some of the witcheries. But not the same type of nails. The ones in the witcheries are more like spikes, are supposed to look antique. And I doubt they're treated with zinc, that they're galvanized."

"Supposedly, iron protects against malevolent spirits, and thus the explanation for Johnny using iron nails. That's his explanation. And his story's completely unoriginal; as you just pointed out, it was one of the theories all over the news the days before he confessed to the murder." Benton pauses, then adds, "Your own office has suggested black magic as a motive, presumably because of the Salem connection."

"It's not our job to offer theories. Our job is to be impartial and objective, so I don't know what you mean when you say we suggested such a thing."

"I'm just telling you it's been discussed."

"With whom?" But I know.

"Jack's always been a loose cannon. But he seems to have lost what little impulse control he had," Benton says.

"I think we've established that Jack is a problem I can no longer attempt to solve. What project?" I go back to what Benton mentioned about Johnny Donahue's female MIT friend. "And what's Johnny's major?"

"Computer science. Since early last summer, he was interning at Otwahl Technologies in Cambridge. As his mother pointed out, he's unusually gifted in some areas. . . ."

"Doing what? What was he doing there?" I envision the solid façade of precast rising up like the Hoover Dam not far from where we just drove past, the part of Cambridge where the SUV with xenon lights was following us before it vanished.

"Software engineering for UGVs and related technologies," Benton says, as if it is no great matter because he doesn't know what I do about UGVs.

Unmanned ground vehicles. Military robots like the prototype MORT in the dead man's apartment.

"What's going on here, Benton?" I say with feeling. "What in God's name is going on?"

7

The storm has settled in, the wind much calmer now, and the snow is already several inches deep. Traffic is steady on Memorial Drive, the weather of little consequence to people used to New England winters.

The rooftops of MIT fraternity houses and playing fields are solid white on the left side of the road, and on the other side the snow drifts like smoke over the bike path and the boathouse and vanishes into the icy blackness of the Charles. Farther east, where the river empties into the harbor, the Boston skyline is ghostly rectangular shapes and smudges of light in the milky night, and there is no air traffic over Logan, not a single plane in sight.

"We should meet with Renaud as soon as possible — the sooner, the better." Benton thinks Essex County District Attorney Paul Renaud should know that there may be something more to Johnny Donahue's confession, that somehow the Harvard senior and a dead man in my cooler could be connected. "But if this involves DARPA?" Benton adds.

"Otwahl gets DARPA funding. But it isn't DARPA, isn't DoD. It's civilian, an international private industry," I reply. "But certainly it's closely tied to government through substantial grants, tens of millions, maybe a lot more than that, since their rather clumsy invention of MORT."

"The question is what else they're focused on. What are they focused on now that could have significance in all this?"

"I honestly can't say, not for a fact. But you know the obvious just by looking at the place." Were we to drive back toward Hanscom, we would pass within a mile of Otwahl Technologies and its adjoining superconducting test facility, a massive self-contained complex with its own private police force. "Neutron science, most likely, because of materials science and how it applies to new technologies."

"Robotics," Benton says.

"Robots, nanotechnology, software engineering, synthetic biology. Lucy knows something about it."

"Probably more than something."

"Knowing her, yes. A lot more than something."

"They're probably making damn humanoids so we never run out of soldiers."

"They might be." I'm not joking.

"And Briggs would know about the robot in this guy's apartment." Benton means the dead man's apartment. "Because of video clips? What else about that? I wonder if he said something to Jack about it, called and alerted him by asking questions."

I explain it further, giving a more detailed account of the man and the recordings Lucy discovered — recordings that Marino inappropriately e-mailed to Briggs before I had a chance to review them first, and when I did get a chance to see them, it was only superficially, en route to the Civil Air Terminal in Dover. I tell Benton all about the ill-fated six-legged robot, the Mortuary Operational Removal Transport, known as MORT, that is parked inside the apartment near the door, and I remind him of the controversies, of the disagreements I had with certain politicians and especially with Briggs over using a machine to recover casualties in theater or anywhere.

I describe the heartlessness, the horror, of a gas-powered metal construction that sounded like a chain saw lurching across the earth to recover wounded or dead human beings by grasping them in grippers that looked like the mandibles of a bull ant. "Think of the message it sends if you're dying on the battlefield and this is what your comrades send for you," I say to Benton. "What kind of message does it send to the victim's loved ones if they see it on the news?"

"You used inflammatory language like that when you testified before a defense appropriations Senate subcommittee," Benton assumes.

"I don't remember what I said verbatim."

"I'm sure you didn't make any friends at Otwahl. You probably made enemies you have no idea about."

"It wasn't about Otwahl or any other technology company. All Otwahl did was create an unmanned robotic vehicle. It was people at the Pentagon that came up with its so-called useful purpose. I think originally MORT was supposed to be a packbot, nothing more. I didn't even remember Otwahl was the company until tonight. They were never a preoccupation of mine. My disagreement was with the Pentagon, and I was going to stand my ground." I almost say *this time.* But I catch myself. Benton doesn't know about the time I didn't stand my ground.

"Enemies who haven't forgotten. Those kinds of enemies never forget. I'm sorry I wasn't privy to all this when it was going on," Benton says, because he wasn't around when I was making enemies on Capitol Hill. He was in a protective witness program and not exactly in a position to give me advice or counsel or even assure me that he wasn't dead. "You must have files on it, records from back then."

"Why?"

"I'd like to take a look, get up to speed. It might explain a few things."

"What things?"

"I'd like to look at what you have from back then," Benton says.

Transcripts from my testimony, video recordings of the segments aired on C-SPAN: What I have would be in my safe in our Cambridge basement — along with certain items I don't want him to see. A thick gray accordion file and photographs I took with my own camera. Bloodstained squares of white cardboard improvised before the days of FTA DNA collection kits, because if blood is air-dried it can last forever, and I knew where technology was headed. Plain white envelopes with finger-nail cuttings and pubic combings and head hair. Oral, anal, and vaginal swabs, and cut and torn bloody underpants. An empty Chablis bottle, a beer can. Materials I smuggled from a dark continent half a world away more than two decades ago, evidence I shouldn't have had, items I shouldn't have had privately tested, but I did. I seriously consider that if Benton was aware of the Cape Town cases, he might not feel the same about me.

"You know the old saying, revenge is best served cold," he goes on. "You fucked a huge multimillion-dollar project, a joint venture between DoD and Otwahl Technologies, and stepped on toes, and although a number of years have passed, I suspect there are people out there who haven't forgotten, even if you have. And now here you are, working with DoD in Otwahl's backyard. A perfect opportunity to calculate revenge, to pay you back."

"Pay me back? A man dropping dead in Norton's Woods is payback?"

"I just think we should know the cast of characters."

Then we stop talking about it, because we have reached the girder bridge that connects Cambridge to Boston, the Mass Ave Bridge, or what the locals refer to as the Harvard Bridge or MIT Bridge, depending on their loyalties. Just ahead, my headquarters rises like a lighthouse, silo-shaped with a glass dome on top, seven stories sided in titanium and reinforced with steel. The first time Marino saw the CFC he decided it looked like a dum-dum bullet, and in the snowy dark, I suppose it does.

Turning off Memorial Drive, away from the river, we take the first left into the parking area, illuminated by solar security lights and surrounded by a black PVC-coated fence that can't be climbed or cut. I dig a remote control out of my bag and push a button to open the tall gate, and we drive over tire tracks that are almost completely covered in fresh white powder. Anne and Ollie's cars are here, parked near the CFC's all-wheel-drive cargo vans and SUVs, and I notice one is missing, one of the SUVs. There should be four, but one of them is gone and has been since before it began to snow, probably the on-call medicolegal investigator.

I wonder who is on duty tonight and why that person is out in one of our vehicles. At a scene, or is the person at home, and I look around as if I've never been here before. Above the fence on two sides are lab buildings that belong to MIT, glass and brick, with antennas and radar dishes on the roofs, the windows dark except for a random few glowing dimly, as if someone left a desk light or a lamp on. Snow streaks the night and is loud like a brittle rain as Benton pulls close to my building, into the space designated for the director, next to Fielding's spot, which is empty and smooth with snow.

"We could put it in the bay," Benton says hopefully.

"That would be a little spoiled, since no one else can," I reply. "And it's unauthorized, anyway. For pickups and deliveries only."

"Dover's worn off on you. Am I going to have to salute?"

"Only at home."

We climb out, and the snow is up to the ankles of my boots and doesn't pack under them because it is too cold, the flakes tiny and icy. I enter a code in a keypad next to a shut bay door that begins to retract loudly as Marino and Lucy drive into the lot. The receiving bay looks like a small hangar sealed with white epoxy paint, and mounted in the ceiling is a monorail crane, a motorized lifter for moving bodies too large for manual handling. There is a ramp inside leading to a metal door, and parked off to the side is our white van-body truck, what at Dover we refer to as a bread truck, designed to transport up to six bodies on stretchers or in transfer cases and to serve as a mobile crime scene lab when needed.

As I wait for Marino and Lucy, I'm reminded I'm not dressed for New England. My tactical jacket was perfectly adequate in Delaware, but now I'm thoroughly chilled. I try not to think about how good it would be to sit in front of the fire with a single-malt Scotch or small-batch bourbon, to catch up with Benton about things other than tragedy and betrayal and enemies with long memories, to get away from everyone. I want to drink and talk honestly with my husband, to put aside games and subterfuge and not wonder what he knows. I crave a normal time with him, but we don't know what that is. Even when we make love we have our secrets and nothing is normal.

"No updates except Lawless." Marino answers a question no one asked as the bay door clanks down behind us. "He e-mailed scene photographs — finally. But says no luck with the dog. No one's called to report a lost greyhound."

"What greyhound?" Benton asks.

I was too busy describing MORT and didn't mention much else I saw on the video clips. I feel foolish. "Norton's Woods," I reply. "A black-and-white greyhound named

Sock that apparently ran off while the EMTs were busy with our case."

"How do you know his name is Sock?"

I explain it to him as I hold my thumb over the glass sensor of the biometric lock so it can scan my print. Opening the door that leads into the lower level of the building, I mention that the dog might have a microchip that could supply useful information about the owner's identification. Some rescue groups automatically microchip former racing greyhounds before putting them up for adoption, I add.

"That's interesting," Benton says. "I think I saw them."

"He stared right at you as you were pulling out of the driveway in your sports car about three-fifteen yesterday afternoon," Lucy tells him as we enter the processing area, an open space with a security office, a digital floor scale, and a wall of massive stainless-steel doors that open into cooler rooms and a walk-in freezer.

"What are you talking about?" Benton asks my niece.

"All that time in the car driving through a blizzard and you didn't catch him up on things?" Lucy says to me, and she's not easy to be around when she gets like this.

I feel a prick of annoyance even though

she's right. *She knows you, too,* enters my mind. *She knows you just as well as you know her.* She knows damn well when something is bothering me that I stubbornly keep to myself, and I've been bothered and feeling stubborn since I left Dover. It was stupid of me not to go into the sort of detail that Benton can do something with. I don't know of anyone more psychologically astute, and he would have plenty to say about the minutiae picked up by the recorders concealed inside the dead man's headphones.

Instead, I obsessed about DARPA because I was really obsessing about Briggs. I can't get past what happened earlier today, about what happened decades ago, about how what he caused never seems to end. He knows about that dark place in my past, a place I take no one, and a part of me will never forgive him for creating that place. It was his idea for me to go to Cape Town. It was his goddamn brilliant plan.

"He and the greyhound walked right past your driveway just minutes before he died," Lucy is telling Benton, but her gaze is steady on me. "If you hadn't left, you would have heard the sirens. You probably would have headed over there to see what was going on and maybe would have some useful information for us."

She looks at me as if she is looking at the dark place. It's not possible she could know about it, I reassure myself. I've never told her, never told Benton or Marino or anyone. The documents were destroyed except for what I have. Briggs promised that decades ago when I left the AFIP and moved to Virginia, and I already knew reports were missing without being told. Lucy doesn't have the combination to my safe, I remind myself. Benton doesn't. No one does.

"If you drop by my lab," Lucy is saying to Benton, "I'll show the video clips to you."

"You haven't seen them," I say to Benton, because I'm not sure. He's acting as if he hasn't seen them, but I don't know if it's just more of the same, more secrets.

"I haven't," he answers, and it sounds like the truth. "But I want to, and I will."

"Weird you're in them," Lucy says to him. "Your house is in them. Really weird. Sort of freaked me out when I saw it."

The night security guard sits behind his glass window, and he nods at us but doesn't get up from his desk. His name is Ron, a big, muscular dark-skinned man with closely shorn hair and unfriendly eyes. He seems afraid of me or skeptical, and it's obvious he's been instructed to maintain his post, not to be sociable, no matter who it is. I can

195

only imagine the stories he's heard, and Fielding enters my thoughts again. What has happened to him? What trouble has he caused? How much has he hurt this place?

I walk over to the security guard's window and check the sign-in log. Since three p.m., three bodies have come in: a motor-vehicle fatality, a gunshot homicide, and an asphyxiation by plastic bag that is undetermined.

"Is Dr. Fielding here?" I ask Ron.

Retired marine corps military police, he is always neat and proud in his midnight-blue uniform with American flag and AFME patches on the shoulders and a brass CFC security shield pinned to his shirt. His face is wary and not the least bit warm behind his glass partition as he answers that he hasn't seen Fielding. He tells me that Anne and Ollie are here but no one else. Not even the on-call death investigator is in. Randy, he informs me in a monotone, and every other word is *ma'am,* and I'm reminded of how cold and condescending *ma'am* this and *ma'am* that can sound and how tired I got of hearing it at Dover. Randy is working from home because of the weather, Ron reports. Apparently, Fielding told him that was okay, even though it's not. That is against the rules I established. On-call investigators don't work from home.

"We'll be in the x-ray room," I inform Ron. "If anybody else shows up, you can find us in there. But unless it's Dr. Fielding, I need to know who it is and give clearance. Actually, I probably should know if Dr. Fielding shows up, too. You know what, no matter who it is, I need to know."

"If Dr. Fielding comes in you want me to call, ma'am. To alert you," Ron repeats, as if he's not sure that's what I meant, or maybe he's arguing.

"Affirmative," I make myself clear. "No one should just walk in, doesn't matter if they work here. Until I tell you otherwise. I want everything airtight right now."

"I understand, ma'am."

"Any calls from the media? Any sign of them?"

"I keep looking, ma'am." Mounted on three walls are monitors, each split into quadrants that are constantly rotating images picked up by security cameras outside the building and in strategic areas such as the bays, corridors, elevators, lobby, and all doors leading into the building. "I know there's some concern about the man found in the park." Ron looks past me at Marino, as if the two of them have an understanding.

"Well, you know where we'll be for now."

I open another door. "Thank you."

A long white hallway with a gray tile floor leads to a series of rooms located in a logical order that facilitates the flow of our work. The first stop is ID, where bodies are photographed and fingerprinted and personal effects not taken by the police are removed and secured in lockers. Next is large-scale x-ray, which includes the CT scanner, and beyond that are the autopsy room, the soiled room, the anteroom, the changing rooms, the locker rooms, the anthropology lab, the Bio4 containment lab reserved for suspected infectious or contaminated cases. The corridor wraps around in a circle that ends where it began, at the receiving bay.

"What does security know about our patient from Norton's Woods?" I ask Marino. "Why does Ron think there's a concern?"

"I didn't tell him anything."

"I'm asking what he knows."

"He wasn't on duty when we left earlier. I haven't seen him today."

"I'm wondering what he's been told," I repeat patiently, because I don't want to squabble with Marino in front of the others. "Obviously, this is a very sensitive situation."

"I gave an order before I left that everyone needed to be on the lookout for the media," Marino says, taking off his leather jacket as we reach the x-ray room, where the red light above the door indicates that the scanner is in use. Anne and Ollie won't have started without me, but it's their habit to deter people from walking into an area where there are levels of radiation much higher than are safe for living patients. "Wasn't my idea for Randy or the others to work from home, either," Marino adds.

I don't ask how long that's been going on or who the "others" are. Who else has been working from home? This is a state government facility, a paramilitary installation, not a cottage industry, I feel like saying.

"Damn Fielding," Marino then mutters. "He's fucking up everything."

I don't answer. Now is not the time to discuss how fucked up everything is.

"You know where I'll be." Lucy walks off toward the elevator, and with an elbow pushes a hands-free oversized button. She disappears behind sliding steel doors as I pass my thumb over another biometric sensor and the lock clicks free.

Inside the control room, forensic radiologist Dr. Oliver Hess is seated at a work station behind lead-lined glass, his gray hair unruly, his face sleepy, as if I got him out of bed. Past him, through an open door, I can see the eggshell-white Siemens Somatom Sensation and hear the fan of its water-cooled system. The scanner is a modified version of the one used at Dover, equipped with a custom head holder and safety straps, its wiring subsurface, its parameter sealed, its table covered by a heavy vinyl slicker to protect the multimillion-dollar system from contaminants such as body fluids. Slightly angled down toward the door to facilitate sliding bodies on and off, the scanner is in the ready status, and technologist Anne Mahoney is placing radio-opaque CT skin markers on the dead man from Norton's Woods. I get a strange feeling as I walk in. He is familiar, although I've never seen him before, only parts of him on recordings I watched on an iPad.

I recognize the tint of his light-brown skin and his tapered hands, which are by his sides on top of a disposable blue sheet, his long, slender fingers slightly curled and stiff with rigor.

In the video clips I heard his voice and saw glimpses of his hands, his boots, his clothing, but I did not see his face. I'm not sure what I imagined but am vaguely disturbed by his delicate features and long, curly brown hair, by the spray of light freckles across his smooth cheeks. I pull the sheet back, and he is very thin, about five-foot-eight and at most one hundred and thirty pounds, I deduce, with very little body hair. He could easily pass for sixteen, and I'm reminded of Johnny Donahue, who isn't much older. Kids. Could that be a common denominator? Or is it Otwahl Technologies?

"Anything?" I ask Anne, a plain-looking woman in her thirties with shaggy brown hair and sensitive hazel eyes. She's probably the best person on my staff, can do anything, whether it is different types of radiographic imaging or helping in the morgue or at crime scenes. She is always willing.

"This. Which I noticed when I undressed him." Her latex-sheathed hands grip the body at the waist and hip, pulling it over so I can see a tiny defect on the left side of the back at the level of the kidneys. "Obviously missed at the scene because it didn't bleed out, at least not much. You know about his bleeding, which I witnessed with my own two eyes when I was going to scan him early this morning? That he bled profusely from his nose and mouth after he was bagged and transported?"

"That's why I'm here." I open a drawer to

retrieve a hand lens, and then Benton is by my side in a surgical mask and gown and gloves. "He's got some sort of injury," I say to him as I lean close to the body and magnify an irregular wound that looks like a small buttonhole. "Definitely not a gunshot entrance. A stab wound made by a very narrow blade, like a boning knife but with two edges. Something like a stiletto."

"A stiletto in his back would drop him in his tracks?" Benton's eyes are skeptical above his mask.

"No. Not unless he was stabbed at the base of his skull and it severed his spinal cord." I think of Mark Bishop and the nails that killed him.

"Like I said at Dover, maybe something was injected," Marino offers as he walks in covered from head to foot with personal protective clothing, including a face shield and hair cover, as if he's worried about airborne pathogens or deadly spores, such as anthrax. "Maybe some kind of anesthesia. A lethal injection, in other words. That could sure as hell drop you in your tracks."

"In the first place, an anesthesia like sodium thiopental is injected into a vein, as are pancuronium bromide or potassium chloride." I pull on a pair of examination gloves. "They aren't injected into the person's back. Same thing with mivacurium, with succinylcholine. You want to kill somebody decisively and quickly with a neuromuscular blocker, you'd better inject it intravenously."

"But if they were injected into a muscle, it would still kill you, right?" Marino opens a cabinet and gets out a camera. He rummages in a drawer and finds a plastic six-inch ruler for size reference. "During executions, sometimes the injection misses the vein and goes into the muscle, and the inmate still dies."

"A slow and very painful death," I reply. "By all accounts, this man's death wasn't slow, and this injury wasn't made by a needle."

"I won't say the prison techs do it on purpose, but it happens. Well, it's probably on purpose. Just like some of them chill the cocktail, making sure the dirtbag feels it hit, the ice-cold hand of death," Marino says for Anne's benefit, because she is passionately anti–capital punishment. His way of flirting is to offend her whenever he can.

"That's disgusting," she says.

"Hey. It's not like they cared about the people they whacked, right? Like they cared if they suffered, right? What goes around comes around. Who hid the damn label maker?"

"I did. I lie awake at night figuring out ways to get you back."

"Oh, yeah? For what?"

"For just being you."

Marino digs in another drawer, finds the label maker. "He looks a hell of a lot younger than what the EMTs said. Anybody notice that besides me? Don't you think he looks younger than his twenties?" Marino asks Anne. "Looks like a damn kid."

"Barely pubescent," she agrees. "But then, all college kids are starting to look like that to me. They look like babies."

"We don't know if he was a college student," I remind everyone.

Marino peels the backing off a label printed with the date and case number, and sticks it on the plastic ruler. "I'll canvas the area over there by the common, see if any supers in apartment buildings recognize him, just do it my damn self to keep the rumor mill quiet. If he lives around there, and it sure seems like it, based on what's on the videos, someone's got to remember him and his greyhound. Sock. What kind of name is that for a dog?"

"Probably not his full name," Anne says. "Race dogs have these rather elaborate registered kennel names, like Sock It to Me or Darned Sock or Sock Hop."

"I keep telling her she should go on *Jeopardy*," Marino says.

"It's possible his name might be in a registry," I comment. "Something with Sock in it, assuming we have no luck with a microchip."

"Assuming you find the damn dog," Marino says.

"We're running his prints, his DNA. Right away, I hope?" Benton stares intently at the body, as if he's talking to it.

"I printed him this morning and no luck, nothing in IAFIS. Nothing in the National Missing and Unidentified Persons System. We'll have his DNA tomorrow and run it through CODIS." Marino's big gloved hands place the ruler under the man's chin. "It's kind of strange about the dog, though. Someone's got to have him. I'm thinking we should put out info for the media about a lost greyhound and a number people can call."

"Nothing from us," I reply. "Right now we're staying away from the media."

"Exactly," Benton says. "We don't want the bad guys knowing we're even aware of the dog, much less looking for it."

" 'Bad guys'?" Anne says.

"What else?" I walk around the table, doing what Lucy calls a "high recon," looking carefully at the body from head to toe.

Marino is taking photographs, and he says, "Before we put him back in the fridge this morning, I checked his hands for trace, collected anything preliminarily, including personal effects."

"You didn't tell me about personal effects. Just that he didn't seem to have any," I reply.

"A ring with a crest on it, a steel Casio watch. A couple keys on a keychain. Let's see, what else? A twenty-dollar bill. A little wooden stash box, empty, but I swabbed it for drugs. The stash box on the video clip. For a second you could see him holding it right after he got to Norton's Woods."

"Where was it recovered?" I ask.

"In his pocket. That's where I found it."

"So he took it out of his pocket at the park and then put it back in his pocket before his terminal event." I remember what I watched on the iPad, the small box held in the black glove.

"I'd say we should be looking for the snorting or smoking variety," Marino says. "I'm betting weed. Don't know if you noticed," he says to me, "but he had a glass pipe in an ashtray on his desk."

"We'll see what shows up on tox," I reply. "We'll do a STAT alcohol and expedite a drug screen. How backed up are they up there?"

"I'll tell Joe to move it to the head of the line," Anne refers to the chief toxicologist, whom I brought with me from New York, rather shamelessly stole him from the NYPD crime labs. "You're the boss. All you've got to do is ask." She meets my eyes. "Welcome back."

"What kind of crest, and what does the keychain look like?" Benton asks Marino.

"A coat of arms, an open book with three crowns," he says, and I can tell he enjoys having Benton at a disadvantage. The CFC is Marino's turf. "No writing on it, no phrase in Latin, nothing like that. I don't know what the crests for MIT and Harvard are."

"Not what you described," Benton answers. "Okay if I use this?" He indicates a computer on the counter.

"The keychain is one of those steel rings attached to a leather loop, like you'd snap around your belt," Marino goes on. "And as we all know, no wallet, not even a cell phone, and I think that's unusual. Who walks around with no cell phone?"

"He was taking his dog out and listening to music. Maybe he wasn't planning to be out very long and didn't want to talk on the phone," Benton says as he types in search words.

I pull the body over on its right side and look at Marino. "You want to help me with this?"

"Three crowns and an open book," Benton says. "City University of San Francisco." He types some more. "An online university specializing in health sciences. Would an online university have class rings?"

"And his personal effects are in which locker?" I ask Marino.

"*Numero uno.* I got the key if you want it."

"I would. Anything the labs need to check?"

"Can't see why."

"Then we'll keep his personal effects until they go to a funeral home or to his family, when we figure out who he is," I reply.

"And then there's Oxford," Benton says next, still searching the Internet. "But if the ring he had on was Oxford, it would have *Oxford University* on it, and you said it didn't have any writing or motto."

"It didn't," Marino replies. "But it looks like someone had it made, you know, plain gold and engraved with the crest, so maybe it wouldn't be as official as what you order from a school and wouldn't have a motto or writing."

"Maybe," Benton says. "But if the ring was made, I have a hard time imagining it's for Oxford University, would be more inclined to think if someone went to an on-line college he might have a ring made because maybe there's no other way to get one, assuming you want to tell the world you're an alum of an online college. This is the City University of San Francisco coat of arms." Benton moves to one side so Marino can see what's on the computer screen, an elaborate crest with blue-and-gold mantling, and a gold owl on top with three gold fleur-de-lis, then below three gold crowns, and in the middle an open book.

Marino is holding the body on its side, and he squints at the computer screen from where he's standing and shrugs. "Maybe. If it was engraved, you know, if the person had it made for him, maybe it wouldn't be that detailed. That could be it."

"I'll look at the ring," I promise as I examine the body externally and make notes on a clipboard.

"No reason to think he was in a struggle, and we might get a perp's DNA or something off the watch or whatever. But you know me." Marino resumes what he was saying to me about processing the dead man's personal effects. "I swabbed every-thing anyway. Nothing struck me as unusual except that his watch had quit, one of those self-winding kind that Lucy likes, a chrono-graph."

"What time did it stop?"

"I got it written down. Sometime after four a.m. About twelve hours after he died. So he's got a nine-mil with eighteen rounds but no phone," he then says. "Okay. I guess so, unless he didn't leave it at home and in fact somebody took it. Maybe took the dog, too. That's what I keep wondering."

"There was a phone on a desk in the video clips I saw," I remind him. "Plugged into a charger near one of the laptops, I believe. Near the glass smoking pipe you men-tioned."

"We couldn't see everything he did in there before he left. I figured he might have grabbed his phone on his way out," Marino supposes. "Or he might have more than one. Who the hell knows?"

"We'll know when we find his apartment," Benton says as he prints what he's found on the Internet. "I'd like to see the scene pho-tos."

"You mean when I find the apartment." Marino puts the camera down on a coun-tertop. "Because it's going to be me poking around. Cops gossip worse than old women. I find where the guy lives, then I'll ask for help."

8

On a body diagram, I note that at eleven-fifteen p.m. the dead man is fully rigorous and refrigerated cold. He has a pattern of dark-red discoloration and positional blanching that indicates he was flat on his back with his arms straight by his sides, palms down, fully clothed, and wearing a watch on his left wrist and a ring on his left little finger for at least twelve hours after he died.

Postmortem hypostasis, better known as lividity or livor mortis, is one of my pet tattletales, although it is often misinterpreted even by those who should know better. It can look like bruising due to trauma when in fact it is caused by the mundane physiological phenomenon of noncirculating blood pooling into small vessels due to gravity. Lividity is a dusky red or can be purplish with lighter areas of blanching where areas of the body rested against a firm surface, and no matter what I'm told about the circumstances of a death, the body itself doesn't lie.

"No secondary livor pattern that might indicate the body moved while livor was still forming," I observe. "Everything I'm seeing is consistent with him being zipped up inside a pouch and placed on a body tray and not moving." I attach a body diagram to a clipboard and sketch impressions made by a waistband, a belt, jewelry, shoes and socks, pale areas on the skin that show the shape of elastic or a buckle or fabric or a weave pattern.

"Certainly suggests he didn't even move his arms, didn't thrash around, so that's good," Anne decides.

"Exactly. If he'd come to, he would have at least moved his arms. So that's real good," Marino agrees, keys clicking as an image fills the screen of the computer terminal on a countertop.

I make a note that the man has no body piercings or tattoos, and is clean, with neatly trimmed nails and the smooth skin of one who doesn't do manual labor or engage in any physical activity that might cause calluses on his hands or feet. I palpate his head, feeling for defects, such as fractures or other injuries, and find nothing.

"Question is whether he was facedown when he fell." Marino is looking at what Investigator Lester Law e-mailed to him. "Or is he on his back in these pictures because the EMTs turned him over?"

"To do CPR they would have had to turn him faceup." I move closer to look.

Marino clicks through several photos, all of them the same but from different perspectives: the man on his back, his dark-green jacket and denim shirt open, his head turned to one side, eyes partly closed; a close-up of his face, debris clinging to his lips, what looks like particles of dead leaves and grass and grit.

"Zoom in on that," I tell Marino, and with a click of the mouse, the image is larger, the man's boyish face filling the screen.

I return to the body behind me and check for injuries of his face and head, noting an abrasion on the underside of the chin. I pull down the lower lip and find a small laceration, likely made by his lower teeth when he fell and hit his face on the gravel path.

"Couldn't possibly account for all the blood I saw," Anne says.

"No, it couldn't," I agree. "But it suggests he hit the ground face-first, which also suggests he dropped like a shot, didn't even stumble or try to break his fall. Where's the pouch he came in?"

"I spread it out on a table in the autopsy room, figured you'd want to have a look," Anne tells me. "And his clothes are air-drying in there. When I undressed him, I put everything in the cabinet by your station. Station one."

"Good. Thank you."

"Maybe somebody punched him," Marino offers. "Maybe distracted him by punching or elbowing him in the face, then stabbed him in the back. Except that probably would have been recorded, would be on the video clips."

"He would have more than just this laceration if someone punched him in the mouth. If you look at the debris on his face and the location of the headphones" — I'm back at the computer, clicking on images to show them — "it appears he fell facedown. The headphones are way over here, what looks like at least six feet away under a bench, indicating to me that he fell with sufficient force to knock them a fair distance and disconnect them from the satellite radio, which I believe was in a pocket."

"Unless someone moved the phones, perhaps kicked them out of the way," Benton says.

"That was my other thought," I reply.

"You mean like somebody who tried to help him," Marino says. "People crowding around him and the headphones ended up under a bench."

"Or someone did it deliberately."

There is something else I notice. Clicking through the slideshow, I stop on a photograph of his left wrist. I zoom in on the steel tachymeter watch, move in close on its carbon-fiber face. The time stamp on the photograph is five-seventeen p.m., which is when the police officer took it, yet the time on the watch is ten-fourteen, five hours later than that.

"When you collected the watch this morning" — I direct this to Marino — "you said it appeared to have stopped. You sure it wasn't simply that the time was different than our local time?"

"Nope, it was stopped," he says. "Like I said, one of those self-winding watches, and it quit at some point early in the morning, like around four a.m."

"Seems it might have been set five hours later than Eastern Standard Time." I point out what I'm seeing in the photograph.

"Okay. Then it must have stopped around eleven p.m. our time," Marino says. "So it was set wrong to begin with and then it quit."

"Maybe he was on another time zone because he'd just flown in from overseas," Benton suggests.

"Soon as we finish up here, I got to find his apartment," Marino says.

I check the quality-control numbers in the quality-control log, making sure standard deviation is zero and the noise level of the system or variation is within normal limits.

"We ready?" I say to everyone.

I'm eager to do the scan. I want to see what is inside this man.

"We'll do a topogram, then collect the data set before going to three-D recon with at least fifty percent overlapping," I tell Anne as she presses a button to slide the table into the scanner. "But we'll change the protocol and start with the thorax, not the head, except, of course, for using the glabella as our reference."

I refer to the space between the eyebrows above the nose that we use for spatial orientation.

"A cross-sectional of the chest exactly correlating with the region of interest you've marked." I go down the list as we return to the control room. "An in situ localization of the wound; we'll isolate that area and any associated injury, any clues in the wound track."

I seat myself between Ollie and Anne, and then Marino and Benton pull up chairs behind us. Through the glass window I can see the man's bare feet in the opening of the scanner's bore.

"Auto and smart MT, noise index eighteen. Point-five segment rotation, point-six-two-five detector configuration," I instruct. "Very thin slice ultra-high resolution. Ten-millimeter collimation."

I can hear the electronic pulsing sounds as detectors begin rotating inside the x-ray tube. The first scan lasts sixty seconds. I watch in real time on a computer screen, not sure what I'm seeing, but it shouldn't be this. It occurs to me the scanner is malfunctioning or that some other patient's scan is displayed, the wrong file accessed. *What am I looking at?*

"Jesus," Ollie says under his breath, frowning at images in a grid, strange images that must be a mistake.

"Orient in time and space, and let's line up the wound back to front, left to right, and upward," I direct. "Connect points to get the penetration of the wound track, well, such as it is. There is a wound track and then it disappears? I don't know what this is."

"What the hell am I looking at?" Marino

asks, baffled.

"Nothing I've ever seen before, certainly not in a stabbing," I reply.

"Well, for one thing, air," Ollie announces. "We're seeing a hell of a lot of air."

"These dark areas here and here and here." I show Marino and Benton. "On CT, air looks dark. As opposed to the brighter white areas, which show higher density. Bone and calcification are bright. You can get a pretty good idea of what something is by the density of the pixels."

I reach for the mouse and move the cursor over a rib so they can see what I mean.

"CT number is one thousand one hundred and fifty one. Whereas this not-so-bright area here" — I move the cursor over an area of lung — "is forty. That's going to be blood. These dullish dark areas you're seeing are hemorrhage."

I'm reminded of high-velocity gunshots that cause tremendous crushing and tearing of tissue, similar to injury caused by the blast wave from an explosion. But this isn't a gunshot case. This isn't from a detonated explosive device. I don't see how either could be true.

"Some kind of wound that travels through the left kidney, superiorly through the diaphragm and into the heart, causing profound devastation along the way. And all this." I point to murky areas around internal organs that are displaced and sheared. "More subcutaneous air. Air in the paraspinal musculature. Retroperitoneal air. How did all this air get inside of him? And here and here. Injury to bone. Rib fracture. Fracture of a transverse process. Hemopneumothorax, lung contusion, hemopericardium. And more air. Here and here and here." I touch the screen. "Air surrounding the heart and in the cardiac chambers, as well as in the pulmonary arteries and veins."

"And you've never seen anything like this?" Benton asks me.

"Yes and no. Similar devastation caused by military rifles, antitank cannons, some semiautomatics using extreme shock-fragmenting high-velocity ammunition, for example. The higher the velocity, the greater the kinetic energy dissipates at impact and the greater the damage, especially to hollow organs, such as bowel and lungs, and non-elastic tissue, such as the liver, the kidneys. But in a case like that, you expect a clear wound track and a missile or fragments of one. Which we aren't seeing."

"What about air?" Benton asks. "Do you see these pockets of air in cases like that?"

"Not exactly," I reply. "A blast wave can

create air emboli by forcing air across the air-blood barrier, such as out of the lungs. In other words, air ends up where it doesn't belong, but this is a lot of air."

"A hell of a lot," Ollie concurs. "And how do you get a blast wave from a stabbing?"

"Do a slice right through those coordinates," I say to him, indicating the region of interest marked by a bright white bead — the radio-opaque CT skin marker that was placed next to the wound on the left side of the man's back. "Start here and keep moving down five millimeters above and below the region of interest specified by the markers. That cut. Yes, that's the one. And let's reformat into virtual three-D volume rendering from inside out. Thin, thin cuts, one millimeter, and the increment between them? What do you think?"

"Point-seventy-five by point-five will do it."

"Okay, fine. Let's see what it looks like if we virtually follow the track, what track there is."

Bones are as vivid as if they are laid bare before us, and organs and other internal structures are well defined in shades of gray as the dead man's upper body, his thorax, begins to rotate slowly in three-dimension on the video display. Using modified software originally developed for virtual colonoscopies, we enter the body through the tiny buttonhole wound, traveling with a virtual camera as if we are in a microscopic spaceship slowly flying through murky grayish clouds of tissue, past a left kidney blown apart like an asteroid.

A ragged opening yawns before us, and we pass through a large hole in the diaphragm. Beyond is shattering, shearing, and contusion. *What happened to you? What did this?* I don't have a clue. It's a helpless feeling to find physical damage that seems to defy physics, an effect without a cause. There's no projectile. There's no frag, nothing metal I can see. There's no exit wound, only the buttonhole entrance on the left side of his back. I'm thinking out loud, repeating important points, making sure everyone understands what is incomprehensible.

"I keep forgetting nothing works down here," Benton comments distractedly as he looks at his iPhone.

"Nothing exited, and nothing is lighting up." I calculate what must be done next. "No sign of anything ferrous, but we need to be sure."

"Absolutely no idea what could have done this," Benton states rather than asks as he gets up from his chair, making rustling sounds as he unties his disposable gown. "You know the old saying, nothing new under the sun. I guess like a lot of old sayings, it's not true."

"This is new. At least to me," I reply.

He bends over and pulls off his shoe covers. "No question he's a homicide."

"Unless he ate some really bad Mexican food," Marino says.

It vaguely drifts through my thoughts that Benton is acting suspiciously.

"Like a high-velocity projectile, but there's no projectile, and if it exited the body, where's the exit wound?" I keep saying the same thing. "Where the hell's the metal? What the hell could he have been shot with? An ice bullet?"

"I saw a thing about that on *MythBusters*. They proved it's impossible because of heat," Marino says, as if I'm serious. "I don't know, though. Wonder what would happen if you loaded the gun and kept it in the freezer until you were ready to fire it."

"Maybe if you're a sniper in the interior of Antarctica," Ollie says. "Where'd that idea come from, anyway? *Dick Tracy?* I'm asking for real."

"I thought it was James Bond. I forget which movie."

"Maybe the exit wound isn't obvious,"

Anne says to me. "Remember that time the guy was shot in the jaw and it exited through his nostril?"

"Then where's the wound track?" I reply. "We need better contrast between tissues, need to be damn sure there's nothing we're missing before I open him up."

"If you need my help with that, I can call the hospital," Benton says as he opens the door. I can tell he's in a hurry, but I'm not sure why.

It's not his case.

"Otherwise, I'll check on what Lucy's found," Benton says. "Take a look at the video clips. Check on a couple other things. You don't mind if I use a phone up there."

"I'll make the call," Anne says to him as he leaves. "I'll get it arranged with McLean and take care of the scan."

It's been a theoretical possibility this day would come, and we are cleared with the Board of Health, and with Harvard and its affiliate McLean Hospital, which has four magnets ranging in strength from 1.5 to 9 Tesla. Long ago I made sure the protocols were in place to do MRIs on dead bodies in McLean's neuroimaging lab, where Anne works as a part-time MR tech for psychiatric research studies. That's how I got her. Benton knew her first and recommended her. He picks well, is a fine judge of character. I should let him hire my damn staff. I wonder whom he is going to call. I'm not sure why he is here at all.

"If that's what you want, we can do it right now," Anne is saying to me. "There shouldn't be a problem, won't be anyone around. We'll just go right up to the front door and get him in and out."

At this hour, psychiatric patients at McLean won't be wandering around the campus. There's little risk of them happening upon a dead body being carried in or out of a lab.

"What if someone shot him with a water cannon?" Marino stares as if transfixed at the rotating torso on the video screen, the ribs curving and gleaming whitely in 3-D. "Seriously. I've always heard that's the perfect crime. You fill a shotgun shell with water, and it's like a bullet when it goes through the body. But it doesn't leave a trace."

"I've not had a case like that," I reply.

"But it could happen," Marino says.

"Theoretically. However, the entrance wound wouldn't be like this one," I reply. "Let's get going. I want him posted and safely out of sight before everyone starts arriving for work." It's almost midnight.

225

Anne clicks on the icon for *Tools* to take measurements and informs me the width of the wound track before it blows through the diaphragm is .77 to 1.59 millimeters at a depth of 4.2 millimeters.

"So what that tells me . . ." I start to say.

"How about inches," Marino complains.

"Some type of double-edged object or blade that doesn't get much wider than half an inch," I explain. "And once it penetrated the body up to an approximate depth of two inches, something else happened that caused profound internal damage."

"What I'm wondering is how much of this abnormality we're seeing is iatrogenic," Ollie says. "Caused by the EMTs working on him for twenty minutes. That's probably the first question we'll get asked. We have to keep an open mind."

"No way. Not unless King Kong did CPR," I reply. "It appears this man was stabbed with something that caused tremendous pressure in his chest and a large air embolus. He would have had severe pain and been dead within minutes, which is consistent with what's been described by witnesses, that he clutched his chest and collapsed."

"Then why all the blood after the fact?" Marino says. "Why wouldn't he have been hemorrhaging instantly? How the hell's it possible he didn't start bleeding until after he was pronounced and on his way here?"

"I don't know the answer, but he didn't die in our cooler." I am at least sure of that. "He was dead before he got here, would have been dead at the scene."

"But we got to prove he started bleeding after he was dead. And dead people don't start bleeding like a damn stuck pig. So how do we prove he was dead before he got here?" Marino persists.

"Who do we need to prove it to?" I look at him.

"I don't know who Fielding's told since we don't even know where the hell he is. What if he's told somebody?"

Like you did, I think, but I don't say it. "That's why one should be careful about divulging details when we don't have all the information." I couldn't sound more reasonable.

"We got no choice about it." Marino won't let it go. "We have to prove why a dead person started bleeding."

I collect my jacket and tell Anne, "A head and full-body CT scan first. And on MR, full-body coil, every inch of him, and upload what you find. I'll want to see it right away."

"I'm driving," Marino says to her.

"Well, pull it into the bay to warm it up. One of the vans."

"We don't want him warming up. Matter of fact, think I'll put the AC on full-blast."

"Then you can ride just the two of you. I'll meet you there."

"Seriously. He warms up, he might start bleeding again."

"You've been watching too much *Saturday Night Live*."

"Dan Aykroyd doing Julia Child? Remember that? *'You'll need a knife, a very, very sharp knife.'* And blood spurting everywhere."

The three of them bantering.

"That was so funny."

"The old ones were better."

"No kidding. Roseanne Roseannadanna."

"Oh, God, I love her."

"I've got them all on DVD."

I hear them laughing as I walk away.

Scanning my thumb, I let myself into the area that is the first stop after Receiving, where we do identifications, a white room with gray countertops that we simply call ID.

Built into a wall are gray metal evidence lockers, each of them numbered, and I use the key Marino gave me to open the top one on the left, where the dead man's personal effects have been safely stored until we receipt them to a funeral home or to a family when we finally know who he is and who should claim him. Inside are paper bags and envelopes neatly labeled, and attached to each are forms Marino has filled out and initialed to maintain chain of custody. I find the small manila envelope containing the signet ring, and initial the form and put down the time I removed it from the locker. At a computer station I pull up a log and enter the same information, and then I think about the dead man's clothes.

I should look at them while I'm down here, not wait until I do the autopsy, which will be hours from now. I want to see the hole made by the blade that penetrated the man's lower back and created such havoc inside him. I want to see how much he might have bled from that wound, and I leave ID and walk along the gray tile corridor, backtracking. I pass the x-ray room, and through its open door I catch a glimpse of Marino, Anne, and Ollie, still in there, getting the body ready for transport to McLean, joking and laughing. I quickly go past without them noticing, and I open the double steel doors leading into the autopsy room.

It is a vast open space of white epoxy paint and white tile and exposed shiny steel tracks with cool filtered lighting running horizontally along the length of the white ceiling. Eleven steel tables are parked by wall-mounted steel sinks, each with a foot-operated faucet control, a high-pressure spray hose, a commercial disposal, a specimen rinse basket, and a sharps container. The stations I carefully researched and had installed are mini-modular operating theaters with down-draft ventilation systems that exchange air every five minutes, and there are computers, fume hoods, carts of surgical instruments, halogen lights on flexible arms, dissecting surfaces with cutting boards, containers of formalin with spigots, and test-tube racks and plastic jars for histology and toxicology.

My station, the chief's station, is the first one, and it occurs to me that someone has been using it, and then I feel ridiculous for thinking it. Of course people would have been using it while I've been gone. Of course Fielding probably did. *It doesn't matter, and why should I care?* I tell myself as I notice that the surgical instruments on the cart aren't neatly lined up the way I would leave them. They are haphazardly placed on a large white polyethylene dissecting board as if someone rinsed them and didn't do it thoroughly. I grab a pair of latex gloves out of a box and pull them on because I don't want to touch anything with my bare hands.

Normally, I don't worry about it, not as much as I should, I suppose, because I come from an old school of forensic pathologists who were stoical and battle-scarred and took perverse pride in not being afraid of or repulsed by anything. Not maggots or purge fluid or putrefying flesh that is bloated and turning green and slipping, not even AIDS, at least not the worries we have now when we live with phobias and federal regulations about absolutely everything. I remember when I walked around without protective clothing on, smoking, drinking coffee, and touching dead patients as any doctor would, my bare skin against theirs as I examined a wound or looked at a contusion or took a measurement. But I was never sloppy with my work station or my surgical instruments. I was never careless.

I would never return so much as a teasing needle to a surgical cart without first washing it with hot, soapy water, and the drumming of hot water into deep metal sinks was a pervasive sound in the morgues of my past. As far back as my Richmond days — even earlier, when I was just starting at Walter Reed — I knew about DNA and that it was about to be admissible in court and become the forensic gold standard, and from that point forward, everything we did at crime scenes and in the autopsy suite and in the labs would be questioned on the witness stand. Contamination was about to become the ultimate nemesis, and although we don't make a routine of autoclaving our surgical instruments at the CFC, we certainly don't give them a cursory splash under the faucet and then toss them onto a cutting board that isn't clean, either.

I pick up an eighteen-inch dissecting knife and notice a trace of dried blood in the scored stainless-steel handle and that the steel blade is scratched and pitted along the edge and spotted instead of razor-sharp and as bright as polished silver. I notice blood in the serrated blade of a bone saw and dried bloodstains on a spool of waxed five-cord thread and on a double-curved needle. I pick up forceps, scissors, rib shears, a chisel, a flexible probe, and am dismayed by the poor condition everything is in.

I will send Anne a message to hose down my station and wash all of its instruments before we autopsy the man from Norton's Woods. I will have this entire goddamn autopsy room cleaned from the ceiling to the floor. I will have all of its systems inspected before my first week home has passed, I decide, as I pull on a fresh pair of gloves and walk to a countertop where a large roll of white paper — what we call butcher paper — is attached to a wall-mounted dispenser. Paper makes a loud ripping sound as I tear off a section and cover an autopsy table midway down the room, a table that looks cleaner than mine.

I cover my AFME field clothes with a disposable gown, not bothering with the long ties in back, then return to my messy station. Against the wall is a large white polypropylene drying cabinet on hard rubber casters with a double clear acrylic door, which I unlock by entering a code in a digital keypad. Hanging inside are a sage-green nylon jacket with a black fleece collar, a blue denim shirt, black cargo pants, and a pair of boxer briefs, each on its own stainless-steel hanger, and on the tray at the bottom are a pair of scuffed brown leather boots, and next to them, a pair of gray wool socks. I recognize some of the clothing from the video clips I saw, and it gives me an unsettled feeling to look at it now. The cabinet's centrifugal fan and HEPA exhaust filters make their low whirring sound as I look at the boots and the socks by picking them up one by one, finding nothing remarkable. The boxer briefs are white cotton with a crossover fly and elastic waistband, and I note nothing unusual, no stains or defects.

Spreading the coat open on the butcher paper–covered table, I slip my hands into the pockets, making sure nothing has been left in them, and I collect a clothing diagram and a clipboard and begin to make notes. The collar is a deep-pile synthetic fur and covered with dirt and sand and pieces of dry brown leaves that adhered to it when the man collapsed to the ground, and the heavy knit cuffs are dirty, too. The sage nylon shell is a very tough material, which appears to be tear-resistant and waterproof with a black fiberfill insulation, none of it easily penetrable unless the blade was strong and very sharp. I find no evidence of blood inside the liner of the coat, not even around the small slit in the back of it, but the areas of the outer shell, the shoulders, the sleeves, the back, are blackened and stiff with blood that collected in the bottom of the body pouch after the man was zipped inside it and then was transported to the CFC.

I don't know how long he might have bled out while he was inside the bag and then the cooler, but he didn't bleed from his wound. When I spread open the denim shirt, long-sleeved, a men's size small, which still smells faintly of a cologne or an after-shave, I find only a spot of dark blood that has dried stiffly around the slit made by the blade. What Marino and Anne have reported seems to be accurate, that the man began bleeding from his nose and mouth while he was fully clothed inside the body bag, his head turned to the side, probably the same side it was turned to when I examined him in the x-ray room a little while ago. Blood must have dripped steadily from his face into the bag, pooling in it and leaking from it, and I can see that easily when I look at it next, an adult-size cadaver pouch, typical of ones used by removal services, black with a nylon zipper. On the sides are webbing handles attached with rivets, and that's often where the problem with leakage oc-curs, assuming the bag is intact with no tears or flaws in the heat-sealed seams. Blood seeps through rivets, especially if the pouch is really cheap, and this one is about twenty-five dollars' worth of heavy-duty PVC, likely purchased by the case.

As I imagine what I just saw on the CT

scan and realize how quickly the damage occurred in what clearly was a blitz attack, the bleeding makes no sense at all. It makes even less sense than it did when Marino first told me about it in Dover. The massive destruction to the man's internal organs would have resulted in pulmonary hemorrhage that would have caused blood to drain out of the nose and mouth. But it should have happened almost instantly. I don't understand why he didn't bleed at the scene. When the paramedics were working to resuscitate him, he should have been bleeding from his face, and this would have been a clear indication that he hadn't dropped dead from an arrhythmia.

As I leave the autopsy room to go upstairs, I envision the video clips again and remember my wondering about his black gloves and why he put them on when he entered the park. Where are they? I haven't seen a pair of gloves. They weren't in the evidence locker or in the drying cabinet, and I checked the pockets of the coat and didn't find them. Based on what I saw in the recordings covertly made by the man's headphones, he had the gloves on when he died, and I envision what I saw on Lucy's iPad when I was riding in the van to the Civil Air Terminal. A black-gloved hand entered the frame as if the man was swatting at something and there was a jostling sound as his hand hit the headphones while his voice blurted out, *"What the . . . ? Hey . . . !"* Then bare trees rushing up and around, then chipped bits of slate looming large on the ground and the thud of him hitting, and then the hem of a long black coat flapping past. Then silence, then the voices of people surrounding him and exclaiming that he wasn't breathing.

The x-ray room door is closed when I get to it, and I check inside, but everyone is gone, the control room empty and quiet, the CT scanner glowing white in the low lights on the other side of the lead-lined glass. I pause to try the phone in there, hoping Anne might answer her cell, but if she's already at McLean and in the neuroimaging lab, it will be impossible to reach her through the thick concrete walls of that place. I am surprised when she answers.

"Where are you?" I ask, and I can hear music in the background.

"Pulling up now," she says, and she must be inside the van with Marino driving and the radio on.

"When you removed his clothing," I say, "did you see a pair of black gloves? He may have been wearing a pair of thick black gloves."

A pause, and I hear her say something to Marino and then I hear his voice, but I can't make out what they're saying to each other. Then she tells me, "No. And Marino says when he had the body in ID first thing, there were no gloves. He doesn't remember gloves."

"Tell me exactly what happened yesterday morning."

"Just sit right here for a minute," I hear her say to Marino. "No, not there yet or they'll come out. The security guys will. Just wait here," she says to him. "Okay," she says to me. "A little bit after seven yesterday morning, Dr. Fielding came to x-ray. As you know, Ollie and I are always in early, by seven, and anyway, he was concerned because of the blood. He'd noticed blood drips on the floor outside the cooler and also inside it, and that the body was bleeding or had bled. A lot of blood in the pouch."

"The body was still fully clothed."

"Yes. The coat was unzipped and the shirt was cut open, the EMTs did that, but he was clothed when he came in and nothing was done until Dr. Fielding went in there to get him ready for us."

"What do you mean, 'to get him ready'?"

I've never known Fielding to get a body ready for autopsy, to actually go to the trouble to move it out of the refrigerator and into x-ray or the autopsy room, at least not since the old days when he was in training. He leaves what he considers mundane tasks to those whom he still calls *dieners* and whom I call autopsy technicians.

"I only know he found the blood and then hurried to get us because he took the call from Cambridge PD, and as you know, it was assumed the guy was a sudden death that was natural, like an arrhythmia or a berry aneurysm or something."

"Then what?"

"Then Ollie and I looked at the body, and we called Marino and he came and looked, and it was decided not to scan him or do the post yet."

"He was left in the cooler?"

"No. Marino wanted to process him in ID first, to get his prints, swabs, so we could get started with IAFIS and DNA, with anything that might help us figure out who he is. The important point is there were no gloves at that time, because Marino would have had to take them off the body so he could print him."

"Then where are they?"

"He doesn't know, and I don't, either."

"Can you put him on, please?"

I hear her hand him the phone, and he says, "Yeah. I unzipped the pouch but didn't take him out of it, and there was a lot of blood in it, like you know."

"And you did what, exactly?"

"I printed him while he was in the pouch, and if there had been gloves, I sure as hell would have seen them."

"Possible the squad removed the gloves at the scene and put them inside the pouch and you didn't notice? And then they got misplaced somehow?"

"Nope. I looked for any personal effects, like I told you. The watch, ring, keychain, the stash box, the twenty-dollar bill. Took everything out of his pockets, and I always look inside the pouch for the very reason you just said. In case the squad or the removal service tucks something in there, like a hat or sunglasses or whatever. The headphones, too. And the satellite radio. They were in a paper bag and came in with the body."

"What about Cambridge PD? I know Investigator Lawless brought in the Glock."

"He receipted it to the firearms lab around ten a.m. That was all he brought in."

"And when Anne put his clothing inside

the drying cabinet, well, obviously she didn't have the gloves if you say they weren't there in the first place."

I hear him say something, and then Anne is back on the phone, saying, "No. I didn't see gloves when I put everything else in the cabinet. That was around nine p.m., almost four hours ago, when I undressed the body to get it ready for the scan, not long before you got to the CFC. I cleaned the cabinet to make sure it was sterile before I put his other clothing in there."

"I'm glad something's sterile. We need to clean my station."

"Okay, okay," she says, but not to me. "Wait. Jesus, Pete. Hold on."

And then Marino's voice in my ear: "There were other cases."

"I beg your pardon?"

"We had other cases yesterday morning. So maybe someone removed the gloves, but I got no friggin' idea why. Unless they maybe got picked up by mistake."

"Who did the cases?"

"Dr. Lambotte, Dr. Booker."

"What about Jack?"

"Two cases in addition to the guy from Norton's Woods," Marino says. "A woman who got hit by a train and an old guy who wasn't under the care of a physician. Jack didn't do shit, was gone with the wind," Marino says. "He doesn't bother with the scene, and so we get a body that starts bleeding in the fridge and now we got to prove the guy was dead."

9

The directorate of what officially is called the Cambridge Forensic Center and Port Mortuary is on the top floor, and I have discovered that it is difficult to tell people how to find me when a building is round.

The best I've been able to do on the infrequent occasions I've been here is to instruct visitors to get off the elevator on the seventh floor, take a left, and look for number 111. It's only one door down from 101, and to comprehend that 101 is the lowest room number on this floor and 111 is the highest requires some imagination. My office suite, therefore, would occupy a corner at the end of a long hallway if there were corners and long hallways, but there aren't. Up here there is just one big circle with six offices, a large conference room, the reading room for voice-recognition dictation, the library, the break room, and in the center a windowless bunker where

Lucy chose to put the computer and questioned documents lab.

Walking past Marino's office, I stop outside 111, what he calls CENTCOM, for Central Command. I'm sure Marino came up with the pretentious appellation all on his own, not because he thinks of me as his commander but rather he's come to think of himself as answering to a higher patriotic order that is close to a religious calling. His worship of all things military is new. It's just one more thing that is paradoxical about him, as if Peter Rocco Marino needs yet another paradox to define his inconsistent and conflicted self.

I need to calm down about him, I say to myself as I unlock my heavy door with its titanium veneer. He isn't so bad and didn't do anything so terrible. He's predictable, and I shouldn't be surprised in the least. After all, who understands him better than I do? The Rosetta stone to Marino isn't Bayonne, New Jersey, where he grew up a street fighter who became a boxer and then a cop. The key to him isn't even his worthless alcoholic father. Marino can be explained by his mother first and foremost, and then his childhood sweetheart Doris, now his ex-wife, both women seemingly docile and subservient and sweet but not harmless. Not hardly.

I push buttons to turn on the flush-mount lighting built into the struts of the geodesic glass dome that is energy-efficient and reminds me of Buckminster Fuller every time I look up. Were the famed architect-inventor still among the living, he would approve of my building and possibly of me but not of our morbid raison d'être, I suspect, although at this stage of things I would have a few quibbles with him, too. For example, I don't agree with his belief that technology can save us. Certainly, it isn't making us more civilized, and I actually think the opposite is true.

I pause on gunmetal-gray carpet just inside my doorway as if waiting for permission to enter, or maybe I'm hesitant because to appropriate this space is to embrace a life I've rather much put off for the better part of two years. If I'm honest about it I should say I've put it off for decades, since my earliest days at Walter Reed, where I was minding my own business in a cramped, windowless room of AFIP headquarters when Briggs walked in without knocking and dropped an eight-by-eleven gray envelope on my desk with *CLASSIFIED* stamped on it.

December 4, 1987. I remember it so

vividly I can describe what I was wearing and the weather and what I ate. I know I smoked a lot that day and had several straight Scotches at the end of it because I was excited and horrified. The case of all cases, and the DoD wanted me, picked me over all others. Or more accurately, Briggs did. By spring of the following year, I was discharged from the air force early, not on good behavior but because the Reagan administration wanted me gone, and I left under certain conditions that are shameful and cause pain even now. It is karmic that I find myself in a building of circles. Nothing has ended or begun in my life. What was far away is right next to me. Somehow it's all the same.

The most blatant sign of my six-month absence from a position I've yet to really fill is that Bryce's adjoining administrative office is comfortably cluttered while mine is empty and stark. It feels forlorn and lonely in here, my small conference table of brushed steel bare, not even a potted plant on it, and when I inhabit a space there are always plants. Orchids, gardenias, succulents, and indoor trees, such as areca and sago palms, because I want life and fragrances. But what I had in here when I moved in is gone and has been gone, overwatered and too much fertilizer. I gave Bryce detailed instructions and three months to kill everything. It took him less than two.

There is virtually nothing on my desk, a bow-shaped modular work station constructed of twenty-two-gauge steel with a black laminate surface and a matching hutch of file drawers and open shelves between expansive windows overlooking the Charles and the Boston skyline. A black granite countertop behind my Aeron chair runs the length of the wall and is home to my Leica Laser Microdissection System and its video displays and accoutrements, and nearby is my faithful backup Leica for daily use, a more basic laboratory research microscope that I can operate with one hand and without software or a training seminar. There isn't much else, no case files in sight, no death certificates or other paperwork for me to review and initial, no mail, and very few personal effects. I decide it's not a good thing to have such a perfectly arranged, immaculate office. I'd rather have a landfill. It's peculiar that being faced with an empty work space should make me feel so overwhelmed, and as I seal Erica Donahue's letter in a plastic bag I finally realize why I'm not a fan of a world that is fast becoming paperless. I like to see the enemy, stacks of what I must conquer, and I take comfort in reams of friends.

I'm locking the letter in a cabinet when Lucy silently appears like an apparition in a voluminous white lab coat she wears for its warmth and what she can conceal beneath it, and she's also fond of big pockets. The oversized coat makes her seem deceptively nonthreatening and much younger than her years, in her low thirties is the way she puts it, but she'll forever be a little girl to me. I wonder if mothers always feel that way about their daughters, even when the daughters are mothers themselves, or in Lucy's case, armed and dangerous.

She probably has a pistol tucked into the back waistband of her cargo pants, and I realize how selfishly happy I am that she's home. She's back in my life, not in Florida or with people I have to force myself to like. Manhattan prosecutor Jaime Berger is included in this mix. As I look at my niece, my surrogate only child, walking into my office, I can't avoid a truth I won't tell her. I'm glad if she and Jaime have called it quits. That's really why I haven't asked about it.

"Is Benton still with you?" I inquire.

"He's on the phone." She shuts the door

behind her.

"Who's he talking to at this hour?"

Lucy takes a chair, pulling her legs up on the seat, crossing them at the ankles. "Some of his people," she says, as if to imply he's talking to colleagues at McLean, but that's not it. Anne is handling the hospital, and she and Marino are there and getting started on the scan. Why would Benton be talking to them or anyone else at McLean?

"It's just the three of us, then," I comment pointedly. "Except for Ron, I assume. But if you want the door shut, I suppose that's fine." It's my way of letting her know that her hypervigilant and secretive behavior isn't lost on me and I wish she would explain it. I wish she would explain why she feels it necessary to be evasive if not blatantly untruthful to me, her aunt, her almost-mother, and now her boss.

"I know." She slides a small evidence pillbox out of her lab coat pocket.

"You know? What do you know?"

"That Anne and Marino went to McLean because you want an MRI. Benton filled me in. Why didn't you go?"

"I'm not needed and wouldn't be particularly helpful, since MR scans aren't my specialty." There is no MRI scanner at Dover's port mortuary, where most bodies

249

are war casualties and are going to have metal in them. "I thought I'd take care of a few things, and when I'm satisfied I know what I'm looking for, I'll get started on the autopsy."

"Kind of a backward way to look at things, when you stop to think about it," Lucy muses, her eyes green and intensely fixed on me. "It used to be you did the autopsy so you knew what you were looking for. Now it's just a confirmation of what you already know and a means of collecting evidence."

"Not exactly. I still get surprises. What's in the box?"

"Speaking of." She slides the small white box across the unobstructed surface of my ridiculously clean desk. "You can take it out and don't need gloves. But be careful with it."

Inside the box on a bed of cotton is what looks like the wing of an insect, possibly a fly.

"Go ahead, touch it," Lucy encourages, leaning forward in her chair, her face bright with excitement, as if she's watching me open a gift.

I feel the stiffness of wire struts and a thin transparent membrane, something like plastic. "Artificial. Interesting. What is this exactly, and where did you get it?"

"You familiar with the holy grail of fly-bots?"

"I confess I'm drawing a blank."

"Years and years of research. Millions and millions of research dollars spent on building the perfect flybot."

"Not intimately aware of it. Actually, I don't think I know what you're talking about."

"Equipped with micro-cameras and transmitters for covert surveillance, literally for bugging people. Or for detecting chemicals or explosives or possibly even biological hazards. The work's been going on at Harvard, MIT, Berkeley, a number of places here and overseas, even before cyborgs, those insects with embedded microelectromechanical systems, machine-insect interfaces. Which then spread to doing shit like that to other living creatures, like turtles, dolphins. Not DARPA's finest moments, you ask me."

I place the wing back on the square of cotton. "Let's back up. Start with where you got this."

"I'm worried."

"You and me both."

"When Marino had him in ID this morning" — Lucy means the dead man from

Norton's Woods — "I wanted to tell him about the recording system I discovered in the headphones, so I go downstairs. He's fingerprinting the body, and I notice what at a glance looks like a fly wing stuck to the guy's coat collar along with some other debris, like dirt and pieces of dead leaves from his being on the ground."

"It didn't get dislodged by the EMTs," I comment. "When they opened his coat."

"Obviously, it didn't. Was snagged on the fur, the fake-fur collar," Lucy says. "Something struck me about it, you know, I got a funny feeling and I took a closer look."

I get a hand lens out of my desk drawer and turn on an examination light, and in the bright illumination the magnified wing doesn't look natural anymore. What one would assume is the base of the wing, where it attaches to the body, is actually some sort of flexure joint, and the veins running through the wing tissue are shiny like wires.

"Probably a carbon composite, and there are fifteen joints in each wing drive, which is pretty amazing." Lucy describes what I'm seeing. "The wing itself is an electroactive polymer frame, which responds to electrical signals, causing the fanfold wings to flap as fast as the real deal, your everyday housefly. Historically, a flybot takes off vertically like a helicopter and flies like an angel, which has been one of its major design obstacles. That and coming up with something micro-mechanical that's autonomous but not bulky — in other words, biologically inspired so it has the necessary power to move around freely in whatever environment you put it in."

"Biologically inspired, like da Vinci's conceptualized inventions." I wonder if she is reminded of the exhibition I took her to in London and if she noticed the poster in the living room of the dead man's apartment. Of course she noticed. Lucy notices everything.

"The poster over the couch," she says.

"Yes, I saw it."

"In one of the video clips, when he was putting the leash on his dog. How creepy is that?" Lucy says.

"I'm not sure I know why it's creepy."

"Well, I had the luxury of looking at the recordings more carefully than you did." Lucy's demeanor again, the nuances I've come to recognize as surely as I detect the subtle changes in tissue under the micro-scope. "It's for the same exhibition you took me to at the Courtauld, has the date on it for that same summer," she says calmly and with a certain goal in mind. "We might have been there when he was, assuming he went."

That's the goal. This is what Lucy thinks. A connection between the dead man and us.

"Having the poster doesn't mean he did," she goes on. "I realize that. It doesn't mean it in a way that would hold up in court," she adds with a hint of irony, as if she's making a dig at Jaime Berger, the prosecutor I'm increasingly suspicious she's no longer with.

"Lucy, do you have some idea of who this man is?" I go ahead and ask.

"I just think it's bizarre to consider he might have been at that gallery when we were. But I'm certainly not saying he was. Not at all."

It's not what she really thinks. I can see it in her eyes and hear it in her voice. She suspects he might have been there when we were. How could she begin to conclude such a thing about a dead man whose name we don't know?

"You're not hacking again," I say bluntly, as if I'm asking about smoking or drinking or some other habit that could be bad for her health.

I've thought more than once that Lucy might have found a way to trace the covertly recorded video files to a personal computer or server somewhere. To her, a firewall and other security measures to protect proprietary data are nothing more than a speed bump on the road to getting what she wants.

"I'm not a hacker," she says simply.

That's not an answer, I think but don't say.

"I just find it an unusual coincidence that he might have been at the Courtauld when we were," she goes on. "And I think it's likely he has that poster because he has some connection to that exhibit. You can't buy them now. I checked. Who would have one unless they went or someone close to them did?"

"Unless he's much older than he looks, he would have been a child then," I point out. "That was in the summer of 2001."

I'm reminded that the time on his watch was five hours ahead of what it should have been for this part of the world. It was set for the United Kingdom's time zone, and the exhibition was in London. That proves nothing. *A consistency but not evidence,* I tell myself.

"That exhibit was exactly the kind of thing a precocious little inventor in the making would love," Lucy says.

"The same way you did," I reply. "I think you walked through it four times. And you bought the lecture series on CD, you were so enthralled."

"It's quite a thought. A little boy in the gallery at the exact moment we were."

"You say that as if it's a fact." I continue to push the same point.

"And almost a decade later I'm here, you're here, and his dead body is here. Talk about six degrees of separation."

It jolts me to hear her refer to something else I was thinking about earlier. First the London exhibit, now the great web that is all of us, the way lives around the planet somehow interconnect.

"I never really get used to it," she is saying. "Seeing someone and then later they're murdered. Not that I can envision him as a boy at a gallery in London, not that I see some little kid's face in my mind. But I might have been standing next to him or even talked to him. In retrospect it's always hard to comprehend that if you had known what was ahead, maybe you could have changed someone's destiny. Or your own."

"Did Benton tell you the man from Norton's Woods was murdered, or did you get that from someone else?"

"We were catching up."

"And you told him about the flybot while you were just now catching up inside your lab." It's not a question.

I feel sure she's told Benton about the robotic fly wing and whatever else she thinks he should know. She's the one who was emphatic in the helicopter a little while ago that he is the only person she really trusts right now, except for me. Although I don't exactly feel trusted. I sense she is sifting through information and selective about what she offers when I wish she wouldn't hold back. I wish she wouldn't be evasive or lie. But one thing I've learned about Lucy is that wishing makes nothing true. I can wish my life away with her and it won't change her behavior. It won't change what she thinks or does.

I turn off the lamp and return the small white box to her. "What do you mean, 'flies like an angel'?"

"Those artistic renderings of angels hovering. I know you've seen them." Lucy reaches for a pad of call sheets and a pen neatly placed next to the phone. "Their bodies are vertical, like someone with a jet pack on, as opposed to insects and birds, whose bodies are horizontal in flight. These little flybots fly vertically, like angels, and that's been one of their flaws, that and their size. Finding the solution is what I mean by 'holy grail.' It's eluded the best and the brightest."

She sketches something to show me, a stick figure that looks like a cross flying through the air.

"If you want an insect like a common housefly to literally be a fly on the wall conducting covert surveillance," she continues, "it should look like a fly, not like a tiny body that's upright with wings attached. If I were having a meeting in Iran with Ahmadinejad and something flew by vertically and landed vertically on a windowsill like a micro–Tinker Bell, I believe I'd notice it and be slightly suspicious."

"If you were meeting with Ahmadinejad in Iran, I'd be slightly suspicious for a lot of reasons. Forgetting why my patient had the wing of one of these things on his coat, assuming this wing is part of an intact flybot —" I start to say.

"Not exactly a flybot," she interrupts. "Not necessarily a spybot, either. That's what I'm getting to. I think this is the holy grail."

"Then whatever it is, what might it have been used for?"

"Let your imagination be the limit," she answers. "I could make quite a list but can't know definitively, not from one wing, although I can tell a few things that are significant. Unfortunately, I couldn't find the rest of it."

"You mean on the body, on his coat? Find it where?"

"At the scene."

"You went to Norton's Woods."

"Sure," she says. "As soon as I realized what the wing was from. Of course I headed straight there."

"We were together for hours." I remind her that she could have told me before now. "Just you and me in the cockpit all the way here from Dover."

"Funny thing about the intercom. Even when I'm sure it's off in back, I'm still not sure. Not if it's something I can't afford having anyone overhear. Marino shouldn't know about this." She indicates the small white box with the wing in it.

"Why exactly?"

"Believe me, you don't want him to know a damn thing about it. It's a very small piece of something a lot bigger, in more ways than one."

She goes on to assure me that Marino knows nothing about her going to Norton's Woods. He is unaware of the tiny mechanical wing or that it was a motivating factor in her encouraging him to bring me home from Dover early, to safely escort me in her helicopter. She didn't mention any of this

259

to me until now, she continues to explain, because she doesn't trust anyone at the moment. Except Benton, she adds. And me, she adds. And she's very careful where she has certain conversations, and all of us should be careful.

"Unless the area has been cleared," she says, and what she means is swept, and the implication is that my office is safe or we wouldn't be having this conversation inside it.

"You checked my office for surveillance devices?" I'm not shocked. Lucy knows how to sweep an area for hidden recorders because she knows how to spy. The best burglar is a locksmith. "Because you think who might be interested in bugging my office?"

"Not sure who's interested in what or why."

"Not Marino," I then say.

"Well, that would be as obvious as a Radio-Shack nanny cam if he did it. Of course not. I'm not worried about him doing something like that. I just worry that he can't keep his mouth shut," Lucy replies. "At least not when it comes to certain people."

"You talked about MORT in the helicopter. You weren't worried about the intercom, about Marino, when it came to MORT."

"Not the same thing. Not even close," she says. "Doesn't matter if Marino runs his mouth to certain people about a robot in the guy's apartment. Other people already know about it, you can rest assured of that. I can't have Marino talk about my little friend." She looks at the small white box. "And he wouldn't mean anything bad. But he doesn't understand certain realities about certain people. Especially General Briggs and Captain Avallone."

"I didn't realize you knew anything about her." I've never mentioned Sophia Avallone to Lucy.

"When she was here. Jack showed her around. Marino bought her lunch, was kissing her uniformed ass. He doesn't get it about people like that, about the fucking Pentagon, for that matter, or someone he stupidly assumes is one of us, you know, is safe."

I'm relieved she realizes it, but I don't want to encourage her to distrust Marino, not even slightly. She's been through enough with him and finally they are friends again, close like they were when she was a child and he taught her to drive his truck and to shoot and she aggravated the hell out of him and it was mutual. She gets science from my genetics, but she gets her affinity

261

for cop stuff, as she refers to it, from him. He was the big, tough detective in her life when she was a know-it-all difficult wunderkind, and he has loved and hated her as many different times as she has loved and hated him. But friends and colleagues now. Whatever it takes to keep it that way. *Be careful what you say,* I tell myself. *Let there be peace.*

"From which I conclude Briggs doesn't know about this." I indicate the small white box on my desk. "And Captain Avallone doesn't."

"I don't see how."

"Is my office bugged right now?"

"Our conversation is completely safe," she replies, and it isn't an answer.

"What about Jack? Possible he knows about the flybot? Well, you didn't tell him."

"No damn way."

"So unless someone's called him looking for it. Or maybe its wing."

"You mean if the killer called here looking for a missing flybot," Lucy says. "And I'm just going to call it that for purposes of simplicity, although it's not just a garden-variety flybot. That would be pretty stupid. That would imply the caller had something to do with the guy's homicide."

"We can't rule out anything. Sometimes

killers are stupid," I reply. "If they're desperate enough."

10

Lucy gets up and goes into my private bathroom, where there is a single-cup coffeemaker on a counter. I hear her filling the tank with tap water and checking the small refrigerator. It is almost one a.m. and the snow hasn't eased up, is falling hard and fast, and when the small flakes blow against the windows, the sound is like sand blasting the glass.

"Skim milk or cream?" Lucy calls out from what is supposed to be my private changing area, which includes a shower. "Bryce is such a good wife. He stocked your refrigerator."

"I still drink it black." I start opening my desk drawers, not sure what I'm looking for.

I think about my sloppy work station in the autopsy room. I think of people helping themselves to what they shouldn't.

"Yeah, well, then why is there milk and cream?" Lucy's loud voice. "Green Mountain or Black Tiger? There's also hazelnut. Since when do you drink hazelnut?" The questions are rhetorical. She knows the answers.

"Since never," I mutter, seeing pencils, pens, Post-its, paper clips, and in a bottom drawer, a pack of spearmint gum.

It is half-full, and I don't chew gum. Who likes spearmint gum and would have reason to go into my desk? Not Bryce. He's much too vain to chew gum, and if I caught him doing it, I would disapprove, because I consider it rude to chew gum in front of other people. Besides, Bryce wouldn't root around inside my desk, not without permission. He wouldn't dare.

"Jack likes hazelnut, French vanilla, shit like that, and he drinks it with skim milk unless he's on one of his high-protein, high-fat diets," Lucy continues from inside my bathroom. "Then he uses real cream, heavy cream, like what's in here. I suppose if you had guests, were expecting visitors, you might have cream."

"Nothing flavored, and please make it strong."

"He's a superuser just like you are," Lucy's voice then says. "His fingerprints are stored in every lock in this place just like yours are."

I hear the spewing of hot water shooting through the K-Cup and use it as a welcome interruption. I refuse to engage in the poisonous speculation that Jack Fielding has been in my office during my absence, that maybe he's been helping himself while he drinks coffee, chews gum, or who the hell knows what he's been up to. But as I look around, it doesn't seem possible. My office feels unlived-in. It certainly doesn't appear as if anyone has been working in here, so what would he be doing?

"I went over to Norton's Woods before Cambridge PD did, you know. Marino asked them to go back because of the serial number being eradicated from the Glock. But I got there first." Lucy talks on loudly from inside the bathroom. "But I had the disadvantage of not knowing exactly where the guy went down, where he was stabbed, we now know. Without the scene photographs, it's impossible to get an exact location, just an approximate one, so I combed every footpath in the park."

She walks out with steaming coffee in black mugs that have the AFME's unusual crest, a five-card poker draw of aces and eights, known as the dead man's hand, what Wild Bill Hickok supposedly was holding when he was shot to death.

"Talk about a needle in a haystack," she continues. "The flybot's probably half the size of a small paper clip, about the size of, well, a housefly. No joy."

"Just because you found a wing doesn't mean the rest of it was ever out there," I remind her as she sets a coffee in front of me.

"If it's out there, it's maimed." Lucy returns to her chair. "Under snow as we speak and missing a wing. But very possibly still alive, especially when it gets exposed to light, assuming it's not further damaged."

" 'Alive'?"

"Not literally. Likely powered by micro-solar panels as opposed to a battery that would already be dead. Light hits it and abracadabra. That's the way everything is headed. And our little friend, wherever he is, is futuristic, a masterpiece of teeny-tiny technology."

"How can you be so sure if you can't find most of it? Just a wing."

"Not just any wing. The angle and flexure joints are ingenious and suggest to me a different flight formation. Not the flight of an angel anymore. But horizontal like a real insect flies. Whatever this thing is and whatever its function, we're talking about something extremely advanced, something

I've never seen before. Nothing's been published about it, because I get pretty much every technical journal there is online, plus I've been running searches with no success. By all indications, it's a project that's classified, top secret. I sure hope the rest of it is out there on the ground somewhere, safely covered with snow."

"What was it doing in Norton's Woods in the first place?" I envision the black-gloved hand entering the frame of the hidden video camera, as if the man was swatting at something.

"Right. Did he have it, or did someone else?" She blows on her coffee, holding the mug in both hands.

"And is someone looking for it? Does someone think it's here or think we know where it is?" I ask that again. "Has anyone mentioned to you that his gloves are gone? Did you happen to notice when you were downstairs while Marino was printing the body? It appears the victim put on a pair of black gloves as he arrived at the park, which I thought was curious when I watched the video clips. I assume he died with the gloves on, and so where are they?"

"That's interesting," Lucy says, and I can't tell if she already knew the gloves are missing.

I can't tell what she knows and if she's lying.

"They weren't in the woods when I was walking around yesterday morning," she informs me. "I would have seen a pair of black gloves, saying they were accidentally left by the squad, the removal service, the cops. Of course, they could have been and were picked up by anybody who happened along."

"In the video clips, someone wearing a long black coat walks past right after the man falls to the ground. Is it possible whoever killed him paused just long enough to take his gloves?"

"You mean if they're some type of data gloves or smart gloves, what they're using in combat, gloves with sensors embedded in them for wearable computer systems, wearable robotics," Lucy says, as if it is a normal thing to consider about a pair of missing gloves.

"I'm just wondering why his gloves might be important enough for someone to take them, if that's what's happened," I reply.

"If they have sensors in them and that's how he was controlling the flybot, assuming the flybot is his, then the gloves would be extremely important," Lucy says.

"And you didn't ask about the gloves

when you were downstairs with Marino? You didn't think to check gloves, clothing, for sensors that might be embedded?"

"If I had the gloves, I would have had a much better chance of finding the flybot when I went back to Norton's Woods," Lucy says. "But I don't have them or know where they are, if that's what you're asking."

"I am asking that because it would be tampering with evidence."

"I didn't. I promise. I don't know for a fact that the gloves are data gloves, but if they are, it would make sense in light of other things. Like what he's saying on the video clip right before he dies," she adds thoughtfully, working it out, or maybe she's already worked it out but is leading me to believe what she's saying is a new thought. "The man keeps saying, 'Hey, boy.' "

"I assumed he was talking to his dog."

"Maybe. Maybe not."

"And he said other things I couldn't figure out," I recall. " 'And for you' or 'Do you send one' or something like that. Could a robotic fly understand voice commands?"

"Absolutely possible. That part was muffled. I heard it, too, and thought it was confusing," Lucy says. "But maybe not if he was controlling the flybot. 'For you' could be *four-two,* maybe, as in the number four?

'And' could be *N,* as in north? I'll listen again and do more enhancement."

"More?"

"I've done some. Nothing helpful. Could be he was telling the flybot GPS coordinates, which would be a common command to give a device that responds to voice — if you're telling it where to go, for example."

"If you could figure out GPS coordinates, maybe you could find the location, find where it is."

"Sincerely doubt it. If the flybot was controlled by the gloves, at least partially controlled by sensors in them, then when the victim waved his hand, probably at the moment he was stabbed?"

"Right. Then what?"

"I don't know, but I don't have the flybot, and I don't have the gloves," Lucy says to me while looking at me intently, her eyes directly on mine. "I didn't find them, but I sure wish I had."

"Did Marino mention that someone may have been following Benton and me after we left Hanscom?" I ask.

"We looked for the big SUV with xenon lights and fog lamps. I'm not saying it means anything, but Jack's got a dark-blue Navigator. Pre-owned, bought it back in October. You weren't here, so I guess you haven't seen it."

"Why would Jack follow us? And no. I don't know anything about him buying a Navigator. I thought he had a Jeep Cherokee."

"Traded up, I guess." She drinks her coffee. "I didn't say he would follow you or did. Or that he would be stupid enough to ride your bumper. Except in a blizzard or fog, when visibility's really bad, a rather inexperienced tail might follow too close if the person doesn't know where the target is going. I don't see why Jack would bother. Wouldn't he assume you were on your way here?"

"Do you have an idea why anyone would bother?"

"If someone knows the flybot is missing," she says, "he or she sure as hell's looking for it, and possibly would spare nothing to find it before it gets into the wrong hands. Or the right hands. Depending on who or what we're dealing with. I can say that much based on a wing. If that's why you were followed, it would make me less likely to suspect that whoever killed this guy found the flybot. In other words, it could very well still be missing or lost. I probably don't need to tell you that a top-secret proprietary technical invention like this could be worth a fortune, especially if someone could steal the idea and take credit for it. If such a person is looking for it and has reason to fear it may have come in with the body, maybe this person wanted to see where you were going, what you were up to. He or she might think the flybot is here at the CFC or might think you have it off-site somewhere. Including at your house."

"Why would I have it at my house? I haven't been home."

"Logic has nothing to do with it when someone is in overdrive," Lucy answers. "If I were the person looking, I might assume you instructed your former FBI husband to hide the flybot at your house. I might assume all kinds of things. And if the flybot is still at large, I'm still going to be looking."

I remember what the man exclaimed, can hear his voice in my head. *"What the . . . ? Hey . . . !"* Maybe his startled reaction wasn't due solely to the sudden sharp pain in his lower back and tremendous pressure in his chest. Maybe something flew at his face. Maybe he had on data gloves, and his startled reaction is what caused the flybot to get broken. I imagine a tiny device mid-flight, and then struck by the man's black gloved hand and crushed against his coat collar.

"If someone has the data gloves and looked for the flybot before the snow started, is it really possible the person wouldn't have found it?" I ask my niece.

"Sure, it's possible. Depends on a number of things. How badly damaged it is, for example. There was a lot of activity around the man after he went down. If the flybot was there on the ground, it could have been crushed or damaged further and rendered completely unresponsive. Or it could be under something or in a tree or a bush or anywhere out there."

"I assume a robotic insect could be used as a weapon," I suggest. "Since I don't have a clue what caused this man's internal injuries, I need to think about every possibility imaginable."

"That's the thing," Lucy says. "These days, almost anything you can imagine is possible."

"Did Benton tell you what we saw on CT?"

"I don't see how a micromechanical insect could cause internal damage like that," Lucy answers. "Unless the victim was somehow injected with a micro–explosive device."

My niece and her phobias. Her obsession with explosives. Her acute distrust of government.

"And I sure as hell hope not," she says. "Actually, we'd be talking about nanoexplosives if a flybot was involved."

My niece and her theories about super-thermite, and I remember Jaime Berger's comment the last time I saw her at Thanksgiving when all of us were in New York, having dinner in her penthouse apartment. "Love doesn't conquer all," Berger said. "It can't possibly," she said as she drank too much wine and spent a lot of time in the kitchen, arguing with Lucy about 9/11, about explosives used in demolitions, nanomaterials painted on infrastructures that would cause a horrendous destruction if impacted by large planes filled with fuel.

I have given up reasoning with my phobic, cynical niece, who is too smart for her own good and won't listen. It doesn't matter to her that there simply aren't enough facts to support what has her convinced, only allegations about residues found in the dust right after the towers collapsed. Then, weeks later, more dust was collected and it showed the same residues of iron oxide and aluminum, a highly energetic nanocomposite that is used in making pyrotechnics and explosives. I admit there have been credible scientific journal articles written about it, but not enough of them, and they don't begin to prove that our own government helped mastermind 9/11 as an excuse to start a war in the Middle East.

"I know how you feel about conspiracy theories," Lucy says to me. "That's a big difference between us. I've seen what the so-called good guys can do."

She doesn't know about South Africa. If she did, she would realize there isn't a difference between the two of us. I know all too well what so-called good guys can do. But not 9/11. I won't go that far, and I think of Jaime Berger and imagine how difficult it would be for the powerful and established Manhattan prosecutor to have Lucy as a partner. Love doesn't conquer all. It really is true. Maybe Lucy's paranoia about 9/11 and the country we live in have driven her back into a personal isolation that historically is never broken for long. I really thought Jaime was the one, that it would last. I now feel certain it hasn't. I want to tell Lucy I'm sorry for that and I'm always here for her and will talk about anything she wants, even if it goes against my beliefs. Now is not the time.

"I think we need to consider that we might be dealing with some renegade scientist or maybe more than one of them up to no good," Lucy then tells me. "That's the big point I'm trying to make. And I mean serious no good, extreme no good, Aunt Kay."

It relieves me to hear her call me Aunt Kay. I feel all is right with us when she calls me Aunt Kay, and she rarely does it anymore. I don't remember the last time she did. When I'm her Aunt Kay I can almost ignore what Lucy Farinelli is, which is a genius who is marginally sociopathic, a diagnosis that Benton scoffs at, nicely but firmly. Being marginally sociopathic is like being marginally pregnant or marginally dead, he says. I love my niece more than my own life, but I've come to accept that when she is well behaved, it is an act of will or simply because it suits her. Morals have very little to do with it. It's all about the end justifying the means.

I study her carefully, even though I won't see what's there. Her face never gives away information that could really hurt her.

I say to her, "I need to go ahead and ask you one thing."

"You can ask more than one." She smiles and doesn't look capable of hurting anything or anyone unless you recognize the strength and agility in her calm hands and the rapid changes in her eyes as thoughts flash behind them like lightning.

"You aren't involved in whatever this is." I mean the small white box and the flybot wing inside it. I mean the dead man who is getting an MRI at McLean — someone we may have crossed paths with at a da Vinci exhibition in London months before 9/11, which Lucy incredibly believes was orchestrated from within our own government.

"Nope." She says it simply and doesn't flinch or look the slightest bit uncomfortable.

"Because you're here now." I remind her she works for the CFC, meaning she works for me, and I answer to the governor of Massachusetts, the Department of Defense, the White House. I answer to a lot of people, I tell her. "I can't have —"

"Of course you can't. I'm not going to get you into trouble."

"It isn't just you anymore —"

"No need to have this conversation," she interrupts again, and her eyes blaze. They are so green they don't look real. "Anyway, he doesn't have thermal injury, right? No burns?"

"None that I can see so far. That's correct," I reply.

"Okay. So if someone poked him with a modified shark bang stick? You know, one of those speargun shafts with something like a shotgun cartridge attached to the tip? Only in this case, a tiny, tiny charge containing nanoexplosives?"

I push the power button to start my desktop computer. "It wouldn't look like what I just saw. It would look like a contact gunshot wound minus the patterned abrasion made by the muzzle of a gun. Even if we're talking about using nanoexplosives as opposed to some type of firearm ammunition on the tip of a shaft or something shaft-like, you're right, you'd see thermal injury. There should be burns at the entrance and also to underlying tissue. I assume you're implying something like a flybot could be used to deliver nanoexplosives. Is that what you fear this so-called renegade scientist or more than one of them might be doing?"

"Deliver. Detonate. Nanoexplosives, drugs, poisons. Like I said, let your imagination be the limit what a device like this might be capable of."

"I need to take a look at the security footage that shows the body bag leaking." As I look for files in my computer. "I'm not going to have to go see Ron for that, am I?"

Lucy comes around to my side of the desk and starts typing on my keyboard, entering her system administrator's password that grants complete access to my kingdom.

"Easy as pie." She taps a key to open a file.

"Nobody could get into my files without your knowing."

"Not in cyberspace. But I can't know if someone's been in your physical space, especially since I'm not up here all the time, in fact, not even most of the time, because I work remotely when I can," she says, but I'm not sure I believe she wouldn't know.

In fact, I don't believe it.

"But no way anyone has gotten into your password-protected files," she says, and that I do believe. Lucy wouldn't permit it. "You can monitor the security cameras from anywhere, by the way. Even from your iPhone if you want. All you need is access to the Internet. I found this earlier and saved it as a file. Five-forty-two p.m. That's what time it was yesterday when this was captured by a closed-caption security camera in the receiving area."

She clicks on play and turns up the volume, and I watch two attendants in winter coats pushing a stretcher bearing a black body bag along the lower level's gray tile hallway.

Wheels click as they park the stretcher in front of the cooler, and now I can see Janelle, stocky with short brunette hair, tough-looking with a surprising number of tattoos, as best I recall. Someone Fielding found and hired.

Janelle opens the massive stainless-steel door, and I hear the rush of blowing air.

"Put it . . ." She points, and I notice she is wearing her coat, a dark jacket with *FORENSICS* in large, bright yellow letters on the back. She's in scene clothes, including a CFC baseball cap, as if she's going out in the cold or just came in.

"That tray there?" an attendant asks as he and his partner lift the body bag off the stretcher. The bag bends freely as they carry it, the body inside it as flexible as in life. "Shit, he's dripping. Dammit. He'd better not have AIDS or something. On my pants, my damn shoes."

"The lower one." Janelle directs them to a tray inside the cooler, stepping out of the way and not interested that blood is dripping from the body bag and spotting the gray floor. She doesn't seem to notice.

"Janelle the magnificent," Lucy comments as the video recording ends abruptly.

"Do you have the MLI log?" I want to see what time the medicolegal investigator — in other words, Janelle — came and went yesterday. "Obviously, she was on call during the evening?"

"She worked a double shift on Sunday, worker bee that she is," Lucy says. "Filled in for Randy, who was scheduled for evenings over the weekend but called in sick. Meaning he stayed home to watch the Super Bowl."

"I hope not."

"And Dandy Randy's not here now because of the weather. Supposedly on call at home. Must be nice to have a take-home SUV and get paid for staying home," Lucy says, and I hear the contempt in her flinty tone and see it in the hardness of her face. "I guess you can tell you got your work cut out for you. Assuming you ever quit making excuses for people."

"I don't make them for you."

"That's because there aren't any."

I look at the log Janelle kept yesterday, a template on my video display that has very few fields filled in.

"I don't mean to state what's as plain as the nose on my face, but there's not much you really know about what goes on," Lucy says. "You don't know the finer points of the day-to-day in this place. How could you?" She returns to her side of the desk and picks up her coffee, but she doesn't sit back down. "You haven't been here. You've sort of never been here since we opened for business."

"This is it? This is the entire log for Sunday?"

"Yup. Janelle came in at four. If what she entered into the log is to be believed." Lucy stands there, drinking her coffee, eyeing me. "And she runs with quite a pack, by the way. Forensic fuck buddies. Most of them cops, a few of them data-entry and clerical. Whoever she can be a hero to. You know she's on a dodgeball team? What kind of person plays dodgeball? Someone with finesse."

"If she came in at four, why is she dressed in scene clothes, including her jacket? As if she just came in from the cold?"

"Like I said, if what she entered in the log is to be believed."

"And David was on before that and didn't respond to anything, either?" I ask. "Jack could have sent him to Norton's Woods. David was sitting right here, so why didn't Jack tell him to go to the scene? It's maybe fifteen minutes from here."

"And you don't know that, either." Lucy walks into the bathroom and rinses her mug. "You don't know if David was sitting right here," she says as she walks back out and hovers near my closed office door. "I don't want to be the one to tell you . . ."

"It would seem you are the only one to tell me. No one else is telling me a damn thing," I reply. "What the hell is happening around here? People just show up when they feel like it?"

"Pretty much. The other MEs, the MLIs, in and out, marching to their own drummer. It trickles down from the top."

"It trickles down from Jack."

"At least on your side of things. The labs are another story, because he's not interested in them. Except firearms." She leans against the closed door, slipping her hands into the pockets of her lab coat.

"He's supposed to be in charge in my absence. Jack's the codirector of the entire CFC Port Mortuary." I can't keep the protest out of my tone, the note of outrage.

"Not interested in the labs, and scientists don't pay any attention to him, anyway. Except firearms, like I said. You know Fielding and guns, knives, crossbows, hunting bows. Never met a weapon he didn't love. So he messes with the firearms and toolmark lab and has managed to fuck them up, too. Piss off Morrow until he's on the verge of quitting. I do know he's actively looking for another job, and there's no good reason his lab didn't finish with the Glock the dead guy had on him. The eradicated serial number. Shit. He bolted out of here this morning and didn't bother."

"He bolted out of here?"

"He was driving off when I was returning from Norton's Woods. This was about ten-thirty."

"Did you talk to him?"

"No. Maybe he wasn't feeling well. I don't know, but I don't understand why he didn't make sure someone took care of the Glock. Using acid on a drilled-off serial number? How long does that take to at least try? He must have known it was important."

"He might not have," I answer. "If the Cambridge detective is the only one who talked to him, why would he think the Glock was important? At that time, no one had a clue the man from Norton's Woods was a homicide."

"Well, I guess that's a relevant point. Morrow probably doesn't even know we went to get you, that you're back from Dover. Fielding vanished, too, when he knew damn well there was a major problem that most people with a brain in their head would decide was his fault. He's the one who took the call about the guy in Norton's Woods. He's the one who didn't go to the scene or make sure somebody did. The reason Janelle is dressed for the great outdoors, in my opinion? She didn't get here at four, the time she entered into the log. She got here just in time to let in the attendants and sign in the body and then turned right around and left. I can find out. There will be an entry for when she disabled the alarm to enter the building. Depends on whether you want to make a federal case out of it."

"I'm surprised Marino hasn't made sure I know the extent of the problems." It's all I can think to say. The inside of my head has gone dark.

"Like the boy crying wolf," Lucy says, and it's true.

Marino complains so much about so many people, I scarcely hear him. Now we're back to my failures. I haven't paid attention. I haven't listened. Maybe I wouldn't have listened no matter who told me.

"I've got a few things to take care of. You know how to find me," Lucy says, and she opens my door and leaves it open after she walks out.

I pick up the phone and try Fielding's numbers again. I don't leave any messages this time, and it crosses my mind that his wife isn't answering their home phone, either. She would see my office name and number on caller ID. Maybe that's why she doesn't pick up, because she knows it's me. Or maybe his family has gone somewhere, is out of town. On a Monday night in the middle of a snowstorm, when he knows damn well I've rushed home from Dover to take care of an emergency case?

I walk out and scan my thumb to unlock the door to the right of mine. I stand inside my deputy chief's office and slowly scan it as if it is a crime scene.

11

I picked his office, insisting on one as nice as mine, generously large, with a private shower. He has a river and city view, although his shades are down, which I find unnerving. He must have closed them when it was still light out, and I don't know why he would do that. Not for a good reason, I think. Whatever Jack Fielding has done, it all bodes badly.

I walk around and open each shade, and through expansive glass that is a reflective gray tint, I can make out the blurred lights of downtown Boston and billowing waves of freezing moisture, an icy snow that clicks and bites like teeth. The tops of high-rises, the Prudential and Hancock towers are obscured, and gusting wind moans in low tones around the dome over my head. Below, Memorial Drive is churned up by traffic, even at this hour, and the Charles is formless and black. I wonder how deep the snow is by now and how deep it will get before it moves off to the south. I wonder if Fielding will ever return to this room I designed and furnished for him, and somehow it feels that he won't, even though there is no evidence he's gone for good.

The biggest difference between our work spaces is his is crowded with reminders of the occupant, his various degrees, certificates, and commendations, his collectibles on shelves, autographed baseballs and bats, tae kwon do trophies and plaques, and models of fighter planes and a piece from a real one that crashed. I go over to his desk and survey Civil War relics: a belt buckle, a mess kit, a powder horn, a few minié balls that I remember him collecting during our early days in Virginia. But there are no photographs, and that makes me sad. In some places I can see what's gone in blank spaces of wall where he's not bothered to fill in the tiny holes left from hanging hooks he removed.

It stings that he no longer displays familiar pictures taken when he was my forensic pathology fellow, candid shots of us in the morgue or the two of us out at death scenes with Marino, the lead homicide detective for Richmond PD in the late eighties, the early nineties, when both Fielding and I were just getting started, although in completely different ways. He was the good-looking doctor beginning his career, while I was shifting mine into the private sector, transitioning into civilian life and the role of chief, doing my best not to look back. Maybe Fielding isn't looking back, although I don't know why. His old days were good days compared to mine. He didn't help cover up a crime. He's never had anything on par with that to hide from. Not that I know of, but I have to wonder. What do I know anymore?

Not much, except I sense he's gotten rid of me, maybe gotten rid of all of us. I sense he's gotten rid of more than he ever has before. It is something I'm convinced of without knowing exactly why. Certainly his personal property is still here, his Gore-Tex rain suit on a hanger, and his neoprene hip waders, his dive bag of scuba gear and scene case stowed in a closet, and his collection of police patches and police and military challenge coins. I remember helping him move into this office. I even helped him arrange his furniture, both of us complaining and laughing and then griping some more as we moved the desk, then his conference table, then moved them again and again.

"What is this, Laurel and Hardy?" he said.

"You going to push a mule up the stairs next?"

"You don't have stairs."

"I'm thinking of getting a horse," he said as we moved the same chairs we'd just moved earlier. "There's a horse farm about a mile from the house. I could board the horse there, maybe ride it to work, to crime scenes."

"I'll add that to the employee handbook. No horses."

We joked and teased each other, and he looked good that day — vital and optimistic, his muscles straining against the short sleeves of his scrubs. He was just incredibly built and healthy-looking then, his face still boyishly handsome, his dark blond hair messy, and he hadn't shaved for several days. He was sexy and funny, and I remember the whispers and giggles of some of the female staff as they walked past his open door, finding excuses to stare at him. Fielding seemed so happy to be here and with me, and I remember both of us placing photographs and reminiscing about our early days together — photographs that now are gone.

In their place are ones I don't recall. The pictures are prominently arranged on his shelves and walls, formal poses of him with politicians and military brass, one with General Briggs and even Captain Avallone, perhaps from the tour Fielding gave her. He looks wooden and bored. In a photograph of him in tae kwon do white, mid-flight and kicking an imagined enemy, he looks angry. He looks red-faced and hateful. As I study recent family portraits, I decide he doesn't look content in them, either, not even when he is holding his two little girls or has his arm around his wife, Laura, a delicate blonde whose prettiness is eroding, as if a trying existence is mapping its course on her physically, etching lines and furrows into a topography that once was graceful and smooth.

She is number three for him, and I can trace his decline as I scan his captured moments in chronological order. When he married her, he looked energetic, with no sign of a rash, and he didn't have any unseemly bald patches. I pause to admire how amazing he was, shirtless and as hard-bodied as stone in running shorts, washing his Mustang, a '67, cherry red with Le Mans stripes down the center of the hood. Then as recently as this past fall, the thickening around his middle; the splotchy, flushed skin; the strands of hair combed back and held in place with gel to hide his alopecia.

At a martial arts competition not even a month ago, he doesn't look as fit or as spiritually balanced in his grandmaster's uniform and black belt. He doesn't look like someone who finds joy in beautiful form or technique. He doesn't look like someone who honors other people or has self-control or respect for anything. He looks dissipated. He looks slightly deranged. He looks perfectly miserable.

Why? I silently ask that earlier photograph of him with his prized car, when he was stunning to behold and seemed carefree and vital, the sort of man it would be easy to fall in love with or to place in charge or to trust with your life. *What changed? What made you so unhappy? What was it this time?* He hates working for me. He hated it the last time, in Watertown, where he didn't stay long, and now the CFC, and he hates that more, it's obvious. This past late summer, when he started looking so bad, is when we finally opened our doors to criminal justice, taking cases. But I wasn't even in Massachusetts then, just one weekend over Labor Day. It can't be my fault. It's always been my fault. I've always blamed myself for Fielding's downfalls, and he's had more of them than I care to count.

I pick him up and he falls again, only

harder each time. It gets uglier. It gets bloodier. Again and again. Like a child who can't walk, and I won't accept it until he's injured beyond fixing. The drama that will always end predictably is the way Benton has described it. Fielding shouldn't be a forensic pathologist, and it's because of me that he is. He would have been better off if he'd never met me in the spring of 1988 when he wasn't sure what he wanted in life and I said I know what you should do. Let me show you. Let me teach you. If he'd never come to Richmond, if he'd never run into me, he might have picked a way to spend his days that would have suited him. His career, his life, would have been about him and not about me.

That really is the bottom line, that he does the best he can in an environment totally destructive to him and finally can't take it any longer and decompensates, disintegrates, and remembers why he is what he is and who shaped him, and then I loom as huge in his wretched life as a billboard. His answer to these crises is always the same. He vanishes. One day he simply drops off the radar, and what I find in his wake is awful. Cases he mishandled or neglected. Memos that show his lack of control and dangerous judgment. Hurtful voicemails he didn't bother to delete because he wanted me to hear them. Damaging e-mails and other communications he hoped I'd find. I sit in his chair and start opening drawers. I don't have to rummage long.

The file folder isn't labeled and contains four pages printed at eight-oh-three yesterday morning, February 8, a speech that based on other information in the header and news section is from the Royal United Services Institute's website. A century-old British think tank with satellite offices strategically located around the world, RUSI is dedicated to advanced innovations in national and international security, and I can't imagine Fielding's interest. I can't fathom him caring about a keynote address given by Russell Brown, the shadow secretary of state for defense, on his views about the "defense debate." I skim the conservative member of Parliament's not-so-startling comments that it isn't a given the UK will always act as part of an alliance and the economic impact of the war is catastrophic. He makes repeated allusions to misinformation methodically propagated, which is as close as the respectable MP is going to come to outright accusing the United States of orchestrating the invasion of Iraq and dragging the UK along for the ride.

Unsurprisingly, the speech is political, as is almost everything right now in Britain, which holds its general election in three months. Six hundred and fifty seats are being contested, and a major campaign issue is the more than ten thousand British troops fighting the Taliban in Afghanistan. Fielding isn't military, has never paid much attention to foreign affairs or elections, and I don't know why he would have the slightest interest in what is happening in the UK. I don't recall that he's ever even been to the UK. He's not the sort to be interested in a general election over there or RUSI or any think tank, and knowing him as well as I do, I suspect he intended for me to find this file. He wanted me to see it after he pulled another one of his vanishing stunts. What is it he wants me to know?

Why is he interested in RUSI? And did he come across the speech himself on the Internet, or did someone send it to him? If it was sent to him, by whom? I consider asking Lucy to go into Fielding's e-mail, but I'm not ready to be that heavy-handed, and I don't want to be caught. I can lock the door, but my superuser deputy chief could still walk in, because I don't have confidence that Ron or anyone else will keep Fielding in the security area if he shows up. I have no faith that Ron, who was unfriendly to me and seems to have little regard for me, will detain Fielding or try to get hold of me to ask for clearance. I don't trust that my staff is loyal to me or feels safe with me or follows my orders, and Fielding could re-appear at any moment.

That would be like him. To vanish without warning, then show up just as unexpectedly and catch me red-handed, sitting at his desk, going through his electronic files. It's just one more thing he'll use against me, and he's used plenty against me over the years. What has he been doing behind my back? Let's see what else I find, and then I'll know what to do. I look at the time stamp again and imagine Fielding sitting in this very chair at eight-oh-three yesterday morning printing the speech, while Lucy, Marino, Anne, and Ollie, while everybody, was in an uproar because of what was in the cooler downstairs.

How odd that Fielding would be up here in his office while that was going on, and I wonder if he even cared that a man might have been locked inside our refrigerator while still alive. Of course, Fielding would have to care. How could he not? If the worst had turned out to be true, he would be blamed. Ultimately, I would be the one all over the news and likely out of a job, but he would go down with me. Yet he was up here on the seventh floor, in his office and out of the fray, as if he already had his mind made up, and it occurs to me that his disappearance may be related to something else. I lean back in his chair and look around, my attention landing on the pad of call sheets and a ballpoint pen near his phone. I notice faint indentations on the top sheet of paper.

Turning on a lamp, I pick up the pad and hold it at various angles, trying to make out indented writing left like a footprint when someone wrote a note on a top sheet of paper that is no longer there. One thing about Fielding, he doesn't have a light touch, not when he's wielding a scalpel or typing on a keyboard or writing something by hand. For a devotee of martial arts, he is surprisingly rough, is easily frustrated and quick to flare up. He has a childish way of holding a pencil or pen with two fingers on top instead of one, as if he's using chopsticks, and it's not uncommon for him to break lead or nibs, and he's hell on Magic Markers.

I don't need ESDA or a Docustat or vacuum box or some other indented writing-recovery unit to detect what I can see the old-fashioned way in oblique lighting with my own eyes. Fielding's barely legible scribble. What appears to be two separate notes. One is a phone number with a 508 area code and "MVF8/18/UK Min of Def Diary2/8." Then a second one: "U of Sheffield today @ Whitehall. Over and out." I look again, making sure I read the last three words correctly. *Over and out.* The end of a radio transmission, like *Roger Wilco over and out* but also a song performed by a heavy-metal band that Fielding used to play in his car all the time when he first came to Richmond. *"Over and out / every dog has its day."* What he'd sing to me when he'd threaten to quit, when he'd had enough, or when he was teasing, flirting, pretending to be fed up. Did he write *over and out* on a call sheet with me in mind or for some other reason?

I find a legal pad in a drawer and write what I've discovered indented on the pad of call sheets and begin doing the best I can to figure out what Fielding was up to and thinking about, what it is he wants me to know. If I came in here to snoop, I was going to find the printout and the indented writing. He knows me. He would think that way, because he knows damn well how my mind works. The University of Sheffield is one of the top research institutions in the world, and Whitehall is where RUSI is headquartered, literally in the former Whitehall Palace, the original location of Scotland Yard.

Logging on to Intelliquest, a search engine Lucy created for the CFC, I type in RUSI and the date February 8 and Whitehall. What comes up is the title of a keynote address, *Civilian-Military Collaboration,* the lecture Fielding must be referring to that was delivered at RUSI at ten a.m. UK time, what is now yesterday morning for me. The speaker was Dr. Liam Saltz, the controversial Nobel laureate whose doomsday opinions about military technology make him a natural enemy of DARPA. I wasn't aware he was on the faculty at the University of Sheffield. I thought he was at Berkeley. He used to be at Berkeley, and now he's at Sheffield, I read on the Internet as I think, rather dazed, of the exhibit at the Courtauld in the summer before 9/11, where Lucy and I heard Dr. Saltz lecture. Not long after that, Dr. Saltz, like me, was a vocal critic of MORT.

I ponder the title of the lecture Dr. Saltz delivered not even twenty-four hours ago. *Civilian-Military Collaboration.* That certainly sounds tame for the rabble-rousing Dr. Saltz, who is as jolting as an air-raid siren in his warnings that America's two-hundred-plus-billion-dollar allocation to future combat systems — specifically, unmanned vehicles — has put us on the road to ultimate annihilation. Robots might seem to make sense when you consider sending them into the battlefield, he rails, but what happens when they come home like used Jeeps and other military surplus? Eventually they will find their way into the civilian world, and what we'll have is more policing and surveillance, more insensate machines doing the jobs of humans, only these machines will be armed and equipped with cameras and recording devices.

I've heard Dr. Saltz on the news, painting terrifying scenarios of "copbots" responding to crime scenes and unmanned "robocruisers" pursuing vehicles to write up occupants for traffic violations or hauling people in for outstanding warrants or, God forbid, getting a message from sensors to use force. Robots Tasering us. Robots shooting us to death. Robots that look like huge insects dragging our wounded and dead off a battlefield. Dr. Saltz testifying before the same Senate subcommittee I did but not at the same time. Both of us wreaking havoc for a technology company named Otwahl that I'd completely forgotten about until just hours ago.

I've met him only once, when both of us happened to be on CNN and he pointed at me and quipped, "Autbotsies."

"I beg your pardon," I answered, unclipping my mike as he walked onto the set.

"Robotic autopsies. Someday they'll take your place, my good doctor, maybe sooner than you think. We should have a drink after the show."

He was a bright-eyed man who looked like a lost hippie with his long, graying ponytail and wasted face, and he had the electricity of an exposed live wire. That was two years ago, and I should have taken him up on his invitation and waited around CNN. I should have had a drink with him. I should have gotten better versed in what he believes, because it isn't all crazy. I haven't seen him since then, although I can't escape his presence in the media, and I try to recall if I've ever mentioned him to Fielding for any reason at all. I don't think so. I can't figure out why I would. Connections. What are they? I search some more.

The University of Sheffield in South Yorkshire has an excellent medical school, that much I already know. *Rerum Cognoscere Causas*, its motto, *To discover the causes of things*, how apropos, how ironic. I need causes. *Research,* and I click on that. Global warming, global soil degradation, rethinking engineering with pioneering computer software, new findings in human embryonic stem cells' DNA changes. I go back to the indented notes on the call sheet.

MVF8/18/UK Min of Def Diary2/8.

MVF is our abbreviation for motor-vehicle fatality, and I instigate another search, this time mining the CFC database. I enter MVF and the date 8/18, August 18 last summer, and a record is returned, the case of a twenty-year-old British man named Damien Patten who was killed in a taxicab accident in Boston. Fielding didn't do the autopsy, one of my other MEs did, and in the narrative I notice that Damien Patten was a lance corporal in the 14th Signal Regiment and was on leave and had come to Boston to get married when he was killed in the taxicab accident. I get a funny feeling. Something registers.

I execute another search using the keywords February 8 and UK Ministry of Defense Diary. I end up on its official news blog, and an entry in the diary lists British soldiers killed in Afghanistan yesterday. I run down the list of casualties, looking for anything that might mean something to me. A lance corporal from 1st Battalion Coldstream Guards. A lance sergeant from 1st Battalion Grenadier Guards. A kingsman from 2nd Battalion Duke of Lancaster's Regiment. Then there is a sapper, or combat engineer, with the Counter-Improvised Explosive Device Task Force, who was killed in the mountainous terrain of northwestern Afghanistan. In the Badghis Province. Where my patient PFC Gabriel was killed on Sunday, February 7.

I execute another search, although one detail I already know without having to look it up is how many NATO troops died in Afghanistan on February 7. At Dover, we always know. It's as routine as preparing for ugly storms, a depressingly morbid report that controls our lives. Nine casualties, and four of them were Americans killed by the same roadside improvised explosive device that turned PFC Gabriel's Humvee into a blast furnace. But again, that was on the seventh, not the eighth. It occurs to me that the British soldier who died on the eighth might have been injured the day before.

I check and I'm right. The IED sapper, Geoffrey Miller, was twenty-three, recently married, and was wounded in a roadside bombing in the Badghis Province early Sunday but died the next day in a military medical center in Germany. Possibly the same roadside bombing that killed the Americans we took care of at Dover yesterday morning — in fact, it's likely. I wonder if Sapper Miller and PFC Gabriel knew each other, and how the British man killed in a taxicab, Damien Patten, might be connected. Was Patten acquainted with Miller and Gabriel in Afghanistan, and what does Fielding have to do with any of this? How are Dr. Saltz or MORT or the dead man from Norton's Woods connected, or are they?

Miller's body will be repatriated this Thursday, returned to his family in Oxford, England. I read on, but I can't find anything else about him, although I certainly am capable of getting more information about a slain British soldier if I need it. I can call the press secretary, Rockman. I can call Briggs, and I should, anyway, I remember. Briggs asked me to — in fact, ordered me — demanding that I keep him informed about the Norton's Woods case, to wake him up if need be the minute I have information. But I won't. No way. Not now. I'm not sure whom I can trust, and as that thought lingers, I realize the trouble I'm in.

What does it say when you can't ask for help from the very people you work with? It says everything, and it's as if the ground is opening up beneath my feet and I'm falling into the unknown, a cold, lightless, empty space where I've been before. Briggs wanted to do an end run, to usurp my authority and transfer the Norton's Woods case to Dover. Fielding has been sneaking around in my absence, meddling in affairs that are none of his business and even using my office, and now he's ducking me, or at least I hope that's all it is. My staff is committing mutiny, and any number of people, strangers to me, seem to know the details of my return home.

It is almost two a.m., and I'm tempted to try the indented telephone number Fielding scribbled on a call sheet and surprise whoever answers, wake the person up and perhaps get a clue as to what is going on. Instead, I do a polite computer search to see who or what the number with the 508 area code might belong to. The report summary shocks me, and for a moment I sit very still and try to calm myself. I try to push back the walls of dismay and confusion crowding in.

Julia Gabriel, mother of PFC Gabriel.

On the screen in front of me are her home and business addresses, her marital status, the salary she earns as a pharmacist in

Worcester, Massachusetts, and the name of her only child and his age, which was nineteen when he died in Afghanistan on Sunday. I was on the phone with Mrs. Gabriel for the better part of an hour before I autopsied her son, trying to explain as gently as I could the impossibility of collecting his sperm while she raised her voice at me and cried and accused me of personal choices that aren't mine to make and ones I didn't make and would never make.

Saving sperm from the dead and using it to impregnate the living isn't something that causes me a moral dilemma. I really have no personal opinion about what truly is a medical and legal question, not a religious or ethical one, and the choice should be up to those involved, certainly not up to the practitioner. What matters to me is that the procedure, which has become increasingly popular because of the war, is done properly and legally, and my supposed views on posthumous reproduction rights were moot in PFC Gabriel's case, anyway. His body was burned and decomposing, his pelvis so charred that his scrotum was gone and the vas deferens containing semen along with it, and I wasn't about to tell Mrs. Gabriel that. I was as compassionate and gentle as I could be and didn't take it personally as she vented her grief and rage on the last doctor her son would ever see on this earth.

Peter had a girlfriend who was willing to have his children just like his friend was doing, it was a pact they'd made, Mrs. Gabriel went on, and I had no idea whose friend or what she was talking about. Peter's friend told him of another friend who got killed in Boston on his wedding day this past summer, only Mrs. Gabriel never mentioned Damien Patten by name, the British man killed in a taxicab this past August 18. *"All three of them dead now, three young, beautiful boys dead,"* Mrs. Gabriel said to me over the phone, and I had no idea who she was talking about. I think I do now. I think she meant Patten for sure, the friend of the friend whom PFC Gabriel had some sort of pact with. I wonder if the friend of Patten's was this other casualty that Fielding seems to have led me to, Geoffrey Miller, an IED sapper.

All three of them dead now.

Did Fielding discuss the Patten case with Mrs. Gabriel, and who did she talk to first, Fielding or me? She called me at Dover at around quarter of eight. I always fill out a call sheet, and I remember writing down the time as I sat in my small office at Dover's Port Mortuary, looking at the CT scans and their coordinates that would help me locate with GPS precision the frag and other objects that had penetrated the badly burned body of her son. Based on what she said to me as I now try to reconstruct that conversation, she likely talked to Fielding first. That might explain her repeated references to "other cases."

Someone had planted an idea in her head about what we do for other cases. She was under the distinct impression that we routinely extract semen from casualties and in fact encourage it, and I recall being puzzled, because the procedure has to be approved and is fraught with legal complications. I couldn't imagine what had given her such an idea, and I might have asked her about it, had she not been so busy castigating me and calling me names. What kind of monster would prevent a woman from having her dead boyfriend's children or stop the mother of a dead son from being a grandmother? We do it for our other cases, why not her son? she wept. *"I have no one left,"* she cried. *"This is bullshit bureaucracy, go on and admit it,"* she yelled at me. *"Bureaucratic bullshit to cover up yet another hate crime."*

"Anyone home?" Benton is in the doorway.

Mrs. Gabriel called me a military bigot.

"You do unto others as long as they're white," she said. *"That's not the Golden Rule but the White Rule,"* she said. *"You took care of that other boy who got killed in Boston, and he wasn't even a U.S. soldier, but not my son, who died for his country. I suppose my son was the wrong color,"* she went on, and I had no idea what she meant or what she was basing such an accusation on. I didn't try to figure it out because it seemed like hysteria, nothing more, and I forgave her for it on the spot. Even though it obviously hurt me badly and I've not been able to put it out of my mind since.

"Hello?" Benton is walking in.

"Another hate crime, only it will be found out and people like you won't get rewarded this time," and she wouldn't explain what she was thinking when she said something so terrible as that. But I didn't ask her to elaborate, and I didn't give her venomous comments much credence at the time, because being yelled at, cursed, threatened, and even attacked by people who are otherwise civilized and sane isn't a new experience. I don't have shatterproof glass installed in the lobbies and viewing rooms of offices where I've worked because I'm afraid of the dead throwing a fit or assaulting me.

"Kay?"

My eyes focus on Benton holding two coffees and trying not to spill them. Why would Julia Gabriel have called here before calling me at Dover? Or did Fielding call her, and in either event, why would he have talked to her? Then I remember Marino telling me about PFC Gabriel being the first casualty from Worcester and the media calling the CFC as if the body was here instead of at Dover, about a number of phone calls here because of the Massachusetts connection. Maybe that's how Fielding found out, but why would he get on the phone with the slain soldier's mother, even if she called here by mistake and needed to be reminded her son was at Dover? Of course she knew that. How could Mrs. Gabriel not know her son was flown into Dover? I can't see any legitimate reason for Fielding to have talked to her or what he possibly could have said that was helpful, and how dare him.

He's not military or even a consultant for the AFME. He's a civilian and has no right to probe into details relating to war casualties or national security or to engage in conversations about such matters, which are plainly defined as classified. Military and medical intelligence are none of his business. RUSI is none of his business. The election in the UK isn't, either. The only thing that should be Fielding's damn business is what he has so resoundingly neglected, which is his enormous responsibility here at the CFC and what should be his damn loyalty to me.

"That's nice of you," I say to Benton in a detached way. "I could use a coffee."

"Where were you just now? Besides in the middle of an imagined fight. You look like you might kill someone."

He comes close to the desk, watching me the way he does when he's trying to read what I'm thinking because he's not about to trust what I say. Or maybe he knows what I have to say is only the beginning of things and that I'm clueless about the rest of it.

"You okay?" He sets the coffees on the desk and moves a chair close.

"No, I'm not okay."

"What's wrong?"

"I think I just discovered what it means when something reaches critical mass."

"What's the matter?" he asks.

"Everything."

12

"Please shut the door." It occurs to me I'm starting to act like Lucy. "I don't know where to begin, so many things are the matter."

Benton closes the door, and I notice the simple platinum band on his left ring finger. Sometimes I'm still caught by surprise that we're married, so much of our lives consumed by each other whether we've been together or apart, and we always agreed we didn't have to do it, to be official and formal, because we're not like other people, and then we did it anyway. The ceremony was a small, simple one, not a celebration as much as a swearing in, because we really meant it when we said until death do us part. After all we'd been through, for us to say it was more than words, more like an oath of office or an ordination or perhaps a summary of what we'd already lived. And I wonder if he ever regrets it. For example, right now does he wish he could go back to how it was? I wouldn't blame him if he thinks about what he's given up and what he misses, and there are so many complications because of me.

He sold his family brownstone, an elegant nineteenth-century mansion on the Boston Common, and he can't have loved some places we've lived or stayed in because of my unusual profession and preoccupations, what is a chaotic and costly existence despite my best intentions. While his forensic psychology practice has remained stable, my career has been in flux these past three years, with the shutting down of a private practice in Charleston, South Carolina, then my office in Watertown closing because of the economy, and I was in New York and then Washington and Dover, and now this, the CFC.

"What the hell is going on in this place?" I ask him as if he knows and I don't understand why he would. But I feel he does, or maybe I'm just wishing it because I'm beginning to experience desperation, that panicky sensation of falling and flailing for something to grab hold of.

"Black and extra-bold." He sits back down and slides the mug of coffee closer. "And not hazelnut. Even though you have quite a

314

stash of it, I hear."

"Jack's still not shown up, and no one has heard from him, I assume."

"He's definitely not here. I think you're as safe in his office as he's been in yours." Benton says it as if he means more than one thing, and I notice how he's dressed.

Earlier he had on his winter coat and in the x-ray room was covered in a disposable gown before heading upstairs to Lucy's lab. I didn't really notice what he was wearing underneath his layers. Black tactical boots, black tactical pants, a dark red flannel shirt, a rubber waterproof watch with a luminescent dial. As if he's anticipating being out in the weather or someplace that might be hard on his clothes.

"So Lucy told you it appears he's been using my office," I say. "For what purpose I don't know. But maybe you do."

"Nobody's needed to tell me there's a looting mentality at — what is it Marino calls this place? CENTCOM? Or does that just refer to the inner sanctum, or what's supposed to be the inner sanctum, your office. No captain of the ship, and you know what happens. The Jolly Roger flag goes up, the inmates run the asylum, the drunks manage the bar, if you'll excuse me for mixing metaphors."

"Why didn't you say something?"

"I don't work at the CFC. Or for it. Just an invited guest on occasion," he says.

"That's not an answer, and you know it. Why wouldn't you protect me?"

"You mean in the manner you think I should," he says, because it's silly to suggest he wouldn't protect me.

"What has been going on around here? Maybe if you tell me, I can figure out what needs to be done," I then say. "I know Lucy's been catching you up. It would be nice if someone would catch me up. In detail, and with openness and full disclosure."

"I'm sorry you're angry. I'm sorry you've come home to a situation that is upsetting. Your homecoming should have been joyful."

"Joyful. What the hell is joyful?"

"A word, a theoretical concept. Like full disclosure. I can tell you what I've witnessed firsthand, what happened when I met here several times. Case discussions. There have been two that involved me." He stares off. "The first was the BC football player from last fall, not long after the CFC took over the Commonwealth's forensic cases."

Wally Jamison, age twenty, Boston College's star quarterback. Found floating in

316

Boston Harbor on November 1 at dawn. Cause of death exsanguination due to blunt-force trauma and multiple cutting injuries. Tom Booker's case, one of my other MEs.

"Jack didn't do that one," I remind him.

"Well, if you ask him, you might get a different impression," Benton informs me. "Jack reviewed the Wally Jamison case as if it was his. Dr. Booker wasn't present. This was last week."

"Why last week? I don't know anything about it."

"New information, and we wanted to talk to Jack, and he seemed eager to cooperate, to offer a wealth of information."

" 'We'?"

Benton lifts his coffee, then changes his mind and sets it back down on Fielding's sloppy desk with all its collectibles that are all about him. "I think Jack's attitude is he may not have done the autopsy, but that's just a technicality. An NFL draft was right up the alley of your ironman freak of a deputy chief."

" 'Ironman freak'?"

"But I suppose it was his bad luck to be out of town when Wally Jamison got beaten and hacked to death. Wally's luck was a little worse."

Believed to have been abducted and murdered on Halloween. Crime scene unknown. No suspect. No motive or credible theory. Just the speculation of a satanic cult initiation. Target a star athlete. Hold him hostage in some clandestine place and kill him savagely. Chatter on the Internet and on the news. Gossip that's become gospel.

"I don't give a shit what Jack's feeling is or what's right up his goddamn alley," says a hard part of me that's old and scarred over, a part of me that is completely fed up with Jack Fielding.

I realize I'm enraged by him. I'm suddenly aware that at the core of my unhealthy relationship with him is molten fury.

"And Mark Bishop, also last week. Wednesday was the football player. Thursday was the boy," Benton says.

"A boy whose murder might be related to some initiation. A gang, a cult," I interject. "A similar speculation about Wally Jamison."

"*Speculation* being the operative word. Whose speculation?"

"Not mine." I think angrily of Fielding. "I don't speculate unless it's behind closed doors with someone I trust. I know better than to put something out there, and then the police run with it, then the media runs with it. Next thing I know, a jury believes it, too."

"Patterns and parallels."

"You're connecting Mark Bishop and Wally Jamison." It seems incredible. "I fail to see what they might have in common besides speculation."

"I was here last week for both case consults." Benton's eyes are steady on me. "Where was Jack last Halloween? Do you know for a fact?"

"I know where I was, that's about the only fact I know. While I've been at Dover, that's all I've known and all I was supposed to know. I didn't hire him so I could goddamn babysit him. I don't know where the hell he was on Halloween. I guess you're going to tell me he wasn't out somewhere taking his kids trick-or-treating."

"He was in Salem. But not with his kids."

"I wouldn't know that and don't know why you do or why it's important."

"It wasn't important until very recently," Benton says.

I stare at his boots again, then at his dark pants with their flannel lining and cargo and rear slash pockets for gun magazines and flashlights, the type of pants he wears when he's working in the field, when he goes to crime scenes or is out on the firing or

319

explosive-ordnance-disposal ranges with cops, with the FBI.

"Where were you before you picked me up at Hanscom?" I ask him. "What were you doing?"

"We have a lot to deal with, Kay. I'm afraid more than I thought."

"Were you dressed in field clothes when you picked me up at the airport?" It occurs to me that he might not have been. He's changed his clothes. Maybe he hasn't done anything yet but is about to.

"I keep a bag in my car. As you know," Benton says. "Since I never know when I might get called."

"To go where? You've been called to go somewhere?"

He looks at me, then out the window at the chalky skyline of Boston in the snowy dark.

"Lucy says you've been on the phone." I continue to prod him for information I can tell I'm not going to get right now.

"I'm afraid nonstop. I'm afraid there's more than I thought," and then he doesn't continue. That's all he's going to say about it. He's headed out somewhere, has someplace to go. It's not a good place. He's been talking to people and not about anything good and he's not going to inform me right now. Full disclosure and joy. When there is such a thing, it is only a taste, a hint of what we don't have the rest of the time.

"You met on Wednesday and then on Thursday. Discussing the Wally Jamison and Mark Bishop cases here at the CFC." I go back to that. "And I assume Jack was in on the Mark Bishop discussion as well. He was involved in both discussions. And you didn't mention this a little while ago when we were talking in the car."

"Not such a little while ago. More than five hours ago. And a lot has happened. There have been developments since we were in the car, as you know. Not the least of which is what we now realize is another murder. Number three."

"You're linking the man from Norton's Woods to Mark Bishop and Wally Jamison."

"Very possibly. In fact, I'd say yes."

"What about the meetings last week? With Jack? He was there," I push.

"Yes. Last Wednesday and Thursday. In your office."

"What do you mean my office? This building? This floor?"

"Your personal office." Benton indicates my office next door.

"In my office. Jack conducted meetings in my office. I see."

"He conducted both meetings in your office. At your conference-room table in there."

"He has his own conference table." I look at the black lacquered oval table with six ergonomic chairs that I got at a government auction.

Benton doesn't respond. He knows as well as I do that Fielding's inappropriate decision to use my personal office has nothing to do with the furniture. I think of what Lucy mentioned about sweeping my office for covert surveillance devices, although she never directly said who might be doing the spying or if anyone was. The most likely candidate for the sort of individual who might bug my office and get away with it is my niece. Maybe motivated by the knowledge that Fielding was helping himself to what isn't rightfully his. I wonder if what's been going on in my private space during my absence has been secretly recorded.

"And you never mentioned this to me at that time," I continue. "You could have told me when it happened. You could have fully disclosed to me that he was using my damn office as if he's the damn chief and director of this goddamn place."

"The first I knew of it was last week when I met with him. I'm not saying I hadn't heard things about the CFC and about him."

"It would have been helpful if I'd known these things you were hearing."

"Rumors. Gossip. I didn't know certain things for a fact."

"Then you should have told me a week ago when you knew it for a fact. On the Wednesday you had your first meeting and discovered it was in my office, in an office Jack didn't have permission to use. What else haven't you told me? What new developments?"

"I'm telling you as much as I can and when I can. I know you understand."

"I don't understand. You should have been telling me things all along. Lucy should have. Marino should have."

"It's not that simple."

"Betrayal is very simple."

"No one is betraying you. Marino and Lucy aren't. I'm certainly not."

"Implying that somebody is. Just not the three of you."

He is quiet.

"You and I talk every day, Benton. You should have told me," I then say.

"Let's see when I might have overwhelmed you with all this, overwhelmed you with a lot of things while you've been at Dover.

When you'd call at five a.m. before you'd head over to Port Mortuary to take care of our fallen heroes? Or at midnight when you'd finally log out of your computer or quit studying for your boards?"

He doesn't say it defensively or unkindly, but I get his not-so-subtle point, and it's justified. I'm being unfair. I'm being hypocritical. Whose idea was it that when we have virtually no time for each other we shouldn't dwell on work or domestic minutiae or they will be all that's left? Like cancer, I'm quick to offer my clever medical analogies and brilliant insights when he's the psychologist, he's the one who used to head the FBI's profiling unit at Quantico, he's the one on the faculty of Harvard's Department of Psychiatry. But it's me with all the wisdom, all the profound examples, comparing work and niggling domestic details and emotional injuries to cancers, to scarring, to necrosis, and my prognostications that if we're not careful, one day there's no healthy tissue left and death will follow. I feel embarrassed. I feel shallow.

"No, I didn't approach certain subjects until we were driving here, and now I'm telling you more, telling you what I can," Benton says to me with stoical calm, as if we are in a session of his and any moment he will simply announce we have to stop.

I won't stop until I know what I must. Some things he must tell me. It's not just fairness, it's about survival, and I realize I'm feeling unsure of Benton as if I don't quite know him anymore. He's my husband, and I'm touched by a perception that something has been altered, a new ingredient has been added to the house special.

What is it?

I study what I'm intuiting as if I can taste what has changed.

"I mentioned my concern that Jack's interpretation of Mark Bishop's injuries is problematic," Benton goes on, and he's guarded. He's calculating every word he says as if someone else is listening or he will be reporting our conversation to others. "Well, based on what you've described about the hammer marks on the little boy's head, Jack's interpretation is just damn wrong, couldn't be more wrong, and I suspected it at the time when he was going over the case with us. I suspected he was lying."

" 'Us'?"

"I told you I've heard things, but I honestly haven't been around Jack."

"Why do you say 'honestly'? As opposed to *dishonestly,* Benton?"

"I'm always honest with you, Kay."

"Of course you aren't, but now is not the time to go into it."

"Now isn't. I know you understand." And he holds my stare for a long moment. He's telling me to please let it go.

"All right. I'm sorry." I will let it go, but I don't want to.

"I hadn't seen him for months, and what I saw for myself was . . . Well, it was pretty obvious during those discussions last week that something's off with him, severely off," Benton resumes. "He looked bad. His thoughts were racing all over the map. He was hyperfluent, grandiose, hypomanic, aggressive, and red-faced, as if he might explode. I certainly felt he wasn't being truthful, that he was deliberately misleading us."

"What do you mean 'us'?" And it begins to occur to me what I'm picking up.

"Has he ever been in a psychiatric hospital, been in treatment, maybe been diagnosed with a mood disorder? He ever mentioned anything like that to you?" Benton questions me in a way that I find unexpected and unnerving, and I'm reminded of what I sensed in the car when we were driving here. Only now it's more pronounced, more recognizable.

He is acting the way he used to when he was still an agent, when he was empowered by the federal government to enforce the law. I detect an authority and confidence he hasn't manifested in years, a sure-footedness he lacked after his reemergence from protective deep cover. He came back feeling lost, weak, like nothing more than an academician, he often complained. *Emasculated,* he would say. *The FBI eats its young, and they've eaten me,* he would say. *That's my reward for going after an organized-crime cartel. I finally get my life back and don't want what's left of it,* he would say. *It's a husk. I'm a husk. I love you, but please understand I'm not what I was.*

"He ever been delusional or violent?" Benton is asking me, and it isn't just a clinician talking.

I'm feeling interrogated.

"He had to expect you would tell me he's been using my office as if it's his. Or that I'd find out." I think of Lucy again, of spying and covert recordings.

"I know he has a temper," Benton says, "but I'm talking about physical violence possibly accompanied by dissociative fugue, disappearing for hours, days, weeks, with little or no recall. What we're seeing with some of these men and women who return from war, disappearances and amnesia triggered by severe trauma and often confused with malingering. The same thing Johnny Donahue is supposedly suffering from, only I'm not sure how much of it has been suggested to that poor damn kid. I wonder where the idea came from, if someone's suggested it to him."

He says it as if he really doesn't wonder it.

"Jack's certainly famous for coming across as a malingerer, of avoiding his responsibilities going back to the beginning of time," Benton then says.

I created Fielding.

"What haven't you told me about him?" Benton goes on.

I made Fielding what he is. He is my monster.

"A psychiatric history?" Benton says. "Off-limits even to me, even to the FBI. I could find out, but I won't violate that boundary."

Benton and the FBI. One and the same again. Not a street agent again. I can't imagine that. A criminal investigative analyst, a criminal intelligence analyst, a threat analyst. The Department of Justice has so many analysts, agents who are a combination academic and tactical. If you're going to go to prison or get shot, may as well be at the hand of a cop who's got a Ph.D.

"What might you know about Jack, your protégé, that I don't?" Benton asks me. "Besides that he's a sick fuck. Because he is. Somewhere some part of you knows it, Kay."

I'm Briggs's monster, and Fielding is mine. Going back to the beginning of time.

"I'm well aware of sexual abuse," Benton says blandly, as if he doesn't care what happened to Fielding when he was a child, as if Benton really doesn't give a damn.

Not a psychologist but something else speaking, and I'm sure. Cops, federal agents, prosecutors, those who protect and punish, are hardened to excuses. They judge "subjects" and "persons of interest" by what they do, not by what was done to them. People like Benton don't give a damn about why or if it couldn't be helped, doesn't matter the definitions, distillations, and predictions he so astutely, so skillfully, renders. In his heart Benton has no sympathy for hateful, harmful people, and his years of being a clinician and consultant have been cruel to him, have been unfulfilling and have felt fake, he's confessed to me more than once.

"That much is a matter of public record since the case went to trial." Benton feels the need to tell me something I've never asked Fielding about.

I don't remember when and how I first heard of the special school Fielding attended as a boy near Atlanta. Somehow I know, and all that comes to mind is references he's made to a certain "episode" in his past, that what he experienced with a certain "counselor" makes it excruciatingly difficult for him to handle any tragedy involving children, especially if they were abused. I'm certain I never pushed him to volunteer the details. Back in those days especially, I wouldn't have asked.

"Nineteen seventy-eight," Benton says, "when Jack was fifteen, although he was twelve when it started, went on for several years until they were caught having sex in the back of her station wagon parked at the edge of the soccer field as if she wanted to be caught. She was pregnant. Anther pathetic story about boarding schools, this one, thank God, not Catholic but for troubled teens, one of these private treatment center–slash–academies that has *Ranch* in its name. What the therapist did to get convicted of ten counts of sexual battery on a minor isn't what you haven't told me about Jack."

"I don't know the details," I finally answer him. "Not all of them or even most of them.

I don't remember her name, if I ever knew it; didn't know she was pregnant. His child? Did she have it?"

"I've reviewed the case transcripts. Yes. She had it."

"I wouldn't have had a reason to look at the case transcripts." I don't ask why Benton has a reason. He's not going to reveal that to me right now, and maybe he never will. "What a shame there's one more child in the world Jack's raised poorly. Or not at all," I add. "How sad."

"Kathleen Lawler hasn't had such a good life, either," Benton starts to say.

"How sad," I repeat.

"The woman convicted of molesting Jack," he says. "I don't know about the child, a girl, born in prison, given up for adoption. Considering the mutant genetic loading, probably in prison, too, or dead. Kathleen Lawler was in one mess after another, currently in a correctional facility for female offenders in Savannah, Georgia, serving twenty years for DUI manslaughter. Jack communicates with her, is a prison pen pal, although he uses a pen name, and that's not what you haven't told me, because I doubt you know about it. Actually, I can't imagine you do."

"Who else was at the meetings last week?"

I'm so cold my fingernails are blue, and I wish I'd brought my jacket in here. I notice a lab coat on the back of Fielding's door.

"It crossed my mind while we were sitting in your office," says Benton, the former FBI agent, the former protected witness and master of secrets, who isn't acting like a former anything anymore.

He's acting like he's investigating a case, not just a consultant on one. I'm convinced that what I suspect is true. He's back with the Feds. Things end where they begin and begin where they end.

"An affective disorder. I've thought hard about it, tried to remember him from the old days. Done a lot of reflecting on the old days." Benton talks matter-of-factly, as if he has no feelings about what he's divulging and accusing me of. "He's never been normal. That's my point. Jack has significant underlying pathology. That's why he was sent off to boarding school. To learn to manage his anger. When he was six years old he stabbed another little kid in the chest with a ballpoint pen. When he was eleven he hit his mother in the head with a rake. Then he was sent to the ranch near Atlanta, where he only got angrier."

"I have no idea what he did when he was growing up," I reply. "It's not a common practice to conduct extensive background checks on doctors one might hire, in fact, was unheard of when I was getting started, when he was getting started. I'm not an FBI agent," I add pointedly. "I don't dig up everything I can about people and go around questioning neighbors they grew up around. I don't question their teachers. I don't track down their pen pals."

I get up from Fielding's desk.

"Although I probably should have. I probably will from now on. But I've never covered up for him," I go on. "Never protected him that way. I admit I've been too forgiving. I admit I've fixed his disasters or tried to. But never covered up something I shouldn't, if that's what you're saying I've done. I would never do anything unethical for him or anyone." *Not anymore,* I add silently. I did it once but never again, and I never did it for Jack Fielding. Not even for myself but for the highest law of the land.

I walk across the office, cold and exhausted and ashamed of myself. I remove Fielding's lab coat from the hook at the top of the closed door.

"I don't know what it is you think I've not told you, Benton. I have no idea what he's involved with or whom. Or his delusions or dissociative states and blackouts. Not in my

333

presence, and he's never shared information like that, if it's true."

I put on the lab coat, and it is huge, and I detect the faint sharp odor of eucalyptus, like Vicks, like Bengay.

"Maybe a mood disorder with a touch of narcissism and intermittent explosive anger," Benton goes on as if I just said nothing. "Or it could be the drugs, maybe his damn performance-enhancement drugs as usual, the sorry bastard. He doesn't represent the CFC well, I'm sorry as hell to make the understatement of the century, and it wasn't lost on Douglas and David, and that got the CFC off on the wrong foot, as long ago as early November, when they got involved in the Wally Jamison kidnapping and murder. You can imagine what's gotten back to Briggs and others. Jack is one inch from ruining everything, and that opens up a place to opportunists. Like I said, it creates a looting mentality."

I pause before a window and look down on the dark, snowy street as if I might find something there that will remind me of who I am. Something to give me strength, something to find comfort in.

"He's done a lot of damage." Benton's voice behind me. "I don't know that it's been intentional. But I suspect some of it

334

has been because of his complicated relationship with you."

Snow is blowing at a sharp angle, hitting the window almost horizontally and making rapid clicks that remind me of fingernails tapping, of something restless and disturbed. When I look at the snow as it hits the glass, it makes me dizzy. It gives me vertigo to look at it and then to look down.

"Is that what this is about, Benton? My complicated relationship with him?"

"I need to know about it. It's better it's me instead of someone else asking you."

"You're saying everything is damaged and ruined because of it. That it's the root of everything wrong." I don't turn around but stare out and down until I can't look at the flying flakes of ice and the road below and the dark river or the volatile winter night any longer. "That's what you believe." I want him to verify what he just said. I want to know if what's been damaged and ruined while I've been gone includes Benton and me.

"I just need to know anything you haven't told me," he answers instead.

"I'm sure you and others need to know." I don't say it nicely as my pulse picks up.

"I understand things from the past don't

get resolved easily. I understand complications."

I turn around and meet his stare, and what I see in it isn't just cases and dead people or my mutinous office or my deranged deputy chief. I see Benton's distrust of me and my past. I see him doubting my character and who I am to him.

"I never slept with Jack," I tell him. "If that's what you're trying to find out so someone else is spared the discomfort of asking me. Or is it my discomfort you're so worried about? I never did. It won't come out because it isn't there. If that's what you're trying to ask me, that's your answer. You can pass it along to Briggs, to the FBI, to the attorney general, to whoever you goddamn want."

"I would understand when Jack was your fellow, when both of you were just getting started in Richmond."

"I try not to make it a practice to have sex with people I mentor," I say with a surprising flare of irritability. "I'd like to think I bear no similarity to what's-her-name Lawler, the former therapist locked up in Georgia."

"Jack wasn't twelve when you met him."

"It never happened. I don't do that with people I mentor."

"And when people mentor you?" Benton's eyes are steady on me as I stand by the window.

"That's not why John Briggs and I have a problem," I answer angrily.

13

I return to Fielding's desk and sit back down in his chair as I finger something slick and filmy inside one of his lab coat pockets. I pull out a square of transparent plastic that is paper-thin.

"The CFC didn't need to make a bad first impression with the Feds, but I'm confident you'll change it." Benton says it as if he regrets what he's just asked me, as if he's sorry about what he just confronted me with in the line of duty.

I sniff what Fielding must have peeled off a eucalyptus-laced pain-relieving patch, and resentfully think, *Yes, indeed, the Feds. I'm so glad I can change what the goddamn Feds must think of me.*

"I don't want you to feel negative about everything here, everything you've come home to," Benton continues. "It wouldn't be helpful if you are. There is a lot to take care of, but we'll get there. I know we will.

I'm sorry our conversation had to move in certain directions. I'm really sorry we had to get into all this."

"Let's talk about Douglas and David." I remind him of names he referred to moments earlier. "Who are they?"

"I have no doubt you'll prevail and make this place work, make it what it was meant to be, which is stellar and unlike anything anywhere. Better than what they have in Australia, in Switzerland, even better than any place where they were doing it first, including Dover, right? I have complete confidence in you, Kay. I don't want you to ever forget that."

The more Benton assures me of his confidence, the less I believe it.

"Law enforcement respects you, the military does," he adds, and I don't believe that, either.

If it were true, he wouldn't have to say it. *So what?* I then think, with hostility that seems to come from nowhere. I don't need people to like or respect me. It isn't a popularity contest. Isn't that what Briggs always says? *It's not a popularity contest, Colonel,* or if he's being more personable, *It's not a popularity contest, Kay,* and he smiles wryly, a steely glint of mischief in his eyes. He doesn't give a shit if anybody likes him, and in fact thrives on people not liking him, and I'm going to start thriving on it, too. The hell with everyone. I know what I need to do, which is something. I will do something, oh, yes, I will. Thinking I'm going to come home to this and just take it, do nothing about it, let whoever it is have his way? No. Hell, no. Not going to happen. Whoever would entertain an idea like that sure as hell doesn't know me.

"Who are Douglas and David?" I again ask, and I sound snappish.

"Douglas Burke and David McMaster," Benton says.

"I don't know them, and who are they to you?" Now I'm the one doing the interrogating.

"FBI's Boston Field Office, Metro Boston Homeland Security. You haven't gotten to know the locals, not key ones, but you will. Including the coast guard. I'm going to help you get to know everyone around here if you'll permit me to. For once I might be useful. I've missed being useful to you. I know you're upset."

"I'm not upset."

"Your face is flushed. You look upset. I don't mean to upset you. I'm sorry I have. But it's something I've needed to know for several reasons."

"And are you satisfied?"

"It's critical to know where you are in all this and who you are in it," he says as I hold the flimsy plastic backing, a square about the size of a cigarette pack.

I lift it up to the light and see Fielding's large fingerprints on the transparent film and smaller ones that must be mine. Fielding is chronically straining muscles, always achy and sore, especially when he's abusing anabolic steroids. When he's back to his old, bad tricks he smells like a damn menthol cough drop.

"What do Homeland Security, the coast guard, have to do with anything we're talking about?" I'm opening desk drawers, looking for Nuprin, Motrin, or Bengay patches, for Tiger Balm, for anything that might confirm what I suspect.

"Wally Jamison's body was floating in the harbor at the coast guard's ISC, their Integrated Support Command. Right there under their nose. Which I believe was the point," Benton replies as he watches me.

"Or the point was the wharf right there that's deserted after dark. One of the few wharves in the area that you can drive a car on. I sure as hell know that area. So do you. We know it, and some of the people who work there probably would recognize us, we've walked around there so many times, right next door to where we stay once in a blue moon when we can get away and be alone and be civil to each other." I sound sarcastic and mean.

"Authorized personnel only. Might I ask what you're looking for? I'm sure it's something that will be in plain view."

"It's my office. This entire place is my office. I'll look at whatever the hell I want. Plain view or not." My pulse is flying, and I feel agitated.

"The wharf isn't open to the public. Not just anybody can drive a car on it," Benton replies as he watches me carefully, worried. "I didn't mean to upset you this much."

"We walk over there all the time and no one asks for our IDs. They're not standing around with submachine guns. It's a tourist area." I'm argumentative and combative, and I don't want to be.

"The coast guard ISC isn't a tourist area. There's a guard gate you have to go through to get out on the pier," Benton says very calmly, very reasonably, and he continues looking at his iPhone. He looks at it and then at me, back and forth, reading both of us.

"I miss it. Let's spend a few days there soon." I try to sound nice because I'm acting awful. "Just the two of us."

"Yes. We will. Soon," he says. "We'll talk and get everything straight."

I imagine it with startling clarity, our favorite suite that reaches out into the water like a fingertip at the Fairmont hotel on Battery Wharf, directly next door to the coast guard ISC. I see the ruffled dark-green water of the harbor and hear it washing against pilings as if I'm there. I hear the creaking of docks, the clanking of rigging lines against masts, and the bass tones of the horns the big ships sound as if all of it is audible inside Fielding's office.

"And we won't answer our phones, and we'll go for walks and get room service and watch the tall ships, the tugboats, the tankers from our window. I would love that. Wouldn't you love it?" But I don't sound nice as I say it. I sound pushy and angry.

"We'll do it this weekend if you want. If we can," he says as he reads something on his iPhone, scrolling down with his thumb.

I move my coffee away and the corner of the desk looks rounded, not squared. Too much caffeine and my heart is beating hard. I feel light-headed and edgy.

"I hate it when you look at your phone all the time," I say before I can stop myself. "You know how much I hate it when we're talking."

"It can't be avoided right now," he says as he looks at it.

"Exit off Ninety-three, get on Commercial Street, and you're right there," I resume arguing. "A convenient way to get rid of a body. Drive it there and dump it in the harbor. Nude, so whatever trace evidence there might have been from the car trunk, for example, was probably washed away." I shut a bottom drawer and sound peculiar to myself as I mutter distractedly, "Pain-relieving patches. None. And I didn't see any in my desk drawers, either. Only chewing gum. I've never been a gum chewer. Well, when I was a little kid. Dubble Bubble at Halloween, with the colorful waxy yellow wrapper that's twisted on the ends."

I see it. I smell it. My mouth waters.

"Here's a secret I've never told anyone. I'd recycle. Chew it and wrap it up again. For days until there was no flavor left."

My mouth is watering, and I swallow several times.

"I stopped chewing gum when I stopped trick-or-treating. See, you've reminded me of trick-or-treating, something I haven't thought of in so many years I can't believe it's just popped into my head. Sometimes I forget I was ever a child. Ever young and stupid and trusting."

My hands are shaking.

"Better not to like something you can't afford, so I didn't make a habit of gum."

I'm trembling.

"Better not to look like you grew up low-class, especially if you did grow up low-class. When have you ever seen me chew gum? I won't. It's low-class."

"Nothing about you is low-class." Benton watches me carefully, guardedly, and I see what is in his eyes. I'm scaring him.

But I can't stop myself. "I've worked damn hard in life not to look low-class. You didn't know me when I was getting started and had no idea what people are really like, people who have complete power over you, people you worship really, and what they're capable of luring you into so that you never feel the same about yourself. And then you bury it like that beating heart under the floorboards in Edgar Allan Poe, but you always know it's there. And you can't tell anyone. Even when it keeps you awake at night. You can't even tell the person you're closest to that there's this cold, dead heart under the floorboards and it's your fault it's under there."

"Christ, Kay."

"It's odd that everything we love seems to

be in close proximity to something hateful and dead," enters my mind next. "Well, not everything."

"Are you all right?"

"I'm fine. Just stressed out, and who the hell wouldn't be? Our house is a stone's throw from Norton's Woods, where someone was murdered yesterday, and he may have been at the Courtauld Gallery at the same time Lucy and I were the summer before Nine-Eleven, which she thinks was caused by us, by the way. Liam Saltz was there, too, at the Courtauld, one of the lecturers. I didn't meet him then, but Lucy has him on CD. I can't remember what he talked about."

"I'm curious why you would bring him up."

"A link on a website that Jack was looking at for some reason."

Benton doesn't say anything, and he doesn't take his eyes off me.

"You and I go in The Biscuit when I'm home on weekends, maybe we've been in there at the same time Johnny Donahue and his MIT friend were," I go on and can't keep up with my thoughts. "We love Salem and the oils and candles in the shops there, the same shops that sell iron spikes, devil's bone. Our favorite getaway in Boston is next

346

to where Wally Jamison's body was found the morning after Halloween. Is someone watching us? Does someone know everything we do? What was Jack doing in Salem on Halloween?"

"Wally's body got where it was by boat, not the wharf," Benton replies, and I don't know where he got the information.

"All these things in common. You'd think we live in a small town."

"You don't look good."

"You're sure it was a boat. I feel like I'm having a hot flash." I touch my cheek, press my hand against it. "Lord. That will be next. So much to look forward to."

"More relevant is the fact that someone deliberately dumped his body where the hundred-foot cutters are homeported with guardsmen on board." Benton watches my every move. "And starting around daybreak, support staff and other personnel show up for work and the wharf is a parking lot. All these people getting out of their cars and seeing a mutilated body floating in the water. That's brazen. Killing a little kid in his own backyard while his parents are inside the house is brazen. Killing someone on Super Bowl Sunday in Norton's Woods while a VIP wedding is going on is brazen. Doing all this in our own neighborhoods is brazen. Yes."

"First you know it's a boat. Next you know it was a VIP wedding, not just a wedding but a VIP wedding." I don't ask but state. He wouldn't say it if he didn't know it. "Why was Jack in Salem? Doing what there? You can't even get a hotel room in Salem on Halloween. You can't even drive, there are so many people."

"Are you sure you're all right?"

"Do you think it's personal?" I ask as I obsess about what a small world it is. "I come home and this is my welcome. To have all this ugliness and death and deceit and betrayal practically in my lap."

"To some extent, yes," Benton says.

"Well, thank you for that."

"I said, 'to some extent.' Not everything."

"You said you think it's personal. I want to know exactly how it is personal."

"Try to calm down. Breathe slowly." He reaches for my hand, and I won't let him touch me. "Slowly, slowly, Kay."

I pull away from him, and he returns his hand to his lap, to the iPhone in it that flashes red every other second as messages land. I don't want him to touch me. It's as if I have no skin.

"Is there anything to eat in this place? I can send out for something," Benton says.

"Maybe it's low blood sugar. When did you eat last?"

"No. I couldn't right now. I'll be fine. Why do you say 'VIP'?" I hear myself ask.

He looks at his phone again, the tiny red light flashing its alert. "Anne," he says to me as he reads what just landed. "She's on her way, should be here in a few minutes."

"What else? I can download the scan in here, take a look."

"She didn't send it. She tried to call you. Obviously, you're not at your desk. There were undercover agents at the wedding. Protecting a VIP, but obviously he wasn't the one who needed it," Benton says. "Nobody was looking for the one who needed protecting. We didn't know he was going to be there."

I take another deep breath, and I try to diagnose a heart attack, if I might be having one.

"Did the agents see what happened?" Mount Auburn would be the closest hospital. I don't want to go to the hospital.

"Ones stationed by the outside doors weren't looking at him and didn't see it. They saw people rushing around him when he collapsed. There was no reason he was of interest, and the agents maintained their posts. They had to. In case it was some

349

diversionary maneuver. You always maintain your post when you're on a protective detail; with rare exception, you don't divert."

I focus on the discomfort in the center of my chest and my shortness of breath. I'm sweating and light-headed, but there's no pain in my arms. No pain in my back. No pain in my jaw. No radiating pain, and heart attacks don't cause altered thinking. I look at my hands. I hold them in front of me as if I can see what's on them.

"When you saw Jack last week, did he smell like menthol?" I ask, and then I say, "Where is he? What exactly has he done?"

"What about menthol?"

"Extra-strength Nuprin patches, Bengay patches, something like that." I get up from Fielding's desk. "If he's wearing them all the time and reeks of eucalyptus, of menthol, it's usually an indication he's abusing himself physically, tearing the hell out of himself physically in the gym, in his tae kwon do tournaments, has chronic and acute muscle and joint pain. Steroids. When Jack's on steroids, well . . . That's always been the prelude to other things."

"Based on what I saw last week, he's on something."

I'm already taking off Fielding's lab coat.

I fold it into a neat square and place it on top of his desk.

"Is there a place you can lie down?" Benton says. "I think you should lie down. The on-call room downstairs. There's a bed. I can't take you home. You can't be there right now. I don't want you going out of this building, not without me."

"I don't need to lie down. Lying down won't help. It will make it worse." I walk into Fielding's bathroom and snatch a trash basket liner from a box under the sink.

Benton is on his feet, watching what I'm doing, keeping an eye on me as I tuck the folded lab coat inside the liner and return to the bathroom. I scrub my hands and face with soap and hot water. I wash any area of skin that might have come into contact with the plastic film I found in Fielding's lab coat pocket.

"Drugs," I announce when I sit back down.

Benton returns to his chair, tensely, as if he might spring up again.

"Something transdermal that certainly isn't Nuprin or Motrin. Don't know what, but I will find out," I let him know.

"The piece of plastic you were touching."

"Unless you poisoned my coffee."

"Maybe a nicotine patch."

351

"You wouldn't poison me, would you? If you don't want to be married anymore, there are simpler solutions."

"I don't see why he'd be on nicotine unless as a stimulant? I guess so. Something like that."

"It's not something like that. I used to live off nicotine patches and never felt like this, not even when I would light up while I still had a twenty-one-milligram patch on. A true addict. That's me. But not drugs, not whatever this is. What has he done?"

Benton stares at his coffee mug, tracing the AFME crest on the black glazed ceramic. His silence confirms what I suspect. Whatever Fielding is involved in, it's connected to everything else: to me, to Benton, to Briggs, to a dead football player, to a dead little boy, to the man from Norton's Woods, to dead soldiers from Great Britain and Worcester. Like planes lit up at night, connected to a tower, connected in a pattern, at times seeming at a standstill in the dark air but having been somewhere and going somewhere, individual forces that are part of something bigger, something incomprehensibly huge.

"You need to trust me," Benton says quietly.

"Has Briggs been in contact with you?"

"Some things have been going on for a while. Are you all right? I don't want to go before I know you are."

"This is what I've trained for, made so many sacrifices for." I decide to accept it. Acceptance makes it easier for me to know what to do. "Six months of being away from you, of being away from everyone, of giving up everything so I could come home to something that's been going on for a while. An agenda."

I almost add *just like in the beginning,* when I was barely a forensic pathologist and was too naïve to have a clue about what was happening. When I was quick to salute authority, and worse, to trust it, and much worse, to respect it, and even worse than that, to admire it, and worst of all, to admire John Briggs so much I would do anything he wanted, absolutely anything. Somehow I've managed to land in the same spot. The same thing again. An agenda. Lies and more lies, and innocent people who are disposable. Crimes as coldly carried out as any I've ever seen. Joanne Rule and Noonie Pieste are graphically in my mind, as real as they've ever been.

I see them on dented gurneys with rust in their welded seams and wheels that stick, and I remember my feet sticking as I walked across an old white stone floor that would not stay clean. It was always bloody in the Cape Town morgue, with bodies parked everywhere, and the week I was there I saw cases as extreme in their grotesqueness as that continent is extreme in its magnificent beauty. People hit by trains and run over on the highway, and domestic and drug deaths in the shantytowns, and a shark attack in False Bay, and a tourist who died from a fall on Table Mountain.

I have the irrational thought that if I go downstairs and walk into my cooler, the bodies of those two slain women will be waiting for me just as they were on that December morning after I'd flown nineteen hours in a small coach seat to get to them. Only they had already been looked at by the time I showed up, and that would have been true if I'd flown Mach II on the Concorde or been a block away from them when they were murdered. It wasn't possible for me to get to them fast enough. Their bodies may as well have been on a movie set, they were so staged. Innocent young women murdered for the sake of a news story, for the sake of power and influence and votes, and I couldn't put a stop to it.

I not only couldn't stop it, I helped make it happen, because I made it possible for it to happen, and I replay what PFC Gabriel's mother said about hate crimes and being rewarded for them. My office at Dover is right next to Briggs's command suite. I remember someone walking past my closed door several times while I was talking to her. Whoever it was paused at least twice. It crossed my mind at the time that someone might be waiting to come in but could hear through the door that I was on the phone and was unwilling to interrupt. The more likely answer is that someone was listening. Briggs has started something, or someone allied with him has, and Benton's right, it's been going on for a while.

"Then these last six months have been nothing more than a political ploy. How sad. How tawdry. How disappointing." My voice is steady, and I sound completely calm, the way I get before I do something.

"Are you okay? Because we should go downstairs if you're okay. Anne is here. We should talk to her, and then I need to go." Benton has gotten up and is near the door, waiting for me with his phone in hand.

"Let me guess. Briggs made sure I got this position so he could keep it open for whomever he really has in mind." I go on and my heart has slowed and my nerves feel steadier, as if they're firing normally again.

"Wanted me to keep the seat warm. Or was I the excuse to get this place built, to get MIT, get Harvard, get everybody on board, to justify some thirty million in grants?"

Benton reads something else as messages drop out of the thin air, one after another.

"He could have saved himself a lot of trouble," I say as I get up from the desk.

"You're not going to quit," Benton says, reading what someone has just sent to him. "Don't give them that satisfaction."

" 'Them.' Then it's more than one."

He doesn't answer as he types with his thumbs.

"Well, it's always been more than one. Take your pick," I say as we walk out together.

"If you quit, you give them exactly what they want." As he reads and scrolls down on his phone.

"People like that don't know what they want." I shut Fielding's door behind us, making sure it's locked. "They just think they do."

We begin our descent in my bullet-shaped building that on dark nights and gloomy days is the color of lead.

I'm explaining to Benton the indented writing on a pad of call sheets as we glide down in an elevator I researched and selected because it reduces energy consumption by fifty percent. It can't be a coincidence that Fielding was interested in a keynote address Dr. Liam Saltz just gave at Whitehall, I say, while numbers change on a digital display, while we gently sink from floor to floor in the soft glow of LEDs in my environmentally friendly hoisting machine that no one who works here appreciates in the least, from what I've heard. Mostly there are complaints because it is slow.

"He's one extreme, and DARPA's certainly the other, neither of them always right, that's for sure." I describe Dr. Saltz as a computer scientist, an engineer, a philosopher, a theologian, whose sport, whose art, most assuredly isn't war. He hates wars and those who make them.

"I know all about him and his art." Benton doesn't say it in a positive way as we stop gently and the steel door slides open with scarcely a sound. "I certainly remember from that time at CNN when you and I got into a spat because of him."

"I don't remember getting into a spat." We are back in the receiving area, where Ron is sternly alert behind his glass partition, exactly as we left him long hours ago.

In split screens of video displays I see cars parked in the lot behind the building, SUVs that aren't covered with snow and have their headlights on. Agents or undercover police, and I remember windows glowing in MIT buildings rising above the CFC fence, I remember noticing it at the time Benton drove us here, and now I know why. The CFC has been under surveillance, and the FBI, the police, aren't making any effort to disguise their presence now. I feel as if the CFC is on lockdown.

Ever since I walked out of Port Mortuary at Dover, I have been accompanied or locked inside a secured building, and the reason isn't what was presented, at least not the only reason. No one was trying to get me home as quickly as possible because of a body bleeding inside the cooler. That was a priority but certainly not the only one and maybe not even the top one. Certain people used that as an excuse to escort me, certain people, such as my niece, who was armed and playing bodyguard, and I can't believe Benton wasn't involved in that decision, no matter what he did or didn't know at the time.

"Maybe you remember him hitting on you," Benton is saying as we follow the gray corridor.

"You seem to think I'm having sex with everyone."

"Not with everyone," he says.

I smile. I almost laugh.

"You're feeling better," he says, touching my arm tenderly as he walks with me.

Whatever got into me has passed, and I wish it wasn't such a godforsaken hour of the morning. I wish someone was in the trace evidence lab so we could take a look at the plastic film I was exposed to, probably try the scanning electron microscope first, then Fourier transform infrared or whatever detectors it takes to figure out what is on Fielding's pain-relieving patches. I've never taken anabolic steroids and don't know firsthand how that would feel, but I can't imagine it's what I felt upstairs. Not that quickly.

Cocaine, crystal methamphetamine, LSD, whatever could get into my system instantly and transdermally, hopefully nothing like that, either, but what would I know about how that would feel? Not an opioid like fentanyl, which is the most common narcotic delivered by a patch. A strong pain reliever like fentanyl wouldn't have caused me to react the way I did, but again, I'm not sure. I've never been on fentanyl. Everybody reacts differently to medications, and uncontrolled substances can be contaminated with impurities and have variable doses.

"Really. You seem like yourself." Benton touches me again. "How are you feeling? You okay for sure?"

"Worn off, whatever it was. I wouldn't do the case if it wasn't, if I felt even remotely impaired," I tell him. "I guess you're coming to the autopsy room." Since we're headed there.

"A drink. Right." He is back to Liam Saltz. "He bumps into you at CNN and asks you to have a drink with him at midnight. That's not exactly normal."

"I'm not sure how to take that. But I don't feel flattered."

"His reputation with women is on a par with certain politicians who will remain unnamed. What's the buzzword these days? A sexual addiction."

"Well, if you're going to have one."

We walk past the x-ray room, and the door is shut, the red light off because the scanner isn't in use. The lower level is empty and silent, and I wonder where Marino is. Maybe he's with Anne.

"He had any contact with you since then? That was what? About two years ago?" Benton asks. "Or maybe with some of your compatriots at Walter Reed or Dover?"

"Not with me. I wouldn't know about others, except no one involved with the armed forces is a fan of Dr. Saltz's. He's not considered patriotic, which really isn't fair if you analyze what he's actually saying."

"Problem is nobody seems to understand what anybody is saying anymore. People don't listen. Saltz isn't a communist. He's not a terrorist. He hasn't committed treason. He just doesn't know how to curb his enthusiasm and muzzle his big mouth. But he's not of interest to the government. Well, he wasn't."

"Suddenly, he is." I assume that's what Benton will tell me next.

"He wasn't at Whitehall yesterday. Wasn't even in London." Benton waits until now to inform me of this as we pause before the locked double steel doors of the autopsy room. "I don't guess you found that part on the Internet when you were trying to make heads or tails of Jack's indented writing," Benton adds in a tone that is shaded with other meanings. A hint of hostility, not directed at me but at Fielding.

"How do you know where Liam Saltz was or wasn't?" I ask at the same time I think about what Benton mentioned upstairs. He referred to the event at Norton's Woods as a VIP wedding and mentioned a security presence. Undercover agents, Benton told me, although it was during an interval when I wasn't thinking as clearly as I should have been.

"Did his keynote address by satellite on a big video screen. Well attended by the audience at Whitehall," Benton says as if he was there. "He had a complication, a family matter, and had to leave the country."

I think of the man beyond these closed steel doors. A man whose wristwatch when he died may have been set to UK time. A man with an old robot called MORT inside his apartment, the same robot that Liam Saltz and I testified against, persuading people in power to disallow its use.

"Is that why Jack was looking him up, looking up RUSI or whatever he was looking at early yesterday morning?" I ask as I scan open the lock to the autopsy room.

"I'm wondering how that happened, if he got a call and then looked him up or maybe knew he was in Cambridge for some reason," Benton replies. "I'm wondering a lot of things that hopefully will get answered soon. What I do know is Dr. Saltz was here for the wedding. The daughter of his current wife, whose biological father was supposed to give her away, then got the swine flu."

"I text-messaged you," Anne tells me, and she's shrouded in blue as she works on a computer that is contained in a waterproof stainless-steel enclosure, the sealed keyboard mounted at a height suitable for typing while standing. Behind her on the autopsy table of station one, which is now shiny and clean, is the man from Norton's Woods.

"I'm sorry," I say to her abstractedly as I think of Liam Saltz and worry what his connection might be to this dead man, beyond robots, particularly MORT. "My phone's in my office, and I've not been in there," I say to Anne, and then I ask Benton, "Does he have other children?"

"He's at the Charles Hotel," Benton replies. "Someone's on the way to talk to him. But to answer your question, yes, he does. He has a number of children and stepchildren from multiple marriages."

"I wanted to let you know I didn't feel comfortable uploading his scans and e-mailing them," Anne then says to me. "Don't know what we're dealing with and thought it was better to play it extra-safe. If you're going to hang around, you need to cover up." She directs this to Benton. "Got no clue what this one's been exposed to, but he didn't set off any alarms. At least

363

he's not radioactive. Whatever he's got in him isn't, thank God."

"I assume all was quiet at the hospital. No incidents," Benton says to her. "I'm not staying."

"Security escorted us in and out, and we didn't see anyone else — no patients or staff, at any rate."

"You found something in him?" I ask her.

"Trace amounts of metal." Anne's gloved hands move on the computer's keyboard and click the mouse, both freshly overlaid with industrial silicone. Fielding's sloppy presence is noticeably gone from the autopsy room, and I see water in the sink of station one — my station — and a big sponge, the surgical instruments bright and shiny and neatly arranged on the dissecting board. I spot a mop that wasn't here earlier, and a whetstone on a countertop.

"I'm amazed," I say to her as I look around.

"Ollie," she says, clicking the mouse. "I called him, and he drove back and spruced up the place."

"You're kidding."

"It's not that we haven't tried while you were gone. Jack's been using this work space, and we've learned to stay away."

"How can there be metal that didn't show

up on CT?" Benton watches her scroll through files she created at the neuroimaging lab, looking for the images she wants from the MRI.

"If it's really small," I explain to him how it's possible. "A threshold size of less than point-five millimeter and I wouldn't expect it to be detected on CT. That's why we wanted to rule out the possibility by using MR, and apparently it's a good thing."

"Although maybe not if he was alive," Anne says, clicking on a file. "You don't want something ferromagnetic in a living person, because it's going to torque. It's going to move. Like metal shavings in the eyes of people involved in professions that expose them to something like that. They may not even know it until they get an MRI. Then they know it; boy, do they ever. Or if they have body piercings they don't tell us about, and we've seen that enough times," she says to Benton. "Or, God forbid, a pacemaker. Metal moves, and it heats up."

"Theories?" I ask her, because I can't imagine an event or a weapon that could create what has just filled the video display.

"Your guess is as good as mine," she answers as we study high-resolution images of the dead man's internal damage, a dark distorted area of signal voids that starts just inside the buttonhole wound and becomes increasingly less pronounced the deeper the penetration inside the organs and soft tissue structures of the chest.

"Because of the magnetic field, even with what must be particles incredibly minute, you're going to get artifact. Right here," I point out to Benton. "These very dark and distorted areas where there's no signal penetration. You get this blooming artifact along the wound track, what's left of the wound track, because the signal's been blown out by metal. He's got some sort of ferromagnetic foreign bodies inside him, all right."

"What could do that?" Benton asks.

"I'm going to have to recover some of it, analyze it." I think of what Lucy said about thermite. It would be ferromagnetic just as bullets are, both metal composites having iron oxide in common.

"Point-five? The size of dust?" Benton's eyes are distracted by other thoughts.

"A little bigger," Anne replies.

"About the size of gunshot residue, grains of unburned powder," I add.

"A projectile like a bullet could be reduced to frag no bigger than grains of gunshot powder," Benton considers, and I can tell he is connecting what I'm saying with something else, and I think of my niece and wonder exactly what she said to him while they were together in her lab earlier. I think of shark bang sticks and nanoexplosives, but there are no thermal injuries, no burns. It wouldn't make sense.

"No projectile I've ever seen," Anne says, and I agree. "Do we know anything more about who he might be?" She means the body on the table. "I wasn't trying to eavesdrop."

"Hopefully soon," Benton replies.

"It sounds like you might have an idea," Anne says to him.

"Our first clue was he showed up at Norton's Woods at the same time Dr. Saltz was inside the building, and that was something to check because of certain interests these two individuals would have in common." He means robots, I suspect.

"I don't think I know who that is," Anne says to him.

"A scientist who won a Nobel Prize and is an expatriate," Benton says, and as I observe him with Anne I'm reminded they are colleagues and friends, that he treats her with an easy familiarity, with trust that he doesn't exhibit around most people. "And if he" — Benton indicates the dead man — "knew Dr. Saltz was coming to Cambridge, the question was how."

"Do we know if he knew that?" I ask.

"Right now we don't for a fact."

"So Dr. Saltz was at the wedding. But this one wasn't dressed for a wedding." Anne indicates the nude dead body on the table. "He had his dog with him. And a gun."

"What I know so far is the bride is a daughter from a different marriage," Benton says as if this detail has been carefully checked. "The daughter's father, who was supposed to give her away, got sick. So she asked her stepfather, Dr. Saltz, at the last minute, and he couldn't physically be in two places at once. He flew into Boston on Saturday and made his appearance at White-hall via satellite. A sacrifice on his part. The last thing he felt like doing, I'm sure, was to reenter the U.S. and show up at Cambridge."

"The undercover agents?" I ask. "For him? If so, why? I know he has enemies, but why would the FBI be offering protection to a civilian scientist from the UK?"

"That's the irony," Benton says. "The security at the event wasn't about him, was about those attending the wedding, most of them from the UK because of the groom's family. The groom is Russell Brown's son, David. Both Liam Saltz's stepdaughter Ruth and David attend Harvard Law, which is one reason the wedding was here."

Russell Brown. The shadow secretary of state for defense, whose speech I just read on the RUSI website.

"He shows up at an event like that and is armed," I say as I move closer to the steel table. "A gun with the serial number eradicated?"

"Right. Why?" Benton asks. "To protect himself, or was he a potential assailant? Or to protect himself for a reason that's unrelated to the wedding and the people I've just mentioned?"

"Possibly top-secret technology he was involved in," I offer. "Technology worth quite a lot of money," I add. "Technology people might kill for."

"And maybe did kill for," Anne says as she looks at the dead young man.

"Hopefully, we'll know soon," Benton says.

I look at the dead man rigid on his back, his curled fingers and the position of his arms, his legs, his hands, his head, exactly as they were earlier, no matter how much he has been disturbed during transport and scans. Rigor mortis is complete, but he won't resist me strenuously as I examine him, because he's thin. He doesn't have much muscle fiber for calcium ions to have gotten trapped in after his neurotransmitters quit. I can break him easily. I can bend him to my will.

"I've got to go," Benton says to me. "I know you want to get this taken care of. I'll need your help with something by the time you're ready to get away from here, and you're not to get away on your own. Make sure she calls me," he says to Anne as she labels test tubes and specimen containers. "Call me or call Marino," he adds. "Give us an hour's advance notice."

"Marino will be with you . . . ?" I start to ask.

"We're working on something. He's already there."

I no longer question what Benton is referring to when he says "we," and he looks one more time at me, his eyes meeting mine with the intimacy of a lingering touch, and he leaves the autopsy room. I hear the receding sound of his brisk footsteps along the hard tile corridor, then his voice and another voice as he talks to someone, perhaps Ron. I can't make out a word they are saying, but they sound serious and intense before silence returns abruptly. I imagine Benton has left the receiving area, and on a video display I'm startled by him.

Picked up by security cameras, he walks through the bay as he zips up the shearling coat I gave him so long ago I don't remember the year, only that it was in Aspen, where he used to have a place.

I watch him on closed-circuit TV opening the side door that is next to the massive bay door, and then another camera picks him up outside my building as he walks past his green SUV parked in my spot. He gets into a different SUV, dark and big with bright headlights that the snow slashes through, the wipers sweeping side to side, and I can't see who is driving. I watch the SUV in my snow-covered lot, backing up, moving forward, and pausing as the big gate opens, and finally out of sight in the bitter weather at the empty hour of four a.m., with my husband in the passenger's seat, driven by someone, maybe his FBI friend Douglas, both of them headed to a destination that for some reason I've not been told about.

14

Inside the anteroom I prepare for battle the way I always do, suiting up in armor made of plastic and paper.

I never feel like a doctor, not even a surgeon, as I get ready to conduct a post-mortem examination, and I suspect only people who deal with the dead for a living can understand what I mean by that. During my medical school residencies I was no different from other doctors, tending to the sick and injured on wards and in emergency rooms, and I assisted in surgical procedures in the OR. So I know what it is to incise warm bodies that have a blood pressure and something vital to lose. What I'm about to do couldn't be more different from that, and the first time I inserted a scalpel blade into cold, unfeeling flesh, made my first Y-incision on my first dead patient, I gave up something I've never gotten back.

I abandoned any notion that I might be

godlike or heroic or gifted beyond other mortals. I rejected the fantasy that I could heal any creature, including myself. No doctor has the power to cause blood to clot or tissue or bone to regenerate or tumors to shrink. We don't create, only prompt biological functions to work or not work properly on their own, and in that regard, doctors are more limited than a mechanic or an engineer who actually builds something out of nothing. My choice of a medical specialty, which my mother and sister still consider morbid and abnormal, probably has made me more honest than most physicians. I know that when I administer my healing touch to the dead they are unmoved by me or my bedside manner. They stay just as dead as they were before. They don't say thank you or send holiday greetings or name their children after me. Of course I was cognizant of all this when I decided on pathology, but that's like saying you know what combat is when you enlist in the marines and get deployed to the mountains of Afghanistan. People don't really know what anything is really like until it really happens to them.

I can never smell the acrid, oily, pungent odor of unbuffered formaldehyde without being reminded of how naïve I was to assume that the dissection of a cadaver donated to science for teaching purposes is anything like the autopsy of an unembalmed person whose cause of death is questioned. My first one took place in the Hopkins hospital morgue, which was a crude place compared to what is beyond this room where I am this minute folding my AFME field clothes and placing them on a bench, not bothering with the locker room or modesty at this hour. The woman whose name I still recall was only thirty-three and left behind two small children and a husband when she died of postoperative complications from an appendectomy.

To this day I'm sorry she was my science project. I'm sorry she was ever put in a position to be any pathology resident's project, and I remember thinking how absurd it was that such a healthy young human being had succumbed to an infection caused by the removal of a rather useless wormlike pouch from the large intestine. I wanted to make her better. As I worked on her, practiced on her, I wanted her to come to and climb off that scratched-up steel pedestal table in the center of the dingy floor inside that dreary subterranean room that smelled like death. I wanted her alive and well and to feel I'd had something to do with it. I'm not a surgeon. What I do is excavate so I can make my case when I go to war with killers or, less dramatically but more typically, with lawyers.

Anne was thoughtful enough to find a pair of freshly laundered scrubs, size medium and the institutional green I'm accustomed to, and I put them on, then over them a disposable gown, which I tie snugly in back before I pull shoe covers out of a dispenser and cover a pair of rubber medical clogs Anne dug up somewhere. Next are protective sleeves, a hair cover, a mask, and a face shield, and finally I double-glove.

"Maybe you could scribe for me," I say to her as I return to the autopsy room, a big, empty vista of gleaming white and bright steel. Only the three of us are here, if I include my patient on the first table. "In the event I don't get to dictate my findings directly afterward, as it appears I may have to leave."

"Not by yourself," she reminds me.

"Benton took the car key," I remind her.

"Wouldn't stop you, since we have vehicles, so don't try to fool me. When it's time, I'm calling him, and there won't be an argument." Anne can say almost anything and not sound disrespectful or rude.

She takes photographs while I swab the

entrance wound on the lower back. Then I swab orifices in the off chance this homicide might involve a sexual assault, although I don't see how, based on what has been described.

"Because we're looking for a unicorn." I seal anal and oral swabs in paper envelopes and label and initial them. "Not your everyday pony, and I'm not going to believe anything, anyway, since I didn't go to the scene."

"Well, nobody did," Anne says. "Which is a shame."

"Even if somebody had, I'd still be looking for a unicorn."

"I don't blame you. I wouldn't trust what anybody says if I were you."

"If you were me." I lock a new blade into a scalpel as she fills a labeled plastic jar with formalin.

"Unless it's me who's talking," she replies without looking at me. "I wouldn't lie or cheat or help myself to things that aren't mine. I would never treat this place as if it belongs to me. Never mind. I shouldn't get into it."

I won't let her get into it. It isn't necessary to put her in a position like that, betraying the people who have betrayed me. I know what it feels like to be put in a position like that. It's one of the worst feelings there is and promotes lying, overtly or by omission, and I know that feeling, too. An untruth that lodges intact in the core of your being like undigested corn found in Egyptian mummies. There's no getting rid of such a thing, of undoing it, without going in to get it, and I'm not sure I have the courage for that, as I think of the worn wooden steps leading down into the basement of the house in Cambridge. I think of the rough stone walls belowground and the fifteen-hundred-pound safe with its two-inch-thick composite triple-lock door.

"I don't suppose you've heard any rumors about where everybody is," I then say. "When you were with Marino at McLean." I begin the Y incision, cutting from clavicle to clavicle, then long and deep straight down with a slight detour around the navel and terminating at the pubic bone in the lower abdomen. "Did you get any idea of who is in our parking lot and what's going on? Since I seem to be under house arrest for reasons no one has been inclined to make completely clear."

"The FBI." Anne doesn't tell me something I don't know as she walks to the wall where clipboards hang from hooks next to rows of plastic racks for blank forms and diagrams. "At least two agents in the parking lot, and one followed us. Someone did." She collects the paperwork she needs and selects a clipboard after making sure the ballpoint pen attached to it by a cord has ink. "A detective, an agent. I don't know who followed us to the hospital, but someone who clearly had alerted security before we got there." She returns to the table. "When we rolled up at the neuroimaging lab, there were three McLean security guys, most excitement they've had in years. And then this person in an SUV, a dark-blue Ford, an Explorer or an Expedition."

Maybe what Benton just drove away in, and I ask Anne, "Did he or she get out of the SUV? I assume you didn't talk to whoever it was?" I reflect back soft tissue. The man is so lean he has just the thinnest layer of yellow fat before the tissue turns beefy red.

"It was hard to see, and I wasn't going to walk right up and stare. The agent was still sitting in the SUV when we left and followed us back here."

She picks up rib cutters from the surgical cart and helps me remove the breastplate, exposing the organs and significant hemorrhage, and I smell the beginning of cells breaking down, the faintest hint of what promises to be putrid and foul. The odors emitted by the human body as it decomposes are uniquely unpleasant. It isn't like a bird or an opossum or the largest mammal one can think of. In death we are as different from other creatures as we are in life, and I would recognize the stench of decaying human flesh anywhere.

"How do you want to do this? En bloc? And deal with the metal after we have the organs on the cutting board?" Anne asks.

"I think we need to synchronize what we're doing inch by inch, step by step. Line things up with the scans as best we can, because I'm not sure I'm going to be able to see whatever these ferromagnetic foreign bodies are unless I'm looking right at them with a lens." I wipe my bloody gloved hands on a towel and step closer to the video display, which Anne has divided into quadrants to give me a choice of images from the MRI.

"Distributed a lot like gunshot powder," she suggests. "Although we can't see the actual metal particles because they canceled the signal."

"True. More blooming artifact, more voids at the beginning than the end. Greatest amount at the entrance." I point my bloody gloved finger at the screen.

"But no residue of anything on the surface," she says. "And that's different from a gunshot wound, a contact wound."

"Everything about this is different from a gunshot wound," I answer.

"You can see that whatever this stuff is, it starts here." She indicates the entrance wound on the lower back. "But not at the surface. Just beneath it, maybe half an inch beneath it, which is really weird. I'm trying to imagine it and can't. If you pressed something against his back and fired, you'd get gunshot residue on the clothes and in the entrance wound, not just an inch inside and then deeper."

"I looked at his clothes earlier."

"No burns or soot, no evidence of GSR," she says.

"Not grossly," I correct her, because not being able to see gunshot residue doesn't mean it isn't there.

"Exactly. Nothing visually."

"What about Morrow? I don't suppose he came downstairs yesterday while Marino had the body in ID, printing him, collecting personal effects. I don't suppose someone thought to ask Morrow to do a presumptive test for nitrites on the clothing, since we didn't know at that time there could be GSR or that there was even an entrance wound that correlates with cuts in the clothing."

"Not that I know of. And he left early."

"I heard. Well, we still can test presumptively, but I'd be really surprised if that's what we're seeing on MR. When Morrow or maybe Phil gets in, let's get them to do a Griess test just to satisfy my curiosity before we move on to something else. I'm betting it will be negative, but it's not destructive, so nothing lost."

It's a simple, quick procedure involving desensitized photographic paper that is treated with a solution of sulfanilic acid, distilled water, and alpha-naphthol in methanol. When the paper is pressed against the area of clothing in question and then exposed to steam, any nitrite residues will turn orange.

"Of course, we're going to do SEM-EDX," I add. "But these days it's a good idea to do more than one thing, since slowly but surely lead is going to disappear from ammunition, and most of these tests are looking for lead, which is toxic to the environment. So we need to start checking for zinc and aluminum alloys, plus various stabilizers and plasticizers, which are added to the gunpowder during manufacturing. Here in the U.S., at any rate. Not so much in combat, where poisoning the environment with heavy metals is considered a fine idea, since the goal is to create dirty bombs, the dirtier the better."

"Not our goal, I hope."

"No, not ours. We don't do that."

"I never know what to believe."

"I do know what to believe, at least about some things. I know what comes back to us when our service people are returned to Dover," I reply. "I know what's in them. I know what isn't. I know what's manufactured by us and what's manufactured by others, the Iraqi insurgency, the Taliban, the Iranians. That's one of the things we do, materials analysis to figure out who is making what, who is supplying it."

"So when I hear these things about weapons or bombs made in Iran . . ."

"That's where it comes from. It's how the U.S. knows. Intelligence from our dead, from what they teach us."

We leave it at that, our talk of the war, because of this other war that has killed a man who is too young to be finished. A man who took an old greyhound for a walk in the civilized world of Cambridge and ended up in my care.

"They've developed some really interesting technology in Texas that I want us to look into." I return to gunshot residue because it is safer to talk about that. "Combining solid phase micro-extraction with gas chromatography coupled with a nitrogen phosphorus detector."

"As Texas should, since it's a state law that everybody carry a gun. Or is it that firearms are tax-deductible, like farming and raising livestock is around here?"

"Well, not quite," I reply. "But we'll want to look into doing something similar at the CFC, since of all places I would expect a growing prevalence of *green* ammunition."

"Of course. Don't pollute the environment while you're doing a drive-by shooting."

"What scientists have come up with at Sam Houston can detect as little as one gunpowder particle, which isn't relevant in this case, since we know this man has metal in him, almost at a microscopic level but plenty of it. Preliminarily, at any rate, Marino should have used a GSR kit on the hands at least. Since this man was armed."

"I do know that he did that much before he printed him," Anne says. "Because of the gun, although no sign it had been fired. But I saw him using a stub on the hands when I walked into ID at one point."

"But not the wound, because you discovered it later. It wasn't swabbed."

"I haven't done anything. I wouldn't have. Not my department."

"Good. I'll take care of it when I get to it, when we turn him over," I decide. "Let's take out the bloc so I can blot the raw surfaces of the injured track. I'm going to use the MRI as my map and blot as much of the metal material as I can, in hopes that even if we can't see it, we're getting some of it. We know it's metal. The question is, what kind of metal and what is it from?"

In wall-mounted steel cabinets with glass doors I find a box of blotting paper while Anne lifts the bloc of organs out of the body and places it on the dissecting board.

"I can't tell you what a problem it is these days, people with metal in them," she comments as she collects organ fragments from the chest cavity, which is opened and empty like a china cup, the ribs gleaming opaquely through glistening red tissue. "Including old bullets of the non-green variety. We get these research subjects in after the hospital's advertised for volunteers, and of course I mean the *normals,* right? All these people who come in and they're just as normal as the day is long, right? And have nothing to report. Uh, right. Like it's real normal to have an old bullet in you."

She returns fragments of the left kidney, the left lung, and the heart to their correct anatomical positions on the bloc of organs as if she's piecing together a puzzle.

"Happens more often than you think," she says. "Well, not more often than someone like you would think, since we see things like that in the morgue all the time. And then you get the old routine that bullets are lead, and lead isn't magnetic, so it's fine to scan the person. Usually, one of the psychiatrists who doesn't know any better and can't seem to remember from one time to the next that, no, wrong again. Lead, iron, nickel, cobalt. All bullets, pellets, are ferromagnetic, I don't care if they're so-called green, they're going to torque because of the magnetic field. That could be a problem if someone's got a fragment in him that's in close proximity to a blood vessel, an organ. God forbid something was left in the brain if some poor person was shot in the head eons ago. Paxil, Neurontin, or the like aren't going to help the poor person's mood disorder if an old bullet relocates to the wrong place."

She rinses a fragment of kidney and places it on the dissecting board.

"We're going to need to measure how much blood is in the peritoneum." I'm looking at the hole in the diaphragm that I saw hours earlier when I followed the wound track during the CT scan. "I'm going to guess at least three hundred MLs, originating through the lacerated diaphragm, and at least fifty MLs in his pericardium, which normally might suggest some time interval before death because of how much he bled. But the severity of these injuries, which are similar to blast injuries? He had no survival time. Only as long as it took for his heart and respiration to quit. If I were willing to use the term *instant death,* this would qualify as one."

"This is unusual." Anne hands me a tiny fragment of kidney that is hard and brown with tan discoloration and retracted edges. "I mean, what is that? It almost looks fixed or cooked or something."

There is more. As I pull a light closer and look at the bloc of organs, I notice hard, dry fragments of the left lung's lower lobe and of the heart's left ventricle. Using a steel beaker, I scoop pooled blood and hematoma out of the mediastinum, or the middle section of the chest cavity, and find more fragments and tiny, hard, irregular blood clots. Looking closely at the disrupted left kidney, I note perirenal hemorrhage and interstitial emphysema, and more evidence of the same abnormal tissue changes in areas closest to the wound track, areas most susceptible to damage from a blast. But what blast?

"Reminds me of tissue that's been frozen, almost freeze-dried," I say as I label sheets of blotting paper with an abbreviation for the location the sample came from. LLL for left lower lobe and LK for left kidney and LV for left ventricle of the heart.

In the strong light of a surgical lamp and the magnification of a hand lens I can barely make out dark silvery specks of whatever was blasted through this man when he was stabbed in the back. I see fibers and other debris that won't be discernible until they are looked at under a microscope, but I feel hopeful. Something was deposited that likely was unintended by the perpetrator, trace evidence that might give me information about the weapon and the person who used it. I turn the fume hood on the lowest setting so there is nothing more than an exchange of air, and I begin gently blotting.

I touch the sterile paper to the surfaces of fragmented tissue and the edges of wounds, and one by one lay the sheets inside the hood, where the gently circulating air will facilitate evaporation, the drying of blood without disturbing anything adhering to it. I collect samples of the freeze-dried-looking tissue and save them in plasticized cartons and also in small jars of formalin, and I tell Anne we're going to want a lot of photographs and that I'll ask colleagues of mine to look at images of internal damage and of the tannish tough tissue. I'll ask if they've ever seen anything like it before, and as I'm saying all this, I'm wondering who I mean. Not Briggs. I wouldn't dare send anything to him. Certainly not Fielding. No one who works here. No one at all comes to mind except Benton and Lucy, whose opinions won't help or matter. It's up to me whether I like it or not.

"Let's turn him over," I say, and empty of organs, he is light in the torso and head-heavy.

I measure the entrance wound and describe what it looks like and exactly where it is, and I examine the wound track through the bloc of organs, finding every area that was punctured by what I'm now certain was a narrow double- and single-edged blade.

"If you look at the wound, you can clearly see the two sharp ends of it, the corners of the buttonhole made by two sharp edges," I explain to Anne.

"I see." Her eyes are dubious behind her plastic glasses.

"But look here, where the wound track

terminates in the heart. Can you see how both ends of the wound are identical, both very sharp?" I move the light closer and hand her a magnifying lens.

"Slightly different from the wound on his back," she says.

"Yes. Because when the blade terminated in the heart muscle, it didn't penetrate as deeply; just the tip went in. As opposed to when these other wounds were made." I show her. "The tip penetrated and was followed by the length of the blade running through, and as you can see, the one end of the wound is just a little blunted and slightly stretched. You especially can see it here, where it penetrated the left kidney and kept going."

"I think I see what you're saying."

"Not what you would expect with a butterfly knife, a boning knife, a dagger, all of which are double-edged, both sides of the blade sharp from tip to handle. This brings to mind something spear-tipped — sharp on both sides at the tip but single-edged after that, like I've seen in some fighting knives or, in particular, something like a bowie knife or bayonet, where the top of the blade has been sharpened on both edges to make penetration easier in stabbings. So what we've got is an entrance that is three-eighths of an inch linear; both ends of the wound are sharp, with one that is slightly more blunted than the other. And the width expands to five-eighths of an inch." I measure, and Anne writes it down on a body diagram.

"So the blade is three-eighths of an inch at the tip, and at its widest it's five-eighths. That's pretty narrow. Almost like a stiletto," she says.

"But a stiletto is double-edged, the entire blade is."

"Homemade? A blade that injects something that explodes?"

"Without causing thermal injury, without causing burns. In fact, what we're seeing is more consistent with frostbite, where the tissue feels hard and is discolored," I remind her as I measure the distance from the wound on the man's back to the top of his head. "Twenty-six inches, and two inches to the left of the mid-spine. Direction is up and anterior, with extensive subcutaneous and tissue emphysema along the track, perforating the transverse process on the left twelfth rib paraspinally. Perforating paraspinal muscle, perirenal fat, left adrenal, left kidney, diaphragm, left lung, and pericardium, terminating in the heart."

"How long a blade for something to

perforate all that?"

"At least five inches."

She plugs in the autopsy saw, and we turn the body on its back again. I place a headrest under the neck and incise the scalp from ear to ear, following the hairline so the sutures won't be visible afterward. The top of the skull is white like an egg as I reflect the scalp back and pull the face down like a sock, like something sad, the features collapsing as if he is crying.

15

I don't realize the sun is up and the arctic front has marched off to the south until I open my office door and am greeted by a clear blue sky beyond tall windows.

I look down seven floors, and there are a few cars moving slowly on the white-frosted furrowed road below, and going the other way, a snowplow truck with its yellow blade held up like a crab claw as it scuttles along, looking for the right spot, then lowering the blade with a clank I can't hear from up here and scraping pavement that's not going to be completely cleared because of ice.

The riverbank is white, and the Charles is the color of old blue bottle glass and wrinkled by the current, and beyond in the distance the skyline of Boston catches the early light, the John Hancock Tower soaring far above any other high-rise, overbearing and sturdy, like a solitary column left standing in the ruins of an ancient temple. I think about coffee, and it is a fleeting urge as I wander into my bathroom and look at the coffeemaker on the counter by the sink and the boxes of K-Cups that include hazelnut.

I'm beyond being helped by stimulants, not sure I'd feel caffeine except in my gut, which is empty and raw. Intermittently, I'm stabbed by nausea, then I'm hungry, then nothing at all, just the gauziness of sleeplessness and the persistent hint of a headache that seems more remembered than real. My eyes burn, and thoughts move thickly but push with force like a heavy surf pounding against the same unyielding questions and tasks to be done. I won't wait for anyone, given a choice. I can't wait. There is no choice. I will overstep boundaries if need be, and why shouldn't I? Boundaries I've set have been stepped on right and left by others. I will do things myself, those things I know how to do. I am alone, more alone than I was because I've changed. Dover has changed me. I will do what is necessary, and it might not be what people want.

It is half past seven, and I've been downstairs all this time because Anne and I took care of other cases after we finished with the Norton's Woods man, whose name we are no closer to discovering, or if it is known, I've not been informed. I know intimate details about him that should be none of my business, but not the most important facts: who he is, what he was and hoped to become, his dreams, and what he loved and hated. I sit down at my desk and check the notes Anne made for me downstairs and add a few of my own, making sure I will remember later he had eaten something with poppy seeds and yellow cheese shortly before he died and the total amount of blood and clot in the left hemithorax was one thousand three hundred milliliters and the heart was disrupted into five irregular fragments that were still attached at the level of the valves.

I will want to emphasize this to the prosecution, it occurs to me, because I'm thinking about court. For me it all ends there, at least on the civilian side of my life. I imagine the prosecutor using inflammatory language I can't use, telling the jury that the man ate cheese and a poppy-seed bagel and took his rescued old dog for a walk, that his heart was blown to pieces, causing him to hemorrhage almost three units of blood or more than a third of all the blood in his body in a matter of minutes. The autopsy didn't reveal the purpose of the man's death, although provisionally, at least the cause of it is simple, and I absently write it down as I continue to ponder and meditate and make plans.

Atypical stab/puncture to the left back.

A pathological diagnosis that seems trite after what I just saw, and one that would give me pause, were I to come across it somewhere. I'd find it cryptic, almost tongue-in-cheek and coy, like a bad joke if one knows the rest of it, the massive blast-like disruption of the organs and that the death is a vicious and calculated homicide. I envision the hem of the long black coat quickly flapping past and what must have happened just seconds before when the person wearing it plunged a blade into the victim's lower back. For an instant he felt the physical response, the shock and pain as he exclaimed, *"Hey . . . !"* and clutched his chest, collapsing on his face on the slate path.

I imagine the person in the black coat quickly bending over to snatch off the man's black gloves and briskly walking away, perhaps tucking the blade up a sleeve or into a folded newspaper or I don't know. But as I imagine it, I believe the person in the long black coat is the killer and was covertly recorded by the dead man's head-phones, and it causes me to wonder again who was doing the spying. Did the killer plant micro–recording devices in the victim's headphones so he could be followed? And I imagine a figure in a long black coat walking swiftly through the shaded woods, coming up behind the victim, who couldn't hear anything but the music in his headphones as he's stabbed in the back, and he falls too fast to turn around. I wonder if he died not knowing who did this to him. And afterward? Is it what Lucy proposed? Did the person in the long black coat view the video files and decide it wasn't necessary to delete them from a webcam site somewhere, that in fact it was clever to leave them?

There are reasons for all things, I tell myself what has always been true but never feels that way while I'm in the middle of the problem. There are answers, and I will find them, and while the physics of how the fatal injury was executed may seem difficult to divine, I assure myself there are tracks the killer left behind. I have captured footprints on blotting paper. I will follow them to who did this. *You won't get away with it,* I think, as if I'm talking to the person in the long black coat. *I hope whoever you are, you have nothing to do with me, that you aren't someone I taught to be meticulous and clever.* I have decided that Jack Fielding is on the run or in custody. It even enters my mind that he might be dead. But I'm exhausted. I'm sleep-deprived. My thoughts aren't as disciplined as they should be. He can't be dead. Why would he be dead? I have seen the dead downstairs, and he wasn't among them.

My other patients of the morning were simple enough and asked little of me as I tended to them: a motor-vehicle fatality, and I could smell the booze and his bladder was full, as if he'd been drinking until the moment he left the bar and climbed behind the wheel in a snowstorm that careened him into a tree; a shooting in a run-down motel, and the needle tracks and prison tattoos of yet one more among us who died the way he lived; an asphyxia by a plastic dry-cleaning bag tied around an old widow's neck with an old red satin ribbon, maybe left over from a holiday during better times, her stomach full of dissolved white tablets, and next to the bed an empty bottle of a benzodiazepine prescribed for sleeplessness and anxiety.

I have no messages on my office and cell phones, no e-mails that matter to me at the moment and under the circumstances. When I checked Lucy's lab, she wasn't there, and when I checked with security, I discovered that even Ron has left, replaced by a guard I've never met, gangly and jug-eared like Ichabod Crane, someone named Phil who says Lucy's car isn't in the lot and the instructions are that the security guards aren't to let anyone into the building, not through the lower level or the lobby, without clearing it with me. Not possible, I let Phil know. Employees should be showing up already, or they will be at any minute, and I can't be the gatekeeper. Let anybody in who has a right to be here, I told him before I came upstairs. Except Dr. Fielding, and when I added that, I could tell it wasn't necessary. The guard named Phil clearly was aware that Fielding can't just show up or won't or maybe isn't able to, and besides, the FBI dominates my parking lot. I can see their SUVs clear as the bright, cold day on the video display on my desk.

I swivel my chair around to the polished black-granite countertop behind me, to my arsenal of microscopes and what accompanies them. Pulling on a pair of examination gloves, I slit open one of the white envelopes I sealed with white paper tape right before I came upstairs, and I pull out a sheet of blotting paper that is stained with a generous smear of dried blood that came from the area of the left kidney where I saw a dense collection of metallic foreign bodies in the

MRI. Turning on the lamp of my materials microscope, a Leica I have depended on for years, I carefully move the paper to the stage. I tilt the eyetubes to a viewing angle that won't strain my neck and shoulders and realize right away that the settings have been changed for someone much taller than me who is right-handed, someone who drinks coffee with cream and chews spearmint gum, I suspect. The ocular focus and interocular distance have been changed, too.

Switching to left-hand operation and adjusting the height so it is better suited for me, I start with a magnification of 50X, manipulating the focus knob with one hand as I use the other to move the sheet of blotting paper on the stage, lining up the bloody smear until I find what I'm looking for, bright whitish-silver chips and flakes in a constellation of other particles so minute that when I bump the magnification up to 100X, I can't make out their characteristics, only the rough edges and scratches and striations on the largest particles, what looks like unburned metal chips and filings that have been milled by a machine or a tool. Nothing I see reminds me of gunshot residue, doesn't even remotely resemble the flakes, disks, or balls I associate with gunpowder or the ragged fragments or particulate of a projectile or its jacket.

More curious is other debris mixed with blood and its obvious elements, the colorful confetti of detritus that constitutes everyday dust tangled with red cells piled up like coins, and granular leukocytes reminiscent of amoeba that are caught as if frozen in time, swimming and cavorting with a louse and a flea that at a magnified size remind me why seventeenth-century London went into a panic when Robert Hooke published *Micrographia* and revealed the piercing mouthparts and claws of what infested cats and mattresses. I recognize fungi and spores that look like sponges and fruit, spiny pieces of insect legs and insect egg cases that look like the delicate shells of nuts or spherical boxes carved of porous wood. As I move the paper on the stage, I find more hairy appendages of long-dead monsters, such as midges and mites and the wide compound eyes of a decapitated ant, the feathery antenna of what may have been a mosquito, the overlapping scales of animal hair, maybe from a horse or a dog or a rat, and reddish-orange flecks that could be rust.

I reach for the phone and call Benton. When he answers, I hear voices in the background and am subjected to a bad connection.

"A knife sharpened or shaped on something like a lathe, possibly a rusty one in a workshop or basement, possibly an old root cellar where there are mold, bugs, decaying vegetables, probably damp carpet," I say right off as I begin an Internet search on my computer, typing the keywords *knife* and *exploding gases.*

"What was sharpened?" Benton asks, and then he says something to someone else, something like *need the keys* or *need to keep.* "I'm moving, not in a good place," he gets back to me.

"The weapon used to stab him. A lathe, a grinder, possibly old or not taken care of, with traces of rust, based on the metal shavings and very fine particulate I'm seeing. I think the blade was honed, perhaps to make it thinner and to sharpen the tip on both edges, to turn the tip into a spear, so whatever might have been used for sharpening and polishing, a rasp, a file."

"You're talking about power tools that are old and rusty. A lot of rust?"

"Metalworking tools of some type, not necessarily power tools; I'm not in a position to be that detailed. I'm not an expert in metalworking and I don't know how much rust. Just that I found what looks like flakes of it." *Exploding intestines. How to clean your spark plugs. Common gases associated with metalworking and hand-forged knives,* I silently read what is on my computer screen as I then say to Benton, "Not that I pretend to be a trace-evidence examiner, but microscopically it's nothing I've not seen before, just never seen it blown into a body. But then I've never really looked. I've never had a reason to look for something like this, am unaccustomed to using blotting paper internally when someone has been stabbed. I suppose there could be all sorts of invisible fibers, debris, particulate, injected inside people who've been shot, stabbed, impaled, or God knows what."

I type *injection knife* into the search field because as I listen to myself, I'm reminded of remote delivery darts, of weapons powered by CO_2 to fire what's basically a long-range immobilization or tranquilizing missile with a small explosive charge and a hypodermic needle. Why couldn't you do the same thing with a knife, as long as it had a way to be powered and a narrow channel bored through the blade with an outlet hole near the tip?

"I'm walking outside to the car now," Benton says. "Will be there in forty-five minutes to an hour if the traffic's not too bad. The roads aren't bad. One-twenty-eight isn't too bad."

"Well, this wasn't hard." I'm disappointed. Nothing with so much potential for lethal damage should be this easy to find.

"What isn't hard?" Benton says as I look in amazement at an image of a steel combat knife with a gas outlet hole near the tip and a neoprene handle in a foam-lined plastic case.

"A CO_2 cartridge screws into the handle. . . ." I skim out loud. "Thrust the five-inch stainless-steel blade into the target as you use your thumb to push the release button, which it appears is part of the guard hub. . . ."

"Kay? Who's with you right now?"

"Injects a freezing ball of gas the size of a basketball or more than forty cubic inches at eight hundred pounds of pressure per square inch," I go on, looking at images on an elaborate website as I wonder how many people have such a weapon in their homes, their cars, their camping gear, or are walking around with it strapped to their sides. I have to admit it is ingenious, possibly one of the scariest things I've ever seen. "Can drop a large mammal in a single stab . . ."

"Kay, are you by yourself?"

"Freezes wound tissue instantly, thus

delaying bleeding and attracting other predators, so if you have to defend yourself against a great white shark, for example, it won't begin bleeding into the water and attracting other sharks until you are well out of the way." I skim and summarize and feel sickened. "It's called a WASP. You can add it to your shopping cart for less than four hundred dollars."

"Let's talk about it when I see you," Benton says over the phone.

"I've never heard of it." I read more about a compressed gas injection knife I can order right now as long as I'm over eighteen years of age. "Advertised for Special Ops, SWAT, pilots who are stranded in open water, scuba divers. Apparently developed to kill large marine predators — as I said, sharks, mammals, maybe whales and those in wet suits. . . ."

"Kay?"

"Or grizzly bears, for example, while you're minding your own business on a friendly hike through the mountains." I make no effort to keep the sarcasm out of my tone, to hide the anger I feel. "And, of course, military, but nothing I've seen in military casualties —"

"I'm on a cell phone," Benton interrupts me. "I'd rather you don't mention this to anyone else. No one in your office, or have you already?"

"I haven't already."

"You're by yourself?" he asks me again.

Why wouldn't I be? But I say, "Yes."

"And maybe you could delete it from your history, empty your cache, in case anybody decides to view your recent searches."

"I can't stop Lucy from doing that."

"I don't care if Lucy does it."

"She's not here. I don't know where she went."

"I know," he says.

"All right, then." He's not going to tell me where she is or where anybody is, it seems. "I'll make evidence rounds, take care of as much as I can and meet you downstairs in back when you get here." I hang up and try to reason through what just happened. I try not to feel hurt by him as I logically sort it out.

Benton didn't sound surprised or especially concerned. He didn't seem alarmed by what I've discovered but by my discovering it and the possibility that I might have told someone else, and that probably means the same thing I've been sensing since I returned home from Dover. Maybe I'm not the one finding things out. Maybe I'm simply the last one to know and nobody wants me to find out anything. What an unexpected predicament to be in, if not an unprecedented one, I think, as I do what Benton asked and empty the cache and clear the history, making it problematic for anyone to see what I've been searching on the Internet. As I do this I wonder who really asked: my husband, or was it the FBI asking? Who was just talking to me and telling me what to do as if I don't know better?

It's almost nine, and most of my staff is already here, those who aren't using the snow as an excuse to stay home or to go somewhere else they'd rather be, such as skiing in Vermont. On the security monitor I've watched cars pull into the lot and seen some people coming through the back door but far more arriving by way of the civilized entrance on the ground floor, through the stone lobby with its formidable carvings and flags, avoiding the dreary domain of the dead on the lower level. The scientists rarely need to meet the patients whose body fluids and belongings and other evidence they test, and then I hear the sounds of my administrator, Bryce, unlocking the door in the hallway that opens onto his adjoining office.

I reseal the blotting paper in a clean envelope and unlock a drawer to gather other items I've been keeping safe as I try not to sink into a dark space, thinking dark thoughts about what I just looked at on a website and what it implies about human beings and their capacity to create imaginative ways to do harm to other creatures. In the name of survival, it crosses my mind, but then rarely is it really about staying alive; instead, it's about making sure something else doesn't, and the power people feel when they can overpower, maim, kill. How terrible, how awful, and I have no doubt about what happened to the man from Norton's Woods, that someone came up behind him and stabbed him with an injection knife, blasting a ball of compressed gas into his vital organs, and if it was CO_2, there is no test that will tell us. Carbon dioxide is ubiquitous, literally as present as the air we exhale, and I envision what I saw on CT, the dark pockets of air that had been blown into the chest and what that must have felt like, and how I will answer the same question I'm always asked.

Did he suffer?

The truthful answer would be no one knows such a thing except the person who is dead, but I would say no, he didn't suffer. I would say he felt it. He felt something catastrophic happening to him. He wasn't conscious long enough to suffer during the agonal last moments of his life, but he would have felt a punch to his lower back accompanied by tremendous pressure in his chest as his organs ruptured, all of it happening at once. That would have been the last thing he felt except possibly a glimmer, a flash, of a panicked thought that he was about to die, and then I stop thinking about it because to obsess and imagine further would become useless and self-indulgent theorizing that is paralyzing and nonproductive. I can't help him if I'm upset.

I'm worthless to anyone if I feel what I feel, just as it was when I took care of my father and became an expert at pushing down emotions that climbed up inside me like some desperate creature trying to get out. "I worry what you have learned, my little Katie," my father said to me when I was twelve and he was a skeleton in the back bedroom, where the air was always too warm and smelled like sickness and light seeped wanly through the slatted shades I kept closed most of the way his last months. "You have learned things you shouldn't ever have to learn but especially at your age, my little Katie," he said to me as I made the bed with him still in it, having learned to wash him religiously so he wasn't overcome by pressure sores, to change his soiled sheets by moving his body, a body that seemed hollowed out and dead except for the heat of his fever.

I would gently rock my father to his side, holding him up on one side, then the other, leaning him against me because he could not get up in the end, couldn't even sit up. He was too weak to help me move him during what his doctor called the blast phase of chronic myeloid leukemia, and at times he enters my mind and I feel the weight of him against me when I'm swathed in protective clothing, peering through protective glasses, at work at my hard steel table.

I fill out lab analysis requests that will need to be signed by each scientist I receipt various items to so I can keep the chain of evidence intact. Then I get up from my desk.

16

Knocking once, I open the door that leads into Bryce's office.

Our shared entrance is directly across from the door to my private bath, which I've learned to keep open a crack. When both gray metal doors are shut I have had a tendency to get mixed up and walk in on Bryce when I'm interested in coffee or washing up or I find myself about to hand paperwork to a toilet and a sink. He is at his desk with his chair rolled back and has taken off his coat, which is draped over the back, but he still has on his big designer sunglasses that look ridiculously heavy, as if drawn on with a dark-brown crayon. He struggles with a pair of L.L.Bean snow boots that don't go with his typically deliberate ensemble, which today is a navy cashmere blazer, tight black jeans, a black turtleneck, and a tooled leather belt with a big silver buckle shaped like a dragon.

"I'll be on the phone and can't be disturbed," I tell him as if I've been here every day for these past six months, as if I've never been gone. "Then I have to leave."

"Is someone going to tell me what's going on around here? And welcome home, boss." He looks up at me, his eyes masked by the big, dark glasses. "I don't suppose the unmarked cars in the parking lot are a surprise party, because I know I'm not throwing one. Not that I wouldn't and wasn't intending to eventually, but whoever they are, they aren't here because of me, and when I asked one of them to be so kind as to give me an explanation and please move his ass so I could park in my spot, he was shall we say *testy?*"

"The case from yesterday morning," I start to say.

"Oh, is that why? Well, no wonder." His face brightens as if what I just said is somehow good news. "I knew it was going to be important, I somehow knew it. But he didn't really die here, please tell me it's not true, that you didn't find anything to suggest anything so outrageous or I guess I'll just start looking for another job right this minute and tell Ethan we're not about to buy that bungalow we've been looking at. I'm sure you've figured out what happened

411

by now, knowing you. You probably figured it out in five minutes."

He pulls off the other boot, moving both of them to the side, and I notice he's spiked his hair and has shaved off the mustache and beard he had when I saw him last. Compactly built, Bryce is slight but strong with a blond choirboy prettiness, to use a cliché, because it happens to be true. He doesn't look like himself with facial hair, which is probably the point, to look like someone else, to be transformed into a formidable and virile character like James Brolin, or to be taken seriously like Wolf Blitzer, heroes of his. My top administrator and trusted right hand has many, a host of famous imagined friends he speaks of easily as if the act of tuning into them on one of his big-screen TVs or saving them with TiVo makes them as real as next-door neighbors.

Seriously good at what he does for me, with degrees in criminal justice and public administration, Bryce Clark at a glance seems misplaced, as if he wandered off the set of *E!,* and I have used this to my advantage over the few years he's worked for me. Outsiders and even people who work here don't always realize that my recovering Mormon compulsive-talking clotheshorse of a chief of staff is not to be trifled with. If nothing else, he's voyeuristic and adores "filling me in," as he puts it. He likes nothing better than to gather information like a magpie and carry it back to his nest. He is dangerous if he detests you. It's unlikely you'll know it. His banter and deliberate affect are a bunker that his more dangerous self hides behind, and in that way he reminds me of my former secretary, Rose. Those who made the mistake of treating her like a silly old woman one day found themselves missing a limb.

"The FBI? Homeland Security? No one I've seen before." Bryce is bent over in his chair as he unzips a nylon gym bag, his stocking feet planted on the floor.

"Probably the FBI —" But he isn't going to let me finish.

"Well, the one who was so rude totally looked the part, all buff in a gray suit and camel-hair coat. I think the FBI fires people if they get fat. Well, good luck hiring in America. Drop-dead good-looking, I'll give him that. Did you see him back there? Do we know his name and what field office he's with? Not anyone I've met from Boston. Maybe he's new."

"Who?" My thoughts run into a wall.

"Lord, you are tired. The agent in that big, bad black Ford Expedition, the spitting image of the football player on *Glee* — oh, you probably don't watch that, either, it's only the best show on TV and I can't imagine you don't love Jane Lynch, unless you don't know who she is, since you probably didn't catch *The L Word,* but maybe *Best in Show* or *Talladega Nights?* My God, what a hoot. The Bureau boy in the black Ford looks exactly like Finn —"

"Bryce . . ."

"Anyway, I saw all the blood, how much the body from Norton's Woods bled inside his pouch, and it was god-awful, and I thought to myself, *This is it. The end of this place.* Meanwhile, Marino's huffing and puffing and about to blow the house down, pitching a fit as only Marino can about someone delivered alive and dying in the fridge. So I told Ethan we might have to tuck away our pennies because I might be unemployed. And the job market right now? Ten percent unemployment or some nightmare like that, and I seriously doubt *Doctor G* is going to hire me because every morgue worker on the planet wants to be on her show, but I would ask you to pick up the phone and recommend me to her, please, if this place goes down the toilet. Why can't we do a reality show? I mean, really. You had your own show on CNN some years ago; why can't we do something here?"

"I need to talk to you about —" But there's no point when he gets like this.

"I'm glad you're here, but sorry you had to come home for something so god-awful. I stayed awake all night wondering what I was going to tell reporters. When I saw those SUVs behind the building, I thought it was the media, was fully expecting television trucks —"

"Bryce, you need to calm down and maybe take your sunglasses off —"

"But nothing in the news that I know of, and not one reporter has called me or left a message here or anything —"

"I need to go over a few things, and you really need to shut up, please," I interrupt him.

"I know." He takes off his sunglasses as he works his foot into a black high-top sneaker. "I'm just a little overwrought, Dr. Scarpetta. And you know how I get when I'm overwrought."

"Have you heard from Jack?"

"Where's the Mouth of Truth when you need it?" As he ties his sneakers. "Don't ask me to pretend, and I would respectfully request that you inform him I don't answer directly to him anymore. Now that you're home, thank God."

"Why do you say that?"

"Because all he does is order me around as if I work in the drive-through window at Wendy's. He barks and snaps as his hair falls out, and then I wonder if he's going to kick someone, maybe me, or strangle me with his umpteenth-degree black belt or whatever the fuck he has, excuse my French. And it's gotten worse, and we weren't supposed to bother you at Dover. I told everybody to leave you alone. Everybody's told everybody to leave you alone or they'll answer to me. I'm just realizing you've been up all night. You look awful." His blue eyes look me up and down, studying the way I'm dressed, which is in the same khaki cargo pants and black polo shirt with the AFME crest that I put on at Dover.

"I came straight here and don't have anything to change into." I finally get a word in edgewise. "I don't know why you bothered replacing your L.L.Beans with an old pair of Converse left over from basketball camp."

"I know you have a better eye than that, and I know you know I never went to basketball camp, because I always went to music camp every summer. Hugo Boss, half price at Endless-dot-com, plus free shipping," he adds, getting up from his chair.

"I'm making coffee, and you want some. And no, I've not heard from Jack, and you don't need to tell me there's a problem and it might have to do with those agents in our parking lot, who obviously have a personality disorder. I don't know why they can't make an effort to be friendly. If I wore a big gun and could arrest people, I'd be Little Miss Sunshine to everyone, smile and be so nice. Why not?" Bryce brushes past me, walking into my office, disappearing into the bathroom. "I can run by your house and pick up a few things if you want. Just tell me. A business suit or something casual?"

"If I get stuck here . . ." I start to say I might take him up on it.

"We really do need to arrange some sort of closet for you, a little haute couture at HQ. Ohhhh, wardrobe?" his voice sings out as he makes coffee. "Now if we had our own show, we'd have wardrobe, hair, makeup, and you'd never find yourself in the same dirty clothes and odiferous of death, not that I'm saying you're . . . Well, anyway. Best of all would be if you went home and straight to bed." As hot water shoots loudly through a K-Cup. "Or I could run out and get you something to eat. I find when I'm tired and sleep-deprived . . ." He emerges from my bathroom with two coffees and says, "Fat. There's a time and a place for everything. Dunkin' Donuts, their croissant with sausage and egg, how 'bout it? You might need two. You actually look a little thin. Life in the military really doesn't suit you, dear boss."

"Are you aware of a woman named Erica Donahue calling here?" I ask him as I return to my desk with a coffee I'm not sure I should drink. Opening a drawer, I search for Advil in hopes there really might be a bottle hiding somewhere.

"She did. Several times." Bryce carefully sips the hot coffee, leaning against the frame of the open doorway that connects us.

When he offers nothing else, I ask, "When did she call?"

"Starting after it was in the news about her son. That was a week ago, I think, when he confessed to killing Mark Bishop."

"You talked to her?"

"Most recently, all I really did was direct her call to Jack again when she was looking for you."

" 'Again'?"

"You should get his part from him. I don't know his details," Bryce says, and it's not like him to be careful with me. He's cautious suddenly.

"But he talked to her."

"This was, let me see. . . ." He has a habit of gazing up at the dome as if the answers to all things are there. It's also a favorite delaying tactic of his. "Last Thursday."

"And you talked to her. Before you transferred her call to Jack."

"Mostly I listened."

"What was her demeanor, and what did she say?"

"Very polite, sounded like the upper-class intelligent woman she is, based on what I hear. I mean, there's a ton of stuff about the Donahue family and Johnny Hinckley Junior. He's almost that notorious. . . . *And when he saw what he had done, he holstered his trusty nail gun.* . . . But you probably don't read all this shit on these gore-sites like Morbidia Trivia, Wicked-whatever-pedia, Cryptnotes, or whatever, and I do have to follow them as part of my job, part of my being informed about what's being said out there in sensational sin-loving cyberland."

He's comfortable again. He's uncomfortable only when I probe him about Fielding.

"Mom was an almost famous concert pianist in a former life, played in a symphony orchestra. I think in San Francisco," Bryce goes on. "I happened to notice some Twittering about her being taught by Yundi

Li, but I seriously doubt Li gives lessons, and he's only twenty-eight, so I don't believe it for a second. Of course she's in an uproar, can you imagine? They say her son is a savant, has these bizarre abilities, like knowing tire treads. The detective from Salem, Saint Hilaire, who is anything but, and you don't know him yet, was talking about it. Apparently, Johnny Donahue can look at a tread pattern in a dirt parking lot and go, 'That's a Bridgestone Battle Wing front motorcycle tire.' I just came up with that because Ethan has those on his BMW, which I wish he didn't love so much, because to me they're all donorcycles. Supposedly, Johnny can do math problems in his head, and I'm not talking if a banana costs eighty-nine cents how much is a bunch of six? More Einsteinian, like what is nine times a hundred and three to the square root of seven or something? But then you probably know all this. I'm sure you've been keeping up with the case."

"What exactly did she want to discuss with me? Did she tell you?" I know Bryce. He wouldn't hand off someone like Erica Donahue without letting her talk until she ran out of words or patience. He's too much of a snoop, his mind a chatterbox gossip mill.

"Well, obviously he didn't do it, and if someone would really look into the facts without having their mind made up, they'd see all the inconsistencies. The conflicts," Bryce replies, blowing on his coffee, not looking at me.

"What conflicts, exactly?"

"She says she talked to him the day of the murder at around nine in the morning, before he headed off to that café in Cambridge that's now become so famous right around the corner from you?" Bryce continues. "The Biscuit? Lines out the door because of all the publicity. Nothing like a murder. Anyway, he wasn't feeling well that day, according to Mom. Has terrible allergies or something and was complaining his pills or shots or whatever weren't working anymore, and he was dosing up big-time and felt *punk* is the word she used. So I guess if someone has itchy eyes and a runny nose, he's not going to kill anyone. I didn't want to tell her that a jury wouldn't put much stock in a sneezy defense —"

"I need to make a call and then make my rounds," I cut him off before he digresses the rest of the day. "Can you check with Trace Evidence and see if Evelyn is in, and if so, please tell her I have a few things that are rather urgent. What I've got needs to start with her and then fingerprints, then DNA, then toxicology, then one item in particular will come back up here to Lucy's lab. There was no one over there a while ago. What about Shane, are we expecting him, because I'm going to need an opinion about a document?"

"It's not like we're a rugby team stranded in a blizzard in the Andes and are going to resort to cannibalism, for God's sake."

"It was quite a storm all night."

"You've been down south too long. There's what? Eight inches? A bit icy but nothing for around here," Bryce says.

"Actually, if you could ask Evelyn to come upstairs immediately and let her into Jack's office." I decide I'm not going to wait as I remember the lab coat folded up inside the trash-can liner.

I explain to Bryce what's in the pocket and that I want it checked right away on SEM and I also want a nondestructive chemical analysis.

"Be very, very careful not to open the bag and touch anything," I say to Bryce. "And tell Evelyn there are fingerprints on the plastic film. Meaning there will also be DNA."

With my administrator silently out of range

on the other side of our shared shut door, I decide to hold off calling Erica Donahue until I have a chance to think about what I'm going to do. I need to think about everything.

I want to reread her letter and make sure of my intentions, and as I ponder and remember what's happened since I left Dover, as I look out at the bright blue sky of a new day, I know I'm still hungover from the last mother I dealt with. I feel poisoned by the memory of Julia Gabriel on the phone as someone loitered outside my closed door at Port Mortuary. The names she called me and what she accused me of were bitter and vile, but I didn't really let it get to me in a way that gave power to her words until I found what I did in Fielding's office. Since then a shadow that is chilled and dark like a sunless part of the moon is at the back of my thoughts and moods. I don't know what is being said or decided about me or what has been resurrected like some cold-blooded thing that never died and now is stirring.

What records have been found, and what has been gone through that I have secretly feared all these years and at the same time forgotten? Although the truth was always there, like something unseemly out of sight in a closet, something that I never look for but, if reminded, I know it's not gone, because it was never thrown out or returned to its rightful owner, which should never have been me. But the ugly matter was handed over as if it was mine. And it was left hanging. As long as what was done in South Africa stayed hidden in my closet instead of where it belonged, I'd be fine, was the message I got when I returned to Walter Reed after working those two deaths and was thanked for my service to the AFIP, to the air force, and was free to leave early. Debt paid in full. They had just the position for me in Virginia, where I would prosper as long as I remembered loyalty and took my dirty laundry with me.

Has it happened again? Has Briggs done the same thing to me again and soon will send me packing? Where this time? Early retirement crosses my mind. It's all coming out with more ugliness piled on, and that's not survivable, I decide, because I don't know what else to think. Briggs has told someone, and someone told Julia Gabriel, who has accused me of hatred, prejudice, callousness, dishonesty, and I must remember that this noxious miasma permeates any decisions I might make right now, that and fatigue. *Be exceedingly careful. Use your head. Don't give yourself up to emotions, and easy as pie* drifts through my mind. What Lucy said about security recordings, and I pick up my phone and buzz Bryce.

"Yes, boss," he says brightly, as if we haven't chatted in days.

"Our security recordings from the closed-circuit cameras everywhere," I say. "When was Captain Avallone here from Dover? I understand Jack gave her a tour."

"Oh, Lord, that was a while ago. I believe November. . . ."

"I recall she went home to Maine the week of Thanksgiving," I tell him. "I know she was gone from Dover that week because I had to stay. We were shorthanded."

"That sounds about right. I think she was here that Friday."

"Were you with them on the grand tour?"

"I was not. I wasn't invited. And Jack spent a lot of time with her in your office, just so you know. In there with the door shut. They ate lunch in there at your table."

"This is what I need you to do," I tell him. "Get hold of Lucy, text-message her or whatever you need to do, and let her know I want a review of every security recording that has Jack and Sophia on it, including anything in my office."

"In your office?"

"How long has he been using it?"

"Well . . ."

"Bryce? How long?"

"Pretty much the entire time. He helps himself when he wants to impress people. I mean, he doesn't use it for his casework very often, mostly when he's being ceremonial. . . ."

"Tell Lucy I want recordings of my office. She'll know exactly what I mean. I want to see what Jack and the captain were talking about."

"How delicious. I'll get right on it."

"I'm about to make an important call, so please don't disturb me," I then say. As I hang up, I realize Benton will be here soon.

But I resist the temptation to rush. Wise to slow down, to allow thoughts and perceptions to sort themselves out, to strive for clarity. *You're tired. Exercise caution, and play it smart when you're this tired.* There's one way to do this right, and every other way is wrong. You won't know the right way until it happens, and you won't recognize it if you're wound up and muddled. I reach for my coffee but change my mind about that, too. It won't help at this point, will only make me jittery and upset my stomach more. Pulling another pair of examination gloves out of a box on the granite counter behind my desk, I remove the document from the plastic bag I sealed it in.

I slide the two folded sheets of heavy paper out of the envelope I slit open in Benton's SUV as we drove through a blizzard what now seems like a lifetime ago but has only been twelve hours. In the light of morning and after so much has happened, it seems more unusual than it did that this classical pianist whom Bryce described as intelligent and reasonable would have used duct tape on her fine engraved stationery. Why not regular tape that is transparent instead of this ugly wide strip of lead-gray across the back? Why not do what I do when I enclose a private memo in an envelope and simply sign your name or initials over the seal of the flap? What was Erica Donahue afraid would happen? That her driver might want to read what she wrote to someone named Scarpetta whom he apparently had never heard of?

I smooth open the pages with my cotton-gloved hand and try to intuit what the mother of a college boy who has confessed to murder transferred to the keys of her typewriter, as if what she felt and believed as she composed her plea to me is a chemical I can absorb that will get me into her mind. It occurs to me I've come up with such an analogy because of the plastic film I found in the pocket of Fielding's lab coat. Hours beyond that unnerving druggy experience, I can see just how bad it really was and that I could not have been myself with Benton, and how uncomfortable it must have been for him. Maybe that's why he's being so secretive and is lecturing me about divulging information to whoever happens to be nearby, as if I, of all people, don't know better. Maybe he doesn't trust my judgment or self-control and fears that the horrors of war changed me. Maybe he's not so sure that the woman who came home to him from Dover is the one he knows.

I'm not who you used to know floats through my head. *I'm not sure you ever knew me* is a whisper in my thoughts, and as I read the neat rows of single-spaced type, I find it remarkable that in two pages there isn't one mistake. I see no evidence of white-out or correction tape, no misspellings or bad grammar. When I think back to the last typewriter I used, a dusky pink IBM Selectric I had in Richmond the first few years I was there, I remember my chronic aggravation with ribbons that broke or having to swap out the golf ball–like element when I wanted to change fonts, and dealing with a dirty platen that left smudges on paper, not to mention my own hurried fingers hitting the wrong keys, and while my spelling and grammar are good, I'm certainly not infallible.

As my secretary Rose used to say when she'd walk in with my latest effort typed on that damn machine, *"And on what page is this in Strunk and White, or maybe it's in the MLA style guide and I just can't find it? I'll redo it, but every time you type something yourself?"* And she'd flap her hand in that characteristic gesture of hers that said to me *Why bother?,* and then I stop those thoughts because it makes me sad when I think about her. I've missed Rose every day since she died, and if she were here right now, somehow things would be different. Things would feel different, if nothing else. For me she was my clarity. For her I was her life. No one like Rose should be gone from this earth, and I still can't believe it, and now is not a good time to think about the blond young man in black high-top sneakers sitting next door instead of her. I need to focus. Focus on Erica Donahue. What will I do with this woman? I am going to do something, but I must be shrewd.

She must have typed her letter to me more than once, as many times as it took to make it impeccable, and I'm reminded that when her driver rolled up in the Bentley he didn't seem to know that the intended recipient of the envelope sealed with duct tape is a woman, and indeed seemed to think a silver-haired man was me. I remind myself that the mother of Johnny Donahue also doesn't seem aware that the forensic psychologist evaluating him, this same silver-haired man, is my husband, and also contrary to what's in her letter, there is no unit for the "criminally insane" at McLean, nor has anyone deemed that Johnny is criminally insane, which is a legal term and not a diagnosis. According to Benton, she also has other facts wrong.

She has confused details that may very well hurt her son, possibly damaging an alibi that potentially is his strongest. Claiming he left The Biscuit in Cambridge at one p.m. instead of at two, as Johnny maintains, she has made it far more believable that he could have found transportation and gotten to Salem in time to kill Mark Bishop around four that afternoon. Then there is her reference to her son reading horror novels and enjoying horror films and violent entertainment, and finally what she said about Jack Fielding and a nail gun and a satanic cult, none of that correct or proven.

Where did she get those dangerous details

— where, really? I suppose Fielding could have put such ideas in her head when he talked to her on the phone, if it's true he's the one now spreading these rumors, that he's lying, which is what Benton seems to think. Regardless of what Fielding did or didn't do or his truths or untruths or his reasons for anything that is happening, my questions come back to the mother of Johnny Donahue. I make myself bring all of it back to her, because what I fail to see is motivation that is logical. Her delivering this letter to me really doesn't sit well at all. It feels off. It feels wrong.

For one so meticulous about typos and sentence construction, not to mention the attention she must pay to her music, it strikes me that she doesn't seem to care nearly as much as she should about the facts of her son's confession to one of the most heinous acts of violence in recent memory. Every detail counts in a case like this, and how could an intelligent, sophisticated woman with expensive lawyers not know that? Why would she take the chance of divulging anything to someone like me, a complete stranger, especially in writing, when her son faces being locked up for the rest of his life in a forensic psychiatric facility like Bridgewater or, worse, in a prison, where a convicted child-killer with Asperger's, a so-called savant who can work the most difficult math problems in his head but is impaired when it comes to everyday social cues, isn't likely to survive very long?

I refresh myself on all these facts and relevant points at the same time I realize I'm feeling and behaving as if they matter to me. And they shouldn't. I'm supposed to be objective. *You don't take sides, and it's not your job to care,* I tell myself. *You don't care about Johnny Donahue or his mother one way or the other, and you're not a detective or the FBI,* I think sternly. *You're not Johnny's defense attorney or his therapist, and there's nothing for you to get involved in,* I then say to myself severely, because I don't feel convinced. I'm struggling with impulses that have become impossibly strong, and I'm not sure how to turn them off or if I can or should. I do know I don't want to.

Some of what I've grown accustomed to not only at Dover but on non-combat-related matters that are the jurisdiction of the AFME or what basically is the federal medical examiner is far too compatible with my true nature, and I don't want to go back to the staid old way of doing things. I'm military and I'm not. I'm civilian and I'm not. I've been in and out of Washington and lived on an air force base and routinely been sent on recovery missions of air crashes and accidents during training exercises and deaths on military installations or fatalities involving special forces, the Secret Service, a federal judge, even an astronaut in recent months, handling a multitude of sensitive situations I can't talk about. What I'm feeling is the *not* part of the equation. I'm not any one thing, and I'm not feeling at all inclined to surrender to limitations, to sit on my hands because something isn't my department.

As an officer involved in medical intelligence, I'm expected to investigate certain aspects of life and death that go far beyond the usual clinical determinations. Materials I remove from bodies, the types of injuries and wound ballistics, the strengths and failures of armor, and infections, diseases, lesions, whether from parasites or sand fleas, and extreme heat, dehydration, and boredom, depression, and drugs are all matters of national defense and security. The data I gather aren't just for the sake of families and usually aren't destined for criminal court but can have a bearing on the strategies of war and what keeps us safe domestically. I'm expected to ask questions. I'm expected to follow leads. I'm expected to pass along information to the surgeon general, the Department of Defense, to be intensely industrious and proactive.

You're home now. You don't want to come across as a colonel or a commander, certainly not as a prima donna. You don't want to get a case null prossed *or thrown out of court. You don't want to cause trouble. Isn't there enough already? Why would you encourage more? Briggs doesn't want you here. Be careful you don't justify his position. Your own staff doesn't seem to want you here or know you're here. Don't make it easy for you not to be. Your only legitimate purpose in contacting Erica Donahue is to ask her kindly not to contact you or your office again, for her own good, for her own protection.*

I decide to use those exact words, and I almost believe my motivation as I call the home phone number typed at the end of her letter.

17

The person who answers doesn't seem to understand what I'm saying, and I have to repeat myself twice, explaining that I'm Dr. Kay Scarpetta and I'm responding to a letter I just received from Erica Donahue, and is she available, please?

"I beg your pardon," the well-modulated voice says. "Who is this?" A woman's voice, I'm fairly sure, although it is low, almost in the tenor range, and could belong to a young man. In the background a piano plays, unaccompanied, a solo.

"Is this Mrs. Donahue?" I'm already getting an uncomfortable feeling.

"Who is this, and why are you calling?" The voice hardens and enunciates crisply.

I repeat what I said as I recognize a Chopin étude, and I remember a concert at Carnegie Hall. Mikhail Pletnev, who was stunning in his technical mastering of a composition that is very hard to play. The music of someone detailed and meticulous who likes everything just so. Someone who isn't careless and doesn't make mistakes. Someone who wouldn't mar a fine engraved envelope by slapping on duct tape. Someone who isn't impulsive but very studied.

"Well, I don't know who this really is," says the voice, what I now believe is Mrs. Donahue's voice, stony and edged with distrust and pain. "And I don't know how you got this number, since it's unlisted and unpublished. If this is some sort of crank call, it's absolutely outrageous, and whoever you are, you should be ashamed of yourself —"

"I assure you this is not a crank call," I interrupt before she can hang up on me as I think about her listening to Chopin, Beethoven, Schumann, worrying her life away, agonizing over a son who probably has caused her anguish since she gave birth to him. "I'm the director of the Cambridge Forensic Center, the chief medical examiner of Massachusetts," I explain authoritatively but calmly, the same voice I use with families who are on the verge of losing control, as if she is Julia Gabriel and about to shriek at me. "I've been out of town, and when I arrived at the airport last night, your driver was there with your letter, which I've carefully read."

"That's absolutely impossible. I don't have a driver, and I didn't write you a letter. I've written no one at your office and have no idea what on earth you're talking about. Who is this? Who really, and what do you want?"

"I have the letter in front of me, Mrs. Donahue."

I look at it on top of my desk and smooth it open again, being careful and deliberate as it nags at me to ask her about Fielding and why she called him and what he said to her. It nags at me that I don't want her to hate me or think I'm unfeeling or anything other than honest. It's possible Fielding disparaged me to her the same way I suspect he did with Julia Gabriel. I'm close to asking, but I stop myself. What has been said, and what has Erica Donahue been led to believe? But not now. *Self-control,* I tell myself.

Mrs. Donahue asks indignantly, "What does it say that's supposedly from me?"

"A creamy rag paper with a watermark." I hold the top sheet of paper up to my desk lamp, adjusting the shade so the bulb shines directly through the paper, showing the watermark clearly, like the inner workings of a soft-shell crab showing through pearly skin. "An open book with three crowns," I say, and I'm shocked.

I don't let her hear it in my voice. I make sure she can't begin to sense what is racing through my mind as I describe to her what I'm seeing, like a hologram, in the sheet of paper I hold up to the light: an open book between two crowns, with a third crown below, and above that three cinquefoil flowers. And it is the flowers Marino neglected to mention that so glaringly aren't Oxford's coat of arms, that so glaringly aren't the coat of arms for the online City University of San Francisco. What I'm looking at isn't what Benton found on the Internet early this morning while all of us were in the x-ray room, but it's what I saw on the gold signet ring I took out of the evidence locker before I came upstairs after looking at the dead man's clothes.

I open the small manila envelope and shake the ring out into the palm of my gloved hand. The gold catches the lamplight and is bright against white cotton as I turn it different ways to look at it, noting it is badly scratched and the bottom of the band is worn thin. The ring looks old, like an antique, to me.

"Well, that sounds like my crest and my paper. I admit it does," Mrs. Donahue is saying over the phone, and then I read to her the Beacon Hill address engraved on the envelope and letterhead, and she confirms it also is hers. "My personal stationery? How is that possible?" She sounds angry, the way people get when they're scared.

"What can you tell me about your crest? Would you mind explaining it to me?" I ask.

I look at the identical crest engraved in the yellow-gold signet ring that I now hold under a hand lens. The three crowns and the open book are large in the magnifying glass, and the engraving is almost gone in spots, the five-petal flowers, the cinquefoils especially, just a ghost of what was once deeply etched because of the age of the ring, which has been subjected to wear and tear by someone, or perhaps by a number of people, including the man from Norton's Woods, who was wearing it on the little finger of his left hand when he was murdered. There can be no mistake he had it on, that the ring came in with his body. There was no mix-up by police, a hospital, a funeral home. The ring was there when Marino removed the man's personal effects yesterday morning and locked them up and kept the key until he turned it over to me.

"My family name is Fraser," Mrs.

Donahue explains. "It's my family coat of arms, that particular emblazon for Jackson Fraser, a great-grandfather who apparently changed the design to incorporate elements such as Azure in base, a border Or, and a third crown Gules, which you can't see unless you're looking at a replica of the coat of arms that displays the tinctures, such as what is framed in my music room. Are you saying someone wrote a letter on my stationery and had a driver hand-deliver it to you? I don't understand or see how it's possible, and I don't know what it means or why someone would do something like that. What kind of car was it? We certainly don't have a driver. I have an old Mercedes, and my husband drives a Saab and isn't in the country right now, anyway, and we've never had a driver. We only use drivers when we travel."

"I'm wondering if your family coat of arms is on anything else. Embroidered, engraved, besides being framed on the wall in your music room, anywhere else it might appear. If it's known or published, if someone could have gotten hold of it." No matter how I phrase it, it sounds like a peculiar thing to quiz her about.

"Get hold of it to do what ultimately? What goal?"

"Your stationery, for example. Let's think about that and what the ultimate goal might be."

"Is what you have engraved or printed?" she then asks. "Can you tell the difference between engraved and printed by looking at what you have?"

You don't know who he is, I'm thinking. *You don't know that the man who died wearing that ring isn't a member of her family, a relative,* and I remember Benton saying Johnny Donahue has an older brother who works at Langley. What if he happened to be in Cambridge yesterday, staying at an apartment near Harvard, maybe a friend's apartment that has an obsolete packbot in it, a friend with a greyhound, a friend who perhaps works in a robotics lab? What if the older brother or some other man significant to Mrs. Donahue had just been overseas, in the UK, and had flown back here unexpected and is dead and she doesn't know, the Donahue family doesn't know? What does Johnny's brother look like?

Don't ask her.

"The stationery is engraved," I answer Mrs. Donahue's question.

What if her family is somehow connected with Liam Saltz or with someone who might have attended his daughter's wedding on

441

Sunday? Might the Donahues have a connection to a member of Parliament named Brown?

Stay away from it.

"Well, you can't pull engraved stationery out of a hat, have it made in a minute," Mrs. Donahue is saying.

Now I'm looking at the envelope, at the duct tape on the back that I didn't cut through, that I thought to preserve.

"Especially if you don't have the copperplates," she adds.

We use sticky-sided tape all the time in forensics, to collect trace evidence from carpet, from upholstery, to lift fibers, paint chips, glass fragments, gunshot residue, minerals, even DNA and fingerprints, from all types of surfaces, including human bodies. Anybody could know that. Just watch television. Just Google "crime scene investigative techniques and equipment."

"If someone got hold of my copperplates? But who? Who could have them?" she protests. "Without those, it would take weeks. And if you do press proofs, which of course I do, add several more weeks. This makes no sense."

She wouldn't put duct tape on the back of her elegant envelope that took many weeks to engrave. Not this precise, proud woman who listens to Chopin études. If someone else did, then I might have an idea why. Especially if it was someone who knows me or knows the way I think.

"And yes, the crest is on a number of things. It's been in my family for centuries," she adds, because she wants to talk. There is much pent up inside her, and she wants to let it out.

Allow it.

"Scottish, but you probably guessed that based on the name," she then says. "Framed on the wall in the music room, as I mentioned, and engraved on some of my family silverware, and we did have some silver stolen years ago by a housekeeper who was fired but never charged with anything because we really couldn't prove it to the satisfaction of the Boston police. I suppose my family silver could have ended up in a pawnshop around here. But I don't see what that could have to do with my stationery. It sounds as if you're implying someone might have made engraved stationery identical to mine with the goal of impersonating me. Or someone stole it. Are you suggesting identity theft?"

What to say? How far do I go?

"What about anything else that might have been stolen, anything else with your family crest on it?" I don't want to directly ask her about the ring.

"Why do you ask? Is there something else?"

"I have a letter that is supposedly from you," I reiterate instead of answering her questions. "It's typed on a typewriter."

"I still use a typewriter," she verifies, and sounds bewildered. "But usually I write letters by hand."

"Might I ask with what?"

"Why, a pen, of course. A fountain pen."

"And the type style on your typewriter, which is what kind? But you might not know the typeface. Not everybody would."

"It's just an Olivetti portable I've had forever. The typeface is cursive, like handwriting."

"A manual one that must be fairly old." As I look at the letter, at the distressed cursive typeface made with metal typebars striking an inked ribbon.

"It was my mother's."

"Mrs. Donahue, do you know where your typewriter is?"

"I'm going to walk over there, to the cabinet in the library where it's kept while I'm not using it."

I hear her moving into another area of the house, and it sounds as if she sets what must

444

be a portable phone down on a hard surface. Then a series of doors shut, perhaps cabinet doors, and a moment later she is back on with me and almost breathless as she says, "Well, it's gone. It's not here."

"Do you remember when you saw it last?"

"I don't know. Weeks ago. Probably around Christmas. I don't know."

"And it wouldn't be someplace else. Perhaps you moved it or someone borrowed it?"

"No. This is terrible. Someone took it and probably took my stationery, too. The same one who wrote to you as if it was me. And I didn't. I most assuredly didn't."

The first person to come to mind is her own son Johnny. But he is at McLean. He couldn't possibly have borrowed her typewriter, her pen, her stationery, and then hired a man and a Bentley to deliver a letter to me. Assuming he could have known when I was flying in last night on Lucy's helicopter, and I'm not going to ask his mother about that, either. The more I ask her, the more information I give.

"What's in the letter?" she persists. "What did someone write as if it's from me? Who could have taken my typewriter? Should we call the police? What am I saying? You are the police."

"I'm a medical examiner," I correct her matter-of-factly as Chopin's tempo quickens, a different étude. "I'm not the police."

"But you are, really. Doctors like you investigate like the police and act like the police and have powers they can abuse like the police. I talked to your assistant, Dr. Fielding, about what's being blamed on my son, as I know you're very well aware. You must know I've called your office about it and why. You must know why and how wrong it is. You sound like a fair-minded woman. I know you haven't been here, but I must say I don't understand what's been condoned, even from a distance."

I swivel around in my chair, facing the curved wall behind me that is nothing but glass, my office shaped exactly like the building if you laid it on its side, cylindrical and rounded at one end. The morning sky is bright blue, what Lucy calls severe clear, and I notice something moving in the security display, a black SUV parking in back.

"I was told you called to speak to him," I reply, because I can't say what is about to boil out of me. What isn't fair? What have I condoned? How did she know I haven't been here? "I can understand your concern, but —"

"I'm not ignorant," Mrs. Donahue cuts me off. "I'm not ignorant about these things, even if I've never been involved in anything so awful ever before, but there was no reason for him to be so rude to me. I was within my rights to ask what I did. I fail to understand how you can condone it, and maybe you really haven't. Maybe you aren't aware of the entire sordid mess, but how could you not be? You're in charge, and now that I have you on the phone, perhaps you can explain how it's fair or appropriate or even legal for someone in his position to be involved in this and have so much power."

The word *careful* flashes in my mind, as if there is a warning light in my head flashing neon-red.

"I'm sorry if you feel he was rude or unhelpful." I abide by my own warning and am careful. "You understand we can't discuss cases with . . ."

"Dr. Scarpetta." Sharp piano notes sound as if responding to her or the other way around. "I would never and I most assuredly did not," she says emotionally. "Will you excuse me while I turn this down? You probably don't know Valentina Lisitsa. If only I could just listen and not have all these other dreadful things banging in my head, like pots and pans banging in my head! My stationery, my typewriter. My son! Oh, God, oh, God." As the music stops. "I didn't ask Dr. Fielding prying questions about someone who was murdered, much less a child. If that's what he's told you I called about, it's absolutely untrue. Well, I'll just say it. A lie. A damn lie. I'm not surprised."

"You called wanting to speak to me," I say, because that's all I really know other than her claims to Bryce about Johnny and his innocence and allergies. She obviously has no idea I've not talked to Fielding, that no one has, it seems. And the more I downplay what she's saying or outright ignore it, the louder she'll get and the more she'll volunteer.

"Late last week," she says with energy. "Because you're in charge and I've gotten nowhere with Dr. Fielding, and of course you understand my concern, and this really is unacceptable if not criminal. So I wanted to complain, and I'm sorry about your coming home to that. When I realized who you are, that it wasn't some crank call, my first thought was it's about my filing a complaint with your office, not anything as official as I'm making it sound, at least not yet, although our lawyer certainly knows and the CFC's legal counsel certainly knows. And now maybe I won't need to file anything. It depends on what you and I agree upon."

Agree upon about what? I think but I don't ask. She knew I was coming home, and that doesn't fit with what she supposedly wrote to me, either. But it fits with a driver meeting me at Hanscom Field.

"What is in the letter? Can you read it to me? Why can't you?" she says again.

"Is it possible someone else in your family might have written to me on your stationery and borrowed your typewriter?" I suggest.

"And signed my name?"

I don't answer.

"I'm assuming I supposedly signed whatever you got or you'd have no reason to think it's from me other than an engraved address, which could be my husband, who unavoidably is in Japan on business, has been since Friday, although it is the most inopportune time to be away. He wouldn't write such a thing, anyway. Of course he wouldn't."

"The letter purports to be from you," I reply, and I don't tell her it is signed "Erica" above her name typed in cursive and that the envelope is addressed in an ornate script in the black ink of a fountain pen.

"This is very upsetting. I don't know why you won't read it to me. I have a right to

449

know what someone said as if they're me. I suppose our attorney will have to deal with you after all, the attorney representing Johnny, and I assume it's about him, this letter that's a lie, a fraud. Probably the dirty trick of the same ones who are behind all this. He was perfectly fine until he went there, and then he became Mr. Hyde, which is a harsh thing to say about your own child. But that's the only way I can think to say it so you understand how dramatically he was altered. Drugs. It must be, although the tests are negative, according to our lawyer, and Johnny would never take them. He knows better. He knows what thin ice he already skates on because of his unusualness. I don't know what else it could be except drugs, that somebody introduced him to something that changed him, that had a terrible effect, to deliberately destroy his life, to set him up. . . ."

She continues to talk without pause, getting increasingly upset, as a knock sounds on my outer door and someone tries the knob, then at the same time Bryce opens our adjoining door and I shake my head no at him. *Not now.* Then he whispers that Benton is at my door, and can he let him in? And I nod, and he shuts one door and another opens.

I put Mrs. Donahue's call on speaker-phone.

Benton closes the door behind him as I hold up the letter to indicate whom it is I'm talking to. He moves a chair close to me while Mrs. Donahue continues to speak, and I jot a note on a call sheet.

Says didn't write it — not her driver or Bentley.

". . . at that place," Mrs. Donahue's voice sounds inside my office as if she is in it.

Benton sits and has no reaction, and his face is pale, drained, and exhausted. He doesn't look well and smells of wood smoke.

"I've never been there because they don't allow visitors unless they have some special event for staff. . . ." her voice continues.

Benton picks up a pen and writes on the same call sheet *Otwahl?* But it seems perfunctory when he does it. He doesn't seem particularly curious.

"And then you have to go through security on a par with the White House, or maybe more extreme than that," Mrs. Donahue says, "not that I know it for a fact, but according to my son, who was frightened and a wreck the last few months he was there. Certainly since summer."

"What place are you talking about?" I ask her as I write another note to Benton.

451

Typewriter missing from her house.

He looks at the note and nods as if he already knew that Erica Donahue's old Olivetti manual typewriter is gone, possibly stolen, assuming what she's just told me is true. Or maybe he somehow knows she's told me this, and then it intrudes upon my thoughts that my office probably is bugged. Lucy's saying she has swept my office for covert surveillance devices likely means she planted them, and my attention wanders around the room, as if I might find tiny cameras or microphones hidden in books or pens or paperweights or the phone I'm talking on. It's ridiculous. If Lucy has bugged my office, I'm not going to know. More to the point, Fielding wouldn't know. I hope I catch him saying things to Captain Avallone, not realizing the two of them were being recorded secretly. I hope I catch both of them in the act of conspiring to ruin me, to run me out of the CFC.

". . . where he had his internship. That technology company that makes robots and things nobody is supposed to know about . . ." Mrs. Donahue is saying.

I watch Benton fold his hands in his lap, lacing his fingers as if he is placid when he's anything but low-key and relaxed. I know the language of how he sits or moves his

452

eyes and can read his restiveness in what seems the utter stillness of his body and mood. He is stressed-out and worn-out, but there is something else. Something has happened.

". . . Johnny had to sign contracts and all these legal agreements promising he wouldn't talk about Otwahl, not even what its name means. Can you imagine that? Not even something like that, what *Otwahl* means. But no wonder! What these damn people are up to. Huge secret contracts with the government, and greed. Enormous greed. So are you surprised things might be missing or people are being impersonated, their identities stolen?"

I have no idea what *Otwahl* means. I assumed it was the name of a person, the one who founded the company. Somebody Otwahl. I look at Benton. He is staring vacantly across the room, listening to Mrs. Donahue.

". . . Not about anything, certainly not what goes on, and anything he did there belongs to them and stays there." She is talking fast, and her voice no longer sounds as though it is coming from her diaphragm but from high up in her throat. "I'm terrified. Who are these people, and what have they done to my son?"

"What makes you think they've done

something to Johnny?" I ask her as Benton quietly, calmly writes a note on the call sheet, his mouth set in a firm, thin line, the way he looks when he gets like this.

"Because it can't be coincidental," she replies, and her voice reminds me of the cursive typeface of her old Olivetti. Something elegant that is deteriorating, fading, less distinct and slightly bleary. "He was fine and then he wasn't, and now he's locked up at a psychiatric hospital and confessing to a crime he didn't commit. And now this," she says hoarsely, clearing her throat. "A letter on my stationery or what looks like my stationery, and of course it's not from me and I have no idea who delivered it to you. And my typewriter is gone. . . ."

Benton slides the call sheet to me, and I read what he wrote in his legible hand.

We know about it.

I look at him and frown. I don't understand.

". . . Why would they want him accused of something he didn't do, and how have they managed to brainwash him into thinking he murdered that child?" Mrs. Donahue then says yet again, "Drugs. I can only assume drugs. Maybe one of them killed that little boy and they need someone as a scapegoat. And there was my poor Johnny, who is gullible, who doesn't read situations the way others do. What better person to pick on than a teenager with Asperger's. . . ."

I am staring at Benton's note. *We know about it.* As though if I read it more than once I'll comprehend what it is he knows about or what it is that he and his invisible others, these entities he refers to as "we," know about. But as I sit here, concentrating on Mrs. Donahue and trying to decipher what she is truly conveying while I cautiously extract information from her, I have the feeling Benton isn't really listening. He seems barely interested, isn't his typically keen self. What I detect is he wants me to end the call and leave with him, as if something is over with and it's just a matter of finishing what has already ended, just a matter of tying up loose ends, of cleaning up. It is the way he used to act when a case had wrung him out for months or years and finally was solved or dropped or the jury reached a verdict, and suddenly everything stopped and he was left harried but spent and depressed.

"You started noticing the difference in your son when?" I'm not going to quit now, no matter what Benton knows or how spent he is.

"July, August. Then by September for sure. He started his internship with Otwahl last May."

"Mark Bishop was killed January thirtieth." It is as close as I dare come to pointing out the obvious, that what she continues to claim about her son being framed doesn't make sense, the timing doesn't.

If his personality began changing last summer when he was working at Otwahl and yet Mark Bishop wasn't murdered until January 30, what she's suggesting would mean someone programmed Johnny to take the blame for a murder that hadn't happened yet and wouldn't happen for many months. The Mark Bishop case doesn't fit with something meticulously planned but as a senseless and sadistic violent attack on a little boy who was at home, playing in his yard, on a weekend late afternoon as it was getting dark and no one was looking. It strikes me as a crime of opportunity, a thrill kill, the evil game of a predator, possibly one with pedophilic proclivities. It wasn't an assassination. It wasn't the black-ops takeout of a terrorist. I don't believe his death was premeditated and executed with a very certain goal in mind, such as national security or political power or money.

". . . People who don't understand Asperger's assume those who have it are violent, are almost nonhuman, don't feel the same things the rest of us do or don't feel anything. People assume all sorts of things because of what I call *unusualness,* not sickness or derangement but unusual. That's the disadvantage I mean." Mrs. Donahue is talking rapidly and with no ordered sequence to her thoughts. "You point out behavior changes that are alarming and other people think it's just him. Just Johnny because of his unusualness, which is a sad disadvantage, as if he needed yet one more disadvantage. Well, that's not what this is, not about his unusualness. Something horrific got started when he did at that place, at Otwahl last May. . . ."

It also enters my mind what Benton mentioned hours earlier, that Mark Bishop's death might be connected to others: the football player from BC, who was found in the Boston Harbor last November, and possibly the man who was murdered in Norton's Woods. If Benton is right, then Johnny Donahue would have to be framed for all three of these homicides, and how could he be? He was an inpatient at McLean when the killing occurred in Norton's Woods, for example. I know he couldn't have committed that homicide, and I fail to see how he could be set up to take the blame for it unless he wasn't on the hospital ward, unless he was on the loose and armed with an injection knife.

Benton writes another note. *We need to go.* And he underlines it.

"Mrs. Donahue, is your son on any medications?" I ask.

"Not really."

"Prescription or perhaps over-the-counter medications?" I inquire without being pushy, and it requires effort on my part, because my patience is frayed. "Maybe you can tell me anything at all he might have been taking before he was hospitalized or any other medical problems he might have."

I almost say "might have had," as if he is dead.

"Well, a nasal spray. Especially of late."

Benton raises his hands palms up as if to say *This isn't news.* He knows about Johnny's medication. His patience is frayed, too, and signs of it are breaking through his imperviousness. He wants me to get off the phone and to go with him right now.

"Why of late? Was he having respiratory problems? Allergies? Asthma?" I ask as I pull a pair of gloves out of the dispenser and hand them to Benton. Then I give him the manila envelope containing the ring.

458

"Animal dander, pollens, dust, gluten, you name it, he's allergic, has been treated by allergists most of his life. He was doing fine until late summer, and then nothing seemed to work very well anymore. It was a very bad season for pollens, and stress makes things worse, and he was increasingly stressed," she says. "He did start using a spray again that has a type of cortisone in it. The name just fled from me. . . ."

"Corticosteroid?"

"Yes. That's it. And I've wondered about it in terms of it affecting his moods, his behavior. Things such as insomnia, ups and downs, and irritability, which, as you know, became extreme, culminating in him having blackouts and delusions, and ultimately our hospitalizing him."

"He started using it again? So he's used the corticosteroid spray before?"

"Certainly, over the years. But not since he started a new treatment, which meant he didn't need shots anymore. For about a year it was like a magical cure; then he got bad again and resumed the nasal spray."

"Tell me about the new treatment."

"I'm sure you're familiar with drops under the tongue."

I'm aware that sublingual immunotherapy has yet to be approved by the FDA, and I ask, "Is your son part of a clinical trial?" I scribble another note to Benton.

Spray and drops to the labs stat. And I underlined *stat,* which means *statim,* or immediately.

"That's right, through his allergist."

I look at Benton to see if he knows about this, and he glances at my note as he puts on the gloves, and next he glances at his watch. He's going to look at the ring only because I asked him to. It's as if he's already seen it or already knows it isn't important or has his mind made up. Something has ended. Something has happened.

". . . What's called an off-label use that his doctor supervises, but no more trips to his office for shots every week," Mrs. Donahue says, and she seems momentarily soothed as she talks about her son's allergies instead of everything else, her pain in remission, but it won't last.

If someone has tampered with Johnny's medications, it might explain why his allergies got bad again. What he was placing under his tongue or spraying up his nose might have been sufficiently altered chemically to render the medications ineffective, not to mention extremely harmful. I look at Benton as he examines the signet ring. He has no expression on his face. I hold up a sheet of stationery so he can see the water-mark. He has no visible reaction, and I notice a cobweb in his hair. I reach over and remove it, and he returns the ring to the envelope. He meets my eyes and widens them the way he does at parties and dinners when he's telegraphing *Let's go now.*

". . . Johnny takes several drops under his tongue daily, and for a while had excellent results. Then it stopped working as well, and he's been miserable at times. This past August he resumed the spray but only seemed to get worse, and along with it were these very disturbing changes in his personality. They were noted by others, and he did get in trouble for acting out, was kicked out of that class, as you know, but he wouldn't have harmed that child. I don't think Johnny was even aware of him, much less would do something. . . ."

Benton takes off the gloves and drops them in the trash. I point at the envelope, and he shakes his head. *Don't ask Mrs. Donahue about the ring.* He doesn't want me to mention it, or maybe it isn't necessary for me to bring it up to her because of what Benton knows that I don't, and then I notice his black tactical boots. They are covered with gray dust that wasn't there earlier when we were talking in Fielding's office. The legs of his black tactical pants also are quite dusty, and the sleeves of his shearling coat are dirty, as if he brushed up against something.

". . . It was the main thing I wanted to ask, more of a personal matter directed at him as a man who teaches martial arts and is supposed to abide by a code of honor," Mrs. Donahue says, grabbing my attention back, and I wonder if I've misunderstood her. I can't possibly have heard what I just did. "It was that more than the other, not at all what you assumed or what he told you. Lying, I'm sure, because as I've said, if he claims I called him to ask for details about what was done to that poor child, then he was lying. I promise I didn't ask about Mark Bishop, who wasn't known to us personally, by the way. We only saw him there sometimes. I didn't ask for information about him. . . ."

"Mrs. Donahue, I'm sorry. You're cutting in and out." It's not really true, but I need her to repeat what she said and to clarify.

"These portable phones. Is this better? I'm sorry. I'm pacing as I talk, pacing all over the house."

"Thank you. Could you please repeat the last few things you said? What about martial arts?"

I listen with another jolt of disbelief as she reminds me of what she assumes I know, that her son Johnny is acquainted with Jack Fielding through tae kwon do. When she called this office several times to talk to Fielding and eventually to complain to me, it is because of this relationship. Fielding was Johnny's instructor at the Cambridge Tae Kwon Do Club. Fielding was Mark Bishop's instructor, taught a class of Tiny Tigers, but Johnny didn't know Mark, and certainly they weren't in the same class, weren't taught together, Mrs. Donahue is adamant about that, and I ask her when Johnny started taking lessons. I tell her I'm not sure about the details and must have an accurate account if I'm to deal appropriately and fairly with her complaint about my deputy chief.

"He's been taking lessons since last May," Mrs. Donahue says while my thoughts scatter and bounce like caroms. "You can understand why my son, who's never really had friends, would be easily influenced by someone he adores and respects. . . ."

"Adores and respects? Do you mean Dr. Fielding?"

"No, not hardly," she says acidly, as if she truly hates the man. "His friend was involved in it first, has been for quite some time. Apparently, a number of women are quite serious about tae kwon do, and when she began working with Johnny and they became friends, she encouraged him, and I wish he hadn't listened. That and, of course, Otwahl, that place and whatever goes on there, and look what's happened. But you can certainly imagine why Johnny would want to be powerful and able to protect himself, to feel less picked on and alone when the irony, of course, is that those days for him really were gone. He wasn't bullied at Harvard. . . ."

She goes on, rambling and less crisp and commanding now, and her despair is palpable. I can feel it in the air inside my office as I get up from my desk.

". . . How dare him. That certainly constitutes a violation of his medical oath if anything does. How dare him continue to be in charge of the Mark Bishop case in light of what we all know the truth is," she says.

"Can you be specific about what truth you're referring to?" I look out my windows at the blindingly bright morning. The sun and the glare are so intense, my eyes water.

"His bias." Her voice sounds behind me, on speakerphone. "He's never been fond of Johnny or particularly nice to him, would make tactless comments to him in front of the others. Things such as 'You need to look at me when I'm talking to you instead of at the goddamn light switch.' Well, as I'm sure you're aware, because of Johnny's unusualness, his attention gets caught up on things that don't make sense to others. He has poor eye contact and can be offensive because people don't understand it's just the way his brain works. Do you know much about Asperger's, or has your husband . . ."

"I don't know much." I don't intend to get into what Benton has or hasn't told me.

"Well, Johnny gets fixated on a detail of no significance to anyone else and will stare at it while you're talking to him. I'll be telling him something important and he's looking at a brooch or a bracelet I'm wearing, or he makes a comment or laughs when he shouldn't. And Dr. Fielding berated him about laughing inappropriately. He belittled him in front of everyone, and that's when Johnny tried to kick him. Here this man has however many degrees of a black belt someone can have, and my son, who weighs all of a hundred and forty pounds, tried to kick him, and that was when he was forced to leave the class for good. Dr. Fielding forbade him from ever coming back and threatened to blackball him if he tried to take lessons anywhere else."

"When was this?" I hear myself as if I'm someone else speaking.

"The second week of December. I have the exact date. I have everything written down."

Six weeks before Mark Bishop was murdered, I think, dazed, as if I'm the one who has been kicked. "And you suggested to Dr. Fielding —" I start to say to the phone on my desk as if I'm looking at Mrs. Donahue and she can see me.

"I certainly did!" she says excitedly, defiantly. "When Johnny started babbling his nonsense about having killed that boy during a blackout and that their tae kwon do instructor did the autopsy! Can you imagine my reaction?"

Their tae kwon do instructor. Who else is she referring to? Johnny's MIT friend, or are there others? Who else might Fielding have been teaching, and what could have caused Johnny Donahue to confess to a murder Benton believes he didn't commit? Why would Johnny think he did something so horrific during a so-called blackout? Who influenced him to the extent he would admit to it and offer details such as the weapon being a nail gun when I know for a fact that isn't true? But I'm not going to ask Mrs.

Donahue anything else. I've gone too far; everything has gone too far. I've asked her more than I should, and Benton already knows the answers to anything I might think of. I can tell by the way he's sitting in his chair, staring down at the floor, his face as hard and dark as my building's metal skin.

18

I hang up the phone and stand before my curved wall of glass, looking out at a patchwork of slate tiles and snow punctuated by church steeples stretching out before me in the kingdom of CFC.

I wait for my heart to slow and my emotions to settle, swallowing hard to push the pain and anger back down my throat, distracting myself with the view of MIT, and beyond it, Harvard and beyond. As I stand inside my empire of many windows and look out at what I'm supposed to manage if the worst happens to people, I understand. I understand why Benton is acting the way he is. I understand what has ended. Jack Fielding has.

I vaguely remember him mentioning not long after he moved here from Chicago that he had volunteered at some tae kwon do club and couldn't always be available to do cases on weekends or after hours because of his dedication to teaching what he referred to as his art, his passion. On occasion he would be gone to tournaments, he told me, and he assumed he would be granted "flexibility." As acting chief during my long absences, he expected flexibility, he reiterated, almost lecturing me. The same flexibility I would have if I were here, he stated, as if it was a known fact that I have flexibility when I'm home.

I remember being put off by his demands, since he's the one who called me asking for a job at the CFC, and the position I foolishly agreed to give him far surpasses any he's ever had. In Chicago he wasn't afforded much status, was one of six medical examiners and not in line for a promotion of any kind, his chief confided in me when we spoke of my hiring Fielding away from there. It would be a tremendous professional opportunity and good for him personally to be around family, the chief said, and I was deeply moved that Fielding thought of me as family. I was pleased that he had missed me and wanted to come back to Massachusetts, to work for me like in the old days.

And the irony that should have infuriated me, and one I certainly should have pointed out to Fielding instead of indulging him as usual, was this notion of flexibility, as if I come and go as I please, as if I take vacations and run off to tournaments and disappear several weekends each month because of some art or passion I have beyond what I do in my profession, beyond what I do every damn day. My passion is what I live every damn day, and the deaths I take care of every damn day and the people the deaths leave behind and how they pick up and go on, and how I help them somehow do that. I hear myself and realize I've been saying these things out loud, and I feel Benton's hands on my shoulders as he stands behind me while I wipe tears from my eyes. He rests his chin on top of my head and wraps his arms around me.

"What have I done?" I say to him.

"You've put up with a lot from him, with way too much, but it's not you who's done anything. Whatever he was on, was taking and probably dealing . . . Well. You had a brush with it earlier, so you can imagine." He means whatever drugs Fielding might have used to saturate his pain-relieving patches, and whatever drugs he might have been selling.

"Have you found him?" I ask.

"Yes."

"He's in custody? He's been arrested? Or

you're just questioning him?"

"We have him, Kay."

"I suppose it's best." I don't know what else to ask except how Fielding is doing, which Benton doesn't answer.

I wonder if Fielding had to be placed in a four-point restraint or maybe in a padded room, and I can't imagine him in captivity. I can't imagine him in prison. He won't last. He will bat himself to death against bars like a panicked moth if someone doesn't kill him first. It also crosses my mind that he is dead. Then it feels he is. The feeling settles numbly, heavily, as if I've been given a nerve block.

"We need to head out. I'll explain as best I can, as best we know. It's complicated; it's a lot," I hear Benton say.

He moves away, no longer touching me, and it is as if there is nothing holding me here and I will float out the window, and at the same time, there is the heaviness. I feel I've turned into metal or stone, into something no longer alive or human.

"I couldn't let you know earlier as it became clear, not that all of it is clear yet," Benton says. "I'm sorry when I have to keep things from you, Kay."

"Why would he, why would anyone . . . ?" I start to ask questions that can never be answered satisfactorily, the same questions I've always asked. Why are people cruel? Why do they kill? Why do they take pleasure in ruining others?

"Because he could." Benton says what he always does.

"But why would he?" Fielding isn't like that. He's never been diabolical. Immature and selfish and dysfunctional, yes. But not evil. He wouldn't kill a six-year-old boy for fun and then enjoy pinning the crime on a teenager with Asperger's. Fielding's not equipped to orchestrate a cold-blooded game like that.

"Money. Control. His addictions. Righting wrongs that go back to the beginning of his time. And decompensating. Ultimately destroying himself because that's who he was really destroying when he destroyed others." Benton has it all figured out. Everybody has it figured out except me.

"I don't know," I mutter, and I tell myself to be strong. I have to take care of this. I can't help Fielding, I can't help anyone, if I'm not strong.

"He didn't hide things well," Benton then says as I move away from the window. "Once we figured out where to look, it's become increasingly obvious."

Someone setting people up, setting up

everything. That's why it's not hidden well. That's why it's obvious. It's supposed to be obvious, to make us think certain things are true when maybe they aren't. I won't accept that the person behind all this is Fielding until I see it for myself. *Be strong. You must take care of it. Don't cry over him or anyone. You can't.*

"What do I need to bring?" I collect my coat off a chair, the tactical jacket from Dover that isn't nearly warm enough.

"We have everything there," he says. "Just your credentials in case someone asks."

Of course they have everything there. Everything and everyone is there except me. I collect my shoulder bag from the back of my door.

"When did you figure it out?" I ask. "Figure it out enough to get warrants to find him? Or however it's happened?"

"When you discovered the man from Norton's Woods was a homicide, that changed things, to say the least. Now Fielding was connected to another murder."

"I don't see how," I reply as we walk out together, and I don't tell Bryce I'm leaving. At the moment I don't want to face anyone. I'm in no mood to chat or to be cordial or even civilized.

"Because the Glock had disappeared from

the firearms lab. I know you haven't been told about that, and very few people are aware of it," Benton says.

I remember Lucy's comments about seeing Morrow in the back parking lot at around ten-thirty yesterday morning, about a half hour after the pistol was receipted to him in his lab, and he couldn't be bothered with it, according to Lucy. If she knew about the missing Glock, she withheld that crucial information, and I ask Benton if she deliberately lied by omission to me, the chief, her boss.

"Because she works here," I say as we wait for the elevator to climb to our floor. It is stuck on the lower level, as if someone is holding open the door down there, what staff members sometimes do when they are loading a lot of things on or off. "She works for me and can't just keep information from me. She can't lie to me."

"She wasn't aware of it then. Marino and I knew, and we didn't tell her."

"And you knew about Jack and Johnny and Mark. About tae kwon do." I'm sure Benton did. Probably Marino, too.

"We've been watching Jack, been looking into it. Yes. Since Mark was murdered last week and I found out Jack taught him and Johnny."

474

I think of the photographs missing from Fielding's office, the tiny holes in the wall from the hanging hooks being removed.

"It began to make sense that Jack took control of certain cases. The Mark Bishop case, for example, even though he hates to do kids," Benton goes on, looking around, making sure no one is nearby to overhear us. "What a perfect opportunity to cover up your own crimes."

Or some other person's crimes, I think. Fielding would be the sort to cover for someone else. He desperately needs to be powerful, to be the hero, and then I remind myself to stop defending him. *Don't unless you have proof.* Whatever turns out to be true, I'll accept it, and it occurs to me that the photographs missing from Fielding's office might have been group poses. That seems familiar. I can almost envision them. Perhaps of tae kwon do classes. Pictures with Johnny and Mark in them.

I wonder but don't ask if Benton removed those photographs or if Marino did, as Benton continues to explain that Fielding went to great lengths to manipulate everyone into believing that Johnny Donahue killed Mark Bishop. Fielding used a compromised, vulnerable teenager as a scapegoat, and then Fielding had to escalate his manipulations further after he took out the man from Norton's Woods. That's the phrase Benton uses. *Took out.* Fielding took him out and then heard about the Glock found on the body and realized he'd made a serious tactical error. Everything was falling apart. He was losing it, decompensating like Ted Bundy did right before he was caught, Benton says.

"Jack's fatal mistake was to stop by the firearms lab yesterday morning and ask Morrow about the Glock," Benton continues. "A little later it was gone and so was Jack, and that was impulsive and reckless and just damn stupid on his part. It would have been better to let the gun be traced to him and claim it was lost or stolen. Anything would have been better than what he did. It shows how out of control he was to take the damn gun from the lab."

"You're saying the Glock the man from Norton's Woods had is Jack's."

"Yes."

"It's definitely Jack's," I repeat, and the elevator is moving now, making a lot of stops on its way up, and I realize it is lunchtime. Employees heading to the break room or heading out of the building.

"Yes. The dead man has a gun that could be traced to Fielding once acid was used on

476

the drilled-off serial number," Benton says, and it's clear to me that he knows who the dead man is.

"That was done. Not here." I don't want to think of yet something else done inside my building that I didn't know.

"Hours ago. At the scene. We took care of the identification right there."

"The FBI did."

"It was important to know immediately who the gun was traced to. To confirm our suspicions. Then it came here to the CFC and is safely locked up in the firearms lab. For further examination," Benton says.

"If Jack is the one who murdered him, he should have realized the problem with the Glock when he first was called about the case on Sunday afternoon," I reply. "Yet he waited until Monday morning to be concerned about a gun he knew could be traced to him?"

"To avoid suspicion. If he'd started asking the Cambridge police a lot of questions about the Glock prior to the body being transported to the CFC, or demanded that the gun be brought in immediately when the labs were closed, it would have come across as peculiar. Antennas would have gone up. Fielding slept on it and by Monday morning was probably beside himself and planning what he was going to do once the gun was brought in. He would take it and flee. Remember, he hasn't been exactly rational. It's important to keep in mind he's been cognitively impaired by his substance abuse."

I think about the chronology. I reconstruct Fielding's steps yesterday morning, based on information from his desk drawer and the indented writing on his call-sheet pad. Shortly after seven a.m. it seems he talked to Julia Gabriel before she called me at Dover, and about a half hour later he entered the cooler, and minutes after that he told Anne and Ollie the body from Norton's Woods was inexplicably bloody. It seems more logical to consider it was at this point that Fielding recognized the dead man and realized the Glock he'd heard about from the police would be traced to him. If he didn't recognize the dead man until Monday morning, then Fielding didn't kill him, I say to Benton, who replies that Fielding had a motive I couldn't possibly know about.

The dead man's stepfather is Liam Saltz, Benton informs me. It was confirmed a little while ago when an FBI agent went to the Charles Hotel and talked to Dr. Saltz and showed him an ID photograph Marino took of the man from Norton's Woods. He was Eli Goldman, age twenty-two, a graduate student at MIT and an employee at Otwahl Technologies, working on special micromechanical projects. The video clips from Eli's headphones were traced to a webcam site on Otwahl's server, Benton tells me, but he won't elaborate on who did the tracing, if Lucy might have.

"He rigged up the headphones himself?" I ask as the elevator finally gets to us and the doors slide open.

"It appears likely. He loved to tinker."

"And MORT? How did he get that? And what for? More tinkering?" I know I sound cynical.

I know when people have their damn minds made up, and I'm not ready for my mind to be made up. Not one damn thing should be decided this fast.

"A facsimile, a model he made as a boy," Benton explains. "Based on photographs his stepfather had taken of the real thing when he was lobbying against it some eight or nine years ago when you and Dr. Saltz testified before the Senate subcommittee. Apparently, Eli was making models of robots and inventing things since he was practically in diapers."

We slowly sink from floor to floor while I

479

ask why Otwahl would hire the stepson of a detractor like Liam Saltz, and I want to know what Otwahl means, because Mrs. Donahue said the name meant something. "O. T. Wahl," Benton replies. "A play on words, because the last name of the company's founder is Wahl. *On the Wall,* as in a fly on the wall, and Eli's last name isn't Saltz," Benton adds, as if I didn't hear him when he told me it's Goldman. Eli Goldman. But Otwahl would have done a background check on him, I point out. Certainly they would have known who his stepfather is, even if their last names aren't the same.

"MORT was a long time ago," Benton says as the elevator doors open on the lower floor. "And I don't know that Otwahl had a clue Eli and his stepdad were philosophically simpatico."

"How long had Eli worked there?"

"Three years."

"Maybe three years ago Otwahl wasn't doing anything that Eli or his stepfather would have been concerned about," I suggest as we walk along gray tile while Phil the security guard watches us from behind his glass partition. I don't wave at him. I'm not friendly.

"Well, Eli was worried and had been for months," Benton says. "He was about to give his stepfather a demonstration of technology that he wasn't going to approve of at all, a fly that could be a fly on the wall and spy and detect explosives and deliver them or drugs or poisons or who knows what."

Nanoexplosives or dangerous drugs delivered by something as small as a fly, I think, as we walk past staff I've not seen in months. I don't stop to chat. I don't wave or say hello or even have eye contact.

"He's about to give his stepfather important information like that and conveniently dies," I reply.

"Exactly. The motive I mentioned," Benton says. "Drugs," he says again, and then he tells me more, gives me details the FBI learned from Liam Saltz just a few hours earlier.

I feel sad and upset again as I envision what Benton is saying about a young man so enamored of his famous stepfather that whenever they were to see each other, Eli always set his watch to it, mirroring Dr. Saltz's time zone in anticipation of their reunion, a quirk that has its roots in Eli's poignant past of broken homes and parental figures missing in action and adored from afar. I remember what I watched on the video clips, Eli and Sock walking to

481

Norton's Woods, and then I imagine Dr. Saltz emerging from the building in the near dark after a wedding Eli wasn't invited to. I imagine the Nobel laureate looking around and wondering where his stepson was, having no idea of the terrible truth. Dead. Zipped up inside a pouch and unidentified. A young man, barely more than a boy. Someone Lucy and I may have crossed paths with at an exhibit in London the summer of 2001.

"Who killed him, and what for?" I say as we pass through the empty bay, the CFC van-body truck gone. "I don't see how what you've just said explains Eli being murdered by Jack."

"It all points in the same direction. I'm sorry. But it does."

"I just don't see why and for what." I open the door leading outside, and it is too beautiful and sunny to be so cold.

"I know this is hard," Benton says.

"A pair of data gloves?" I say as we begin to pick our way over snow that is glazed and slick. "A micromechanical fly? Who would stab him with an injection knife, and why?"

"Drugs." Benton goes back to that again. "Somehow Eli had the misfortune of getting involved with Jack or the other way around. Strength-enhancing, very dangerous drugs. Probably was using and selling, and Eli was the supplier, or someone at Otwahl was. We don't know. But Eli being killed while he was out there with a flybot and about to meet his stepfather wasn't a coincidence. It's the motive, I mean."

"Why would Jack be interested in a flybot or a meeting?" I ask as we move very slowly, one step at a time, my feet about to go out from under me. "A damn ice-skating rink," I complain, because the parking lot wasn't plowed and it needs to be sanded. Nobody has been running this place the way it ought to be run.

"I'm sorry, we're way over here." We head slowly toward the back fence. "But that's all there was. The drug connection," Benton then says. "Not street drugs. This is about Otwahl. About a huge amount of money. About the war, about potential violence on an international and massive scale."

"Then if what you're saying is right, it would seem to imply Jack was spying on Eli. Rigged up the headphones with hidden recording devices and followed him to Norton's Woods. That would make sense if the murder was to stop Eli from showing his stepfather the flybot or turning it over to him. How else would Jack know what Eli was about to do? He must have been spying on him, or someone was."

"I doubt Jack had anything to do with the headphones."

"My point exactly. Jack wouldn't be interested in technology like that or capable of it, and he wouldn't be interested in a place like Otwahl. You're not talking about the Jack I know. He's much too limbically driven, too impatient, too simple, to do what you've just described." I almost say *too primitive,* because that has always been part of his charm. His physicality, his hedonism, his linear way of coping with things. "And the headphones don't make sense," I insist. "The headphones make me think someone else might be involved."

"I understand how you feel. I can understand why you'd want to think that."

"And did Dr. Saltz know his adoring stepson was into drugs and had an illegal gun?" I ask. "Did he happen to mention the headphones or other people Eli might have been involved with?"

"He knew nothing about the headphones and not much about Eli's personal life. Only that Eli was worried about his safety. As I said, he'd been worried for months. I know this is painful, Kay."

"Worried about what, specifically?" I ask as we walk very slowly, and someone is going to get hurt out here. Someone is going to slip and break bones and sue the CFC. That will be next.

"Eli was involved in dangerous projects and surrounded by bad people. That's how Dr. Saltz described it," Benton says. "It's a lot to explain and not what you might imagine."

"He knew his stepson had a gun, an illegal one," I repeat my question.

"He didn't know that. I assume Eli wouldn't have mentioned it."

"Everyone seems to be doing a lot of assuming." I stop and look at Benton, our breath smoking out in the brightness and the cold, and we are at the back of the parking lot now, near the fence, in what I call the hinterlands.

"Eli would know how Dr. Saltz feels about guns," Benton says. "Jack probably sold the Glock to him or gave it to him."

"Or someone did," I reiterate. "Just as someone must have given him the signet ring with the Donahue crest on it. I don't suppose Eli was also involved in tae kwon do." I look around at SUVs that don't belong to the CFC, but I don't look at the agents inside them. I don't look at anyone as I shield my eyes from the sun.

"No," Benton answers. "The football

player wasn't, either, Wally Jamison, but he used the gym where they're held, used Jack's same gym. Maybe Eli had been to that gym, too."

"Eli doesn't look like someone who uses a gym. Hardly a muscle in his body," I comment as Benton points a key fob at a black Ford Explorer that isn't his and the doors unlock with a chirp. "And if Jack killed him, why?" I again ask, because it makes no sense to me, but maybe it's my fatigue. No sleep and too much trauma, and I'm too tired to comprehend the simplest thing.

"Or maybe the connection has to do with Otwahl and Johnny Donahue and other illegal activities Jack was involved in that you're about to find out. What he was doing at the CFC, how he was earning his money while you were gone." Benton's voice is hard as he says all that while opening my door for me. "Don't know everything but enough, and you were right to ask what Mark Bishop was doing in his backyard when he was killed. What kind of playing he was doing. I almost couldn't believe it when you asked me that, and I couldn't tell you when you asked. Mark was in one of Jack's classes, as Mrs. Donahue implied, for three- to six-year-olds, had just started in December and was practicing tae kwon do in his yard when someone, and I think we know who, appeared, and again, you're probably right about how it happened."

As he goes around to the driver's side to get in, and I dig in my bag for my sunglasses, impatient and frustrated as a lipstick, pens, and a tube of hand cream spill on the plastic floor mat. I must have left my sunglasses somewhere. Maybe in my office at Dover, where I can scarcely remember being anymore. It seems like forever ago, and right now I am sickened beyond what I could possibly describe to anyone, and it doesn't please me to hear I was right about anything. I don't give a damn who is right, just that someone is, and I don't think anybody is. I just don't believe it.

"A person Mark had no reason to distrust, such as his instructor, who lured him into a fantasy, a game, and murdered him," Benton goes on as he starts the SUV. "And then trumped up a way to blame it on Johnny."

"I didn't say that part." I stuff items back into my bag as I grab my shoulder harness and fasten up, then I decide to take my jacket off, and I undo the seat belt.

"What part?" Benton enters an address in the GPS.

"I never said Jack trumped up a way to make Johnny believe he drove nails into

Mark Bishop's head," I reply, and the SUV is warm from when Benton drove it here, and the sun is hot as it blazes through glass.

I take off my jacket and toss it in back, where there is a large, thick box with a FedEx label. I can't tell whom it is for and I'm not interested, probably some agent Benton knows, probably whoever Douglas is, and I suppose I'll find out soon enough. I fasten my shoulder harness again, working so hard I'm practically out of breath, and my heart is pounding.

"I didn't mean that part was from you. There are a lot of questions. We need you to help us answer everything we possibly can," Benton says.

We begin backing up, pulling out of my parking lot, waiting for the gate to open, and I feel handled. I feel humored. I'm not sure I remember ever feeling so nonessential in an investigation, as if I'm an obstruction and a nuisance people have to be politically correct with because of my position, but not taken seriously and unwanted.

"I thought I'd seen it all. I'm warning you, it's bad, Kay." Benton's voice has no energy as he says that. It sounds hollow, like something gutted.

19

The gray frame house with the old stone foundation and a cold cellar in back were built by a sea captain in centuries past. The property is scrubbed and eroded by harsh weather, directly exposed to what blows in from the sea, and sits alone at the end of a narrow, icy street coarsely sanded by city emergency crews. Where branches have snapped, ice is shattered on the frozen earth and sparkles like broken glass in a high sun that offers no warmth, only a blinding glare.

Sand makes a gritty sound against the underside of the SUV while Benton drives very slowly, looking for a place to park, and I look out at the brightness of the sandy road and the heaving deep blue of the sea and the paler blue of the cloudless sky. I no longer feel the need for sleep or that I could if I tried. Having last gotten up at quarter of five yesterday morning in Delaware, I have been awake some thirty hours since, which isn't unheard of for me, isn't really remarkable if I pause to calculate how often it happens in a profession where people don't have the common courtesy to kill or to die during business hours. But this is a different type of sleeplessness, foreign and unfamiliar, with the added excitement bordering on hysteria from being told, or having it implied at least, that I've lived much of my life with something deadly and I'm the reason it turned deadly.

No one is stating such a thing in exactly those words, but I know it to be true. Benton is diplomatic, but I know. He's not said it's my fault people are brutally dead and countless others have been disrespected and defiled, not to mention those harmed by drugs, people whose names we may never know, guinea pigs or "lab rats," as Benton put it, for a malevolent science project involving a potent form of anabolic steroid or testosterone laced with a hallucinogenic to build strength and muscle mass and enhance aggression and fearlessness. To create killing machines, to turn human beings into monstrosities with no frontal cortex, no concept of consequences, human robots that savagely kill and feel no remorse, feel virtually nothing at all, including pain. Benton has been describing what

Liam Saltz told the FBI this morning, the poor man bereft and terrified.

Dr. Saltz suspects Eli got involved with a treacherous and unauthorized technology at Otwahl, found himself in the midst of DARPA research gone bad, gone frighteningly wrong, and was about to warn his humanitarian Nobel laureate stepfather and to offer proof and to beg him to put a stop to it. Fielding put a stop to Eli because Fielding was using these dangerous drugs, perhaps helping to distribute them, but mostly my deputy chief with his lifelong lust for strength and physical beauty and his chronic aches and pains was addicted. That's the theory behind Fielding's vile crimes, and I don't believe it is that simple or even true. But I do believe other comments Benton has continued to make. I was too good to Fielding. I've always been too good to him. I've never seen him for what he is or accepted his potential to do real harm, and therefore I enabled him.

Snow turned to freezing rain where the ocean warms the air, and the power is still out from downed lines in this area of Salem Neck called Winter Island, where Jack Fielding owns a historic investment property I had no idea about. To get to it you have to pass the Plummer Home for Boys, a lovely mossy green mansion set on a gracious spread of lawn overlooking the sea, with a distant view of the wealthy resort community of Marblehead. I can't help but think about the way things begin and end, the way people have a tendency to run in place, to tread water, to really not get beyond where and how it all started for them.

Fielding stopped his life where it took off for him so precipitously, in a picturesque setting for troubled youths who can no longer live with their families. I wonder if it was deliberate to pick a spot no more than a stone's throw from a boys' home, if that factored into his subconscious when he decided on a property I'm told he intended to retire to or perhaps sell for a profit in the future when the real-estate market turns around and after he'd finished much-needed improvements. He'd been doing the work on the house and its outbuilding himself and doing it poorly, and I'm about to see the manifestation of his disorganized, chaotic mind, the handiwork of someone profoundly out of control, Benton has let me know. I'm about to see the way my enabled protégé lived and ended.

"Are you still with us? I know you're tired," Benton says as he touches my arm.

"I'm fine." I realize he's been talking and I tuned him out.

"You don't look fine. You're still crying."

"I'm not crying. It's the sun. I can't believe I left my sunglasses somewhere."

"I've said you can have mine." His dark glasses turn toward me as he creeps along the sandy, gritty-sounding road in the glaring sun.

"No, thank you."

"Why don't you tell me what's going on with you, because we're not going to have a chance to talk for a while," he says. "You're angry with me."

"You're just doing your job, whatever it is."

"You're angry with me because you're angry at Jack, and you're afraid to be angry at him."

"I'm not afraid of what I feel about him. I'm more afraid of everyone else," I reply.

"Meaning what, exactly?"

"It's something I sense, and you don't agree with me, so we should leave it at that," I say to him as I look out the window at the cold, blue ocean and the distant horizon, where I can make out houses on the shore.

"Maybe you could be a little more specific. What do you sense? Is this a new thought?"

"It isn't. And it's nothing anybody wants

to hear," I answer him as I stare out at the bright afternoon while we continue to troll for a place to park.

I'm not really helping him look for a spot. Mostly I'm sitting and staring out the window while my mind goes where it wants to, like a small animal darting about, looking for a safe place. Benton probably thinks I'm pretty useless. He's aided and abetted my uselessness by waiting this long to come get me for something that's been going on for hours. I'm showing up in medias res, as if this is a musical or an opera and it's no big deal for me to wander in during the middle or toward the end, depending on which act we're in.

"Christ, this is ridiculous. You would think someone would have left us something. I should have had Marino put cones out, save us something." Benton vents his anger at parked cars and the narrow street, then says to me, "I want to hear whatever it is. New thought or not. Now, while we have a minute alone."

There is no point in saying the rest of it, of telling him again what I sense, which is a calculating, cruel logic behind what was done to Wally Jamison, Mark Bishop, and Eli Goldman, behind what happened to Fielding, behind everything, a precisely

494

formulated agenda, even if it didn't turn out as planned. Not that I know the plan in its entirety, maybe not even most of it, but what I sense is palpable and undeniable, and I won't be talked out of it. *Trust your instincts. Don't trust anything else. This is about power. The power to control people, to make them feel good or frightened or to suffer unbearably. Power over life and death.* I'm not going to repeat what I'm sure sounds irrational. I'm not going to tell Benton yet again that I sense an insatiable desire for power, that I feel the presence of a murderous entity watching us from a dark place, lying in wait. Some things are over, but not everything is, and I don't say any of this to him.

"I'm just going to have to tuck it in here, and the hell with it." He isn't really talking to me but to himself, easing as close to a rock wall as he can so we don't stick halfway out into the slick, sandy street. "We'll hope some yahoo doesn't hit me. If so, he'll be in for an unpleasant surprise."

I suppose he means it wouldn't be fun to realize the door you just dinged or the bumper you just scraped or the side you just swiped is the property of the FBI. The SUV is a typical government vehicle, black with tinted glass and cloth seats, and emergency strobes hidden behind the grill, and on the floor in back are two coffee cups neatly held in place inside their cardboard to-go box along with a balled-up food bag. The war wagon of a busy agent who is tidy but not always in a convenient spot to toss out trash. I didn't know that Douglas was a woman until Benton referred to the special agent who's assigned this car as "she" a little while ago while he was telling me about *her* running the license plate of the Bentley that met us at Hanscom last night, a 2003 four-door black Flying Spur personally owned by the CEO of a Boston-based niche service company that supplies "discreet concierge-minded chauffeurs" who will drive any vehicle requested, explaining why the Bentley didn't have a livery license plate.

The reservation was made online by someone using an e-mail address that belongs to Johnny Donahue, an inpatient at McLean with no Internet access when the e-mail was sent yesterday from an IP address that is an Internet café near Salem State College, which is very close to here. The credit card used belongs to Erica Donahue, and as far as anybody knows, she doesn't do anything online and won't touch a computer. Needless to say, the FBI and the police don't believe she or her son booked the Bentley or the driver.

The FBI and the police believe Fielding did, that he likely got access to Mrs. Donahue's credit card information from payments she made to the tae kwon do club for lessons her son took until he was told not to come back after he tried to kick his instructor, my deputy chief, a grandmaster with a seventh-degree black belt. It isn't clear how Fielding might have gained access to Johnny's e-mail account unless he somehow manipulated the vulnerable and gullible teenager into giving him the password at some point or learned it by some other means.

The chauffeur, who isn't suspected of anything except not bothering to research Dr. Scarpetta before he delivered something to her, received the assignment from dispatch, and according to dispatch, no one who works at the elite transportation company ever met the alleged Mrs. Donahue or talked to her over the phone. In the notes section of the online reservation, an "exotic luxury car" was requested for an "errand," with the explanation that further instructions and a letter to be delivered would be dropped off at the private driving company's headquarters. At approximately six p.m., a manila envelope was slipped through the mail slot in the front door, and some three hours later, the chauffeur showed up at Hanscom Field with it and decided that Benton was me.

We get out into the cold, clean air, and ice is everywhere, lit up by the sun as if we are inside an illuminated crystal chandelier. Shielding my eyes with my hand, I watch the dark-blue sea as it rolls and contracts like muscle, pushing itself inland to smash and boil against a rock-strewn shore where no one lives. Right here a sea captain once looked out at a view that I doubt has changed much in hundreds of years, acres of rugged coastline and beach with copses of hardwood trees, untouched and uninhabitable because it is part of a marine recreational park, which happens to have a boat launch.

A little farther down, past the campground, where the Neck wraps around toward the Salem Harbor, is a yacht yard where Fielding's twenty-foot Mako was shrink-wrapped and on a jack stand when police found it this morning. I'm vaguely aware he has a dive boat because I've heard him mention it, but I didn't know where he keeps it. I never would have imagined twenty-four hours ago that it might become the focus of a homicide investigation, or that his dark-blue Navigator SUV with its missing front license plate would, or that his Glock pistol with its drilled-off serial number would, or that everything Fielding owns and has done throughout his entire existence would.

Overhead, an orange Dauphin helicopter, an HH-65A, also known as a Dolphin, beats low across the cold blue sky, its enclosed Fenestron ten-bladed tail rotor making a distinctive modulated sound that is described as low noise but to me has a quiet high pitch, is ominously whiny, reminding me a bit of a C-17. Homeland Security is conducting air surveillance, and I've been told that, too. I don't know why federal law enforcement has taken to the air or the land or the sea unless there is a concern about the overall security of the Salem Harbor, a significant port with a huge power plant. I have heard the word *terrorism* mentioned, just in passing by Benton and also by Marino when I had him on the phone a few minutes ago, but these days I hear that word a lot. In fact, I hear it all the time. Bioterrorism. Chemical terrorism. Domestic terrorism. Industrial terrorism. Nanoterrorism. Technoterrorism. Everything is terrorism if I stop to think about it. Just as every violent crime is hateful and a hate crime, really.

I continue going back to Otwahl, everything leading me back to Otwahl, my
thoughts carried on the wing of a flybot or,
as Lucy puts it, not a flybot but the holy
grail of flybots. Then I think about my old
nemesis MORT, a life-size model of it
perched like a giant mechanical insect inside
a Cambridge apartment rented by Eli Goldman, and next I worry about the controversial scientist Dr. Liam Saltz, who must be
heartbroken beyond remedy. Maybe he
simply got caught in one of those ghastly
coincidences that happens in life, his tragic
misfortune to be the stepfather of a brilliant
young man who slipped into bad science,
bad drugs, and illegal firearms.

A kid too smart for his own good, as
Benton puts it, murdered while wearing an
antique signet ring missing from Erica
Donahue's house, just as her stationery is
missing, and her typewriter and a fountain
pen, items that Fielding must have gotten
hold of somehow. He must have gotten his
hands on all sorts of things from the rich
Harvard student he bullied, Johnny
Donahue, and it doesn't matter if it all feels
wrong to me. I can't prove that Fielding
didn't exchange the gold ring for drugs. I
can't prove he didn't exchange the Glock

for drugs. I can't say that's not why Eli had the ring and the gun, that there's some other reason far more nefarious and dangerous than what Benton and others are proposing.

I can say and have said that Eli Goldman was an obstruction to the mercenary progress of a company like Otwahl, and Otwahl is the common denominator in everything, more so than tae kwon do or Fielding. As far as I'm concerned, if Fielding is as directly and solely responsible as everyone is claiming, then we should be taking a very hard and different look at Otwahl and wonder what he had to do with the place beyond being a user or a research subject or even someone who helped distribute experimental drugs until they brought about his complete annihilation.

"Otwahl and Jack Fielding," I said to Benton a little while ago. If Fielding is guilty of murder and case-tampering and obstruction of justice and all sorts of lies and conspiracies, then he's intimately connected with Otwahl, right down to its parking lot, where his Navigator likely got tucked out of sight last night during a blizzard. "You have to make that connection in a meaningful way," I repeatedly told Benton on our drive to this desolate spot that is achingly beautiful and yet ruined, as if Fielding's property is an ugly stain on the canvas of an exquisite seascape.

"Otwahl Technologies and an eighteenth-century sea captain's house on Salem Neck," I said to my husband, and I asked his opinion, his honest and objective opinion. After all, he should have a very well-informed and completely objective opinion because of his alliance with the well-informed and completely objective *we*'s, as I stated it, these anonymous comrades of his, the shadowy rank and file of an FBI he doesn't belong to anymore, he claims, and of course I don't believe him. He is FBI, all right, as secretive and driven as I remember him from times long past, and maybe I could put up with that if I didn't feel so utterly alone.

He's not even listening to me anymore, pretty much checked out when I made the comment a few minutes ago that Fielding must have some link to Otwahl beyond his teaching martial arts to a few brainy students who had internships with the technology behemoth. The connection must be more than just drugs, I said. Drug-impregnated pain-relieving patches can't be the entire explanation for what I'm about to find inside a tiny stone outbuilding that

Fielding was turning into a guest quarters before he supposedly found another use for it that has earned it several new names.

The Kill Cottage, I think darkly, bitterly. *The Semen's House,* I think cynically.

Destined to be Salem's latest attraction during Halloween, which lasts all of October, with a million people making a pilgrimage here from all over the land. Another example of a place made famous by atrocities that don't seem real anymore, tall tales, almost cartoonish, like the witch on her broom depicted on the Salem logo that is on police patches and even painted on the police cruiser doors. Be careful what you hate and murder, because one day it will own you. The Witch City, as people have dubbed the place where those men and women were herded up to what is now called Gallows Hill Park, a spot similar to where Fielding bought a sea captain's house. Places that don't change much. Places that are now parks. Only Gallows Hill is ugly, and it should be. An open field ravaged by the wind, and barren. Mostly rocks, weeds, and patchy, coarse grass. Nothing grows there.

Thoughts like these are solar flares, and peak and spike with a timing I can't seem to control, as Benton touches my elbow, then grips it firmly, while we cross the sandy dead-end street that has turned into a parking lot of law-enforcement vehicles, marked and unmarked, some with the Salem logo, silhouettes of witches straddling their brooms. Pulled up close to the sea captain's house, almost right up against the back of it, is the CFC's white van-body truck that Marino drove here hours earlier while I was in the autopsy room and then upstairs, having no idea what was happening some thirty miles northeast. The back of the truck is open, and Marino is inside, wearing green rubber boots and a bright yellow hard hat and a bright yellow level-A suit, what we use for demanding jobs that require protection from biological and chemical hazards.

Cables snake over the diamond-steel floor and out the open metal doors, over the unpaved icy drive, and disappear through the front of the stone cottage, what must have been a charming, cozy outbuilding before Fielding turned it into a construction site of exposed foundation blocks, the ground frozen with ice that is gray. The area behind the sea captain's house is an eyesore of spilled cement and toppled piles of lumber and bricks, and rusting tools, shingles, weather stripping, and nails everywhere. A wheelbarrow is covered loosely with a black tarp that flaps, the entire perimeter strung with yellow crime scene tape that shakes and jumps in the wind.

"We got enough juice in this thing for lights and that's it, got about a hundred and twenty minutes of run time left," Marino says to me as he digs inside a built-in storage bin.

What he's referring to is the auxiliary power unit, the APU, which can keep the truck's electrical system running while the engine is off and supplies a limited amount of emergency power externally.

"Assuming the power doesn't come back on, and maybe we'll get lucky. I've heard it could anytime, the main problem being those poles knocked over by snapped-off trees you probably drove past on Derby Street on your way here. But even if we get the electricity back, it won't help much in there." He means in the stone outbuilding. "No heat in there. It's cold as shit, and after a while it gets to you, I'm just telling you," he says from inside the truck while Benton and I stand outside in the wind and I flip up the collar of my jacket. "Cold as our damn fridge at the morgue, if you can imagine working in there for hours."

As if I've never worked a scene in frigid

weather and am unfamiliar with a morgue cooler.

"Course, there are some advantages to that if the power goes out, which it's going to do in these parts when you get storms, and he didn't have a backup generator," Marino continues.

He means that Fielding didn't.

"And that's a lot of money to lose if the freezer quits. Which is why plugging in a space heater and turning it on high was for the obvious reason of ruining the DNA so we'd never know who he'd taken the shit from. Do you think that's possible?" he asks me.

"I'm not sure which part of it —" I start to say.

"That we won't ID them. Possible we won't?" Marino continues talking nonstop, as if he's been drinking coffee since I saw him last. His eyes are bloodshot and glassy.

"No," I reply. "I don't think it's possible. I think we'll find out."

"So you don't think it's as worthless as tapioca."

"Christ," Benton says. "I could have done without that. Christ, I wish you'd stop with the fucking food analogies."

"Low copy number." I remind Marino we can get a DNA profile from as little as three

506

human cells. Unless virtually every cell is degraded, we'll be okay, I assure him.

"Well, it's only fair we really try." Marino talks to me as if Benton's not here, directing his every comment to me as if he's in charge and doesn't want to be reminded of my FBI or former FBI husband. "I mean, what if it was your son?"

"I agree we have to ID them and let their next of kin know," I reply.

"And get sued, now that I think of it," Marino reconsiders. "Well, maybe we shouldn't tell anyone. Seems to me we just need to know who it came from. Why tell the families and open a can of worms?"

"Full disclosure," Benton says ironically, as if he really knows what that is. He is looking at his iPhone, reading something on it, and he adds, "Because a lot of them probably already know. We're assuming Fielding arranged with them up front to pay for the service he was offering. It's not possible to hide anything."

"We're not going to," I answer. "We don't hide things, period."

"Well, I'll tell you. I'm thinking we really should install cameras inside our cooler, not just outside in the hall and the bay and certain rooms but actually in there," Marino says to me, as if it has always been his belief that we should have cameras inside the coolers, probably inside the freezer, too. In fact, he's never mentioned the idea before now. "I wonder if cameras would work in a cooler. . . ." he is saying.

"They work outdoors. It gets colder in the winter around here than it is in the cooler," Benton comments dully, barely listening to Marino, who is full of himself, enjoying his role in the drama that has unfolded, and he's never liked Fielding. I can't think of a bigger *I told you so.*

"Well, we got to do it," Marino says to me. "Cameras and no more of this shit, of people doing shit they think they can get away with."

I look behind us at boots and shoes lined up outside the opening that leads into the cottage. The Kill Cottage, the Semen's Cottage. Some cops are calling it the Little Shop of Horrors.

"Cameras," I hear Marino as I stare at the stone cottage. "If we had them in the cooler, we'd have it all on tape. Well, hell, maybe it's a good thing. Shit, imagine if something like that got leaked and ended up on You-Tube. Fielding doing that to all these dead bodies. Jesus. I bet you have cameras like that at Dover, though."

He hands us folded bright yellow suits like his.

"Dover must have cameras in the coolers, right?" he goes on. "I'm sure DoD would spring for it, and nothing like the present to ask, right? In light of the circumstances, I don't think anything's off the table when it comes to beefing up security at our place. . . ."

I realize Marino is still talking to me, but I don't answer because I'm worrying about what's in the cab of the truck. I'm suddenly overwhelmed by pity as I stand outside in the cold and wind and glare, my level-A suit folded up and tucked under my arm while Benton is putting his on.

And Marino goes on quite cheerfully, as if this is quite the carnival. ". . . Like I said, a good thing it's cold. I can't imagine working this on one of those ninety-degree days like we used to get in Richmond, where you can wring water out of the air and nothing's stirring. I mean, what a fucking pig. Don't even look at the toilet in there; probably the last time it was flushed was when they were still burning witches around here. . . ."

"They were hanged," I hear myself say.

Marino looks at me with a blank expression on his big face, and his nose and ears are red, the hard hat perched on top of his bald head like the bonnet of a yellow fire-plug.

"How's he doing?" I indicate the cab of the truck and what's inside it.

"Anne's a regular Dr. Dolittle. Did you know she wanted to be a vet before she decided to be Madame Curie?" He still says *curry,* like curry powder, no matter how many times I've told him it's *Cure-ee,* like the element curium that's named after Madame *Cure-ee.*

"I tell you what, though," he then says to me. "It's a good thing the heat hadn't been off in the house more than five, six hours before anybody got here. Dogs like that don't have much more hair than I do. He'd dug himself under the covers in Fielding's rat's nest of a bed and was still shivering like he was having a seizure. Of course, he was scared shitless. All these cops, the FBI storming in with all their tactical gear, the whole nine yards. Not to mention I've heard that greyhounds don't like to be left alone, have, what do you call it, separation anxiety."

He opens another storage bin and hands me a pair of boots, knowing my size without asking.

"How do you know it's Jack's bed?" I ask.

510

"It's his shit everywhere. Who else's would it be?"

"We need to be sure of everything." I'm going to keep saying it. "He was out here in the middle of nowhere. No neighbors, no eyes or ears, the park deserted this time of year. How do you know for a fact he was alone out here? How can you be absolutely certain he didn't have help?"

"Who? Who the hell would help him do something like this?" Marino looks at me, and I can see it on his big face, what he thinks. I can't be rational about Fielding. That's exactly what Marino thinks, probably what everybody thinks.

"We need to keep an open mind," I reply, then I indicate the cab of the truck again and ask again about the dog.

"He's fine," Marino says. "Anne got him something to eat, chicken and rice from that Greek diner in Belmont, made him a nice comfy bed, and the heat's blasting, feels like an oven, probably sucking up more to keep his skinny ass warm than we're using in the cellar. You want to meet him?"

He hands us heavy black rubber gloves and disposable nitrile ones, and Benton blows on his hands to warm them as he continues text-messaging and reading whatever is landing on his phone. He doesn't seem interested in anything Marino and I are saying.

"Let me take care of things first," I tell Marino, because I don't have it in me at the moment to see an abandoned dog that was left alone in a pitch-dark house with no heat after his master was murdered by the person who stole him. Or so the theory goes.

"Here's the routine," Marino then says, grabbing two bright yellow hard hats and handing them to us. "Over there, where you'll see plastic tubs for decon." He points at an area of dirt near a sheet of plywood that serves as the cottage's front door. "You don't want to track anything beyond the perimeter. Suits and boots go on and off right over there."

Lined up next to three plastic tubs filled with water is a bottle of Dawn dishwashing detergent and rows of footwear, the boots and shoes of the people inside, including what I recognize as a pair of tan combat boots, men's size. Based on what I'm seeing, there are at least eight investigators working the scene, including someone who might be army, someone who might be Briggs. Marino bends over to check the status display on the diamond-steel-encased APU in the back of the truck, then thuds down the diamond-steel steps out into the glare and sparkle of ice that coats bare trees as if they have been dipped in glass. Hanging everywhere are long, sharp icicles that remind me of nails and spears.

"So what you can do is put your gear on now," Marino says for my benefit as Benton wanders off, busy with his phone, communicating with someone and not listening to us.

Marino and I begin walking to the cottage, careful not to slip on ice that is frozen unevenly over rutted dirt and mud and debris that Fielding never cleaned up.

"Leave your shoes here," Marino tells me, "and if you need to use the facilities or go out for fresh air, just make sure you swish your boots off before you go back in. There's a lot of shit in there you don't want to be tracking everywhere. We don't even know exactly what shit, could be shit we don't know about, my point is. But what we do know isn't something you want to be tracking all over, and I know they say the AIDS virus can't live very long postmortem or whatever, but don't ask me to find out."

"What's been done?" I unfold my suit, and the wind almost blows it out of my hands.

"Things you're not going to want to do and shouldn't be your problem." Marino works his huge hands into a pair of purple gloves.

"I'll do anything that needs to be done," I remind him.

"You're going to need your heavy rubber gloves if you start touching a lot of stuff in there." Marino puts those on next.

I feel like snapping at him that I'm not here to sightsee. Of course I'll be touching things. But I don't intend to stoop to saying I've shown up to work a crime scene as if I'm one of the troops reporting to Marino and will be saluting him next. It's not that I don't understand what Marino is doing, what Benton is doing, what everyone is doing. Nobody wants me guilty of the very thing Mrs. Donahue accused Fielding of, ironically. Not that I want to have a conflict, either, and I understand I shouldn't be the one examining someone who worked for me and who, as rumor has it, I had sex with at some point in my life.

What I don't understand is why I'm not bothered more than I am. The only sadness I'm aware of right now is what I feel about a dog named Sock who is sleeping on towels in the cab of the CFC truck. If I see the dog I'm afraid I'll break down, and every other thought is an anxious one about him. Where will he go? Not to an animal shelter.

I won't allow that. It would make sense if Liam Saltz took him, but he lives in England, and how would he get the dog back to the UK unless it is in the cargo area of a jet, and I won't permit that, either. The pitiful creature has been through enough in this life.

"Just be careful." Marino continues his briefing as if I don't know a damn thing about what is going on around here. "And just so you know, we got the van making runs back and forth like clockwork."

Yes, I know. I'm the one who set it up. I watch Benton wander back toward the truck, talking to someone on his phone, and I feel forgotten. I feel extraneous. I feel I'm not helpful or of interest to anything or anyone.

"Pretty much nonstop, already thirty or forty DNA samples in the works, a lot of it not completely thawed, so maybe you're right and we'll be lucky. The van makes an evidence run and then turns around and comes right back, is on its way back here now even as we speak," Marino says.

I bend over and untie one of my boots.

"Anne drives like a damn demon. I didn't know that. I always figured she'd drive like an old lady, but she's been sliding in and out of here like the damn thing's on skis.

It's something," Marino says, as if he likes her. "Anyway, everybody's working like Santa's helpers. The general says he can bring in backup scientists from Dover. You sure?"

At the moment I don't know what I want, except a chance to evaluate the situation for myself, and I've made that clear.

"It's not your decision," I answer Marino, untying my other boot. "I'll handle it."

"Seems like it would be helpful to have AFDIL." Marino says it in a way that makes me suspicious, and I eye the tan combat boots by the decon tubs.

It's awkward enough that Briggs is here, and it enters my mind that he might not be the only one who's shown up from Dover.

"Who else?" I ask Marino as I lean against cinder blocks for balance. "Rockman or Pruitt?"

"Well, Colonel Pruitt."

Another army man, Pruitt is the director of the Armed Forces DNA Identification Laboratory, AFDIL.

"He and the general flew in together," Marino adds.

I didn't ask either of them to come, but they didn't need me to ask, and besides, Marino asked, at least he admitted to inviting Briggs. Marino told me about it during the drive here, over the phone. He said by the way he hoped I didn't mind that he took the liberty, especially since Briggs supposedly had been calling and I supposedly hadn't been answering, so Briggs hunted down Marino. Briggs wanted to know about Eli, the man from Norton's Woods, and Marino told him what was known about the case and then told him "everything else," Marino informed me, and he hoped I didn't mind.

I replied that I did mind, but what's done is done. I seem to be saying that a lot, and I said as much to Marino while I was on the phone with him during the car ride here. I said certain things were done because Marino had done them, and I can't run an office like that, although what was implicit but not stated was that Briggs is here for that very reason. He's here because I can't run an office. Not like that. Not at all. If I could run the CFC as the government and MIT and Harvard and everyone expected, nobody would be working this crime scene, because it wouldn't exist.

My yellow suit is stiff and digs into my chin as I pull my green rubber boots on, and Marino moves the makeshift plyboard door out of the way. Behind it is a wide sheet of heavy translucent plastic nailed to the top of the door frame, hanging like a curtain.

"Just so we're clear, I'm maintaining the chain of custody," I tell him the same thing I said earlier. "We're doing this the way we always do it."

"If you say so."

"I do say so."

I have a right to say so. Briggs isn't above the law. He has to honor jurisdiction, and for better or for worse, this case is the jurisdiction of Massachusetts and the principalities where the crimes have occurred.

"I just think any help we can get . . ." Marino says.

"I know what you think."

"Look, it's not like there's going to be a trial," he then says. "Fielding saved the Commonwealth a lot of fucking money."

20

The air is heavy with the smell of wood smoke, and I notice that the fireplace in the far wall is crammed with partially burned pieces of lumber topped by billowy clouds of whitish-gray ash, delicate, as if spun by a spider, but in layers. Something clean-burning, like cotton cloth, I think, or an expensive grade of paper that doesn't have a high wood-pulp content.

Whoever built the fire did so with the flue closed, and the assumption is that Fielding did, but no one seems quite sure why, unless he was out of his mind or hoping that eventually his Little Shop of Horrors would burn to the ground. But if that was his intention, he certainly didn't go about it in the right way, and I make a mental note of a gas can in a corner and cans of paint thinner and rags and piles of lumber. Everywhere I look I see an opportunity for starting a conflagration easily, so the fireplace makes no sense unless he was too deranged in the end to think clearly or wasn't trying to burn down the building but to get rid of something, perhaps to destroy evidence. Or someone was.

I look around in the uneven, harsh illumination of temporary low-voltage extension lights hanging from hooks and mounted on poles, their bulbs enclosed in cages. Strewn over an old scarred, paint-spattered workbench are hand tools, clamps, drill bits, paintbrushes, plastic buckets of L-shaped flooring nails and screws, and power tools, such as a drill with screwdriver attachments, a circular saw, a finishing sander, and a lathe on a metal stand. Metal shavings, some of them shiny, and sawdust are on the bench and the concrete floor, everything filthy and rusting, with nothing protecting Fielding's investment in home improvement from the sea air and the weather but heavy plastic and more plyboard stapled and nailed over windows. Across the room is another doorway that is wide open, and I can hear voices and other sounds drifting up from stairs leading down into the cellar.

"What have you collected in here?" I ask Marino as I look around and imagine what I saw under the microscope. If I could magnify samples from Fielding's work space, I suspect I would see a rubbish dump of rust, fibers, molds, dirt, and insect parts.

"Well, it's obvious when you look at the metal shavings some of them are recent because they haven't started rusting and are really shiny," Marino replies. "So we got samples, and they've gone to the labs to find out if under the scope they look anything like what you found in Eli Saltz's body."

"His last name isn't Saltz," I remind him for the umpteenth time.

"You know, to compare tool marks," Marino says. "Not that there's much of a reason to doubt what Fielding did. We found the box."

The box the WASP came in.

"A couple spent CO-two cartridges, a couple extra handles, even the instruction book," Marino goes on. "The whole nine yards. According to the company, Jack ordered it two years ago. Maybe because of his scuba diving." He shrugs his big shoulders in his big yellow suit. "Don't know, except he didn't order it two years ago to kill Eli. That's for damn sure. And two years ago Jack was in Chicago, and I guess you might ask what he needed a WASP for." Marino walks around in his big green boots and keeps looking at the opening to the stairs leading down, as if he's curious about what's being said and done down there. "The only thing that will kill you in the Great Lakes that I know of is all the mercury in the fish."

"It's with us. We have the box and the CO-two cartridges. We have all of it." I want to know which labs. I want to make sure Briggs isn't sending my evidence to the AFME labs in Dover.

"Yeah, all that stuff. Except the knife that was in the box, the WASP itself. It still hasn't shown up. My guess is he ditched it after stabbing the guy, maybe threw it off a bridge or something. No wonder he didn't want anyone going to the Norton's Woods scene, right?" Marino's bloodshot eyes look at me, then distractedly look around, the way people act when nothing they are looking at is new. He'd been here many hours before I showed up.

"What about in here?" I squat in front of the fireplace, which is open and built of old firebrick that is probably original to the building. "What's been done here?" My hard hat keeps slipping over my eyes, and I take it off and set it on the floor.

"What about it?" Marino watches me from where he's standing.

I move my gloved finger toward the whitish ashes, and they are weightless, lifting and stirring as the air moves, as if my thoughts are moving them. I contemplate the best way to preserve what I'm seeing, the ashes much too fragile to move in toto, and I'm pretty sure I recognize what has happened in the fireplace, or at least some of what occurred. I've seen this before but not recently, maybe not in at least ten years. When documents are burned these days, usually they were printed, not typed, and were generated on inexpensive copying paper with a high wood-pulp content that combusts incompletely, creating a lot of black sooty ash. Paper with a high cotton-rag content has a completely different appearance when it is burned, and what comes to mind immediately is Erica Donahue's letter that she claims she never wrote.

"What I recommend," I say to Marino, "is we cover the fireplace so the ashes aren't disturbed. We need to photograph them in situ before disturbing them in any way. So let's do that before we collect them in paint cans for the documents lab."

His big booted feet move closer, and he says, "What for?"

What he's really asking is why I am acting like a crime scene investigator. My answer, should I give one, which I won't, is because somebody has to.

"Let's finish this the way it should be done, the way we know how and have always done things." I meet his glassy stare, and what I'm really saying is nothing is over. I don't care what everyone assumes. It's not over until it is.

"Let's see what you've got." He squats next to me, our yellow suits making a plastic sound as we move around, and their faint odor reminds me of a new shower curtain.

"Typed characters on the ash." I point, and the ashes stir again.

"Now you're a psychic and ought to get a job in one of the magic shops around here if you can read something that's been burned."

"You can read some of it because the expensive paper burns clean, turns white, and the inked characters made by a typewriter can be seen. We've looked at things like this before, Marino. Just not in a long time. Do you see what I'm looking at?" I point, and the air moves and the ashes stir some more. "You can actually see the inked engraving of her letterhead, or part of it. Boston and part of the zip code. The same zip code on the letter I got from Mrs. Donahue, although she says she didn't write it and her typewriter is missing."

"Well, there's one in the house. A green one, an old portable on the dining-room table." He gets up and bends his legs as if his knees ache.

"There's a green typewriter next door?"

"I figured Benton told you."

"I guess he couldn't tell me everything in an hour."

"Don't get pissed. He probably couldn't. You won't believe all the shit next door. Appears when Fielding moved here he never really moved his shit in. Boxes everywhere. A fucking landfill over there."

"I doubt he had a portable typewriter. I doubt that's his."

"Unless he was in cahoots with the Donahue kid. That's the theory of where a lot of shit has come from."

"Not according to his mother. Johnny disliked Jack. So how does it make sense that Jack would have Mrs. Donahue's typewriter?"

"If it's hers. We don't know it is. And then there's the drugs," Marino says. "Obviously, Johnny's been on them since about the time he started taking tae kwon do lessons from Fielding. One plus one equals two, right?"

"We're going to find out what adds up and what doesn't. What about stationery or paper?"

"Didn't see any."

"Except what seems to be in here." I remind him it appears some of Erica Donahue's stationery might have been burned, or maybe all of it was, whatever was left over from the letter someone wrote to me, pretending to be her.

"Listen . . ." Marino doesn't finish what he's about to say.

He doesn't need to. I know what he's going to say. He's going to remind me I can't be reasonable about Fielding, and Marino thinks he should know, all right. Because of our own history. Marino was around in the early days, too. He remembers when Fielding was my forensic pathology fellow in Richmond, my protégé, and in the minds of a lot of people, it seems, a lot more than that.

"This was here just like this?" I then ask, indicating a roll of lead-gray duct tape on the workbench.

"Okay. Sure," he says as he squats by an open crime scene case on the floor and gets out an evidence bag, because the roll of tape can be fracture-matched to the last strip torn off it. "So tell me how the hell he might have gotten hold of it, and what for?"

He means Fielding. How did Jack Fielding get hold of Erica Donahue's typewriter, and what was his purpose in writing a letter allegedly from her and having it hand-delivered to me by a driver-for-hire who usually works events like bar mitzvahs and weddings? Did Johnny Donahue give Fielding the typewriter and stationery? If so, why? Maybe Fielding simply manipulated Johnny. Lured him into a trap.

"Maybe a last-ditch effort to frame the kid," Marino then says, answering his own question and voicing what I'm pondering and about to dismiss as a possibility. "A good question for Benton."

But Benton is off somewhere, talking on his phone or maybe conferring with his FBI compatriots, maybe with the female agent named Douglas. It bothers me when I think about her, and I hope I'm just paranoid and raw and have no reason to be concerned about the nature of his relationship with Special Agent Douglas. I hope the extra coffee cup in the back of her SUV wasn't Benton's, that he hasn't been riding around with her, spending a lot of time with her while I was at Dover and then before that, in and out of Washington. Not just an enabler and a bad mentor, now I'm a bad wife, it occurs to me. Everything feels wrecked. It feels over with. It feels as if I'm working my own death scene, as if the life I knew somehow didn't survive while I was away, and I'm investigating, trying to reconstruct what did me in.

"This is what we need to do right now," I tell Marino. "I assume no one has touched the typewriter, and is it an Olivetti, or do you know?"

"We've been pretty tied up over here." What he's saying is that the police have more important matters to tend to than an old manual typewriter. "We found the dog in there, like I told you. And a bedroom it appears Fielding was using, and you can tell he was in and out living here, but this is where it happened." He indicates the outbuilding we're in. "The typewriter's in a case on the dining-room table. I opened it to see what was inside, but that's it."

"Swab the keys for DNA before you pack it up and transport it to the labs, and I want those swabs going out on the next evidence run the van makes. I want those swabs analyzed first, because they might tell us who wrote that letter to me," I tell him.

"I think we know who."

"Then the typewriter goes to Documents so we can compare the typeface to what's on the letter I got, a cursive typeface, and we'll analyze the duct tape that's on the envelope and see if it came from the roll we just found and what trace is on it or DNA or fingerprints or who knows what. Don't be surprised if it points to the Donahues. If trace is from their house or fingerprints or DNA is from that source."

"Why?"

"Framing their son."

"I didn't know Jack was that damn smart," Marino says.

"I didn't say he framed anyone. I've not tried and convicted him or anyone," I reply flatly. "We have his DNA profile and fingerprints for exclusionary purposes, just as we have all of ours. So he should be easy to include or exclude, and any other profiles, and if there are? If we find DNA from more than one source, which we certainly should expect? We run the profiles through CODIS immediately."

"Sure. If that's what you want."

"We run them right away, Marino. Because we know where Jack is. But if anyone else is involved, including the Donahues? We can't waste time."

"Sure, Doc. Whatever you want," Marino says, and I can read his thoughts.

This is Jack Fielding's house, it's his Kill Cottage, his Little Shop of Horrors. Why go to all this trouble? But Marino's not going to say it to me. He's assuming I'm in denial.

I'm holding out the remote and irrational hope that Fielding didn't kill anyone, that someone else magically was using his property and his belongings and is responsible for all of this, someone other than Fielding, who is the victim and not the monster everyone now believes he is.

"We don't know if his family's been here," I remind Marino patiently and quietly, but in a sobering tone. "His wife, his two little girls. We don't know who's been in the house and touched things."

"Not unless they've been coming here from Chicago to stay in this dump."

"When exactly did they move out of Concord?" That's where his family was living with him, in a house Fielding had rented that I helped him find.

"Last fall. And it fits with everything," Marino makes yet one more assumption. "The football player and what happened after Fielding's family moved back to Chicago and he came here, fixing up this place while he was living in it like a hobo. He could have sent you a goddamn e-mail and let you know it wasn't working out for him personally around here. That his wife and kids bolted not long after the CFC started taking cases."

"He didn't tell me. I'm sorry he didn't."

"Yeah, well, don't say I should have." Marino seals the roll of duct tape in a plastic evidence bag. "It wasn't my business. I wasn't going to start out my new career here by ratting on the staff and telling you that Fielding was the usual fuck-up right out of the box and you sure as hell should have expected it when you thought it was such a brilliant idea to take him back."

"I should have expected this?" I hold Marino's bloodshot, resentful stare.

"Put on your hard hat before you go down. There's a lot of shit hanging from the ceilings, like all these damn lights strung up like it's Christmas. I got to go back out to the truck, and I know you need a minute."

I adjust the ratchet of my hard hat, making it tighter, and the reason Marino isn't going into the cellar with me isn't because I need a minute. It isn't because he's sensitive enough to offer me a chance to deal with what's down there without him by my side, breathing down my neck. That might be what he's talked himself into, but as I listen to him swishing his boots in the tubs just outside the door, stepping in and out of the water, I can only imagine how distasteful a scene like this must be to him. It has little to do with the unpleasantness of body fluids thawing and breaking down or even

531

his squeamishness about hepatitis or HIV or some other virus and everything to do with how the body fluids got here. Marino's ablution in the plastic tubs filled with water and dishwashing fluid are his attempt to cleanse himself of the guilt I know he feels.

He never saw Fielding doing any of it, and that's the problem Marino faces. The way he would think about it is he should have noticed, and as I've explained to Benton while we were driving here and then explained to Marino over the phone, the extraction of sperm isn't much different from a vasectomy, except when such a procedure is performed on a dead body, it's even quicker and simpler, for obvious reasons. No local anesthesia is needed, and the doctor doesn't have to be concerned with how the patient is feeling or if he might have second thoughts or any other emotional response.

All Fielding had to do was make a small puncture on one side of the scrotum and inject a needle into the vas deferens to extract sperm. He could have done this in minutes. He probably didn't do it during the autopsy but before it by going into the cooler when nobody was around, making certain he got to the body as quickly after death as possible, which in retrospect might explain why he noticed the man from Norton's Woods was bleeding before anybody else did. Fielding went into the cooler first thing when he got to the building early Monday morning to acquire his latest involuntary sperm donation, and that's when he noticed blood in the tray under the body bag. So he walked rapidly down the corridor and notified Anne and Ollie.

If anybody would have noticed something like this going on during the six months I was at Dover it was Anne, I told Marino. She never saw what Fielding was doing or had a clue, and we know he extracted sperm from at least a hundred patients based on what has been found in a freezer in the cellar and what's broken all over the floor, potentially a hundred thousand dollars, maybe much more, depending on what he charged and if he did it on a sliding scale, taking into account what the family or other interested party could afford. Liquid gold, as cops are calling what Fielding was selling on a black market of his own creation, and I can't stop thinking about his choice of Eli as an involuntary donor, assuming this was Fielding's intention, and we'll never really know.

But at the time Fielding went into the cooler yesterday morning, there was only one young male body fresh enough to be a suitable candidate for a sperm extraction, and that was Eli Goldman. The other male case was elderly, and it's highly unlikely he had loved ones who might be interested in buying his semen, and a third case was a female. If Fielding murdered Eli with the injection knife, would he then be so brazen and reckless as to take the young man's sperm, and who was he planning to sell it to without incriminating himself? If he'd tried something like that, he may as well have confessed to the homicide.

It continues to tug at my thoughts that Fielding didn't know who the unidentified dead young male was when he was notified about the case on Sunday afternoon. Fielding didn't bother going to the scene, wasn't interested, and had no reason at that time to be interested. I continue to suspect he didn't have a clue until he walked into the cooler, and then he recognized Eli Goldman because they had a connection somehow. Maybe it was drugs, and that's why Eli had one of Fielding's guns. Maybe Fielding had given or sold the Glock to Eli. For sure someone did. Drugs, the gun, maybe something else. If only I could have been in Fielding's mind when he walked into the cooler at shortly after seven yesterday morning. Then I would know. I would know everything.

I move a hanging light out of my way so it doesn't knock my hard hat as I go down stone steps in my bulky yellow suit and big rubber boots.

A cold sweat is rolling down my sides, and I am worrying about Briggs and what it will be like when I'm confronted with him, and I'm worrying about a greyhound named Sock. I am worrying about everything I can possibly worry about because I can't bear what I'm about to see, but it is better this way, and as much as I complain about Marino, he really did do the right thing. I wouldn't have wanted Fielding's body transported to the CFC. I wouldn't want to see it for the first time in a pouch on a steel gurney or tray. Marino knows me well enough to decide that given the choice, I would demand to see Fielding the way he died, to satisfy myself that it was exactly as it appears, and that what Briggs determined when he examined the body hours earlier is the same thing I observe and that Briggs and I share the same opinion about Fielding's cause and manner of death.

The cellar is whitewashed stone with a vaulted stone ceiling and no windows, and it is too small a space for so many people, all of them dressed the way I am, in bright yellow with thick black gloves and green rubber boots and bright yellow hard hats. Some people have on face shields, others surgical masks, and I recognize my own scientists, three from the DNA lab, who are swabbing an area of the stone floor that is littered with shattered glass test tubes and their black plastic stoppers. Nearby is the space heater Marino mentioned, and an upright stainless-steel laboratory cryogenic freezer, the same make and model that we use in labs where we have to store biological samples at ultra-low temperatures.

The freezer door is open wide, the adjustable shelves inside empty because someone, presumably Fielding, removed all the specimens and smashed them to the stone floor, then turned on the space heater. I notice partial labels adhering to glass fragments on a floor that is otherwise clean, the cellar appearing whitewashed with something non-glossy, like primer, like a winemaker's cave that has been turned into a laboratory with a steel sink and steel countertop, racks for test tubes, and large steel tanks of liquid nitrogen, and central to the main room I'm in, a long metal table that Fielding probably was using for shipping and several chairs, one of them pulled out a little, as if someone might have been sitting in it. I look at the chair first, and I look for blood, but I don't see any.

The table is covered with white butcher paper, and arranged on it are pairs of elbow-length bright-blue cryogloves, ampoules, rollerbases, smudge-proof pens, and long corks and measuring sticks for storage canisters, and stacked underneath are white cardboard boxes called CryoCubes, which are inexpensive vapor shippers we typically use for sending biological materials that are placed inside an aluminum canister, where they can remain frozen at minus 150 degrees centigrade for up to five days. These special packing containers can also be used to ship frozen semen, and in fact are often referred to as "semen tanks" and are favored by animal breeders.

I can only assume that Fielding's equipment and materials for his illegal and outrageous cottage industry were purloined from the CFC, that in the dark of night or after hours, he somehow managed to sneak what he wanted out of the labs without security batting an eye. Or it is possible he simply ordered what he needed and charged it to us but had it shipped directly here, to the sea captain's house. Even as I'm piecing together what he might have done, he is so close to me I could touch him, under a disposable blue sheet on his clean white primer–painted floor that is stained with blood at one edge of the plasticized paper, a spot of blood that is part of a large pool under his head, based on what I know. From where I'm standing, I can see the blood has begun to separate and coagulate, is in the early stages of decomposition, a process that would have been dramatically slowed because of the ambient temperature in the cellar. It is cold enough to see your breath, as cold as a morgue refrigerator.

The flashgun of a camera goes off, and then goes off again as a broad-shouldered figure in blaze yellow photographs the one area of whitewashed wall down here that is blackened and foul, where a total station on a bright yellow tripod has been set up, and I'm guessing the electro-optical distance-measuring system has already mapped the scene, recording the coordinate data of every feature, including what Colonel Pruitt is photographing. He catches me looking at him and lowers the camera to his side as I walk over to a wall where I smell death, the faintest musty, pungent stench of blood that has broken down and dried over months in a sunless, cold environment. I smell mildew.

I smell dust, and I notice piles of torn dirty carpet and plywood nearby against a different wall, and I can tell by dust and dirt on the white floor that the carpet and wood was recently dragged to where it is.

Bolted into stone at the height of my head are a series of steel screw-pin anchor shackles that I associate with sling assemblies used in hoisting. Based on coils of rope, grease guns, clamps, a cargo trolley, and grab hooks and swivel rings in the ceiling, I surmise that Fielding devised a creative rig for changing out the heavy tanks of liquid nitrogen, and at some point the system was perverted into one I suspect he never intended when he began extracting semen and selling it.

"From what I'm able to figure out so far, the main thing used was the splitting maul, which would account for both the blunt-force and cutting injuries," Pruitt begins without so much as a hello, as if our meeting here is normal, nothing more than a continuum of our time together at Dover. "Basically, a long-handled sledgehammer on one side, the other side sharp like an ax. It was under carpet and wood, along with a Boston College letter jacket, a pair of sneakers, other items of clothing that we think were Wally Jamison's. This entire area was under that stuff over there." He indicates the carpet and wood that was moved, what I surmise was used to cover the crime scene. "All of it, including the splitting maul, of course, has been packaged and sent to your place already. Did you see the weapon yet?" Pruitt says, shaking his head.

"No."

"Can't imagine someone coming after me with something like that. Jesus. Shades of Lizzie Borden. And pieces of bloody rope from being strung up." He points to the shackles and rings bolted into stone that is crusty and black with old blood, and I almost imagine I can smell fear down here, the unimaginable terror of the football player tortured and murdered on Halloween.

"Why didn't he clean this up?" I ask the first question that comes to mind as I look at a scene that doesn't appear to have been touched after Wally Jamison was brutally and sadistically murdered down here.

"I guess he took the path of least resistance and just covered everything up with plyboard and old carpet," Pruitt replies. "That's why there's a lot of dirt and fibers everywhere. Appears after the homicide, he didn't bother washing things down at all. Just heaped old carpet on top and leaned

540

all these boards against the wall." He points again to the pile of old torn carpet of different colors, and near it, the large sheets of plyboard stacked on the white floor near a closed access door that leads outside the cellar.

"I don't know why he wouldn't have washed it down," I repeat. "That was three months ago. He just left a crime scene, practically left it like a time capsule? Just threw carpet and plyboard over it?"

"One theory is he got off on it. Like people who photograph or film what they do so they can continue getting off on it after the fact. Every time he came down here, he knew what was behind the boards and carpet, what was hidden under them, and got off on it."

Or someone got off on it, I think. Jack Fielding has never gotten off on gore. For a forensic pathologist, he was actually rather squeamish. Benton will say it was the influence of drugs. Everyone is probably saying that, and maybe it's true. Fielding was altered, that much I don't doubt.

"Some of us can help you with this, you know," Pruitt then says, looking at me through a plastic face shield that clouds up intermittently as he breathes the cold cellar air. His hazel eyes are alert and friendly as they look at me, but he is troubled. How could anybody not be, and I wonder if he senses what I do. I wonder if he has a feeling in his gut that something is wrong with all this. I wonder if he's asking the question I am right now as I look at the blackened whitewashed wall with the rusting shackles bolted into the stone.

Why would Jack Fielding do something like this?

Extracting semen to sell to bereft families is almost understandable. One can easily blame greed or even a lust for the gratification, the power he must have felt when he was able to give back life where it had been taken. But as I envision the photographs, video recordings, and CT scans I've seen of Wally Jamison's mutilated body, I'm reminded of what went through my thoughts at the time. His murder seemed sexually and emotionally driven, as if the person who swung the weapon at him had feelings for him, certainly had a rage that didn't quit until Wally was lacerated, sliced, cut, and contused beyond recognition and bled to death. Afterward, his nude body was transported, probably by boat, probably by Fielding's boat, and dumped in the harbor at the coast guard station, an act that Benton describes as brazen, as a taunt to law enforcement. And that doesn't sound like Fielding, either. For such a fierce, muscle-bound grandmaster, he was rather much a coward.

"Thank you. Let's see what's needed," I say to Pruitt.

"Well, you know the DNA that's needed. Hundreds of samples already, not just the semen that needs to be reconnected with its donor but everything else being swabbed."

"I know. It's a huge job and will go on for quite a while because we don't know what's happened in here. Just part of it. What was in the freezer and then whatever else was done in addition to what I'm supposing must have been the homicide of the BC student, Wally Jamison." As I say his name I envision him, square-jawed with curly black hair and bright blue eyes, and powerfully built. Then what he looked like later. "What time did you get here?"

"John and I flew in early, got here about seven hours ago."

I don't ask him where Briggs is now.

"He did the external exam and will go over those details with you when you're ready," Pruitt adds.

"And nobody had touched him prior to that?" Fielding's body was discovered shortly after three a.m. Or that's what I've

543

been told.

"When John and I got here, the body was covered just like he is now. The Glock isn't here. After the FBI restored the eradicated serial number, the gun was bagged and is now at your labs," Pruitt tells me what Benton did.

"I didn't know about it until a little while ago. When I was being driven here."

"Look. If I'd been here at three a.m. and it was up to me?" He starts to say he would have told me everything that was going on. "But the FBI wanted to keep things contained, since no one's been sure if he was a lone wolf." He means if Fielding was. "Because of all the other factors, like Dr. Saltz and the MP and so on. The fear of terrorism."

"Yes. Only not the brand of terrorism the Bureau usually has to worry about. This is a different brand of terrorism," I comment. "It feels personal. Doesn't it feel personal? What are you thinking about all this?"

"Nobody had touched the body when the police, the FBI found it." Pruitt doesn't want to tell me what he thinks about it. "I do know he was the same temperature as the room by then, had been down here for a while, but you should talk to John about it."

"You're saying his body was the same temperature as the ambient air at three a.m."

"It's forty degrees, or around that. Maybe a few degrees warmer because of all the people down here. But you need to get the details from John."

Pruitt stares off at the human-shaped mound draped with a blue sheet on the other side of the cellar, near the freezer, near thawing fluids on the stone floor, where investigators have knee pads on and are collecting one shard of glass at a time and swabbing, and packaging each item separately in paper envelopes that they label with permanent markers. I won't do the calculations until I check the body, but already what I'm hearing adds to what I suspect. Something is wrong.

21

The stain on the whitewashed wall is an ugly darkness some six feet above the stone floor, probably where Wally Jamison's head and neck were when he was shackled and beaten and cut to death.

Spraying out from the largest stain are a constellation of pinpoint spatters, tiny black marks that at close inspection are elongated, are angled, the cast-off blood from the weapon as it was repeatedly swung, as it was repeatedly bloodied from impacting with human flesh, and I envision the wood-splitting maul Pruitt mentioned, and I agree with him. What a terrible way to die. Then I think of the injection knife. Another horrendous way to die. Sadism.

"He should have had a system of keeping track of the samples," I say to Pruitt as I watch the investigators in bright yellow, on their hands and knees, some of them people I don't know. Maybe Saint Hilaire from

Salem. Maybe Lester "Lawless" Law from Cambridge. I'm not sure who is here, really, just that the FBI is working in conjunction with a special task force comprising investigators from various departments who are members of the North Eastern Massachusetts Law Enforcement Council, NEMLEC. "If he really was selling extracted semen," I continue my train of thought, "I would assume he had a way of logging the specimens." I direct his attention to bits of gummy labels still adhering to broken glass on the floor. "Finding information like that will help us with identification, maybe preliminarily supply it, and then we can verify through DNA. If all of the specimens came from CFC cases, we should have DNA on blood-spot cards in each case file."

"I know Marino is looking into that, has somebody pulling every case of young males who would have been viable candidates. Especially if Fielding did the autopsies."

"With all due respect, that was my direction, not Marino's." I hear the defensiveness I can't keep out of my tone, but I've had enough of my new self-appointed acting chief Pete Marino. I've had enough references that imply he runs my office.

"We've not found a log yet," Pruitt adds. "But Farinelli's over there with his laptop, which was as dead as he was when we got here. Maybe the log will be on that."

It always seems strange when investigators refer to my niece by her last name. Lucy must be next door in the house, where there are no lights or heat, unless the power has come back on. I realize that down here I might not know, since we are using auxiliary lights brought in and set up. I walk over to an open Pelican case near the bottom of the stairs and find a flashlight, then return to the wall to shine the light over bloodstains to see what else they have to tell me before I look at the person who supposedly caused them, my deputy chief, working alone in his Kill Cottage. *My deputy chief, the lone wolf who had no help in all this,* I think skeptically and with growing anger at the police, the FBI, at everyone who started working the scene without me.

Below the darkest area on the white-washed wall is a corresponding dark area on the whitewashed floor, a myriad of drips that combine into a solid stain, what I can tell was a pool of blood that is almost black and flaking, much of it having soaked into the porous whitewashed stone. Some of the drops at the edge of the large stained area are perfectly round, with only a small amount of distortion or scalloping around the edges from the roughness of the stone, passive spatters from the victim bleeding. Other stains are smeared from someone, possibly the assailant, stepping on them or dragging something over them while they were still wet. Maybe dragging carpet and plyboards over them, I think. The only bloodstains that show a direction of travel are those on the wall and the ceiling, black and elongated or with a teardrop shape, and I believe most of these were projected by the repeated swings and impacts of the weapon.

The victim was upright when he bled, shackled to the wall, it would seem, and what I can't tell is the timing of at least one blow that I know was fatal. Did it happen early on or later? *The earlier, the better,* I can't help but think as I imagine what was done, as I reconstruct the pain and suffering and most of all his terror. I hope he hadn't been subjected to the abuse for long when an artery was breached, most likely the carotid on the left side of his neck. The distinctive wave pattern on the wall is from arterial blood spurting out under high pressure in rhythm to the beats of his heart, and I remember photographs I saw, the deep gashes to his neck.

Wally Jamison would have lived only

minutes after receiving such an injury, and I wonder how long the cutting and beating went on after it was too late to hurt him anymore. I wonder about the rage and what the connection might have been between Wally Jamison and Jack Fielding. It had to be more than that they simply went to the same gym. Wally wasn't involved in martial arts, and as far as anyone knows, he wasn't acquainted with Johnny Donahue or Eli Goldman or Mark Bishop. He didn't work or intern at Otwahl, either, and apparently had nothing to do with robotics or other technologies. What I know about Wally Jamison is that he was from Florida, a senior at BC, where he was majoring in history and somewhat of a celebrity because of football, and a partier, a ladies' man. I can't come up with a single reason why Fielding might have known him, unless it was some chance encounter they had, perhaps because of the gym and then perhaps drugs, the hormonal cocktail Benton mentioned.

Wally Jamison's toxicology was negative for illegal or therapeutic drugs or alcohol, but we don't routinely test for steroids unless we have reason to suspect a death may be related to them. Wally's cause of death wasn't a question. There certainly was no reason to think steroids killed him, at least not directly, and now it may be too late to go back. We're not going to get another sample of his urine, although we can try testing his hair, where the molecules of drugs, including steroids, might have accumulated inside the hair shaft. A test like that would be a long shot for detecting steroids, and it isn't going to tell us if Wally got them from Fielding or knew Fielding or was murdered by him. But I'm willing to try anything, because as I look around this cellar and see the shape of Fielding's body under a sheet on the floor, I want to know why. I have to know and won't accept that he was crazy, that he'd lost his mind. That's just not good enough.

Returning to the Pelican case near the stairs, I find a pair of knee pads and put them on before kneeling by the rounded blue sheet, and when I pull it back from Jack Fielding's face, I'm not prepared for how present he looks. That's the word that comes to mind, *present,* as if he's still here, as if he's asleep but not well. There is nothing vital or vibrant about him, and my brain races through the details I'm seeing, the stiff strands of hair from the gel he used to hide his baldness, the red splotches on his face, which is puffy and pale, and I pull the sheet off, and it rustles as I move it out of my way. I sit back on the heels of my rubber boots and look him over, taking in his gelled sandy-brown hair that was thinning on top and gone in spots, and the dried blood around his ear and pooled under his head.

I imagine Fielding pointing the barrel of the Glock inside his left ear and pulling the trigger. I try to get into his mind, try to conjure up his last thoughts. Why would he do that? Why his ear? The side of the head is common in gunshot suicides, but not the ear, and why his left side and not his right? Fielding was right-handed. I used to tease him about having what I called "extreme handedness" because he couldn't do anything useful with his left hand, nothing that required any degree of dexterity or skill. He certainly didn't shoot himself in his left ear while holding the pistol in his right hand, not unless he'd become a contortionist in my absence, and maybe that will be one more speculation everyone will come up with. But I need to check the angle. I point my right finger into my left ear canal as best I can, pretending my index finger is the barrel of the Glock.

"Things really aren't that bad," a deep voice says. "It hasn't come to that, has it?" General John Briggs says.

I look up at him standing over me, his legs

spread, his hands behind his back, big and bulky in bright yellow, but he's not wearing a face shield or gloves or a hard hat, his face ruggedly compelling, hawklike, it's been described as, and shadowed with stubble. He's a dark man, and no matter how often he shaves, he always looks as if he needs to, his eyes the same dark gray as the titanium veneer on my building, his black hair thick with very little gray for his age, which is exactly sixty.

"Colonel," he then says, and he squats next to me and picks up the flashlight I was using earlier and had left upright on the stone floor. "I imagine you're wondering the same thing I am." He turns on the light.

"I seriously doubt it," I reply as he shines the light inside Fielding's left ear.

"I'm wondering where he was," Briggs says. "Looking for high-velocity spatter, something to indicate if he was right here? Because why? Was he standing by his cryo-genic freezer and just stuck a gun in his ear?"

I take the light from him so I can direct it where I want as I look inside Fielding's ear, and mostly what I see is dark dried blood that is crusty, but as I lean closer I can make out the small black entrance wound, a contact wound, and that is elongated. It is angled. A large amount of blood is under his head, a dried pool of it that is thick and looks sticky because the cellar is moist, and I smell blood that is beginning to break down, the sweetish foul odor that is faint, and I detect alcohol. It wouldn't surprise me if Fielding was drinking in the end. Whether he shot himself or someone else did, he probably was compromised, and I remember the big SUV with the xenon lights that tailed Benton and me some sixteen hours ago while we were driving through a blizzard to the CFC. The current assumption is that Fielding was in that SUV, that it was his Navigator and he'd removed the front plate so we couldn't tell who was behind us.

Nobody has satisfactorily offered why he might have decided to tail Benton and me or how he managed to disappear instantly, seemingly into thin air, after Benton stopped in the middle of the snowy road in hopes whoever was on our bumper would pass us. I seem to be the only one consumed by the fact that Otwahl Technologies is very close to the area where the big SUV with xenon lights and fog lamps vanished, and if someone had a gate opener or code to that place or was familiar to the private police, that person could have tucked the Navigator in there, rather much like vanishing in the Bat Cave, is how I described it to Benton, who didn't seem impressed. *"Why would Jack Fielding have that kind of access to Otwahl?"* I asked Benton as we were driving here. *"Even if he was involved with some of the people who work there, would he have access to its parking lot? Could he have pulled in so quickly and been confident the private police who patrol the grounds would have been fine with it?"*

"With all the white-painted surfaces in here," Briggs is saying to me, "you'd think we could find something that might indicate where the shooting occurred."

I look at Fielding's hands. They are as cold as the stone in the cellar, and he is completely rigorous. As muscle-bound as he is, it is like moving the arms of a marble statue as I shine the flashlight on his thick, strong hands, examining them, noting his clean, trimmed nails and surprised by them. I expected them to be dirty, as crazy and out of control as everyone believes he was. I notice his calluses, which he's always had from using free weights in the gym or working on his cars or doing home repairs. It appears he died holding the pistol in his left hand, or it is supposed to look like he did, his fingers curled tightly and the impression in his palm made by the Glock's nonslip stippled grip. But I don't notice a fine mist of blood that might have blown back on his skin when he pulled the trigger. Back spatter is an artifact that can't be staged or faked.

"We'll do GSR on his hands," I comment, and I notice that Fielding isn't wearing his wedding band. The last time I saw him, he had it on, but that was in August, and he was still living with his family, from what I understand.

"The muzzle of the gun had blood," Briggs tells me. "Internal muzzle staining from blood being sucked in."

The phenomenon is caused by explosive gases when the barrel of a gun is pressed against the skin and fired.

"The ejected cartridge case?" I inquire.

"Over there." He indicates an area of the whitewashed floor about five feet from Fielding's right knee.

"And the gun? In what position?" I slide my hands under Fielding's head and feel the hard lump of jagged metal under the scalp above his right ear, where the bullet exited his skull and is trapped under his skin.

"Still gripped in his left hand. I'm sure you noticed the way his fingers are curled and the impression of the grip in his palm. We had to pry the gun out of his hand."

"I see. So he shot himself with his left hand even though he's right-handed. Not impossible but unusual, and he either was already lying right here on the floor when he did it or fell with the gun still gripped in his hand. A cadaveric spasm and he clenched it hard. And fell neatly on his back just like this. Well, that's quite a thing to imagine. You know me and cadaveric spasms, John."

"They do happen."

"Like winning the lottery," I answer. "That happens, too. Just never to me."

I feel fractured bone shift beneath my fingers as I gently palpate Fielding's head and envision a wound path that is upward and slightly back-to-front, the bullet lodging approximately three inches from the lower angle of his right jaw.

"He shot himself like this?" I turn my left hand into a gun again, and point my purple nitrile–gloved index finger at an awkward angle, as if I'm going to shoot myself in the left ear. "Even if he held the pistol in his left hand when he wasn't left-handed, it's slightly awkward and unusual, the way my elbow has to be down and behind me, don't you think? And I might expect a fine mist of back spatter on his hand. Of course, these things aren't set in stone," I say inside Fielding's white-painted stone cellar.

"Odd thing about shooting yourself in the ear," I comment, "is people generally are squeamish because of the anticipated noise, not rational, because you're about to die anyway, but it's human nature. Like shooting yourself in the eye. Almost nobody does."

"You and I need to talk, Kay," Briggs says.

"And most of all, the timing of when the cryogenic freezer was gone into," I then say. "And the space heater turned on and what was burned upstairs, possibly Erica Donahue's stationery. If Jack did all that before he killed himself, then why is there no semen or broken glass on the floor under him?" I am manipulating Fielding's big body, and he is deadweight, completely stiff and unwilling as I move him a little, looking under him at a floor that is white and clean. "If he came down here and broke all these test tubes and then shot himself in the ear, there should be glass and semen under his body. It's all around him but none under him. There's a shard of glass in his hair." I pick it out and look at it. "Someone broke all this after he was dead, after he was already lying here on the floor."

"He could have gotten glass in his hair when he broke test tubes, violently smashed everything," Briggs says, and he sounds patient and kind, for him. He almost seems to feel sorry for me. My insecurities again.

"Do you have your mind made up, John? You and everyone else?" I look up into his compelling face.

"You know damn better than that," he says. "We have a lot to talk about, and I'd rather not do it here in front of the others. When you're ready, I'll be next door."

The power came back on in Salem Neck at about half past two, about the time I was finishing with Jack Fielding, kneeling next to him on that cold stone floor until my feet started tingling and my knees were aching and burning, despite the pads I had on.

The flush-mounted lights in his old outdated kitchen are illuminated, the house quite chilly but with the promise of warmth in the forced air I feel coming out of floor vents as I walk around in my tactical boots and field clothes and jacket, having taken off my protective gear except for disposable gloves. The white porcelain sink is filled with dishes, and the water is scummy with soap, a coagulated slick of yellowish grease floating on it, and the sheer yellow curtain covering the window over the sink is stained and dingy.

Wherever I look I find remnants of food and garbage and hard drinking and am reminded of the squalor of countless scenes I've worked, of their rot and spoilage, their musty, mildewy smells, of how often it is that the life preceding the death was the real crime. Fielding's last months on earth were far more tortured than he deserved, and I can't accept that he wanted anything he made for himself. This is not what he scripted for his ultimate destiny, it's not what he was born to, and I continue thinking of that favorite phrase of his when he would remind me he wasn't *born to* this or *born to* that, especially if I asked him to do something he found distasteful or boring.

I pause by a wooden table with two wooden chairs beneath a window that faces the icy street and the choppy dark-blue water beyond it, and the table is deep in old newspapers and magazines that I spread around with my gloved hand. The *Wall Street Journal,* the *Boston Globe,* the *Salem News,* as recent as Saturday, I note, and I recall seeing several papers covered with ice on the sidewalk in front, as if they were tossed there and no one brought them inside the house before the big storm. There

are about half a dozen *Men's Health* magazines, and I notice the mailing labels are for
Fielding's Concord address. The January
and February issues were forwarded here,
as was a lot of other mail in the pile I sift
through. I recall that Fielding's rental of the
house in Concord began almost a year ago,
and based on the clutter and furniture I
recognize as his and what I've been told
about his domestic problems, it would make
sense that he didn't renew the lease. He
relocated to a drafty antique house that is
completely lacking in charm because of the
run-down condition it's in, and while I can
imagine what he envisioned when he fell in
love with the place, something changed for
him.

What happened to you? I look around at
the squalor he's left in his wake. *Who were
you in the end?* I envision his dead hands
and remember their coldness and their rigor
and how heavy they felt as I held them.
They were clean, his nails well kempt, and
that very small detail doesn't seem to fit
with everything else I'm seeing. *Did you
make this appalling mess? Or did someone
else? Has some other person who is slovenly
and crazed been inside your house?* But I
also know that consistency really is the
hobgoblin of little minds, that what Ralph

Waldo Emerson wrote is true. People aren't easily explained or defined, and what they do isn't always consistent. Fielding may very well have been falling apart along with everything around him but was still vain enough to have good hygiene. It could be true.

But I'm not going to know. His CT scan, his autopsy won't tell me. There's so much I won't know, including why he never told me about his place in Salem. Benton says that Fielding purchased the house right after he moved to Massachusetts, which was a year ago this past January, but he never mentioned it to me. I'm not sure he was hiding anything criminal he was up to or intended to be up to, but rather I have a feeling he wanted something that was just his, something that didn't concern me and that I had no opinion about and wasn't going to improve or change or help him with. He didn't want my mentoring him as he set about to turn an eighteenth-century sea captain's safe harbor into his own or into an investment or whatever he originally dreamed of having all to himself.

If that's the truth, then how sad, I think as I look out at water sparkling like sapphires, rolling and crashing against the gray, rocky shore across the icy, sandy street. I walk through a wide opening that once had pocket doors, into a dining room of exposed dark oak beams in a white plaster ceiling that is water-stained, noting that the tarnished brass hanging onion lantern belongs in an entryway, not over the walnut table, which is dusty and surrounded by chairs that don't match and need new upholstery. I don't blame Fielding for not wanting me here. I'm too critical, too sure of my goddamn good taste and informed opinions, and it's no wonder I drove him to distraction. Not just an enabler but also a bad mother when I had no right to even be a good one. It wasn't my place to be anything to him except a responsible boss, and if he were here I would tell him I'm sorry. I would ask him to forgive me for knowing him and caring, because what help was it? What damn good did I do?

I focus on a disturbed area of dust at one end of the table, where someone was eating or working, perhaps where the Olivetti typewriter was, and the chair in front of it is in better shape than the others. Its faded, threadbare red-velvet cushion is intact and probably safe to sit on, and I think about Fielding in here typing. I try to place him at this table with its old casement windows, the view in here a dreary one of the gravel drive, and it's impossible for me to envision him hunched over in a small chair beneath a hanging lantern, typing a two-page letter over and over on engraved watermarked paper until he had a final version that was flawless.

Fielding and his big, impatient fingers, and he was never much of a typist, was self-taught, what he called "hunt and pick" instead of hunt and peck, and the point of that document supposedly from Erica Donahue is illogical if it came from him. Considering the condition Fielding was in, based on what Benton saw when he met with him last week in my office, it doesn't seem plausible to me that my deputy chief would have gone to such lengths to set up and frame a Harvard student for Mark Bishop's homicide. Why would Fielding have killed that six-year-old boy? I don't buy what Benton says, that Fielding was killing himself as a child when he drove nails into Mark Bishop's head. Fielding was putting an end to his own childhood of abuse, Benton told me, and I'm not persuaded.

But I have to remind myself that there are many things in life that make sense to the people who are doing them while the rest of us never figure it out. Even when we're told why, the explanation often doesn't fit with any template that has rhyme or reason. I pause before a casement window, not quite ready to leave this room and enter the next one, where I can hear Briggs walking around in his desert boots. He is talking to someone on his phone, and I pull out mine to check my text messages and see that there is one from Bryce.

Can U call Evelyn!?

I try her in the trace evidence lab and another microscopist answers, a young scientist named Matthew.

"You anywhere near a computer?" Matthew's voice, confident and tense with excitement. "Evelyn's just down the hall in the ladies' room, but we want to send you something totally weird, and I keep thinking it's a mistake or like the weirdest contamination ever. You know a hair is about eighty thousand nanometers, right? So imagine something four nanometers, in other words, a hair would be twenty thousand times the diameter of what we found. And it's not organic, even though the elemental fingerprint is mostly pure carbon, but we've also detected trace residues of what appears to be phencyclidine. . . ."

"You found PCP?" I interrupt his breathless talk.

"PCP, angel dust, a really trace amount,

just a minuscule amount. Using FTIR. At a magnification of one hundred, just plain ol' light microscopy, and you can see the granules and a lot of other microscopic debris, especially cotton fibers, on the backing of the pain-relieving patch, okay? Probably some of these granular structures are PCP, maybe Nuprin, Motrin, too, whatever the patch originally was, possibly other chemicals there."

"Matthew, slow down."

"Well, at one hundred and fifty thousand X with SEM you'll see what I'm talking about as big as a bread box, Dr. Scarpetta, what we want to send you."

"Go ahead, and if nothing else, I'll go out to the truck and log in. Send PDFs, though, and I'll try on my iPhone. What are you talking about, exactly?"

"Sort of like buckyballs, like a dumbbell made out of buckyballs but with legs. It's definitely man-made, about the size of a strand of DNA, like I said, four nanometers and pure carbon, except for whatever it was meant to deliver. And also traces of polyethylene glycol that we're conjecturing was the outer coating for what was meant to be delivered."

"Explain the *meant-to-deliver* part. Something built on nanoscale to deliver a trace amount of PCP or what?"

"This isn't my area, obviously, and we don't have an AFM, an atomic force microscope, here, hint, hint. Because I'd say we've just entered a new day where we have to start looking for things like this, things you might need to magnify millions of times. And in my opinion, something like an AFM would have to have been used to assemble this, do the nanoassembly, to manipulate the nanotubes, the nanoparticles, while you're trying to get them to stick together, using a nanoprobe or whatever. Well, we could probably handle a lot of this with SEM, but an AFM would be a good idea if this is what's headed down the pike and about to slam into us head-on, Dr. Scarpetta."

"You don't know what you've found, but it's a nanobot of some type, possibly, in your opinion, for the delivery of a drug or drugs? You found one on the film backing that was in the lab coat pocket?" I don't say whose lab coat.

"Just one admixed with the particulate and fibers and other debris because we didn't analyze the entire piece of film, just the specimen we mounted on a stub. The rest of the plastic film's at fingerprints right now, and then it's going to DNA, then to

GC-Mass-Spec," Matthew says. "And it's broken or degraded."

"What is?"

"The nanobot. Or it looks broken, or maybe it's deteriorating, like it was supposed to have eight legs but I'm seeing four on one side and two on the other. I'm e-mailing this to you now, a couple photographs we took so you can see it for yourself."

I'm able to pull up the images on my iPhone, and it is an inexplicable feeling to note the eerie symmetry, to have it enter my mind that the nanobot looks like a molecular version of a micromechanical fly. I can't know if Lucy's holy grail of flybots looks like this nanobot magnified thousands of times, but the artificial structure in the photographs is insectlike with its grayish, buckyball elongated body. The delicate nanowire arms or legs that are still intact are bent at right angles with gripperlike appendages on the tips, possibly for grabbing onto the walls of cells or burrowing into blood vessels or organs, to find the target, in other words, and adhere to it while delivering medicine or perhaps illegal drugs destined for certain brain receptors.

No wonder Johnny Donahue's drug screen was negative, it occurs to me. If nanobots were added to his sublingual allergy extracts or, better yet, to his corticosteroid nasal spray, the drugs might have been below the level of detection. More astonishingly, the drugs may not have penetrated the blood-brain barrier at all, but would have been programmed to bind to receptors in the frontal cortex. If the drugs never entered the bloodstream, they wouldn't have been excreted in urine. They wouldn't have ended up in hair, and that's the point of nanotechnology's use in medicine, to treat diseases and disorders with drugs that aren't systemic and therefore are less harmful. As is true with everything else, whatever can be used for good most assuredly will be used for evil.

Fielding's living room is bare floors and walls, and stacked almost to the ceiling are dusty brown boxes, all the same size, with the moving company Gentle Giant's logo on the sides, scores of cartons in cubed piles as if they've never been touched since they were carried in here.

In the midst of this cardboard bunker Briggs sits, reminding me of a Matthew Brady photograph of a Civil War general, in his muted sandy-green fatigues and boots, a Mac notebook in his lap, his broad-shouldered back straight against the straight-back chair. I decide it would be like him to sit and make me stand, to choreograph our conversation so I feel small and subservient to him, but he gets up, and I tell him no, thank you, I'll stand. So both of us do, moving to a window, where he places his laptop on a sill.

"I find it interesting he has a wireless network in here," Briggs says right off, looking out at the view of the ocean and the rocks across the icy street that is covered with tan sand. "With all you've seen in here, would you expect him to have wireless?"

"Maybe he wasn't the only person in here."

"Maybe."

"At least you'll entertain the possibility. That's more than anybody else seems to be doing." I place my iPhone on the windowsill so he can see what is in the small display, and he looks at it, and then he looks away.

"Imagine two types of nanobots," he says, as if he's talking to someone on the other side of the wavy old window, as if his attention is out there on the sunlight and sparkling water and not on the woman standing next to him, a woman who always feels young and insecure with him, no matter her age or who she grew up to become.

"A nanobot that is biodegradable," he says, "that vanishes at some point after delivering a minute dose of a psychoactive drug, and then a second type of nanobot that self-replicates."

I always feel like someone else with Briggs, someone other than myself, and as I stand next to him, our sleeves touching and feeling his heat, I think of the wonderful and the terrible ways he has shaped me.

"The self-replicating one is what worries us most. Imagine if you got something like that inside you," he says, and what's inside me is the irresistible force that is General John Briggs, and I understand what Fielding felt and how much he must have revered and resented me.

I understand how awful and wonderful it is to be overwhelmed by someone. Like a drug, it occurs to me. An addiction you desperately want to get over and desperately want to keep. Briggs will always have the same effect on me, I think. I won't get over it in this life.

"And the self-replicating nanobot enables the sustained release of something like testosterone," Briggs says, and I feel his energy, the intensity of him, and I'm aware of how close we are standing to each other, drawn to each other, just as we've always been and should never have been. "A drug like PCP couldn't replicate, of course, so that would be a dead-end hit, would be repeated only as the subject repeats his or her nasal spray or injections or applies a new transdermal patch impregnated with biodegradable nanobots. But something your body naturally produces could be programmed to replicate, so the nanobot is replicating, flowing freely through the body, through your arteries, latching onto target areas, like the frontal cortex of your brain, without the need of a battery. Self-propelled and replicating."

Briggs looks at me, and his eyes are hard but there is something in them that he's always held for me, an attachment that is as constant as it is conflicted. I'm vividly reminded of who we were at Walter Reed, when our futures held mystery and limitless possibility, when he was older and profoundly formidable to me and I was a prodigy. He called me Major Prodigy, and then I returned from South Africa and went to Richmond and he didn't call me at all, not for years. What we had with each other was complex and unfathomable, and I'm reminded all over again when I'm with him.

"We wouldn't need wars anymore," he says. "Not the sort of wars you and I know,

Kay. We're on the threshold of a new world where our old wars will seem easy and humane."

"Jack Fielding wasn't that kind of scientist," I reply. "He didn't manufacture those patches and probably would have been extremely resistant and unnerved had someone attempted to entice him into using drugs delivered by nanobots. I would be stunned if he even knew what a nanobot is or would have a clue this was what he was letting loose in his system. He probably thought he was taking some new form of steroid, a designer steroid, something that would help him in his bodybuilding, help alleviate his chronic pain from decades of overuse, help him fight aging. He hated getting older. Getting old wasn't an option to him."

"Well, he won't have to worry about it."

No, he won't, that's for sure. What I say is, "I don't accept that he killed himself because he didn't want to get old. I haven't accepted he killed himself, and have extreme doubts about it."

"I understand you got an exposure to one of his patches," Briggs then says, "and I'm sorry about that, but if you hadn't, you wouldn't know the rest of it. Kay Scarpetta high. Now, that's quite a thought. I'm sorry

I wasn't there to see that."

Benton must have told him.

"This is what we're up against, Kay," Briggs says. "Our brave new world, what I call neuroterrorism, what the Pentagon is calling it, the big fear. Make us crazy and you win. Make us crazy enough and we'll kill ourselves, saving the bad guys the trouble. In Afghanistan, give our troops opium, give them benzodiazepines, give them hallucinogenics, something to take the edge off their boredom, and then see what happens when they climb into their choppers and fighter jets and tanks and Humvees. See what happens when they come home addicts, come home deranged."

"Otwahl," I comment. "We're developing weapons like this?"

"*We* aren't. That's not what DARPA's paying all these millions for, dammit. But someone at Otwahl is, and we don't think it's just one. A cell of superbrains engaging in experiments not authorized or approved, and in fact as dangerous as it gets."

"I assume you know who."

"Damn kids," he says, gazing out at the bright afternoon. "Seventeen, eighteen, with IQs off the charts and full of passion but nothing home up here." He taps his forehead. "I don't need to tell you about boys

574

especially, their frontal lobes not done, like a half-baked cookie until they're in their early to mid-twenties, and yet there they are, fucking around in nanotech labs or with superconductors and robotics and synthetic biology, you name it. Difficult enough we give them guns and throw them into stealth bombers, but we have rules," he says in a hard tone. "We have structures, regimens, leadership, the strictest of supervision, but what the hell do you think goes on at a place like Otwahl where the objective isn't national security and discipline but money and ambition? Those damn whiz kids like Johnny Donahue and his gang over there don't know shit about Afghanistan or Pakistan or Iraq, for Christ's sake. They've never set foot on a military base."

"I don't see Jack's connection to it beyond his teaching martial arts to a few of them." The sky is a spotless deep turquoise, and below it, the blue ocean heaves.

"He got tangled up with them, and my guess is unwittingly became a science project. You know all too well what goes on with research projects and clinical trials, only the type we're familiar with are supervised and strictly monitored by human-study review boards. So where do you get volunteers if you're an eighteen-year-old

Harvard or MIT technical engineer at Ot-wahl? We can only guess that Jack made his contacts likely through the gym, through tae kwon do. All of us are painfully aware of his lifelong problems with substance abuse, mainly steroids, so now someone is going to deliver the elixir of life, the fountain of youth, through pain-relieving patches. But he sure as hell didn't get what he bargained for. Neither did Wally Jamison, Mark Bishop, or Eli Goldman."

"Wally Jamison didn't work at Otwahl."

"For a while he dated someone who does. Dawn Kincaid, another one of the neuro-terrorists over there."

"Johnny Donahue's best friend," I say. "And where is she right now?" I ask. "It seems everyone you've mentioned is dead. Except her." I feel an alarm going off inside me.

"Missing in action," Briggs says. "Didn't show up at Otwahl yesterday or today, sup-posedly is on vacation."

"I'm sure."

"Exactly. We'll find her and get the rest of the story, because no question she's going to be the one to tell it, since her expertise is nanoengineering, nanoscale chemical syn-thesis. Based on what we've learned, she's likely the one developing these nasty little

nanobots that found their way to Jack Fielding and turned him into a Mr. Hyde, to put
it mildly."

"Mr. Hyde," I repeat. "The same thing
Erica Donahue says happened to her son,"
I point out. "Only I doubt Johnny killed
anyone."

"He didn't kill that boy."

"You're convinced Jack did."

"Out of control, sloppy," Briggs says.

"And then he killed Eli." My comment
hangs in the air, and I wonder if it sounds
as hollow to Briggs as it does to me. I
wonder if he can hear how strongly I don't
believe it.

"You realize this is because of the damn
swine flu." He continues staring out at the
day blazing beyond dusty old glass. "If the
stepdaughter's biological father hadn't gotten sick, Liam Saltz wouldn't have had the
pleasure of giving her away at her wedding,
and he wouldn't have come to the U.S., to
Cambridge, to Norton's Woods, at the last
minute. And Jack wouldn't have had to
stab Eli in the back with a damn injection
knife."

"To stop him from telling Dr. Saltz what
you're telling me."

"We can't ask Jack, unfortunately."

"Maybe I could understand it if Eli was

going to tell Dr. Saltz or someone that Jack was selling semen he was stealing from dead bodies. Maybe that would be a motive."

"We don't know what Eli knew. But he likely was aware of Jack and his drugs, obviously was well enough acquainted with him to have one of his guns. That must have been a bad feeling when Jack found out from the Cambridge police that the dead man had a Glock on him with an eradicated serial number."

"Sounds like Marino's filled you in. Told you all this as if it's an irrefutable case history. And it's not. It's a theory. We don't have tangible evidence that Jack killed anyone."

"He knew he was in trouble. That much I think is safe to say," Briggs replies.

"As much as anything is safe to say. I agree he wouldn't have removed the Glock from the lab had he not feared he had a problem. My question is whether he was covering for himself or for someone else."

"He knew damn well we'd restore the serial number, that we'd trace the pistol to him."

" 'We,' " I reply. "I've been hearing that word a lot of late."

"I know how you feel about it." Briggs plants his hands on the windowsill and leans forward, as if his lower back aches. "You think I'm trying to take something away from you. You believe it." He smiles grimly. "Captain Avallone came here last fall."

"Someone that junior? So it wouldn't raise suspicions?"

"Exactly, to appear casual, an informal drop-in while she was on her way somewhere else. When the fact is we were hearing things we didn't like about how your second in command was running the CFC. And I don't need to tell you we have a vested interest. The AFME does, DoD does, a lot of people do. It isn't yours to ruin."

"It isn't mine at all," I answer. "Obviously, I did a terrible job before I even started —"

"You haven't done a terrible job," he cuts me off. "I'm just as much to blame. You picked Jack or, better put, gave in to his wish to come back, and I didn't get in your way, and I sure as hell should have. I didn't want to step on you, and I should have stepped all over you about that decision you made. I figured in four months you'd be home, and I honestly didn't imagine the havoc that man could cause in such a short period of time, but he was mixed up with the Otwahl Technologies Rat Pack, doing drugs and losing it."

"Is that why you delayed my leaving

Dover? So you could find time to replace the leadership at the CFC? Find time to replace me?" I say it as bravely as I can.

"The opposite. To keep you out of it. I didn't want you tarred by it. I delayed you as many times as I could without an out-and-out abduction, and then the father of the bride in London gets the damn swine flu, and a dead body starts bleeding. And your niece shows up in her chopper at Dover, and I tried to get you to stay by offering to transport the body to Dover, but you wouldn't, and that was the end of it. And here we are again."

"Yes, again."

"We've been in our messes before. And we probably will again."

"You didn't send Lucy to pick me up."

"I did not. And I don't think she's likely to take orders from me. Thank God she never thought about enlisting. Would end up in Leavenworth."

"You didn't ask her to bug my office."

"A suggestion made in passing so we could know exactly what Jack was doing."

"Your making a suggestion in passing is like a cannibal offhandedly inviting someone to dinner," I reply.

"Quite an analogy."

"People pay attention to your suggestions,

and you know it."

"Lucy pays attention if it suits her."

"What about Captain Avallone? Did she conspire with Jack, conspire against me?"

"Never. I told you why she showed up last November for her tour. She's quite loyal to you."

"So loyal that she told Jack about Cape Town." I surprise myself by saying it out loud.

"That never happened. Sophia knows nothing about Cape Town."

"Then how did Julia Gabriel know?"

"When she was yelling at you? I see," he says, as if I've just answered a question I didn't know he'd asked. "I stopped outside your door to have a word with you and could hear you talking on the phone, could hear you were somewhat intensely involved. She talked to me, too. Talked to a number of people after getting word on the grapevine that we routinely extract semen at Dover, that every medical examiner's office does this routinely, which is utter bullshit. We would never do such a thing unless it was absolutely proper and approved. She got this impression because Jack was covertly doing that at the CFC and had done so in the case of the man who got killed in a Boston taxicab on his wedding day. Someone connected to Mrs. Gabriel's son. And I think you can understand how she got the idea that her son Peter should get the same special treatment."

"She knows nothing about me personally. She didn't mean it personally. You're sure."

"Why would you believe these negative things about you personally?" he says.

"I think you know why, John."

"No damn way she was referring to anything specific. She's an angry, militant woman and was just venting when she called you the same names she called me, called several other people at Dover. Bigots. Racists. Nazis. Fascists. A lot of staff got christened a lot of ugly names that morning."

Briggs steps back away from the window and collects his laptop off the sill, his way of saying he has to go. He can't have a conversation that lasts more than twenty minutes, and in fact the one we just had is lengthy for him and has tried his patience and gotten too close to too many things.

"One favor you could do for me that would be greatly appreciated," he says. "Please stop telling people I thought MORT was the best thing since sliced bread."

Benton, I think. I guess the two of them have gotten quite cozy.

"Not so, but I understand your remembering it that way, and I'm sorry we butted heads about it," Briggs goes on. "However, given a choice of a robot dragging a dead body off the battlefield and a living person risking his life and limb to do it? That's what I call a Sophie's choice. No good choice, only two bad ones. You weren't right, and I wasn't, either."

"Then we'll leave it at that," I answer. "Both of us made bad decisions."

"It's not like we hadn't made them before," he mutters.

He walks with me out of the sea captain's house, passing through rooms I've already been in. Every space seems empty and depressing, as if there never was anybody home. It doesn't feel that Fielding ever lived here, just parked himself as he worked demonically on his renovations and labored secretly in his cellar, and I just don't know what drove him. Maybe it was money. He'd always wanted money and was never going to get it in our trade, and that bothered him about me, too. I do better than most. I plan well, and Benton has his inheritance, and then there is Lucy, who is obscenely rich from computer technologies she's been selling since she was no older than the neuro-terrorists Briggs just talked about. Thank

God Lucy's inventions are legal, as best I know.

She's inside the CFC truck with Marino and Benton, and the yellow suits and hard hats are off, and everyone looks tired. Anne has driven off in the van again, making another delivery to the labs while more evidence waits for her here, white boxes filled with white paper evidence bags.

"There's a package for you in your car," Briggs says to me in front of the others. "The latest, greatest level four-A armor, specifically designed for females in theater, which would be fine if you ladies would bother with the plates."

"If the vest isn't comfortable," I start to say.

"I think it is, but I'm built a little different from you. Problem's going to be if it won't completely close on the sides. We've seen that too many times, and the projectile finds that one damn opening."

"I'll try it out for you," Lucy offers.

"Good," Marino says to her. "You put it on, and I'll start shooting, see if it works."

"Or trauma from blunt force, which is what most people seem to forget about," I tell Briggs. "The round doesn't penetrate the body armor, but if the blunt force from the impact goes as deep as forty-four millimeters, it's not survivable."

"I haven't been to the range in a while," Lucy chats with Marino. "Maybe we can borrow Watertown's. You been to their new one?"

"I bowl with their range master."

"Oh, yeah, your team of cretins. What's it called? Gutter Balls."

"Spare None. You should bowl with us sometime," Marino says to Briggs.

"Would it be acceptable to you, Colonel, if AFDIL sends in backup scientists to help out at the CFC, for God's sake?" Briggs is saying to me. "Since it seems we have an avalanche of evidence that just keeps coming."

"Any help would be greatly appreciated," I reply. "I'll work on the vest right away."

"Get some sleep first." Briggs says it like an order. "You look like hell."

22

Massachusetts Veterinary Referral Hospital has twenty-four-hour emergency care, and although Sock doesn't seem to be in any distress as he snores curled up like a teacup dog, a Chihuahua or poodle that can fit in a purse, I need to find out what I can about him. It is almost dark, and Sock is in my lap, both of us in the backseat of the borrowed SUV, driving north on I-95.

Having identified the man who was murdered while walking Sock, I intend to bestow the same kindness toward the rescued race dog, because no one seems to know where he came from. Liam Saltz doesn't know and wasn't aware his stepson Eli had a greyhound, or any pet. The superintendent of the apartment building near Harvard Square told Marino that pets aren't allowed. By all accounts, when Eli rented his unit there last spring, he didn't have a dog.

"This doesn't really need to be done tonight," Benton says as we drive and I pet the greyhound's silky head and feel great pity for him. I'm careful about his ragged ears because he doesn't like them touched, and he has old scars on his pointed snout. He is quiet, like something mute. *If only you could talk,* I think.

"Dr. Kessel doesn't mind. We should just do it while we're out," I reply.

"I wasn't thinking about whether some vet minded or not."

"I know you weren't." As I stroke Sock and feel that I might want to keep him. "I'm trying to remember the name of the woman who is Jet Ranger's nanny."

"Let's not go there."

"Lucy's never home, either, and it works out just fine. I think it's Annette, or maybe Lanette. I'll ask Lucy if Annette or Lanette could stop by during the day, maybe first thing each morning. Pick up Sock and take him to Lucy's place so he and Jet Ranger can keep each other company. Then Annette or whatever her name is could bring Sock back to Cambridge at night. What would be so hard about that?"

"We'll find Sock a home when the time is right." Benton takes the Woburn exit, the sign illuminating an iridescent green as our

587

headlights flash over it and he slows down on the ramp.

"You're going to have a lovely home," I tell Sock. "Secret Agent Wesley just said so. You heard him."

"The reason you can't have a dog is the same reason it's always been a bad idea," Benton's voice says from the dark front seat. "Your IQ drops about fifty points."

"It would be a negative number, then. Minus ten or something."

"Please don't start baby talk or gibberish or whatever it is you speak to animals."

"I'm trying to figure out where to stop for food for him."

"Why don't I drop you off and I'll run to a convenience store or market and pick up something," Benton then says.

"Nothing canned. I need to do some research first about brands, probably a small-batch food for seniors because he's not a spring chicken. Speaking of, let's do chicken breasts, white rice, whitefish like cod, maybe a healthy grain like quinoa. So I'm afraid you'll need a real grocery store. I think there's a Whole Foods somewhere around here."

Inside Mass Vet Referral, I'm shown along a long, bright corridor lined with examination rooms, and the technician who accompanies us is very kind to Sock, who is rather sluggish, I notice. He is light on his small feet, slowly ambling along the corridor as if he's never run a race in his life and couldn't possibly.

"I think he's scared," I say to the tech.

"They're lazy."

"Who would think that of a dog that can run forty miles an hour?" I comment.

"When they have to, but they don't want to. They'd rather sleep on the couch."

"Well, I don't want to tug him. And his tail's between his legs."

"Poor baby." The tech stops every other second to pet him.

I suspect Dr. Kessel alerted the staff of the greyhound's sad circumstances, and we've been shown nothing but consideration and compassion and quite a lot of attention, as if Sock is famous, and I sincerely hope he won't be. It wouldn't be helpful if news of him became public, becoming chatter on the Internet and voyeurism or the usual tasteless jokes that seem to crop up around me. Do I take Sock to the morgue? Is Sock being trained as a cadaver dog? What does Sock do when I come home smelling like dead bodies?

He doesn't have a fever, and his gums and teeth are healthy, his pulse and respiration are normal, and no sign of a heart murmur or dehydration, but I won't allow Dr. Kessel to draw blood or urine. We'll reserve a thorough checkup for another time, I suggest, because the dog doesn't need more trauma. "Let him get to know me before he associates me with pain and suffering," I suggest to Dr. Kessel, a thin man in scrubs who looks much too young to have finished veterinary school. Using a small scanner he calls a wand, he looks for a microchip that might have been implanted under the skin of Sock's bony back as the dog sits on the examination table and I pet him.

"Well, he's got one, a nice little RFID chip right where it ought to be over his shoulders," Dr. Kessel says as he looks at what appears in the wand's display. "So what we have is an ID number, and let me give the National Pet Registry a quick call and we'll find out who this guy belongs to."

Dr. Kessel makes the call and takes notes. Momentarily, he hands me a piece of paper with a phone number and the name Lost Sock.

"That's quite a name for a race dog, huh, boy?" the vet says to him. "Maybe he lived up to it and that's why he got put out to pasture. A seven-seven-zero area code. Any idea?"

"I don't know."

He goes to a computer on a countertop and types the area code into a search field and says, "Douglasville, Georgia. Probably a vet's office there. You want to call from here and see if it's open? You're a long way from home," he says to Lost Sock, and I already know I won't call him that.

"You won't be lost ever again," I tell him as we return to the car, because I don't want to make the phone call in front of an audience.

The woman who answers simply says hello, as if I've reached a home number, and I tell her I'm calling about a dog that has this phone number on a microchip.

"Then he's one of our rescues," she says, and she has a Southern drawl. "Probably from Birmingham. We get a lot of them retired from the racetrack there. What's his name?"

I tell her.

"Black and white, five years old."

"Yes. That's correct," I reply.

"Is he all right? Not hurt or anything? He hasn't been mistreated."

"Curled up in my lap. He's fine."

"A sweetheart, but they all are. The nice thing about him is he's cat- and small dog–tolerant and does fine with children as long as they don't yank or tug on his ears. If you hold on a minute, I'll pull him up on my computer and see what I can find out about where he's supposed to be and with whom. I remember a student took him but can't think of her name. Up north. He was wandering loose or what? And where are you calling from? I know he's been trained and socialized, went through the program with flying colors, so you have a really nice dog, and I'm sure his owner must be just beside herself looking for him."

" 'Trained and socialized'?" I ask as I think about Sock being owned by a female student. "What program? Is your rescue group involved in a special program of some sort that takes greyhounds to retirement communities or hospitals, something like that?"

"Prisons," she says. "He was released from the racetrack last July and went through our nine-week program where inmates do the actual training. In his case, he went to the Georgia Prison for Women in Savannah."

I remember Benton telling me about the woman incarcerated in a prison located in Savannah, the therapist convicted of molesting Jack Fielding when he was a troubled boy and sent to live on a ranch near Atlanta.

"We got involved with them because they

were already training bomb-sniffing dogs, and we thought why not see if they want to do something a little more warm and fuzzy," the woman says, and I put her on speakerphone and turn up the volume, "like taking one of these sweet babies. The inmate learns patience and responsibility, and what it feels like to be loved unconditionally, and the greyhound learns commands. Anyway, Lost Sock was trained by a female inmate at the Georgia Prison for Women who said she wanted him when she finally gets out, but I'm afraid that won't be for a while. He was then adopted by someone she recommended, the young woman in Massachusetts. Do you have something to write with?"

She gives me the name Dawn Kincaid and several phone numbers. The address is the one where we just were in Salem, Jack Fielding's house. I seriously doubt Dawn Kincaid lived there all of the time, but she may have been there often. I doubt she was living with Eli Goldman all of the time, either, but it could be that he babysat her dog. Obviously, he knew her, both of them at Otwahl, and I remember that Briggs said Dawn Kincaid's area of expertise was chemical synthesis and nanoengineering. Anyone who is an expert in nanoengineering likely would consider it child's play to rig a pair of headphones with hidden micro audio and video recorders. She likely would have had easy access to Eli's headphones and portable satellite radio. She worked with him. Her dog was in his apartment, meaning she may have been a frequent visitor there. She may have stayed there. She might have a key.

Bryce is still at the CFC when I reach him, and I tell him I made a photocopy of Erica Donahue's letter before it was submitted to the labs, and to please find the file and read the phone numbers. I jot them down and ask what's going on with the DNA lab.

"Working around the clock," Bryce says. "I hope you're not coming back here tonight. Get some rest."

"Did Colonel Pruitt return to Dover, or is he at the labs?"

"I saw him a little while ago. He's here with General Briggs, and some of their people are coming from Dover. Well, they're your people, too, I guess. . . ."

"Get hold of Colonel Pruitt and ask him if per my directive the profiles from the typewriter are going into CODIS immediately, before everything else. Maybe they already have? He'll know what I mean. But what's really important is I want a familial search done, checking any profiles against Jack Fielding's exclusionary DNA, and a familial search done in CODIS that includes a comparison with the profile of an inmate at the Georgia Prison for Women in Savannah. Her name is Kathleen Lawler." I spell the name for him. "A repeat offender . . ."

"Where?"

"The women's prison near Savannah, Georgia. Her DNA should be in the CODIS database. . . ."

"What's that got to . . . ?"

"She and Jack had a child together, a girl. I want a familial search to see if we get a match with anything recovered. . . ."

"He what? He what with who?"

"And the latent prints on the plastic film . . ." I start to say.

"Okay. Now you're scrambling my brains. . . ."

"Bryce. Get unscrambled and be quiet, and you'd better be writing this down."

"I am, boss."

"I want the prints from the film compared to Fielding and to me, and I want DNA done ASAP on that, too. See who else might have touched the film. Maybe whoever made or altered the patch the film came from. And my guess is Otwahl might print its employees, have their prints on file over there. A place that security-minded. It's really important we know exactly who supplied those tampered-with patches. Colonel Pruitt and General Briggs will understand all this."

Next I get Erica Donahue on the phone as Benton drives through Cambridge, taking the same roads Eli did the last time he walked here with Sock on Sunday, on his way to meet his stepfather, to blow the whistle on Otwahl Technologies to a man who could do something about it.

"A welcome guest meaning how often?" I ask Mrs. Donahue after she tells me over speakerphone that Dawn Kincaid has been to the Donahues' home on Beacon Hill many times and is always a welcome guest. The Donahues adore her.

"For dinner or just dropping by, especially on the weekends. You know she came up the hard way, had to work for everything and has had so much misfortune, her mother killed in a car crash, and then her father dying tragically, I forget from what. Such a lovely girl, and she's always been so sweet to Johnny. They met when he started at Otwahl last spring, although she's older, in a Ph.D. program at MIT, transferred from Berkeley, I believe, and just incredibly bright and so attractive. How do you know her?"

"I'm afraid I don't. We've not met."

"Johnny's only friend, really. Certainly the closest one he's ever had. But not romantic, although I've hoped for it, but I don't think that will ever be. I believe she's seeing someone else at Otwahl, a scientist she's working with there."

"Do you know his name?"

"I'm sorry, I don't recall it if I ever knew. I think he's originally from Berkeley as well, and then ended up here because of MIT and Otwahl. A South African. I've heard Johnny rather rudely refer to the Afrikaans nerd Dawn dates, and some other names I won't repeat. And before that it was a dumb jock, according to my son, who's a bit jealous. . . ."

"A dumb jock?" I ask.

"A terribly rude thing to say about someone who died so tragically. But Johnny lacks tact. That's part of his unusualness."

"Do you know the name of the man who died?"

"I don't remember. That football player they found in the harbor."

"Did Johnny talk about that case with you?"

"You're not going to imply that my son had something to do with —"

I calmly reassure her I'm not implying anything of the sort, and I end the call as the SUV crunches through the frozen snow blanketing our Cambridge driveway. At the end of it, under the bare branches of a huge oak tree, is the carriage house, our remodeled garage, its double wooden doors illuminated in our headlights.

"You heard that for yourself," I say to Benton.

"It doesn't mean Jack didn't do it. It doesn't mean he didn't kill Wally Jamison or Mark Bishop or Eli Goldman," he says. "We need to be careful."

"Of course we need to be careful. We're always careful. None of this you already knew?"

"I can't tell you what a patient told me. But let's put it this way, what Mrs. Donahue just said is interesting, and I didn't say I'm convinced about Fielding. I'm saying we just need to be careful because we don't know certain things for a fact right now. But we will. I can promise you that. Everyone's looking for Dawn Kincaid. I'll pass this latest information along," Benton says, and what he's really saying is there's nothing we can do about it or nothing we should do about it, and he's right. We can't go out like a two-party posse and track down Dawn

Kincaid, who probably is a thousand miles from here by now.

Benton stops the SUV and points a remote at the garage. A wooden door rolls up, and a light goes on inside, illuminating his black Porsche convertible and three other empty spaces.

He tucks the SUV next to his sports car, and I slip the lead over Sock's long, slender neck and help him out of my lap, then out of the backseat and into the garage, which is very cold because of the missing window in back. I walk Sock across the rubberized flooring and look through the gaping black square and at our snowy backyard beyond it. It is very dark, but I can make out disturbed snow, a lot of footprints, the neighborhood children again using our property as a shortcut, and that's going to stop. We have a dog, and I will get the backyard walled or fenced in. I will be the mean, crabby neighbor who doesn't allow trespassing.

"What a joke," I comment to Benton as we walk out of the detached garage and onto the slick, snowy driveway, the night sharply cold and white and very still. "You decide to get an alarm system for the garage. So we have one that doesn't work and anybody could climb right in. When are we getting a new window?"

We head to the back door, walking carefully over crusty snow, which Sock clearly doesn't like, snatching his paws up as if he's walking over hot coals and shivering. Dark trees rock in the wind, the night sky scattered with stars, the moon small and bone-white high above the roofs and treetops of Cambridge.

"It sucks," he says, shifting the bag of groceries to his other arm as he finds the door key. "I'll make sure to get them out here tomorrow. It's just I haven't been around and someone has to be home."

"How big a deal to get fencing in back for Sock? So we can let him out and not be afraid he'll run off."

"You told me he doesn't like to run." Benton unlocks the door of the glassed-in porch.

Beyond it are the dark shapes of trees in Norton's Woods. The timber building with its three-tiered metal roof hulks darkly against the night, no lights on inside. I feel sad as I look at the American Academy of Arts and Sciences headquarters and think of Liam Saltz and his slain stepson. I wonder if the maimed flybot is still out there somewhere, buried and frozen, no longer alive, as Lucy put it, because the sun can't find it. I have a funny feeling someone has it. Maybe the FBI, I decide. Maybe people from DARPA, from the Pentagon. Maybe Dawn Kincaid.

"I think we need boots for him," I say. "They make little booties for dogs, and he needs something like that so he doesn't cut his paws on the ice and frozen snow."

"Well, he won't go very far in this cold." Benton opens the door and the alarm begins to beep. "Trust me. You'll have a hard time making him go out in this weather. I hope he's housebroken."

"He needs a couple of coats. I'm surprised Eli or Dawn or whoever didn't have coats for him. Greyhounds need them up here. This really isn't the right part of the world for greyhounds, but it is what it is, Sock. You're going to be warm and well fed and fine."

Benton enters the code on the keypad and resets the alarm the instant he's shut the door behind us, and Sock leans against my legs.

"You build a fire, and I'm making drinks," I tell Benton. "Then I'll cook chicken and rice or maybe switch to cod and quinoa but not right now. He's been eating chicken and rice all day, and I don't want him sick. What would you like? Or maybe I should ask what's in the house."

"Some of your pizza's still in the freezer."

I turn on lights, and the stained-glass windows in the stairwell are dark but will be gorgeous from the outside, backlit by lights inside the house. I imagine the French wildlife scenes brilliantly lit up when I take Sock out at night and how cheerful that will be. I imagine playing with him in the backyard in the spring and summer, when it's warm, and seeing the vibrant windows lit up at night and of how peaceful and civilized that will be. Living on the edge of Harvard and coming home from the office to my old dog, and I'll plant a rose garden in back, and I think how good that sounds.

"Nothing to eat for me right now," Benton says, taking off his coat. "First things first. A very strong drink, please."

He goes into the living room, and Sock's nails click against hardwood, then are silent on rugs as we pass from room to room and into the kitchen, where I feel him leaning against my legs as I open dark cherry cabinets above stainless-steel appliances. Wherever I move, he moves and presses against me, pushing against the back of my legs as I get out tumblers, then ice from the freezer, and then a bottle of our very best

Scotch, a Glenmorangie single-malt aged twenty-five years that was a Christmas gift from Jaime Berger. My heart aches as I pour drinks and think of Lucy and Jaime breaking up and of people who are dead, and of what Fielding did to his life, and now he's dead. He'd been killing himself all along, and then someone finished it for him, stuck a Glock in his left ear and pulled the trigger, most likely when he was standing near the cryogenic freezer, where he stored ill-gotten semen before shipping it to wives, mothers, and lovers of men who died young.

Who would Fielding trust so much as to allow the person into his cellar, to share his illegal venture capitalism with, to let borrow his sea captain's house and probably everything he owned? I remember what his former boss told me, the chief in Chicago. He commented he was glad Jack was moving to Massachusetts to be near family, only he wasn't referring to Lucy, Marino, and me, not to any of us, not even to his current wife and their two kids. I have a feeling the chief meant someone I never knew existed before now, and if I weren't so selfish and egotistical, maybe the thought would have occurred to me sooner.

How typical of me to assume such importance in Fielding's life, and he wasn't thinking of me at all when he told his former chief what he did about family. Fielding probably meant the daughter from his first love, probably the first woman he ever had sex with, the therapist at the ranch near Atlanta who bore his daughter, and then gave her up just as Fielding was given up. A girl with genetic loading, as Benton put it, that would land her in prison if she didn't end up dead. And she moved here last year from Berkeley, and then Fielding moved back here from Chicago.

"Nineteen seventy-eight," I say as I walk into the dark, cozy living room of built-in bookcases and exposed old beams. The lights are out, and a fire crackles and glows on the brick hearth, and sparks swarm as Benton moves a log with the poker. "She would be about Lucy's age, about thirty-one." I hand him a tumbler of Scotch, a generous pour with only a few cubes of ice. The whisky looks coppery in the firelight. "Do you think it's her? That Dawn Kincaid is his biological daughter? Because I do. I hope you didn't already know about her."

"I promise I didn't. If it's true."

"You really weren't focused on Dawn Kincaid or a child Fielding had with the woman in prison."

"I really wasn't. You need to remember

604

how recent this all has been, Kay." We settle next to each other on the sofa, and then Sock settles in my lap. "Fielding wasn't on anybody's radar until last week, at least not for anything criminal, nothing violent. But I should have gone to the trouble to find out about the baby adopted," Benton says, and he sounds slightly angry with himself. "I know I would have eventually, and I hadn't yet because it didn't seem important."

"In the grand scheme of things and at the time, it wasn't. I'm not trying to put you on the defensive."

"I knew from the records I reviewed that the baby, a girl, was given up for adoption while the mother was in prison the first time. An adoption agency in Atlanta," he says. "Maybe like some adopted children, she set about to find out who her biological parents were."

"As smart as she is, that probably wasn't hard."

"Christ." Benton takes a swallow of Scotch. "It's always the one thing you think doesn't matter, the one thing you think can wait."

"I know. That's almost always how it works out. The detail you don't want to bother with."

We sit on the sofa, looking at the fire, and

Sock is curled up on top of me. He is attached to me. He won't let me out of his sight. He has to be touching me, as if he's certain I'll disappear and he'll be abandoned in a run-down house again where horrible things happen.

"I think there is a very good probability that's what the DNA is going to tell us about Dawn Kincaid," Benton continues in a flat tone. "I wish we could have known it before, but there wasn't a reason to look."

"You don't have to keep saying that. Why would you have looked? What would a baby he fathered when he was a teenager have to do with what's gone on?"

"Obviously, it might have."

"Twenty-twenty hindsight."

"I knew he was writing Kathleen Lawler, e-mailing her, but there's nothing criminal about that, nothing even suspicious, and no mention of anyone by the name of Dawn, just an *interest* they had in common. I recall that phrase, the interest they shared. I thought he fucking meant crime, maybe their old crime and how it changed who they were forever, that was the *interest* they had in common," he says ruefully, trying to figure it out as he talks. "Now I have to wonder if the interest they shared might be their child, might even be Dawn Kincaid.

Just unfortunate that Jack never got past that part of his life, that he was still connected to Kathleen Lawler, and probably she to him. And then a daughter who got his intelligence, his good parts and his bad parts. And the mother's good and really bad parts. And who the hell knows all the places that daughter's been bounced around to but never lived with her father, who I suspect she never knew while she was growing up. Of course, this is complete speculation on our part."

"Not really. It's like an autopsy. Most of the time it tells me what I already know."

"I'm afraid we might know. I'm afraid we really might, and it's a horror story, really. Talk about bad seed and the sins of the father."

"Some would say it was the sins of the mother in this case."

"I should make some phone calls," Benton says as he drinks and sits in front of the fire, staring into it.

He is angry with himself. He can't tolerate missing that one thing, as he calls it. In his mind, he should have made it a burning priority to track down a baby born to a woman in prison more than thirty years ago, and that really is unreasonable. Why would he think it mattered?

"Jack never mentioned Dawn Kincaid to me or a daughter who was given up for adoption, absolutely nothing like that. I had no idea." The whisky has heated me up, and I pet Sock, feeling the bumps of his ribs, like a washboard, and feeling the sadness that has settled inside me and won't go away. "I seriously doubt she ever lived with him until maybe very recently, don't see how. Not in Richmond, absolutely not. And it's unlikely his wives would have allowed a daughter from that early criminal liaison to be part of their lives, assuming they knew. He probably didn't tell them, except to allude to his difficulty with cases involving dead children. If he even said that much to the women in his life."

"He said it to you."

"I wasn't just a woman in his life. I was his boss."

"That's not all."

"Please not again, Benton. Really. It's getting to be ridiculous. I know you're in a mood and both of us are tired."

"It's the thought of you not being honest with me. I don't care what you did back then. I don't have a right to care about what you did before we were together."

"Well, you do care, and you have a right to care about anything you want. But how many times do I have to tell you?"

"I remember the first time we socialized."

"How dated that sounds, no pun intended. Like two people on a Sunday night in the fifties." I reach for his hand.

"Nineteen eighty-eight, that Italian place in the Fan. Remember Joe's?"

"Every time I was out with the cops, that's where we'd end up. Nothing like a big plate of baked spaghetti after a homicide scene."

"You hadn't been the chief long." Benton talks to the fire, and he strokes my hand gently, both of our hands resting on top of Sock. "I asked you about Jack because you were so industrious about him, so vigilant, so focused, and I thought it was unusual. The more I probed, the more evasive you got. I've never forgotten it."

"It wasn't because of him," I answer. "It was because of the way I felt about me."

"Because of Briggs. Not an easy man to be under. And I don't mean that the way it just came out. Not that you would necessarily be the one under him or anyone. Probably on top."

"Please don't be snide."

"I'm teasing you, and both of us are too tired and frayed around the edges for teasing. I apologize."

"What happened is my fault, anyway. I

won't blame him or anyone," I continue. "But he was God back then. To someone like me. I was really very sheltered. I think all I'd ever done was go to school, study, consumed by residencies, Lord, how many years of them, like a long dream of working hard and rarely sleeping, and of course doing what I was told by people in authority. In the early days hardly questioning it. Because I felt I didn't deserve to be a doctor. I should have run my father's small grocery store, been a wife and mother, lived simply, like everyone else in my family."

"John Briggs was the most powerful person you'd ever come across. I can see why," Benton says, and I sense he might know Briggs better than I've imagined. I wonder how much they've talked these past six months, not only about Fielding but about everything.

"Please don't be threatened by him," I'm saying as I wonder what Benton knows about Briggs and, most of all, what Benton knows about me. "My past with him doesn't matter anymore. And it was about my perception, anyway. I needed him to be powerful. I needed that back then."

"Because your father was anything but powerful. All those years he was ill, with you taking care of him, taking care of everyone. You wanted someone who would take care of you for once."

"And when you get what you want, guess what happens. John took terrible care of me. Or it would be more accurate if I said that I took terrible care of myself. I knew — better yet, was persuaded — to go against my conscience and to be led into something that wasn't right."

"Politics," Benton says as if he knows.

"What would you know about what happened back then?" I look at him, and shadows move on his keenly handsome face in the firelight.

"I think it's something like two years' service for every year of medical or law school paid for by the military. So unless my math is really bad, you owed the U.S. government eight years of service with the air force, more specifically, the AFIP, AFME."

"Six. I finished Hopkins in three years."

"Okay, that's right. But you served what, a year? And every time I've asked about it, you give me the same song and dance about the AFIP wanting to set up a fellowship program in Virginia and they decided to plant you there as chief."

"We did start an AFIP fellowship program. In those days there weren't that many

611

offices if you were AFIP and wanted to specialize in forensics. So we added Richmond. And now, of course, us. The CFC. We'll be gearing up for that soon. Any minute I've got to get that going."

"Politics," Benton says again as he takes a drink of Scotch. "You've always felt guilty about something, and for the longest time I thought it was Jack. Because you'd had an affair with him, repeating his original injury. A powerful woman in charge of him has sex with him, victimizing him again, returning him to the scene of the original crime. For you? That would have been unpardonable."

"Except I didn't."

"You promise."

"I promise."

"Well, you did something." He's not going to stop until we have it before us.

"Yes, I did, but it was before Jack," I answer.

"You did what you were ordered to do, Kay. And you've got to let it go," he says, because he knows. It's obvious he does.

"I never told their families," I reply, and Benton doesn't say anything. "The two women murdered in Cape Town. I couldn't call their families and tell them what really happened. They think it was racism, gang members during Apartheid. A high crime rate of blacks killing whites suited certain political leaders back then. They wanted it to be true. The more, the better."

"Those leaders are gone now, Kay."

"You should make your phone calls, Benton. Call Douglas or whoever and tell them about Dawn Kincaid and who she probably is and the tests I've ordered."

"The Reagan administration is long gone, Kay." Benton's going to make me talk about it, and I'm convinced it's been talked about before. Briggs probably said something to him because Briggs knows damn well how haunted I am.

"What I did isn't long gone," I reply.

"You didn't do a damn thing that was wrong. You had nothing to do with their deaths. I don't have to know all the details to say that much," Benton says as he laces his fingers in mine, our joined hands gently rising and sinking in rhythm to Sock's breathing.

"I feel as if I had everything to do with it," I answer.

"You didn't," he says. "Other people did, and you were forced to be silent. Do you know how often it is I can't tell what I know? My whole life has been like that. The alternative is to make things worse. That's the test. Does telling make it worse and

613

cause others to be persecuted and killed. *Primum non nocere.* First, do no harm. That's what I weigh everything against, and I sure as hell know you do the same."

I don't want a lecture right now.

"Do you think she did it?" I ask as Sock breathes slowly, contentedly, as if he's lived here always and is home. "Killed all of them?"

"Now I'm wondering." He looks at his drink, and it turns the color of honey in the firelight.

"To put Jack out of his misery?"

"She probably hated him," Benton says. "That's why she would have been drawn to him, wanted to get to know him as an adult, if that's what she did."

"Well, I don't think he shackled Wally Jamison in his cellar and hacked him to death. If Wally came to the house in Salem willingly, probably it was upon Dawn's invitation, to see her. Maybe play out some fantasy, a game, a macabre sex game on Halloween. Maybe she did a similar thing to Mark Bishop, and when she has them under control, under her spell, exactly where she wants them, she strikes. A rush, a thrill, for someone diabolical like that."

"Liam Saltz's second wife, Eli's mother, is South African," Benton says. "As is her husband from that earlier marriage, Eli's biological father, and Eli was wearing a ring that likely was taken from the Donahue house, likely taken by Dawn along with the typewriter, the stationery. Maybe used the duct tape to collect fibers, trace evidence, DNA from the Donahue house, while she was at it. Make it look like the letter really did come from the mother, making sure that Johnny's alibi was weakened further by it."

"Now you're thinking irrationally like me," I reply wryly. "That's what I believe happened, or close to it."

"The game," Benton muses in that tone he has when he hates what someone has done. "Games and more games, elaborate, intricate dramas. I can't wait to meet the fucking bitch. I really can't wait."

"Maybe you've had enough Scotch."

"Not half enough. Who better to manipulate Johnny Donahue than someone like that, some attractive brain trust of a woman who's older? To plant the idea in that poor kid's head that he murdered a six-year-old while he was delusional and having memory lapses because of drugs she was spiking his meds with? Spiking Fielding's meds with. Who knows who else? A poisonous person who destroys the people she's supposed to love, pays them back for every crime committed against her, and you pile on her genetic predisposition and maybe the same cocktail Fielding was on?"

"That would be the perfect storm, as they say."

"Let's see what kind of killing machine I can be and get away with it," he says in that tone of his, and if I could look into his eyes, I know what would be in them. Complete contempt. "And after it's ended, no one is left standing but her. Fucking bulletproof."

"You could be right." And I remember the box I left in the car. "Why don't you make your phone calls."

"Borderline, sadistic, manipulative, narcissistic."

"I guess some people are everything." I set down my glass on the coffee table and ease Sock off my lap and onto the rug.

"Some people just about are."

"I forgot the box Briggs left for me," I say as I get up from the sofa. "And I'll take Sock out back. You ready to go potty?" I ask the dog. "Then I'll warm up pizza. I don't suppose we have anything for salad. What the hell have you eaten the entire time I've been gone? Let me guess. You run over to Chang An for Chinese food and live on that for the next three days."

"That would be really good right now."

"You've probably been doing it every week."

"I'd rather have your pizza anytime."

"Don't try to be nice," I reply.

I walk into the kitchen for Sock's lead and slip it around his neck and find a flashlight in a drawer, an old Maglite that Marino gave me aeons ago, long and black aluminum, powered by fat D batteries, reminding me of the old days, when police used to carry flashlights the size of nightsticks instead of everything being so small, like the SureFire lights Lucy likes and what Benton keeps in his glove box. I disarm the alarm system and worry about Sock, about how cold it is, realizing as we go down the back steps in the dark that I didn't bother with a coat for me, and I notice that the motion-sensor light attached to the garage is out. I try to remember if it was out an hour or so ago when we got home, but I'm not sure. There is so much to fix, so much to change, so much to do. Where will I start when tomorrow comes?

Benton didn't lock the door to the detached garage, because what would be the point with an open window the size of a big-screen TV? Inside the remodeled carriage house it is dark and bitterly cold, and air blows in through the open black square that I can barely make out, and I turn on the Maglite and it doesn't work. The batteries must be dead, and how stupid of me not to check before I left the house. I point the key at the SUV, and the lock chirps but the interior light doesn't go on because it's a damn Bureau car, and Special Agent Burke isn't about to have an interior light that comes on. I feel around on the backseat for the box, which is quite large, and I realize it won't be easy to carry it and deal with Sock. In fact, I can't.

"I'm sorry, Sock," I say to the dog as I feel him shivering against my legs. "I know it's cold in here. Just give me a minute. I'm so sorry. But as you're discovering, I'm a very stupid person."

I use the car key to slit the tape on top of the box and pull out a vest that is familiar even if I've not examined this particular brand, but I recognize the feel of tough nylon and the stiffness of ceramic-Kevlar plates that Briggs or someone has already inserted into the internal pockets. I tear open the Velcro straps on the sides to open up the vest so I can sling it over my shoulder. I feel the weight of the vest draped over me as I shove the car door shut, and Sock jumps away from me like a rabbit. He yanks the lead out of my hand.

"It's just the car door, Sock. It's all right, come here, Sock. . . ." I start to call out at the same time something else moves inside the garage near the open window, and I turn around to see what it is, but it is too dark to see anything.

"Sock? Is that you over there?"

The dark, frigid air moves around me, and the blow to my back feels like a hammer hitting me between my shoulder blades, as if a loud hissing dragon is attacking me, and I lose my balance.

A piercing scream and hissing, and a warm, wet mist spatters my face as I fall hard against the SUV and swing with all my might at whatever it is. The Maglite cracks like a bat against something hard that gives beneath the weight of the blow and then moves, and I swing again and hit something again, something that feels different. I smell the iron smell of blood and taste it on my lips and in my mouth as I swing again and again at air, and then the lights are on and the glare is blinding and I'm covered with a fine film of blood as if I've been spray-painted with it. Benton is inside the garage, pointing a pistol at the woman in a huge black coat facedown on the rubberized floor. I notice blood pooling under her bloody right hand, and near it, a severed fingertip with a glittery white French nail, and near that, a knife with a thin steel blade and a thick black handle with a release button on the shiny metal guard.

"Kay? Kay? Are you all right? Kay! Are you all right?"

I realize Benton is shouting at me as I crouch by the woman and touch the side of her neck and find her pulse. I make sure she is breathing and turn her over to check her pupils. Neither of them is fixed. Her face is bloody from the Maglite smashing into it, and I am startled by the resemblance, the dark blond hair cut very short, the strong features, and the full lower lip that look like Jack Fielding's. Even the small ears close to the sides of her head look like his, and I feel the strength in her upper body, her shoulders, although she isn't a large person, maybe five-foot-six or -seven and slender but with large bones like her dead father. All this is flooding my senses as I tell Benton to rush into the house and call 911, and to bring a container of ice.

23

A warm front moved in during the night and brought more snow, this time a gentle snow that falls silently, muting all sound, covering everything that is ugly, softly rounding whatever is sharp and hard.

I sit up in bed inside the master bedroom on the second floor of the house in Cambridge, and snow is coming down, piling in the bare branches of an oak tree on the other side of the big window nearest me. A moment ago a fat gray squirrel was there, perfectly balanced on the smallest twig, and we were eye to eye, his cheeks moving as he stared through the window at me while I sifted through the paperwork and photographs in my lap. I smell old paper and dust and the medicine smell of the wipes I used on Sock, who I suspect hadn't had his ears cleaned in recent memory, maybe not ever, not the way I cleaned them. He didn't like it at first, but I talked him into it with a soft voice and a sweet-potato treat that Lucy brought by when she gave me a container of the same wipes she uses on her bulldog. The miconazole-chlorhexidine is good for pachydermatis, I made the mistake of mentioning to my niece very early this morning when she stopped by to check on me.

Jet Ranger wouldn't appreciate being called a pachyderm, Lucy retorted. He's not an elephant or a hippopotamus, and there's only so much one can do about his weight. She has him on a new diet for seniors, but he can't exercise because of his bad hips, and the snow gives him a rash on his paws for some reason, and his legs are too short for snow this deep, so he can't go on even the briefest walk this time of year, she went on and on, and I'd truly offended her. But that's the way Lucy can get when she's worried and scared, and most of all she's upset she wasn't here last night. She's angry she wasn't here to deal with Dawn Kincaid, but I'm not sorry in the least. I can't say I'm proud of myself for giving someone a linear skull fracture and a concussion, but if Lucy had been in the garage instead of me, there would be one more person dead. My niece would have killed Dawn Kincaid for sure, probably shot her, and there are enough people dead.

It's also possible that Lucy wouldn't have survived the encounter, I don't care what she says. It depends on two details that made the difference in my still being here and Dawn Kincaid being locked up on the forensic ward of an area hospital. I don't think she was expecting me to walk into the garage. I think she was lurking on the other side of the gaping window, waiting for me to take Sock into the dark backyard. But I surprised her by entering the garage first to get what I'd left in the car, and by the time she slipped through the big space where the window was supposed to be, I'd already opened the box and slung the level IV-A tactical vest over my shoulder. When she stabbed at my back with the injection knife, it hit a nylon-covered ceramic-Kevlar plate, and the terrific jolt caused by that absolute stopping action caused her fingers to slide along the blade. She cut three fingers to the bone and severed the tip of her pinkie at the same time she was releasing the CO_2, and a mist of her blood sprayed all over me.

My point to Lucy was that unless she'd caused Dawn to lose the surprise element for the attack and unless Lucy also just happened to have on body armor or at least have it draped over her torso, she might not have been as fortunate as I was. So my niece should stop saying it's a damn shame she wasn't here last night, claiming that she sure as hell would have taken care of things, as if I didn't, because I did, even though it was luck. I think I took care of things just fine and only hope I can take care of a far more important matter that hasn't killed me yet but at times has certainly felt like it might.

"She'd told me there had been catcalls and ugly comments," Mrs. Pieste is telling me over the phone as I go over her daughter's case with her. "Calling her a Boer. Telling the Boers to go home, and as you know, that's Afrikaans for farmer but it's really meant to disparage all white South Africans. And I kept telling the man from the Pentagon that I didn't care about the reason, whether it was Noonie and Joanne being white or American or assumed to be South African. And, of course, they weren't South African. I didn't care why. I just didn't want to believe the suffering he described."

"Do you remember who that man from the Pentagon was?" I ask.

"A lawyer."

"It wasn't a colonel in the army," I hope out loud.

"It was some young lawyer at the Pentagon who worked for the secretary of defense. I don't remember his name."

Then it wasn't Briggs.

"A fast-talking one," Mrs. Pieste adds disdainfully. "I remember I didn't like him. But I wouldn't have liked anybody who told me the things he did."

"The only comfort I can offer out of all of this," I repeat, "is Noonie and Joanne didn't suffer the way you've been led to believe. I can't say with absolute certainty that they weren't aware of being smothered, but it is extremely likely they weren't aware because they were drugged."

"But that would have been tested for," Mrs. Pieste's voice says, and she has a Massachusetts accent, can't pronounce R's, and I didn't realize she's originally from Andover. After Noonie's murder, the Piestes moved to New Hampshire, I just found out.

"Mrs. Pieste, I think you understand nothing was tested as it was supposed to be," I reply.

"Why didn't you?"

"The medical examiner in Cape Town —"

"But you signed the death certificate, Dr. Scarpetta. And the autopsy report. I have copies that lawyer from the Pentagon sent me."

"I didn't sign them." I refused to sign documents that I knew were a lie, but knowing they were a lie made me guilty of it anyway. "I don't have copies, as hard as that probably is for you to believe," I then say. "They weren't supplied to me. What I have are my own notes, my own records, which I mailed back to the U.S. before I left South Africa because I worried my luggage would be gone through, and it was."

"But you signed what I have."

"I promise I didn't," I reply calmly but firmly. "My guess is certain people made certain my signature was forged on those falsified documents in the event I decided to do what I'm doing now."

"If you decided to tell the truth."

It's so hard to hear it stated so bluntly. The truth. Implying what I've told or not told over the years makes me a liar.

"I'm sorry," I tell her again. "You had a right to know the truth back then, at the time of your daughter's death. And the death of her friend."

"I can see why you didn't say anything back then, though," Mrs. Pieste says, and she sounds only slightly upset. Mostly she sounds interested and relieved to be talking about something that has dominated her life for most of it. "When people do things like this, no telling where they'll stop. Well, there's no limit. Other people would have gotten hurt. Including you."

"I wouldn't have wanted anybody else to get hurt," I reply, and I feel worse if what she's saying is that I was silent out of fear for my own safety. I was afraid of a lot of things and a host of people I couldn't see. I was afraid of other people dying, of people being wrongly accused.

"I hope you understand that when I read the death certificate and autopsy report, not that I understand most of the medical terms, well, one would think the findings are yours," Mrs. Pieste says.

"They absolutely weren't, and they are false. There was no tissue response to the injuries. All of it was postmortem. In fact, hours after the deaths, Mrs. Pieste. What was done to Noonie and Joanne occurred many hours after they had died."

"If there wasn't a test for drugs, then how can you be sure they were given something?" her voice goes on, and I hear the sound of another phone being picked up.

"This is Edward Pieste," a man's voice says. "I'm on, too. I'm Noonie's father."

"I'm so sorry for your loss." It sounds weak, perfectly insipid. "I wish I had exactly the right words to say to both of you. I'm sorry you were lied to and that I permitted it, and although I won't make excuses . . ."

"We understand why you couldn't say what happened," the father replies. "The feelings back then, and our government secretly in collusion with those who wanted to keep Apartheid alive. That's why Noonie was making that documentary. They wouldn't let the film crew into South Africa. Each of them had to go in as if they were tourists. A big dirty secret, what our government was doing to support the atrocities over there."

"It wasn't that big of a secret, Eddie." Mrs. Pieste's voice.

"Well, the White House put on the good face."

"I'm sure they told you about the documentary Noonie was making? She had such a future," Mrs. Pieste says to me as I look at a picture of her daughter that I wouldn't want the Piestes to ever see.

"About the children of Apartheid," I reply. "I did see it when it aired here."

"The evils of white supremacy," she says. "Of any supremacy, period."

"I missed the first part of what the two of you have been talking about," Mr. Pieste says. "Was out shoveling the driveway."

"He doesn't listen," his wife says. "A man his age shoveling snow, but he's the hard head." She says it with sad affection. "Dr.

Scarpetta was telling me Noonie and Joanne were drugged."

"Really. Well, that's something." He says it with no energy in his tone.

"I got to the apartment several days after their deaths and did a retrospective. It was staged, of course; their crime scene was staged," I explain. "But there were beer cans, plastic cups, and a wine bottle in the kitchen trash, a bottle of white wine from Stellenbosch, and I managed to get the cans, the bottle, and cups along with other items, and have them sent back to the States, where I had them tested. We found high levels of GHB in the wine bottle and two of the cups. Gamma hydroxybutyric acid, commonly known as a date-rape drug."

"They did say there was rape," Mr. Pieste says with the same empty affect.

"I don't know for a fact that they were raped. There was no physical sign of it, no injuries except staged ones inflicted post-mortem, and swabs I had tested privately here in the U.S. were negative for sperm," I reply, looking through photographs of the nude bodies bound to chairs I know the women weren't sitting in when they were murdered. I look at close-ups showing a livor mortis pattern that told me the women were lying in bed on rumpled sheets for at least twelve hours after death.

I go through photographs I took with my own camera of hacking and cutting injuries that barely bled, and ligatures that scarcely left a mark on the skin because the brutes behind all this were too ignorant to know what the hell they were doing, someone hired or assigned by government or military operatives to spike a bottle of local wine and have drinks with the women, possibly a friend or they thought the person was friendly or safe, when, of course, he was anything but, and I tell them that serology tests I had done after I got home indicated the presence of a male. Later, when I had DNA testing done, I got the profile of a European or white male who remains unknown. I can't say for a fact it is the profile of the killer, but it was someone drinking beer inside the apartment, I add.

As much as one can reconstruct anything, I tell the Piestes what I think happened, that after Noonie and Joanne were drugged and groggy or unconscious, their assailant helped them to bed and smothered them with a pillow, and I based this on pinpoint hemorrhages and other injuries, I explain. Then for some reason this person must have left. Maybe he wanted to come back later with others involved in the conspiracy, or it could be that he waited inside the apartment for his compatriots to arrive, I don't know. But by the time the women were bound and cut and mutilated so savagely, they had been dead for a while, and it couldn't have been more obvious to me when I finally saw them.

"Up here we got about four inches already," Mr. Pieste says after a while, after he's heard enough. "That on top of ice. Did you get the ice down there in Cambridge?"

"I guess we should complain about this to someone," Mrs. Pieste says. "Does it matter how long it's been?"

"It never matters how long it's been when you're talking about the truth," I reply. "And there's no statute of limitation on homicide."

"I just hope they didn't lock up someone who shouldn't have been," Mrs. Pieste then says.

"The cases have remained unsolved. Attributed to black gang members but no arrests," I tell them.

"But it was probably someone white," she says.

"Someone white was drinking beer inside the apartment, that much I can say with reasonable certainty."

"Do you know who did it?" she asks.

"Because we would want them punished," her husband says.

"I only know the type of people who likely did it. Cowardly people all about power and politics. And you should do what you feel, what's in your heart."

"Eddie, what do you think?"

"I'll write a letter to Senator Chappel."

"You know how much good that will do."

"Then to Obama, Hillary Clinton, Joe Biden. I'll write everyone," he says.

"What will anybody do about it now?" Mrs. Pieste says to her husband. "I don't know that I can live through it again, Eddie."

"Well, I need to go clear the walk again," he says. "Got to stay on top of the snow, and it's really coming down. Thank you for your time and trouble, ma'am," he says to me. "And for going ahead and telling us. I know that wasn't an easy decision, and I'm sure my daughter would appreciate it if she was here to tell you herself."

After I hang up, I sit on the bed for a while, the paperwork and photographs back in the gray accordion file they've been in for more than two decades. I'll return the file to the safe in the basement, I decide. But not now. I don't feel like going down into the basement and into that safe right now, and I think someone has just pulled into our driveway. I hear snow crunching, and I'm not in a good state of mind to see whoever it is. I'll stay up here for a little while longer. Maybe make a grocery list or contemplate errands or just pet Sock for a minute or two.

"I can't take you for a walk," I tell him.

He is curled up next to me, his head on my thigh, unperturbed by the sad conversation he just overheard and having no idea what it says about the world he lives in. But then he knows cruelty, maybe knows it better than the rest of us.

"No walks without a coat," I go on, petting him, and he yawns and licks my hand, and I hear the beeping of the alarm being disarmed, then the front door shuts. "I think we're going to try boots," I tell Sock as Marino's and Benton's voices drift up from the entryway. "You probably aren't going to like these little shoes they make for dogs and are likely to get quite annoyed with me, but I promise it's a good thing. Well, we have company." I recognize Marino's heavy footsteps on the stairs. "You remember him from yesterday, in the big truck. The big man in yellow who gets on my nerves most of the time. But for future reference, you have no reason to be afraid of him. He's not a bad person, and as you may be aware, people who have known each other for a very long time tend to be ruder to each other than they are to people they don't like half as much."

"Anybody home?" Marino's big voice precedes him into the bedroom as the doorknob turns, and then he knocks as he opens the door. "Benton said you was decent. Who were you talking to? You on the phone?"

"He's clairvoyant, then," I reply from the bed, where I'm under the covers, nothing but pajamas on. "And I'm not on the phone and wasn't talking to anyone."

"How's Sock? How ya doing, boy?" he then says before I can answer. "How come he smells funny? What did you put on him, flea medicine? This time of year? You look okay. How are you feeling?"

"I cleaned his ears."

"So, how are you doing, Doc?"

Marino looms over me, and his presence seems larger than usual because he's in a heavy parka and a baseball cap and hiking boots while I'm in nothing but flannel, modestly tucked under a blanket and a duvet. He has a small black case in his hands that I recognize as Lucy's iPad, unless he's managed to get one of his own, which I doubt.

"I didn't get hurt. There's nothing wrong with me. I've just been staying in this morning, taking care of a few things," I say to him. "I'm assuming Dawn Kincaid is fine. Last I heard, she was stable."

"Stable? You're joking, right?"

"I'm talking about her physical condition. The reattachment of her finger and the damage to the rest of them, the other three that were cut so severely. It's probably a good thing for her it was so cold in the garage. And, of course, we thought to pack her hand and her severed finger in ice. I'm hoping that helped. Do you know? I haven't heard a word. What's her status? I've not heard any reports since she was admitted last night."

"You're kidding, right?" Marino's eyes look at me, and they're just as bloodshot as they were yesterday in Salem.

"I'm not kidding. Nobody's told me a word. Benton said earlier he would check, but I don't think he has."

"He's been on the phone with us all morning."

"Maybe you'd be so kind as to call the hospital and check."

"Like I give a flying fuck if she loses a

635

finger or all of her damn fingers," Marino says. "Why would you give a fuck? You afraid she'll sue you? That must be it, and wouldn't that figure? She probably will. Will sue you for maybe losing the use of her hand so she can't build nanobots or whatever anymore, a psycho like that. I guess psychopaths are stable in the mental illness sense of the word. Can you be crazy and a psychopath? And still be put together well enough to work at a place like Otwahl? Her case is going to be one big damn problem. If she gets out, well, can you imagine?"

"Why would she get out?"

"I'm just telling you the case is going to be a problem. You won't be safe if she's on the loose again. None of us will be."

He helps himself to the foot of the bed, and the bed sinks and it feels like I'm suddenly sitting uphill as he makes himself comfortable, petting Sock and informing me that the police and the FBI found the "rat hole" Dawn Kincaid had rented, a one-bedroom apartment in Revere, just outside of Boston, where she stayed when she wasn't with Eli Goldman or with her biological father, Jack Fielding, or whoever else she had entangled in her web at any point in time. Marino slips the iPad out of its case and turns it on as he lets me know that he and Lucy and quite a number of other investigators have been searching the rat-hole apartment for hours, going through Dawn's computer and everything she has, including everything she's stolen.

"What about her mother?" I ask. "Has anybody talked to her?"

"Dawn's been in contact with her for a number of years, visiting her in prison down there in Georgia now and then. Reconnected with her and with Fielding on and off over the years. Latches on when she wants something, a first-class manipulator and user."

"But does the mother know what's happened up here?"

"Why do you care what a fucking child molester thinks?"

"Her relationship with Jack wasn't that simple. It's not as easily explained as you so eloquently just put it. I'd hate for her to hear about him on the news."

"Who gives a shit."

"I never want anybody to find out that way," I reply. "I don't care who it is. Her relationship with him wasn't simple," I repeat. "Relationships like that never are."

"Plain and simple to me. Black and white."

"If she hears it on the news," I reply, and

I realize I'm perseverating. "I always hate for that to happen. Such an inhumane way for people to find out terrible things like this. That's my concern."

"A klepto," Marino then says, because his only interest is the case and what the investigators have been discovering at Dawn Kincaid's apartment.

Apparently, she is a bona fide klepto, to quote Marino. Someone who seemed to have taken souvenirs from all sorts of people, he goes on, including items stolen from people we have no idea about. But some of what investigators have found so far has been identified as jewelry and rare coins from the Donahue house, and also several rare autographed musical manuscripts that Mrs. Donahue had no idea were missing from the family library.

Recovered from a locked chest in a closet in Dawn's apartment were guns believed to have been removed from Fielding's collection, and his wedding band. Also in this same trunk, a martial-arts carry bag, I'm told, and inside it, a black satin sash, a white uniform, sparring gear, a lunch bag filled with rusty L-shaped flooring nails, and a hammer, and a pair of boy's Adidas tae kwon do shoes believed to be the ones Mark Bishop was wearing while practicing kicks in his backyard the late afternoon he was killed. Although no one is quite certain how Dawn lured the boy into lying facedown and allowing her to play some gruesome game with him that included "pretending" to hammer nails into his head, or more specifically, the first nail.

"The one that went in right here," Marino continues speculating, pointing to the space between the back of his neck and the base of his skull. "That would have killed him instantly, right?"

"If we must use that phrase," I reply.

"I mean, she probably helped him in some of Fielding's Tiny Tiger classes, maybe?" he continues to spin the story. "So the kid's familiar with her, looks up to her, and she's hot, I mean really good-looking. If it was me, I'd tell the kid I'm going to show him a new move or something and to lie down in the yard. And of course the kid's going to do what an expert says, what someone teaching him says, and he lies down and it's almost dark out and then boom! It's over."

"Someone like that can never get out," I reply. "She'll do more and do it worse next time, if that's even possible."

"Denying everything. She's not talking, except to say Fielding did it all and she's innocent."

"He didn't."

"I'm with you."

"She's going to have a hard time explaining what's in her apartment," I point out, as I continue going through photographs. Marino must have taken hundreds.

"She's good-looking and charming and smart as hell. And Fielding's dead."

"Incriminating." I've said this several times as I look through the photographs on the iPad. "Should be very helpful to the prosecution. I'm not sure why you think the case will be a problem."

"It's going to be. The defense will pin it all on Fielding. The psycho bitch will get a dream team of big-shot lawyers, and they'll make the jury believe Fielding did all of it." Marino leans closer to me, and the slope of the bed changes again, and Sock is snoring quietly, not interested in his former owner or her rat hole, which has a dog bed in it, Marino shows me.

He leans close to me, clicking through several photographs of the dog's plaid bed and several toys, and I indicate I'd rather look at the photographs myself. He and Sock are on top of me, and I'm feeling smothered.

"I just thought I'd show you, since I'm the one who took them," Marino says.

"Thank you. I'll manage. You did a very good job with the photographs."

"Point is, it's obvious the dog stayed here." Marino means Sock stayed in Dawn Kincaid's rat hole. "And also with Eli and with Fielding," he adds. "To give her credit, I guess she liked her dog."

"She left him in Jack's house with no heat and all alone." I click through photographs that are overwhelmingly incriminating.

"She doesn't give a shit unless it suits her. When it doesn't, she gets rid of it one way or another. So she cared about him when it suited her."

"That's the more likely story," I agree.

I look at photographs of an unmade double bed, then other pictures of a tiny bedroom shockingly filled with junk, as if Dawn Kincaid is a hoarder.

"Plus, she had another reason to leave him," Marino goes on. "If she leaves the dog at Fielding's house, then maybe we think he's the one who killed everyone, then killed himself. The dog is there. His red leash is there. The boat that was probably used to dump Wally Jamison's body is there, and Wally's clothes and the murder weapon are in Fielding's basement. The Navigator with the missing front plate is there. You're supposed to think Fielding was following you and Benton when you left Hanscom. Fielding's deranged. He's watching you. He's following you, trying to intimidate you, or spying, or maybe he was going to kill you, too."

"He was dead by the time we were followed. Although I can't be exact about time of death, I'm calculating he'd been dead since Monday afternoon, probably was murdered not long after he got home to Salem after leaving the CFC with the Glock he'd removed from the lab. It was Dawn in the Navigator tailing us Monday night. She's the one deranged. She rode our bumper to make sure we knew we were being followed, then disappeared, probably ducked out of sight in Otwahl's parking lot. So eventually we'd think it was Jack, who in fact already had been murdered by her with a pistol she probably gave to her boyfriend, Eli, before she murdered him, too. But you're right. It's likely she tried to set things up so all of it got blamed on Jack, who isn't around to defend himself. She set up Jack and made it look like he was setting up Johnny Donahue. It's terrifying."

"You got to make the jury buy it."

"That's always the challenge, no matter the case."

"It's bad the dog was at Fielding's house,"

Marino repeats. "It connects him to Eli's murder. Hell, it's on video clips that Eli was walking the dog when he was whacked."

"The microchip," I remind him. "It traces back to Dawn, not to Jack."

"Doesn't mean anything. He kills Eli and then takes the dog, and the dog would know Fielding, right?" Marino says, as if Sock isn't inches away from him, sleeping with his head on my leg. "The dog would be familiar with Fielding because Dawn was staying over there in Salem, had the dog at Fielding's house some of the time or whatever. So Fielding kills Eli, then takes the dog as he walks off, or this is what Dawn wants us to think."

"It's not what happened. Jack didn't kill anyone," as I conclude that Dawn's apartment has the same brand of squalor that I observed at Fielding's house in Salem.

Clutter and boxes everywhere. Clothes piled in mounds and strewn in odd places. Dishes piled in the sink. Trash overflowing. Mounds of newspapers, computer printouts, magazines, and on a dining-room table, a large number of items tagged and placed there by police, including a GPS-enabled sports watch that is the same model as one I gave Fielding for his birthday several years ago, and a Civil War military dissection set in a rosewood case that is identical to one I gave him when he worked for me in Richmond.

There is a close-up of a pair of black gloves, one of them with a small black box on the wrist, what Marino describes as lightweight flexible wireless data gloves with built-in accelerometers, thirty-six sensors, and an ultra-low-profile integrated transmitter-receiver, only I have to infer all this, sift it out of his mispronunciations and mangled descriptions. The gloves, which were closely examined by both Briggs and Lucy at the scene, are clearly intended for gesture-based robotic control — specifically, to control the flybot that Eli had with him when he was murdered by the woman who had given him the stolen signet ring he was wearing when his body came to the CFC.

"Then the flybot was in her apartment," I presume. "And did Benton offer you any coffee?"

"I'm coffeed out. Some of us haven't been to bed yet."

"I'm in bed working. Doesn't mean I've slept."

"Must be nice. I'd like to stay home and work in bed." He takes the iPad from me and searches through files.

"Maybe we could adjust your job description. You can stay home and work in bed a certain number of days each year, depending on your age and decrepitude, which we'll have to evaluate. I suppose I'll be the one to evaluate it."

"Oh, yeah? Who's gonna evaluate yours?" He finds a photograph he wants me to see.

"Mine doesn't need evaluating. It's obvious to one and all."

He shows me a close-up of the flybot, only at a glance it's hard to know what it is, just a shiny, wiry object on a square of white paper on Dawn Kincaid's dining-room table. The micromechanical device could be an earring, it occurs to me. A silver earring that was stepped on, which is exactly what is suspected, Marino tells me. Lucy thinks the flybot was stepped on while the EMTs were working on Eli, then later Dawn found it when she returned to Norton's Woods, possibly wearing the same long black wool coat that she had on in my garage, a coat that I believe was Fielding's. A witness claims to have observed a young man or woman, the person wasn't sure which, in a big black coat walking around Norton's Woods with a flashlight, several hours after Eli Goldman died there. The individual in the big coat was out there alone, and the person who saw him or her thought it was strange because he or she did not have a dog and seemed to be looking for something while making odd hand gestures.

"It must have been huge on her and practically dragged on the ground," Marino says, getting up from the bed. "I'm not saying she was trying to look like a man, but with her short hair and the big coat, and a hat and glasses on or whatever? As long as you don't see her rack. She's got quite a rack. Has that in common with her dad, right?"

"I've never known Jack to have large breasts."

"I mean both of them built."

"So she returned when she assumed it was safe to do so, and even though the flybot was badly damaged, it responded to radio frequency signals sent by the data gloves?" I turn off the iPad and hand it to him.

"I think she just saw it on the ground, think it was shiny in the flashlight and she found it that way. Lucy says the bug is DOA. Squashed."

"Do we know exactly what it does or was supposed to do?"

Marino shrugs, towering over me again, still in his parka, which he hasn't bothered to unbutton, as if he didn't intend to stay long. "This isn't my area of expertise, you know. I didn't understand half of what they were talking about, Lucy and the general. I just know the potential for whatever this thing is supposed to do is something to be concerned about, and DoD intends to do some sort of inspection of Otwahl to see what the hell is really going on over there. But I'm not sure we don't already know exactly what the hell is going on over there."

"Meaning what?"

He returns the iPad to its case and says, "Meaning I worry there's R-and-D going on that the government damn well knows about but just doesn't want anyone else to know, and then you get kids out of control and the shit hits the fan. I think you get my drift. When are you coming back to work?"

"Probably not today," I tell him.

"Well, we got a shitload of things to do and undo," he says.

"Thanks for the warning."

"Buzz me if you need something. I'll call the hospital and let you know how the psycho's doing."

"Thanks for stopping by."

I wait until the sound of his heavy footsteps stops at the front door, and then the door shuts again, and then a pause, and Benton resets the alarm. I hear his footsteps, which are much lighter than Marino's, as he walks past the stairs, toward the back of the house where he has his office.

"Come on, let's get up," I say to Sock, and he opens his eyes and looks at me and yawns. "Do you know what bye-bye means? I guess not. They didn't teach you that at the prison. You just want to sleep, don't you? Well, I've got things to do, so come on. You're really quite lazy, you know. Are you sure you ever won a race or even ran in one? I don't think I believe it."

I move his head and put my feet on the floor, deciding there must be a pet shop around here that has everything a skinny, lazy old greyhound might need for this kind of weather.

"Let's go for a ride." I talk to Sock as I find my slippers and a robe. "Let's see what Secret Agent Wesley is doing. He's probably in his office on the phone again, what do you bet? I know, he's always on the phone, and I agree, it's quite annoying.

"Maybe he'll take us shopping, and then I'm going to make a very nice pasta, home-made pappardelle with a hearty Bolognese sauce, ground veal, red wine, and lots of mushrooms and garlic.

"I need to explain up front that you only get canine cuisine; that's the rule of the house. I'm thinking quinoa and cod for you today." I continue talking as we go down the stairs. "That will be a nice change after all that chicken and rice from the Greek diner."

ABOUT THE AUTHOR

Patricia Cornwell is author of seventeen previous novels featuring Dr. Kay Scarpetta. Her most recent bestsellers include *The Scarpetta Factor, Scarpetta, The Front, Book of the Dead, At Risk,* and *Portrait of a Killer: Jack the Ripper—Case Closed.* Her earlier works include *Postmortem*—the only novel to win the Edgar, Creasey, Anthony, and Macavity awards and the French Prix du Roman d'Aventure in a single year—and *Cruel and Unusual,* which won Britain's prestigious Gold Dagger Award for the best crime novel in 1993. *Book of the Dead* won the 2008 Galaxy British Book Awards' Books Direct Crime Thriller of the Year award, making Cornwell the first American to win this prestigious U.K. award. Dr. Kay Scarpetta herself won the 1999 Sherlock Award for the best detective created by an American author.